NEW WORLD

Warwick Collins has led a varied life. Ever since several of his poems were published in *Encounter*, he has combined a literary interest with earning his daily bread. Amongst various occupations have been those of defence specialist and yacht designer. In 1979 he was invited to address the House of Lords All Party Defence Study Group on future airborne anti tank systems, and the House of Commons Defence Committee on the same subject in 1980. He counts yachting as his main obsession and is the inventor of the internationally famous Tandem Keel. *New World* is the second novel in a trilogy which began with *Challenge*, and is due for completion with a third novel in 1992.

WARWICK COLLINS

New World

PAN BOOKS
LONDON, SYDNEY AND AUCKLAND

First published in Great Britain in 1991 by Pan Books Ltd
This paperback edition published 1992 by Pan Books Ltd,
a division of Pan Macmillan Limited,
Cavaye Place, London SW10 9PG
Associated companies throughout the world

9 8 7 6 5 4 3 2 1

ISBN 0 330 31685 0

Phototypeset by Intype, London
Printed in England by Clays Ltd, St Ives plc

Introduction

The function of a novel set in the future is not to predict that future in detail, but to generate a coherent, alternative reality. Readers who come fresh to *New World* might bear in mind that the manuscript was completed in July 1989, some months before the East European revolutions, and has been changed hardly at all since then. For all of us who have lived through these momentous times, it requires a considerable effort of mind to consider the almost unimaginable changes which have occurred since it was written.

At the time of writing, the Soviet bloc was still intact, effectively monolithic, and (despite some signs of restlessness in Eastern Europe) the Communist Party remained in effective control of its great empire. *New World* looked forward to a time when the Soviet empire had dissolved into its constituent republics.

Now that the unimaginable has occurred, I find myself in an opposing position to many of those who appear to believe that the former Soviet republics will effect an immediate and direct transition into Western-style liberal democracies. Russia has always been centralized. As the economic crisis deepens, increasingly it will be subject to political pressures to return to some form of strong leadership. Its path towards liberal democracy will be a rough and difficult one, with many diversions and changes of direction.

I also wanted to explore a world in which the future is haunted by the past, in which new ideas are framed by the remnants (often disguised) of old institutions. As I write, the KGB may have been divested of its internal security functions, but until further notice it remains in charge of Russian national security. The Army, once the flag carrier of socialism, is no longer so powerful, but is the least affected of the old Soviet institutions, and presents the most continuous and cogent threat to the democratic process. This too was foreseen in *New World*. I have suggested one or two additional illustrations of a partial return to old ways. For example, there is even a sentimental reversion to the use of the word 'Comrade' after many years of disuse, if only because of the disadvantages of other terms of address.

To my mind at least, the belief that Estonia's declaration of independence (following the 1991 August coup) will presage the easy formation of a Western-style Baltic democracy, like Sweden, also appears naïve. Strong and terrible links remain with Russia. Estonia has a resident Russian population of approximately forty per cent of the total. Its industry, particularly its power and raw materials, remains locked into the Russian economy. Even after independence, it is likely there will be Russian troops on its soil for many years to come. Perhaps (like the Americans in Europe) there will be a permanent garrison, albeit discreetly positioned, to maintain Russian 'security' in the region. It is this potential future era, more difficult and ambiguous than popular journalism depicts, in which *New World* is set.

One aspect of the *Challenge* trilogy has also, I think, shown early signs of coming true. In the absence of high level military confrontation, sport becomes a major arena for the expression of national rivalry and status. In a curious parody of the theme of *New World*, both Russia and Estonia have shown signs of wishing to participate in the most exclusive of capitalist sports, the America's Cup. We have not yet reached a position in which the Russian military, bored by years of relative peace, throws its technical and research weight behind an America's Cup challenge. But perhaps this too will emerge as we move towards the next century.

Warwick Collins
January 1992

One

When Ivan Illich stepped off the Aeroflot flight from New York, he was affected by a feeling of *déjà vu*. The new international airport at Plashkaya, outside Moscow, was the apparently willing host of advertising boards, several of which flashed cheerful but lugubrious messages of goodwill. 'Greetings from the people' read one; beneath it was the logo of the State Tractor Company. Another showed, in unintentional cubist planes of lights, a girl brushing her teeth. The toothpaste had a new brand name he had not seen before. There was still only one such company in Russia who would produce such commodities, Government supported like the State Tractor Company. To Illich, there was something comical about this self-conscious imitation of Western mores in advertising, like an elephant in a ballerina's tutu. Even so it was considered necessary and appropriate to introduce these forms of the new economics.

Illich was a simple man. He was prone to a certain nostalgia for the old certainties. In the old days capitalism was denounced. Now the United States, once the *glavnyi vrag*, the main enemy, was the colleague of Russia, or so the newspapers would have one believe.

A full colonel in the Russian Army, these days he was obliged to travel, as were his brother officers, on civilian flights. Admittedly because of his status as a Hero of Russia, he was treated as a VIP; he enjoyed, therefore, special privileges. But these were not the same as in the old days, when an officer, merely by virtue of his profession, could jump queues, could, in certain circumstances, arrogate a section or even an entire aircraft for himself and his colleagues. Then there were numerous other privileges. There was, until recently, a shop in the basement of Voyentorg, the army-navy store on Kalinin Prospekt in Moscow, stocked with export-quality vodka, French cognac and

Armenian brandy, caviar, sturgeon and salmon. It was now open to the general public. Admittedly, one could use the *Beriozka*, hard currency shops, for Japanese hi-fis and cameras, American film or English woollens, but in this too the military had no special privilege.

In the name of the new economics such things had been abolished. It was not their abolition *per se* which disturbed him and his brother officers. It was, rather, the assumptions behind their cessation that perplexed him – the assumption that the Russian Army, once the élite of élites, was no longer the foremost flag carrier of socialism, no longer its sole, powerful guarantor. And so he found himself in the passport queue, standing beside two Armenian fur-traders, in the trail of their expensive cologne, waiting for his passport to be processed. In this case the official was a white faced young man from the Interior Ministry who glanced at Illich's passport, blushed in embarrassment, and – standing ostentatiously to the side – waved him through.

This sudden access of humility on the part of the official was understandable. Colonel Ivan Illich was no mere serving colonel. Four times Olympic gold medalist, Flying Dutchman sailing class, and most recently, victor over the United States in the America's Cup, 2001. Enough to impress a youth from Petrovsk.

He walked through to the main airport arrivals and departures complex. A group of cleaners was working on the staircases, clad in scruffy blue overalls – a *mélange* of racial types, Caucasians, West Ukrainians, Uzbeks, Tartars, and others. At first he thought they were from the *stroibaty*, the construction battalions that are slum postings for army recruits, those without talent for anything else. But sewn on their right sleeves were two dots and a dash, the insignia of low-grade offenders, small-time hustlers, black marketeers, currency dealers, pimps, petty fraudsters, gangsters, some of the unwanted humanity that had crawled from beneath the stones of the new economic policy. Rather than serve their terms inside prison, they were given menial work. This was another aspect of the new, more liberal line in Russian policy. One of the cleaners, a tall Armenian or Azerbaijani, rested on his broom, and surveyed the great hall below him. Illich noticed that the overseer condoned this special privilege. Had the man bribed the overseer? The offender in question stood looking out over the gigantic reception Hall, and Illich had the impression that, although the man's gaze was general, he was surveying, from his position high on the stairs, Illich's own progress through the crowds below. It was still easy to become prey to such suspicions in Russia. Old habits died hard. With a small click of disgust at the lack of discipline allowed by the overseer, Illich walked through the grey, smoked-glass doors and out into the cold street.

A line of taxis waited on the other side. Several drivers had moved in to the first car in line to conserve fuel and warmth in the brisk spring air. Its engine breathed soft blue plumes of low-grade black-market petrol. To their right a single black Chaika waited, the outline of its chauffeur just discernible behind the darkened glass. As Illich began to walk across the tarmac towards the taxis, he noticed the chauffeur had emerged from the Chaika and was now moving towards him, waving, clearly trying to attract his attention. Illich stopped to watch the man. The chauffeur continued to advance, making small bows and nods, stretching out his hand as if offering to take Illich's luggage. 'Sir,' the man said as he drew closer, 'I've been instructed by Comrade Pridilenko to bring you and your luggage to the Foreign Ministry without delay.' Then he added, perhaps because of Illich's blank stare, 'Forgive me, sir, but Comrade Second Secretary Pridilenko asked me to tell you it's urgent.'

Illich was tempted to ignore him, literally to brush him aside and take a taxi instead. Something inside him objected to being summoned peremptorily in this manner. The faces of the three taxi drivers in the front car –

Georgians, he guessed, like most of them these days – surveyed this scene with cool but unaffected interest.

Illich decided instead to permit the chauffeur to take his luggage, and without a further glance towards the row of taxis, followed behind him to the Chaika. Opening the rear door himself, he slammed it shut before the hurrying chauffeur had time to stow his suitcase in the boot and return to the door. It was his last, small gesture of defiance before, beneath the eyes of the Georgians, the Chaika swept out of the parking lot and, keeping to the privileged lane, took the long, straight highway to Moscow.

Two

The driver had referred to 'Comrade' Pridilenko. Changing terms of address caused in Illich a certain wry consideration. The increasing use of the word *tovarich*, 'comrade', was especially interesting, a reflection of Russian social development. It had been the imprimatur of the Communist Party, a formal term of address between cadres and those who served them. With the demise of the Party there had been a number of years in which 'comrade' had fallen into ostentatious disuse amongst the public at large. But alternative terms of common address contained their own grave difficulties. The Russian word for 'mister', *gospodin*, was a pre-revolutionary term heavy with respect for the merchant class. During Communist rule it was sometimes used with foreigners, particularly Westerners, usually in somewhat dry recognition of their bourgeois status. But in the post-*perestroika* Russia it had too many archaic shadows to find a comfortable foothold as a term of popular address. The term *grazhdanin*, 'citizen', was another which might have found favour. But *grazhdanin* too had its dark overtones. In Communist times it was used by state prosecutors to address an individual outside the pale of Soviet society, a class enemy, and it retained this chilling premonition of remorseless justice.

In the absence of alternatives *tovarich*, comrade, had returned to common usage. It entailed a recognition of the historical past, but was employed now with a certain lightness, an ironic inflection, a cheerful goodwill. *Tovarich* said 'we are individuals with a common history, a history of struggle and suffering, but we are alive today'. So terms, laden with cultural associations, subtly evolve.

Illich noticed that the driver took a longer route than normal, perhaps to avoid traffic. They entered central Moscow. Now the Chaika was travelling down river, passing the huge building of the Defence Ministry, from inside which were ordered the lives of five million servicemen. It was sobering to realize, as the limousine accelerated through a red traffic light, that his own fate lay within the compass of those who worked in those myriad offices. The building itself was huge, monolithic, a typical product of former Soviet architecture. Off-duty officers of one of the two Moscow-based parade and ceremonial divisions strolled about the Frunzenskaya embankment, several with girls. On the other side of the river lay Gorky Park and the Lenin Hills.

They turned right along Gogolevsky Boulevard, leaving the huge Moskva Swimming Pool on their right, and then continued along Volkhonka Street. Crossing Borovitskaya Plaza, the crenelated walls and golden domes of the Kremlin were now on their immediate right.

As an Estonian, at least on his mother's side, Illich was something of a rarity in the armed forces. After the revolution in 1917 attempts had been made to establish a broad representation of races within the forces. But it had always been overwhelmingly Slav and predominantly Russian.

During the manpower cuts in the Kruschev era, the general staff took the opportunity to weed out further numbers of non-Slav officers. The Russian share of officers had reached over eighty cent, with most of the rest made up of Ukrainians and Byelorussians. During the late 1980s and 1990s, with signs of unrest and increasing independence amongst the national minorities, the proportion of Russian officers had, if anything, increased further. Now it was something of a rarity to see an Uzbek, a Tartar or a Kazakh face amongst the crisp uniforms of the officer corps. Service slang, with its brutally simple language of racial difference – *kosglazyi* (slant eyes), *zheltoe govno* (yellow shit) – exhibited the contempt for those who were collectively called *nerusskie*, non-Russians. Russian was the natural language of command. Even in the *stroibaty*, the construction battalions, all training manuals, regulations, and documents were in Russian and soldiers were expected to speak it on duty.

It was strange, sometimes even amusing, what tensions these racial differences generated. It was a widely held view, for example, that Estonians were a nation of heavy drinkers. A Russian who, assuming this, was inclined to make comradely overtures to an Estonian by means of a bottle of vodka would be unsure whether his gesture would be welcomed or treated as casting a mortal slur upon Estonian nationality.

The Chaika moved into lower gear. A car had been seen approaching the same red lights from the right, a Zil with two motor-cycle outriders – the limousine of a senior government official. Respectfully they waited while the little convoy crossed in front of them.

In this, the central part of the capital, one was aware of the movement of the elements of control. Other officers went by – MVD troops in bright red flashings in a carrier, perhaps on their way to the changing of the guard at the Kremlin.

'Here we are,' said the chauffeur as they pulled up outside, a square building of dazzling white concrete with grey glass embrasures; the flag of Russia fluttered on a giant pole at the side of the main entrance. This time the chauffeur opened the door for Illich, and added, 'I'll take your baggage around to your hotel.'

'The Porodny,' Illich said.

'They have already booked you in at the Kalinin,' the chauffeur replied. Illich had seen the Kalinin, a palace of vertical grey glass and huge suites for VIPs, much more luxurious than the Porodny, which was frequented by his fellow officers. He could have objected to this regulatory treatment, but it would merely have placed the chauffeur in a difficult position, and he decided to bide his time before making any protestation.

One of Pridilenko's assistants was walking down the steps towards him, holding out his hand in greeting, Western style. A typical diplomat, thought Illich, noting the young man's manners, his perfectly cut hair, his air of obsequious confidence. 'Please follow me, Comrade Colonel.'

Pridilenko's suite was on the fifteenth floor. Unlike most Moscow lifts, which sounded as if their motive power was supplied by a chain-gang of chanting Transbaikal convicts, this one ascended with hardly more disturbance than the sigh of wind in the wings of an angel. A little purr, a courteous murmur of deceleration, and the doors opened on the fifteenth floor.

The corridor into which they stepped was lined with expensive paintings. They were of a curious style, abstracted though not abstract, in muted colours which did not clash with the décor, the preferred background of a new élite acquainted with international tastes and preferences. They entered through swing doors into a large reception area with several smart desks and working surfaces ornamented by sculptured metal ashtrays and elegant flower vases. A middle-aged secretary, dressed smartly in a white trouser suit, emerged from behind a steel and glass desk to take Illich's coat and lead him turn to an ante-room at the side of the reception area. 'Comrade Pridilenko is in a meeting, but he will see you shortly.' The young diplomat shook hands again and disappeared into one of the inner offices that lay beyond the reception area.

Illich sat down in one of the green leather chairs. Spread over a modern glass table were a series of exotic plants, one clearly a form of cactus, and several others with which he was unfamiliar. On the table were copies of *Pravda* and *Izsvestiya*. There was also a Russian translation of the International *Herald Tribune*. For light relief a copy of the satirical magazine *Krokodyl* was laid out neatly to one side. Illich noticed on the cover of *Krokodyl* a cartoon of a cigar-smoking bureaucrat or senior official in a plush office. In front of him sat his mother, a small woman in a shawl. 'Mother,' the bureaucrat was saying, 'I can assure you that I am keeping very well here.' 'But Aleksey,' the mother was replying, 'what will happen to you if the Reds come to power?'

It was an old joke, an uneasy reference to the puritan phase of socialism, constantly recycled. Nevertheless, Illich allowed himself the faintest of smiles. He was still smiling a few seconds later when Pridilenko came in.

Distinguished, white-haired, Pridilenko was one of those handsome men whose natural proclivity it was to assume an almost unaffected, indeed spontaneous, pride in their appearance. He embraced Illich, patted him on the shoulder, and stood back to regard him from under his white eyebrows. Indicating with a quick, conspiratorial gesture that Illich should follow him, he walked through the open doors into a conference room, at the centre of which was a large table. Some six figures were gathered around it.

They stood up as Illich entered with a creak of chairs – except for one, the heavy figure of General Chernavin. He was also the only one that Illich recognized. In his introductions Pridilenko started with the seated officer. 'General Chernavin,' announced Pridilenko. 'We've met,' Illich said politely. Was it with hostility that the general regarded him? Illich turned to the second man who was reaching out a square hand to shake his. 'Valentin

Osborov, Second Secretary, Naval Intelligence.' Pridilenko
continued. 'Arkady Virusk, Interior Ministry. Andrey
Veronin, Second Department, Scientific Research. Sergei
Mamayev, Chairman of the Committee of Sport Resources.
Vera Ahktova . . .' Illich was surprised by the presence of a
woman – the Russian political hierarchy was still domi-
nated by men – ' . . . Head of Secretariat, Office of the
President. Please be seated.'

Illich had no time to look around, however. Pridilenko
was tapping the table quietly with a silver paperknife,
bringing the meeting to order.

Three

While Pridilenko spoke, Illich glanced at General Chernavin's face at the end of the table, hoping for some explanation
of his apparent hostility. Chernavin returned a blank-faced
stare.

'My distinguished colleagues,' Pridilenko began. 'The
purpose of this meeting is to discuss the defence by Russia
of the America's Cup. As each of us here is aware, this
piece of bourgeois silver has an important symbolic function
between states . . .' Pridilenko paused to glance around
him. As on previous occasions, Illich was impressed by his
confidence, by the tone of carefully modulated irony which
he added to the last sentence. 'It is perhaps the only sporting competition which is not merely between individual
sportsmen or teams, but which is also a direct confrontation
of technologies. That is why we are pleased to see here
our colleagues, Comrades Osborov and Veronin, who will
shortly tell us what technical facilities can be brought to
bear on our defence of the America's Cup. General Cherna-

vin has also joined our committee as representative of the highest military circles. Comrade Mamayev, in his administration of the sporting facilities of Russia, will shortly outline his plans for the site of the defence, and also for generating the most able crew in this sporting endeavour.' Pridilenko paused, inclined his head towards the slim, erect shape of Vera Ahktova. 'Before we proceed further, may I also thank Comrade Ahktova for her presence. She will be summarizing the work of the committee to the Office of the President.'

It seemed to Illich that a chill entered the room at that stage. This was no ordinary committee. Pridilenko, the cunning fox, had provided this piece of information last to remind them of their responsibilities to the highest authorities. Woe betide anyone whose attendance on this committee was half-hearted. Illich could not help glancing again at General Chernavin. Was the sentence not also perhaps a reminder to Chernavin that he must behave himself?

'Comrade Mamayev,' said Pridilenko. 'Perhaps you would begin.'

Illich turned his attention towards Sergei Mamayev. A short, square man, with thick brows and dark, sleek hair, Mamayev had the look of a Georgian. In fact, he reminded Illich of the photographs he had seen of Stalin, the infamous one. Appearances in this case were perhaps deceptive. Mamayev folded his hands on the table.

'Permit me to deal with the siting of the defence first. The factors which are involved are, firstly, reasonable weather conditions, particularly prevailing winds. It would be unfortunate to place the defence in an area of unpredictable or unfavourable winds. Secondly, there is the matter of the facilities which are available, but I shall deal with that in a short while.

'In assessing the weather conditions, we were able to draw upon the weather-predicting facilities of the Naval Research Institutes over our entire coastal areas, and also upon satellite information from the Space Research Bureau.

16

For the detailed analysis provided I thank Comrade Osborov and his colleagues.' Osborov nodded his head in acknowledgement. 'A choice existed between a site on the Baltic and one on the Black Sea. Average wind strengths are not dissimilar, but those found in the Black Sea are more irregular, with a greater percentage of calms and gales. For this reason there is a strong argument in favour of siting the defence in the Baltic. The question is, which part of the Baltic?

'There are other factors which should be taken into account. As this committee is aware, a very high proportion of our best sailors come from Estonia. Furthermore, some of the best Olympic sailing training facilities are currently situated in Tallinn. The weather conditions there are reasonable in summer, characterized by relatively persistent, moderate winds.

'An alternative is St Petersburg. The problem here is that, in the areas under consideration, there is heavy shipping, both commercial and military. While it would be possible to site a defence here, on the southern shore of the bay, there is no doubt it would entail some form of disruption to both naval and commercial routes. More importantly than this, however, in the course of our investigations we were informed of new, sensitive navy installations in the local area to the north of St Petersburg. We are informed, and again I thank Comrade Osborov for his information from Naval Intelligence, that to allow free access to a host of nationalities in this general area may not be recommended.

'This returns us to the consideration of Estonia. Since the majority of our crew, following past precedents, are likely to come from Estonia, and will know the local waters and wind conditions well, this is a further incentive to consider this location as our first choice.' Sergei Mamayev cleared his throat. The next phase in his introduction was sensitive.

'Naturally, there are other matters – other than wind strengths, the local geographical knowledge of sailors, and the best existing facilities – which must be considered. There is also, comrades, the political factor.'

Illich was aware of the chill again, the silence of concentration.

'I am only able to make recommendations on what can be established with regard to, so to speak, the physical and human factors. I merely say that, if it is considered that Estonia would be a politically sensitive area in which to hold an America's Cup defence, we should seek, through Comrade Chairman of the Committee Pridilenko, clarification of this matter from the highest authorities.'

A brief silence descended on the table. Pridilenko again took the initiative.

'Thank you, comrade. I agree that we should seek clarification on this matter. As to your summary, we note that the overwhelming body of your research points to Estonia, and Tallinn in particular, as the best area for the defence of the America's Cup.'

Pridilenko would have continued, but General Chernavin had broken his immobility and raised a hand. Illich watched Pridilenko pause, consider, and give in gracefully to this interruption.

'General Chernavin.'

'Comrade Chairman,' the General began. 'Before we move on to further points, I have a comment on the aspect of choosing a location in Estonia.'

The others froze. Pridilenko sensed that the General would not be stopped. He glanced towards Vera Ahktova, who was looking towards the General, her face composed, her pencil poised.

'Comrade Chairman, I have been asked to represent the military, and in this respect I will fulfil my function. On the matter of the choice of Estonia as a location, the outstanding question would appear to be one of security. The view of the military, if asked, would be clear.' Chernavin's stare encompassed the whole table. 'There can be no question that, from the military point of view, we have the resources to ensure security in this region.'

General Chernavin leaned back. An intense silence invaded the room. Estonia, already economically independent, was currently objecting to the continued strong Soviet military presence on her soil. The issue was highly sensitive. The general's comments appeared to those gathered there like an assertion of continued military strength against local wishes. Vera Ahktova's pencil made several brief flourishes on her writing pad. Pridilenko, visibly shaken, gathered together the fragments of the meeting. Having been caught off balance, he recovered fast.

'Thank you, General.' Pridilenko turned again to Sergei Mamayev. 'Perhaps we could move on to the second area of discussion, the arrangements you have made to select crew for the campaign.'

Sergei Mamayev continued, 'The Central Sports Committee was asked to vote on who should represent us as skipper and helmsman. On this matter the committee voted unanimously. It is our collective view that there was only one suitably qualified candidate for the task. Comrade Colonel Illich is the helmsman who is considered our greatest sailor, and the only one who has direct experience of an America's Cup challenge, a highly successful challenge. This selection was the easiest part of our task.' Sergei Mamayev turned towards Illich. 'I offer Colonel Illich my congratulations on his selection as helmsman for Russia in the defence of the America's Cup.'

Pridilenko was quick to seize on this opportunity. He turned towards Illich, and clapped his hands. The committee followed suit politely. All except General Chernavin. It was this refusal to participate with the others in commending Illich's reselection that finally indicated to Illich that he had an important and powerful enemy.

'In the matter of crew,' Mamayev continued, 'we have instituted a competition for winchgrinders throughout

Russia. It will be open to all athletes in the weight-training categories. With regard to other crew, we have instituted a search across the country, in collaboration with all sailing clubs and sailing associations, for new crew to provide a selection pool for the next America's Cup. In this we have the full collaboration of the Olympic organizations, and the use of their selection procedures and training facilities.'

On this subject, Mamayev was at home. He flourished lists and tables, spread the full panoply of Russian sports resources before them, promised action and funds. Eventually Pridilenko said, 'Thank you, comrade. Let us now move on to the research matters. Comrade Osborov.'

Where Mamayev was short and dark, Valentin Osborov was blond, long-boned and somewhat ascetic in appearance. He had a Tartar look about the eyes. Illich, used to racial categorization in the sprawling Russian hinterland, placed him from the northern forests. In style of presentation, the Navy prided itself on understatement.

'The research facilities of the Naval Institute are at the disposal of the design team. We can supply tank test facilities, computational model cutting, and access to naval research computer mainframes. More importantly, in the matter of technical response, we have coded the research effort as Priority 1, equal with the most important naval research programmes.'

Pridilenko said, 'Thank you for your succinct summary, comrade. Comrade Veronin.'

Andrey Veronin leaned forward. 'My function is to ensure access to ancillary research facilities, in structures, high-level build tolerances, and in complex engineering composites. I have also clarified access to certain other facilities, in particular the use of advanced materials in our Space Programme. We have developed, in our *Mir* research, a series of astonishingly light, strong structures in which almost every molecule is aligned for maximum effect. These areas of research will become available on demand, subject to the necessary personnel clearances.'

20

'Thank you. Comrade Virusk . . .' Pridilenko pressed on, inclining his head towards a small, thin man with a mild manner ' . . . will now address us on the contribution of the Interior Ministry.'

Arkady Virusk's delivery was so quiet it was almost necessary to lean forward to hear him.

'We also have placed the programme in the highest importance category. Any worker, manager, or scientist from the civilian sector who may be required by the programme will be released immediately from existing duties on full pay.'

'Thank you. I now turn to General Chernavin.'

Chernavin had sat quietly through the speeches of the previous speakers. He turned towards Pridilenko and addressed him directly.

'Comrade Chairman, in the matter of the overall organization of the defence of the America's Cup against the United States I wish to place the following on record. In the course of our successful challenge last year, the task of organizing that challenge was directly that of the military. We accepted that duty and responsibility, and we did our best to achieve a successful conclusion. In this matter of the defence, we note that our role is somewhat secondary. In this secondary role we will contribute what is required of us.'

For a few seconds, those present assimilated the contents of this little speech. It could have been interpreted as a formal objection, directed at the Chairman, against the fact that overall control was no longer to be exercised by the military. Perhaps Pridilenko hoped, for a brief moment, that the portentous nature of this statement would be lost on Vera Ahktova. But he could see immediately that it was a false hope. She was writing steadily and fluently. By that evening General Chernavin's statement would be processed and ready to pass on to the Presidential Council the following day. Pridilenko must have groaned inwardly. His committee was fast becoming a battleground between the political and military. It seemed the first salvo had been fired.

'Comrades,' Pridilenko said at last. 'This meeting is now over. We will be gathering, as agreed, once every two months to review progress and assess priorities. In view of the importance of the committee and its activities, it cannot be stressed too highly that full attendance is required for all sessions. Thank you, comrades, for your contributions.'

The various parties stood up. Pridilenko touched Illich's shoulder and drew him aside.

'My personal congratulations on your new appointment. A message has been left at my office that you must report back to Tallinn as soon as possible to start your sail-training.'

A voice from behind them said, 'Colonel Illich.'

Illich turned and saluted General Chernavin.

'Now that your tour of the provinces is over,' Chernavin said, 'be so kind as to attend my office at the Defence Ministry at three o' clock this afternoon.'

Illich nodded, saluted again.

The General walked past him and out into the corridor. They waited until his footsteps had died away.

'An angry man,' Pridilenko commented. He made as if to dust some hair or fluff from his perfectly tailored suit, though Illich could see nothing that needed cleaning. 'I have no objection to his attending our committee, but I wish he would leave his armoured divisions outside.'

Four

Pridilenko's Chaika saloon was again on hand to transport Illich to his hotel. The Kalinin was much as he expected. Sheets of tinted glass, stark; a modern skyscraper in the style of Mies van der Rohe. Again the lift proved fast and silent. These new hotels were designed to international standards, with all their advantages and disadvantages. There were shops in the foyer filled with goods which would have been impossible to buy in Moscow five years earlier. The hotel staff might have been from any major city hotel in the Western world – they were efficient, cool, detached. Processed, one travelled to one's rooms with the impression of time suspended.

He washed and shaved. His eyes were still red from the overnight plane travel, but his appearance he judged to be otherwise passable.

This time he caught a taxi to the Defence Ministry and was security-cleared by means of a finger imprint technique using modern machinery imported from Germany. A sergeant led him upstairs to the offices of General Chernavin. The sergeant seated him in the ante-room. On the walls were the expected paraphernalia of military offices everywhere – a tall diagram of official uniforms and correct dress, a warning on security precautions, a safety procedure in case of fire alarm. There was also, on the wall opposite him, a blown up black and white photograph of General Chernavin shaking hands with the Polish and Hungarian Defence Ministers at a European military conference; beneath that, a row of certificates and medals.

From the inner office he could hear, occasionally, the

murmur of voices in discussion. Footsteps approached the door. The face of a senior officer, not General Chernavin but that of a major-general, appeared.

'Colonel Illich,' the officer shook his hand. 'Major-General Vassily Org. It is a pleasure to meet you.'

He followed Major-General Org through into a huge office overlooking the Moscow river, with fine views over Gorky Park and the Lenin Hills beyond. Seated round the desk were three generals, whom he recognized almost at once. None stood up, though they nodded as he entered. So, Illich thought to himself, I am in trouble. This meeting already had the atmosphere of a tribunal.

Major-General Org indicated a seat. Illich saluted and sat down.

The Major-General pulled up a chair, and enunciated on a wall intercom to the neighbouring clerical offices the categorical instruction that they were not to be disturbed. Even more serious, Illich thought to himself; a closed session, no assistants or secretaries.

General Chernavin began: 'In case you have not met my colleagues, General Zholudev, on my right, is head of the Department of Ordnance and Machinery. General Litski is head of the Department of Military Strategy and Coordinated Movement.'

The Department of Military Strategy and Coordinated Movement was the supervisory department of the land forces, the centre of Russian Army doctrine. Another nerve sent its message of apprehension and caution to Illich's brain. Russian Army doctrine was built round the concept of fast, lightning war. The concept demanded overwhelming force, with high degrees of mobility. In the course of the major armed forces reductions of the last decade, the Army had fought a bitter rearguard action to preserve its capabilities. In the skirmishes which rumbled between the politicians and the Defence Ministry on financial allocations, the argument centred on the availability of resources – men, machines, fuel, transport – required for the support of this

doctrine. Remove the doctrine, and you removed the justification for such high levels of military readiness. General
Litski, as guardian of Soviet Army doctrine, occupied a key
position.

Chernavin, however, was clearly in charge of this meeting. He leaned forward, his hands spread on the table:
'Before we proceed, let me inform you that this is not
an official meeting. No official records will be kept. My
colleagues here happen to be present as a result of other
matters. Do you understand?'

Illich understood only too well. The meeting would not
even have the status of a closed or secret tribunal. Afterwards, there would be no written record and, subsequently,
no means of redress in respect of any statements or accusations made at the meeting.

Illich understood, too, that he was being warned that if
he disagreed with the informal meeting, he should say so
now. As a colonel, he had a right to a formal, recorded
meeting if his career or prospects seemed to him to be in
danger. It was a decision which he must make rapidly. If he
were to demand a record of the meeting, he would be
placing himself in a defensive position. Since, up till now, he
had not been accused of anything, he had no reason to be
defensive.

There was a second consideration. Outside the formal
constraints of recorded notes, the group in front of him
might speak more freely. It was curiosity, more than anything, which decided him to incline his head.

'I understand.'

General Chernavin paused for a moment, glanced at his
colleagues on either side. Each man nodded his agreement
to the procedure.

Chernavin said, 'Then perhaps we can begin.' He
nodded to General Litski.

Litski was short, bald, with a scar ranged diagonally from
the right corner of his mouth to his right cheek. Illich knew
that he had received this wound in Afghanistan, when in

charge of an armoured division. This was the purest kind of record. It was fitting, therefore, that in enunciating principles Litski should speak.

'Comrade Colonel, we are pleased that, once again, a member of the Army has been chosen to represent Russia in the defence of the America's Cup. In the absence of overt hostilities between the East and West, and the temporary peace on the international front, it is fitting that we should be engaged in this type of peaceful competition.

'As you know, this peace is guaranteed by the strength and capacity of the Russian armed forces. It is because we are eternally vigilant that such conditions of temporary peace persist. As you also know, this peace must never be taken for granted. Peace is a balancing movement, it is like an acrobat on a wire. One false move, and we plunge into hostilities.'

General Litski paused. There were movements of assent on the part of Generals Chernavin and Zholudev. Illich glanced at Major-General Org, but could see no sign other than a frozen attention to Litski's words.

'Unfortunately, the press, our own press, has sometimes seen fit to misinterpret our position. *Izvestiya*, for example, published recently a series of articles in which it was suggested that we of the Defence Ministry are in conflict with the government. A so-called defence correspondent, A. Aleksovitch, portrayed the military as a source of reaction, even a source of agitation. As you may surmise, Colonel, these and other speculations have introduced an unnecessary element of tension into the generally excellent relations between the armed forces and the government.

'We ourselves must take special care not to be influenced by these tactics. That is to say, while accepting our role as the servant of the government, we must also point out what we know to be true, that the armed forces are the guarantor of peace, that our constant readiness is the surest defence of the peace.

'Such matters are obvious. But sometimes, it seems to us

that certain elements are guilty of falling into the trap of appearing to believe that the readiness of the armed forces is a threat against peace, that in order to pursue peace we must disarm the armed forces. This,' Litski said heavily, 'is to stand cause and effect on its head.'

Through the grey-tinted windows overlooking the Moscow river, Illich could see a tug laboriously pulling a row of barges against the current. It seemed to him symbolic of this ponderous polemic. Somewhere in the room a fly buzzed. Far away, beyond the city to the south-west, he could still see traces of spring snow on the ground. There was no sign of snow now in Gorky Park.

'Now, Comrade Colonel,' Litski continued with unexpected gentleness, 'in what respect does this affect you? We say to you, collectively, and on behalf of the Defence Ministry, that you should remember these facts, keep them constantly in mind in all your dealings with the other ministries.

'We remind you further, that great though your achievements may be in the sporting field, and exalted though your contributions may be to the international prestige of the *Rodina*, you are first a soldier.'

Illich glanced from Litski to Chernavin, from Chernavin to Zholudev. Stony faces returned his glance.

Zholudev it was who now spoke. He was the popular archetype of a general, a powerful animal, and his voice seemed to carry within it the undertones of a low, rumbling snarl.

'Do you have anything to say, Colonel?'

'Nothing,' Illich replied.

'Then we may take it,' persisted General Zholudev, 'that you are in full agreement.'

'I understand what you say.'

'That is not sufficient.' This was Chernavin.

Sufficient for what? Illich asked himself. Three implacable faces studied him.

'I accept that I am first and foremost a soldier,' Illich said.

27

It seemed the stillness gathered round him like crystalline precipitation, that it was colder in this room than on the snow-meadows. Several seconds passed, seconds of a most intense silence.

He had let them down, now, as in other matters. Given the opportunity to confess his inadequacies, he had remained silent. He could sense the anger behind their faces.

At length General Litski said, 'I must proceed to another meeting.'

Chernavin gave Illich a final cold stare. Then the three senior officers stood up with a creaking of chairs. Illich stood and saluted as they walked past him. They did not acknowledge him except with a brief nod of the head. It was, he thought afterwards, like a formal ballet of disapproval.

When they had left, Major-General Org said mildly, 'If I may offer some advice, Colonel. You should write a note addressed to General Chernavin, indicating that you did not understand the full import of the meeting, and that in retrospect, having thought about the matter further, you are fully in agreement with the advice offered by him and his distinguished colleagues. And you should add, finally, that you are honoured that he should have seen fit to direct this attention towards you.'

Illich replied, 'Thank you for your kind and well-meant advice, sir.'

'That's another thing,' Major-General Org observed. 'Not once did I hear you use the word "sir" in your entire interview.'

Illich saluted. He felt Org's eyes follow him as he walked across the room and closed the door behind him. Outside, in the ante-room, the sergeant was waiting to escort him back to the entrance.

Five

An uneasy night at the Kalinin hotel. The air-conditioning was on and he couldn't find a means of regulating it. He preferred to sleep in a cold room. None of the windows would open. He woke with a flat headache.

He breakfasted in the main dining-room, amongst the trade delegates and the visiting heads of tractor factories. As a Hero of Russia he had been almost continuously on tour at the behest of the Interior Ministry, giving talks to dutiful groups of undermanagers in Smolensk, opening a new post office in Dnepropetrovosk, addressing a conference of Mothers of the Russian Union in Rostov. He realized now that his body felt clogged with hospitality and his mind satiated, numbed with adulation.

He ordered only fruit juice and rolls, ate rapidly, then caught a taxi to the new railway station at Chimki. For a moment he felt free. No delegation came to see him off. He was only just in time. The whistle was going for the departure when he flung his single suitcase on board and sprang in after it. He made his way to the first-class compartments in the forward part of the train. The first three compartments were occupied but the door of the fourth was open and he slid the door gratefully closed behind him.

Through Klin, Kalinin, Vysnij Volocok, leaving the Valdaskaja mountains, still capped with snow, on the right. Then north, the line running some fifty kilometres to the west of Novgorod. There were repairs on the line at Malaja Visera, causing a delay of two hours, and by the time they reached Leningrad it was dark. Military movement on the line to Narva caused a further delay. The train set off west towards Tallinn early in the morning. He found it easier to sleep while the train was in movement. In the dawn he caught glimpses of the sea to the north, the Baltic, home waters.

Estonia is a flat land, a part of the great European plain stretching from the Baltic to the Ural mountains. It is a land of inland lakes, more than 1,500, and islands (some 818 in all). The highest point is the hill of Suur-Munamagi, lying south of the town of Voru. Illich, seated in the mahogany comfort of a first-class carriage on the train to Tallinn, had cause to be reminded of this. Flatlanders are given to depression and drinking. It is as if the monotony of the horizontal can only be dispelled by the vertical soar of the spirit. Estonians were closest to Finns, and shared with them some of their melancholy.

Flatlands are also highways. No great natural obstacles hold back invaders. From the sea came Swedes and Danes, Norman Vikings; from the land Poles, Germans and Russians. The Soviet annexation had been distinguished from the others only by being the most recent and, in terms of the spirit of the country, perhaps the most superficial, despite the thoroughness of the Stalinist purges and deportations. In the eyes of the older generation of Estonians, the Soviet Union had been like a brutal lover who had never fully possessed a mistress, a mistress who in turn hankered after former lovers. For them the heart of Estonia lay in the Baltic; it remained a small, northern European state, until recently held captive by the dark heart of Asia. Thus it was still the case that the older people would talk openly of the 'good old Swedish' days, despite the fact that the newly granted economic freedoms gave Estonia self-rule in all matters excepting military security.

The train, moving fast now, swept across the Estonian border. On one of the two towers of Narva, the blue, black and white Estonian tricolour coruscated slowly in the Baltic breeze. He could smell the sea to the north. It came through the open window, a savour of salt. He caught further occasional glimpses of it, before the train began to move inland again at Jovi. Its significance was emotional. In the traditional saying, the sea was as salty as tears, and by its shores they had suffered.

Just as Estonia's heart was in the Baltic, there was one human resource in which Estonia was rich, and that was in sailors. Nearly all the great sailing champions of Russia had come from Estonia, far more than could possibly be explained by its proportion of seaboard. Illich had explored the northern coast by boat in some detail, its currents and idiosyncrasies of wind. Remembering the words of Sergei Mamayev over the choice of location for the next America's Cup, he prayed that the final choice of venue for the defence would be in Estonia. In their home waters, the mainly Estonian crew would be almost invincible.

There was a knock at the carriage door, then the door slid open.

'Anything to drink, sir?' The white-uniformed waiter held a tray with vodka, spirits, a tall jar of tea.

'Tea.'

This was clearly a shock to the steward. Illich was a colonel in the Army, a hero to all Russians, and half Estonian – three clear excuses for alcoholism. There was a saying amongst higher circles of the military, those who had the luxury of personal servants: No man is a hero to his orderly. Illich considered that there should be another. No teetotaller is a hero to the drinks steward.

'Thank you,' he said. The carriage door was peremptorily shut again. In the corridor the steward recovered from this cultural shock.

The last snows still lay on the ground as they passed through Kivioli, Rakvere, Tapa. Emerging from a cutting Illich looked up through the carriage windows and glimpsed above him the antlers of a reindeer. It was a poetic image. Following the decentralization of the collective farms, the peasant smallholdings had taken increasingly to

31

farming deer. They were hardy in the cold climate, converting the mossy grasses into milk and flesh with impressive efficiency.

In the course of the train journey he had time to turn over in his mind the attitude and statements of General Chernavin. He knew, as all Russian soldiers knew, that in the previous decade the power of the military had been gradually but inexorably reined in. Not only were its armaments budgets severely restricted, but all the associated privileges of the military had come under closer scrutiny by the political establishment. The virtual monopoly of scientific research and individual talents by the armed forces had been questioned, checked, placed in slow but inexorable reverse. The government's new priority had been to divert the flow of production from military to civilian consumer goods. It was a policy whose effects were becoming clearer, albeit more slowly than its architects would have wished. New graduates of the scientific academies had been encouraged into the civilian sector. Now the prize postings were executive functions in the General Machine Ministry, overseeing the design and production of refrigerators, combine harvesters, television and hi-fi equipment. The military organs of production were forced to build up adjuncts for the civilian market. Thus the Aviation Ministry turned out Raketa vacuum cleaners and children's prams in addition to its normal quotas of fighter aircraft. And this movement of personnel left its mark on the structure of the armed forces. Increasingly, the bulk of the Army was in reserve, called into the *kadrirovannye* or skeleton divisions, where a handful of regulars were fleshed out with reservists on mobilization.

The train passed a gang of men constructing a road, a group from the *stroibaty*, the construction battalions. He guessed that the road was civilian, not military, no doubt aimed at providing better communications between outlying marketing towns and villages. Such diversions of military manpower provided further reason, Illich thought, for the anger of Chernavin and his fellow generals. The men were working in conjunction with a bulldozer, flattening and filling gravel behind it with their shovels. Several of them rested on their shovels to watch the train go by.

After Aegviidu it was only another half hour to Tallinn. The magnificent medieval city came into view, his home town, the scene of his youth and his sailing. The central hill of the town, with its fringe of trees on the slopes, was partly obscured by a low-lying sea mist. At Tallinn railway station he got out. A porter, recognizing him, waddled over towards him, panting with the effort.

'Ivan Ivanovitch,' the old man hailed him. Illich recognized the man as Talun Kana, the father of one of the reserve crew on the *Leningrad*.

He embraced the old man.

'Are you returning for good?' Kana asked

'I think so,' said Illich. Subject to the Defence Ministry, he thought to himself.

'Where have you been all these months?'

'Sleeping,' said Illich, searching for a phrase that would please the old man, 'on the enormous breasts of Mother Russia.'

'That sounds pleasant enough work to me.'

'It's pleasant for a while.'

At the exit, the old man gave him a friendly shove, and partly propelled by this, Illich passed through the decorated wooden gates into Tallinn.

Six

He walked through the streets carrying his suitcase, scenting the sea. His legs felt light. The longueurs of the journey seemed to fall away from him. Illich could walk for hours in this mood, lightheaded. He decided to walk around the walled city, taking a long route.

He kept to the small streets, away from the crowded main thoroughfares. At least here, in Tallinn, he was able to be himself, not to be constantly on parade. They knew his parents, his family, and familiarity bred a relaxed attitude. Storekeepers would call out to him from a doorway; elderly people, pensioners, would raise their hands in greeting from the tiny windows of their small converted flats on the third and fourth floors. Schoolchildren paused to watch him go by, but they did not crowd him for autographs as in other cities.

An attitude of calm cosmopolitanism pervaded the new shopping areas. Old men wandered with medals from the past, smartly dressed housewives in the latest fashions moved from street stall to shop, a smattering of Western tourists, American, German, Japanese, with their expensive automatic cameras, ambled on the pavements. The greater economic freedom of Estonia brought with it a certain lightness to its capital city, a dilution of the grey depression of other former Soviet cities. Greater diversity brought greater tolerance. It was pleasant to walk on a spring morning around the outside of the old town.

The streets grew narrower in the old quarters – medieval thoroughfares, hardly wide enough for four people abreast. He walked past the house where his late uncle had lived with his family. After his uncle's death, the younger family – his cousin Tarde and his wife and children – had moved to Smolensk where a new computer factory was under construction, and the flat now stood empty, with its windows boarded.

His own flat was at the top of the newly named Laidoner Street. It had been renamed after General Johan Laidoner who, with the help of 2,000 Finnish volunteers, had led the Estonians in a campaign which drove out the invading Red Army in 1919. It was a prestigious flat, one of ten which were once occupied by members of the Russian *vlasti* on postings in the outer republics. Above him was the flat of the Head of the Russian Trade Delegation, who held lavish parties for the leaders of the new burgeoning businesses in Estonia. Sometimes Illich could hear the sound of balalaikas or the heavy beat of Western pop music, and the excited squeal of female party-goers. His former wife had imagined elaborate orgies conducted in the name of commerce, a free trade of bodies. She had asked him on many occasions to complain, because the noise kept the children awake.

That was what he dreaded on entering the flat, the faded echo of his family's voices. After twelve years of marriage his wife had departed, first to Tartu where she lived with her parents, both professors at the university; then, having married a visiting professor of computer studies, she moved to her new husband's home city of Kharkov. She had been granted custody of the children, a ruling he had never contested. The grounds for divorce were his almost permanent absence. In the central republics of the Russian hinterland, a court would have sympathized with him and almost certainly would have taken his side. In Tartu, the Estonian jury looked critically upon a husband who was in the Russian Army.

The entrance hall of the flat was empty. It contained the usual pile of official brown envelopes. He placed these on the dining-room table, and went through the flat, opening

35

its wooden shutters to let in the light. It was four months since he had lived there, four months of constant touring which was only now, thankfully, drawing to an end. There were still half a dozen more engagements to speak in various parts of the Soviet Union, but they were reasonably well spaced. The tours were coming to a natural end. Public interest in the America's Cup had reached a climax a year previously, after the Soviet Union had won, and only recently had started to fall away. He was grateful. Now at least he could begin the serious preparation and training for the next one.

Seven

Amongst the pile of official letters was one, marked 'delivered by hand', sealed in an unobtrusive brown envelope. 'IMPORTANT' had been stamped on it in red against a background of black and white stripes.

He cleared a place on the dining-room table, opened the envelope, and read the letter carefully:

It was headed: *Defence Ministry: Personnel*:

Comrade Colonel Illich,

Your instructions are as follows:

1.   Your appointment as captain and helmsman of the defending yacht representing Russia in the America's Cup has been confirmed.

2.   Report to Major-General S. Vorolov at the People's Sports Palace, Pirita, Tallinn, on 2 April at 9 a.m. A new sailing base has been under construction.

3.   New offices have been established adjacent to the sailing base and fleet harbour. You have been allocated office 2, in the administration centre.

4. *The yacht* Leningrad *has finished its tour of the provinces of the Russian Republics. It is being refitted and made ready for sailing.*

5. *A new yacht, to be named* Kirov, *will be arriving shortly from the construction factory in Pskov, delivery date 14 May. Please ensure readiness for launch.*

6. *Make all haste to begin training your crew for the defence of the America's Cup which is herewith agreed to take place beginning 1 May 2003 (Challenger eliminations). America's Cup races between defender and challenger are scheduled to begin on 1 August, 2003.*

7. *The winter training camp will be at Odessa, 1 September to 1 April. Facilities are currently under completion outside Iljicovsk.*

8. *Clarification has been obtained from the authorities in regard to the siting of the America's Cup defence. Taking into account the sensitivity of military establishments outside St Petersburg on the north of the bay, it has been decided to site the defence west of St Petersburg, on the southern arm of the bay.*

9. *Major-General S. Vorolov will apprise you of further details.*

The letter was signed by Major-General Org, Assistant to General Chernavin. Illich stared briefly at the forward sloping letters like waves, or perhaps troops advancing against cold winds.

There were several things that intrigued him about the arrangements. Firstly, although the northern training camp was at Tallinn, the defence was not to be held within Estonia, but had been shifted eastwards along the coast to a point some miles outside St Petersburg, in the Russian motherland. Did this, he reflected, denote a certain nervousness about Estonia? Secondly, the winter training location in Odessa coincided with the training school set up, several years ago, to train promising sailors of Russian or Slav extraction, a 'counterweight' to the domination of the sport of sailing by Estonians.

Both these arrangements, with their hints of larger, political considerations, confirmed something which he had always noted in reports about the America's Cup. It was a highly political forum. It might begin as a sport but it ended in politics. About all things associated with it lay the shadow, or at least the penumbra, of political manoeuvre. The forthcoming arrangements suggested that things were likely to be no different this time.

When he turned on the bathroom tap there was a sound of shuddering and shaking; a squeal, but no water. Cursing, he picked up the empty kettle on the stove and went down to see the janitor.

He knocked on the blue door of the janitor's ground floor flat. There was a shuffling behind the door, which opened slowly to reveal the janitor's wife, a child in her arms.

'Is Comrade Irkut in?'

She called into the adjacent room, where the sound of a television was loud.

Irkut, a big sallow man with a permanent downturn to his mouth, came to the door in his trousers and vest.

'I have just returned,' Illich said. 'My plumbing is not working.'

Irkut's reaction to such news was an expression of great astonishment. Illich had seen this expression a hundred times before on the faces of Army clerks and quartermasters. He knew that Irkut once had held such a post.

'Your plumbing?'

'Yes.'

'Not working?'

'No.'

'I will tell the plumber immediately.'

'He was supposed to have fixed the plumbing four months ago, before I left.'

'Excuse me, Comrade Colonel.' Irkut disappeared temporarily in order to consult a timetable behind the door. 'You were not scheduled to return for another week.'

'I came home early.'

Another expression developed on Irkut's face, that of a man who has just been told something slightly odd, something a little unbelievable. This was followed by a third expression, one which said, Don't worry, sir, I understand these little foibles of yours. Just let me see to it and everything will be all right.

'I will make sure that it is attended to tomorrow,' Irkut assured him.

'Thank you. In the meantime, may I request that you fill this kettle from your own tap?'

'Certainly, sir,' Irkut said. In a few moments he returned with a filled kettle.

'Is that all I can do, sir?'

Irkut's final expression said, Surely you cannot expect me to put myself out further, after everything I have now done for you?

'Thank you, comrade,' Illich replied.

That evening he telephoned his ex-wife in Kharkov. A new, efficient local telephone exchange had been installed in Estonia, but the main telephone system across Russia and the Ukraine was still archaic. He tried several times, receiving a no-number signal on the first two occasions, and a series of odd clicks on the third. He waited ten minutes and tried again.

This time the voice of a man came to the phone.

'Professor Varilev?'

'Who is that, please?' The voice was diffident.

'Ivan Illich.'

There followed a disapproving silence. What did Anna tell him, that he sounded so offhand?

'May I speak to Anna?'

Again no answer. The phone was put down beside the receiver.

Forty seconds? Fifty seconds? While the phone bill mounted.

'Hello,' his ex-wife's voice.

'Anna?'

'It's you.'

Yes, it is me.

'I have to give a talk in Kharkov on the 24th of April, to the Association of Ukrainian Postal Officers. Would you object if, the following day, the 25th, I took the girls out?'

Another long silence.

'I'll have to see.'

The sound of the phone being put down. Voices in the background, A girl's voice, almost certainly Natasha, saying. 'Is it daddy?' Anna's answering comment, too low to be heard clearly. The sound of her husband, the professor. A series of exchanges between husband and wife: a serious meeting was in progress, of Cabinet proportions.

'Hello.' Her voice again, tinged with defiance.

'I'm here,' Illich said.

'It's not much warning.'

'Three weeks?' he asked.

Another pause.

'Only for two hours, in that case. In the afternoon. After school.'

'Four o'clock?'

A pause.

'Four o'clock,' she confirmed.

'Thank you,' Illich said. 'Goodbye, Anna.'

Another pause, then the phone went dead.

There was something that caused him more discomfort than the monotony of travelling or the life of a people's hero, away from the sea. This was the recurrence of the dream, the dream which was also a nightmare.

He had experienced its return in the Kalinin hotel in Moscow, though not, curiously, on the train journeys. Perhaps the motion of the train had soothed his mind. The dream instead came to him in the new air-conditioned hotels, when his body had the solid rest of land beneath it – or now as he lay with a blanket over himself in the empty, cold flat. It varied, but its central core was always the same.

He had, for the first time in his life, resigned himself in the course of a sailing race to the knowledge that he would be beaten. More than that, he would be beaten by a better man. They were approaching the finishing line, he in second place, the other boat ahead. In the sphere of sailing, no race is decided until the finish line is crossed, but even so he had been beaten, outmanoeuvred and outfought, on three consecutive races, and in this one his opponent had again drawn inexorably into the lead position. And then, as if that were not enough, the nightmare itself.

The leading boat paused right in front of the finishing line, where it seemed to hesitate; then it began to turn, to rotate slowly back. It pivoted gracefully, of its own accord, spinning on its own axis, picking up momentum, bearing away forcefully before the finishing line. His mouth and throat were dry, he could not speak. The turning boat struck a crest and developed a brief mane of spray. Turning still, the wind behind, it passed a critical angle, and he could hear the vicious crash of its boom at the gybe. It accelerated, picking up a bone of spray in its teeth, and descended on him like a ghost.

That was when he woke up, dry-mouthed and sweating.

Eight

Major-General Stefan Vorolov stood up to shake hands with Illich. Illich noted the force of his grip, the immensely strong, squat frame, the square face with its Tartar cheekbones.

Vorolov's eyes indicated a chair. Illich knew, from the insignia at Vorolov's chest, that he had been seconded to this post from the Strategic Rocket Forces, an élite of the armed forces.

Vorolov said: 'As we are to collaborate closely over the next two years, I suggest we call each other by our first names.'

Vorolov's office was large, a veritable suite. Illich glanced at several framed photographs. One showed Vorolov among a group of other officers. The rubric beneath it read: 'General S. Vorolov, Senior Instructor', and beneath that, the general heading 'College of the Strategic Rocket Forces'.

There are certain positions which are steps on the ladder to the very highest commands. To be entrusted with teaching the younger staff officers, reflected Illich, was a classic vantage point in the rise to highest command.

Vorolov noted the direction of his glance. 'My appointment here was created by special meeting of the Armed Forces Committee.' He smiled. 'It seems a somewhat formal procedure if they merely wish to bury an officer in the provinces.'

Beneath this apparent modesty there was another, hidden message. This was that the armed forces had placed one of their best officers in control of the defence of the America's Cup, that absurd silver ewer created by Victorian craftsmen.

Vorolov extended a leather case towards him. 'A cigarette?'

Illich noticed that Vorolov's fingers were stained with nicotine.

'No thanks.'

'I admire your dedication.'

Vorolov lit his own cigarette and, casting away the match, he blew a thoughtful plume.

After a brief pause, Vorolov said, 'Instead of international conflict, we enjoy a period of sustained peace. In place of war, we have . . . what? A yacht race?'

'Perhaps.'

'It is a charming thought.' Vorolov nodded to himself. 'Yachts at least have the virtue of being more aesthetic than rockets.'

Another plume, another pause.

'And you?' Vorolov asked politely, almost shyly. 'You chose it because it is at the forefront of the battle with the West?'

Illich knew now that he was being teased. At least Vorolov had a sense of humour.

'I am surprised, General, that a College of Strategic Yacht Forces has not already been established.'

'Perhaps this will be our task,' Vorolov said. He stood up. 'Let us go and survey our little empire.'

The administration building had been purpose-built. A *stroibaty* battalion had been assigned the task, with engineering expertise supplied by the Armed Forces Central Coordination.

Beside Vorolov's extensive suite, an office had been set aside for Illich. Vorolov pushed open a door. 'Your home,' he said. Illich took note of the medium-sized office, the large standard issue metal desk, the walls currently bare. It would remain almost unused, he reflected, except perhaps for the first few weeks. His function was to be out on the water.

They walked down the corridor towards the exit.

A tall, immensely gaunt man emerged from a nearby office.

'Major Vitaly Archem,' Vorolov introduced him.

Archem must have been well over two metres in height. Illich had only seen such heights when the Moscow basketball team, the Rockets, had come to Tallinn several years ago for a demonstration match against a Finnish team.

Vorolov and Archem, then; one short and square, built like a refrigerator; the other tall as a telephone pole.

Like many tall men, an inbuilt courtesy made Major Archem almost bow to shake hands as if, by virtue of his physique, he were reintroducing the formal procedures of the pre-Revolutionary Tsarist army.

'Major Archem is in charge of organization and supply,' Vorolov was saying. 'We have a high priority Direct Access pass to the Ministry of Machinery. Ask,' he summarized, 'and you shall receive.'

As they left, Major Archem bowed again.

At the end of the corridor, the exit door was guarded by two military policemen.

The progress made in constructing the purpose-built harbour and shoreside maintenance facilities had been rapid. Some four or five hundred men were toiling on the site. To reach the harbourside, Vorolov walked through a storage site for bulldozers and trucks.

The two embracing arms of the harbour wall were already complete, enclosing an area of water approximately the size of two football fields. An array of pontoons and docking facilities was in place. Around the entire perimeter of the base a solid wall, three metres high, had been constructed, topped with guard wire and electrification. Military police and NCOs were organizing its final stages.

At the centre of the site the cantilevered shells of two huge engineering and building sheds were also in the final stages of construction. Immense doors, some five metres high by ten metres wide, were being installed by teams of engineers. Two parallel steel tracks, like railway lines, led from the water into the nearest of the two buildings. The tracks continued through the rear door of this building into the second great covered area. Engineering Administration offices were being set up in the form of army prefabrication units. More permanent harbour administration buildings were at the roof stage. The dormitory buildings, with associated leisure areas, were already complete. Men swarmed everywhere. Vorolov and Illich had to move aside to let through a large delivery truck carrying stressed metal cross-beams.

'Completion date in six weeks,' Vorolov said. 'Then business in earnest. In the meantime, the crews will be arriving and settling in. I naturally leave entirely to you, Comrade, the matter of their training.'

A breeze was blowing from the west, surprisingly warm for this time of year. Vorolov moved into the shadow of a temporary site building to light another cigarette. He threw the match aside and inhaled deeply, staring out to sea reflectively.

'You are pleased with progress?'

This was an odd question between military men. The Army could achieve, if it so wished, virtual miracles of construction merely by throwing men in vast numbers at the problem. Rather, the question should be translated into 'Are you pleased the authorities have given the project such priority?'

To both questions, overt and implicit, Illich replied 'Yes.'

In the shelter of the makeshift building, staring out to sea, Vorolov seemed to pause before formulating another question.

An eddy of wind shook the makeshift building behind which they sheltered. Vorolov expelled a puff of smoke between his lips.

'You are aware that a political dimension exists.'

Illich did not know how to respond. It was a statement more than a question, though it had been cast across him carefully in order, no doubt, to elicit his response. Illich had the feeling that his every small movement was being studied. He simply nodded, as if to say 'I hear you.'

'I am merely a soldier, of course,' Vorolov added casually, between exhalations. Like many such statements, it carried myriad undercurrents. On its surface was a statement of fact. On another level there was a further addition, a part left unsaid, a 'but . . .'

The 'but . . .' which Illich would have liked to add was, 'You were also, until recently, the Chief Instructor of staff officers at the College of Strategic Rocket Forces, in charge of teaching doctrine and tactics to future senior military commanders – a military position of a high strategic grade. You are therefore more than a simple soldier.'

Facing outwards to sea, Vorolov drew on his cigarette while Illich stood with his hands folded behind his back. Each waited for the other to make his move. He is inviting me, Illich thought, to declare myself. Should I, too, say that I am a simple soldier? At the very least, he reflected, such a declaration would have the virtue of being somewhat truer than Vorolov's statement about himself.

Vorolov lowered his cigarette and, in the time-honoured tradition of the Russian Army everywhere, pinched its glowing ember between thumb and forefinger. It was, Illich remembered, a gesture he had seen many thousands of times, in hundreds of different places. But in this case was there a hint of a threat in it, a warning?

They made their way back to the administration offices, Vorolov uncommunicative, Illich silent at his side.

Nine

There seemed little time to settle down before he was scheduled to fly again on his final series of talks and lectures in the southern republics of the former Soviet Union.

The headquarters of the combined sailing clubs of the Foreign and Interior Ministries was situated at Sevastopol, on the Black Sea. Illich's old henchman Alexandre Brod, tactician on the *Leningrad*, was the 'professional' in charge of sailing activities, including the fleet of over 200 Laser dinghies.

On 12 April, in Odessa, several hours' drive from Sevastopol, Illich gave a lecture on team spirit to the association of Ukrainian Municipalities. After his lecture he was scheduled to stay two days in Odessa before taking the Aeroflot flight back to Moscow. To fill in time, he arranged to visit his old friend Brod's house overlooking the sea at Kucek a few kilometres outside Sevastopol.

Illich decided to surprise Brod by arriving half a day earlier than scheduled. Shortly after the lecture had finished, somewhat the worse for wear after the lavish fare provided by the munificent Odessa municipality, he took a taxi provided *gratis* from the pool of the Odessa municipality for the purposes of sightseeing that day.

His Azerbaijani driver, a silver ring threading his right ear, pushed his five-year-old Fiat at great speed past Nikolajev, Cherson, through Navaja Kachovka. They crossed the long bridge between Genicesk and Dzankol, and detoured around Simferpol to Sevastopol. Several miles to the north of Sevastopol, the new shining clubhouse of the Foreign and Interior Ministries obtruded its cube-like architecture onto the beach. On the north side, several new hotels were nearing completion. Having tipped the driver, Illich disembarked and, carrying his suitcase and holdall, made his way down to the beach. There was a copse of trees standing a little back from the shore. In their privacy he changed from his army uniform to his sailor's drysuit and put on, over that, his tracksuit. He repacked his uniform carefully into his suitcase. The April breeze had a chill in it, even in these southern latitudes. To disguise his blond locks, he put on a woolly hat. These changes completed, he emerged from the little copse of trees, and made his way to the clubhouse.

At the entrance of the clubhouse he showed the security guard his Interior Ministry pass. To Illich's relief, the man evinced no sign of recognition. Or perhaps he assumed this unexpected stranger was simply a namesake of the sailing hero. Illich pointed to the line of waiting dinghies.

'When does the race start?'

The security guard consulted a schedule inside his office. 'Three fifteen.'

'Thank you, comrade. Could I perhaps leave my things with you?'

'You can leave them in my office. I'm on duty until seven.'

Illich deposited the suitcase in the small adjoining office.

'Are you sailing?' the man called out after him, when he was walking away.

Illich turned, shrugging his shoulders. 'It depends.'

'You should see Comrade Brod.'

'What does he look like?'

The security guard drew a square shape in the air; a perfect description, Illich thought, of the squat, explosive Brod.

A line of Laser dinghies were waiting to be launched, their masts and sails nearby. Several others were in the process of being rigged. He fixed on an unattended dinghy and began to rig it. At the other end of the beach, Brod's square figure was at the centre of a little flurry of launching boats. Keeping his back to Brod, he wheeled the trailer down to the beach, and launched the boat.

There followed one of those epiphanies of sensation. Shortly after he had pushed off, a little gust of wind caught the sail. He pulled the tiller towards him; the boat bore off and picked up speed. Even clogged with the generous hospitality of the Ukrainian Republic, he felt that glow of expectation which he always, for unfathomable reasons, experienced on the water. So as not to draw attention to himself, he loitered close by the shore in the company of the other launched dinghies.

Keeping his head low, he noticed out of the corner of his eye that Brod himself had now launched a dinghy, and was leading a little fleet of Lasers towards the starting line.

Illich turned to pursue a parallel course towards the waiting committee boat launch three hundred metres from shore.

The breeze was moderate, somewhat cold, and its denseness made the boat heel a little more than expected. He sheeted in and let his instinct inform him about speed, then sheeted out a little, cajoling a response. He was caught up in this when he realized that Brod was staring at him across the water. Deliberately, he let the boat come too far into the wind, so that the sail fluttered; he pushed it back on course, heeled, overcompensated by bringing it back on the wind. It was, he hoped, a good enough imitation of a beginner.

Brod, to Illich's relief, turned away, shouting to several other boats close by. The ten-minute gun sounded. Brod chose the launch end of the line, so Illich stayed at the other, the pin end, even though the changing wind direction created a bias in favour of the other end.

The five-minute gun went.

There were some eighty or so dinghies now, enough to hide among. He kept a wary eye out for Brod, in case he switched to the pin end of the line. But Brod disappeared from view amongst the mêlée at the launch end. Illich glanced at his watch, then mentally began to count off the seconds. Twenty, nineteen, eighteen . . .

He sheeted in and started to accelerate towards the line, close reaching past the outer mark. Three seconds to spare, he thought. He made a little low swoop, picked up speed, sheeted in, and accelerated through the line two seconds after he had seen the puff of smoke from the starting launch.

A good start. At the other end, Brod came out of the pack fast. The line bias put Brod ahead, however, and on this beat Illich would be forced to concentrate merely on reducing his losses. He anticipated a small windshift, tacked, and started to close in on Brod's leading group. He managed to traverse most of the fleet without interference. At the windward mark he was fifth boat after Brod. Half-way along the downwind leg he had overtaken the fourth boat and was closing in on the third. Out ahead, Brod seemed unconcerned.

It was when Illich overtook the third boat that Brod turned round to stare at him. Illich would remember that swift glare, the wide, dark eyes, the furrowed eyebrows. Brod had been a great ladies' man, able to send powerful glances across a crowded room. He was one of that minority of Estonians who are so dark they seem like Latins. To Illich, Brod's intensity sometimes bordered on the comical.

Hidden in his bulky tracksuit, his woollen hat and his sunglasses, Illich nevertheless still felt undetected, despite further dark glances from Brod.

He was drawing level with the second boat as they approached the downwind mark. It was one of those choices, based on intuition and ruthlessness, which were to him the heart of racing. The wind had veered and they were on a broad reach. He could sail upwind of the other boat, try to take its wind, or (the riskier alternative) attempt an inside overlap as they closed with the buoy. Only three boat lengths separated them. In the end he feinted an upwind drive. The other boat responded by luffing up, which in turn opened up a small gap to leeward. Illich bore off, driving hard for the inside overlap. He hissed out 'water!' when it was technically dubious, claiming right of way at a psychological moment timed, not to convey information, but to intimidate the other helmsman. A stronger-nerved man would have ignored him, but this one held back. Illich slipped through on the inside, rounded the buoy, and there ahead of him, ten lengths up, was Brod.

Illich split tacks immediately, putting distance between them. He felt, on the previous beat, there was more wind on the port side of the course, towards the shore. In his experience, the wind accelerated as it followed the curve of a promontory, though it was a risky surmise. Perhaps Brod knew better.

Illich decided to bite the bullet and keep going. In such circumstances it was necessary to forget the peripatetic nature of the decision and concentrate entirely on speed. If you glanced sideways and sensed the other boat's better position, you were finished. He hoped this determined pursuit of a different course would unsettle Brod, pitched suddenly into a battle of nerves with an unknown opponent.

Brod it was who tacked first, the first small sign of a loosening nerve, even though it seemed to Illich that Brod had gained by his own tactic of keeping out to sea. Illich remained on his course towards the shore. A line of whitecaps moved tantalizingly ahead of him. Before Brod travelled more than fifty metres on parallel tack, Illich experienced the lift and rise of the wind.

Now he was gripped by concentration. Fifty metres in, he felt the wind slacken, and tacked back into the wind corridor. He and Brod were closing. A minute later he tacked again, eating up a few more feet at a time.

Brod was sailing well, reliably. As they approached the finishing line there was nothing between them. Nothing, that is, except that Illich was on port tack and they were on a collision course. Brod had clear right of way. Just before they were about to meet, Illich, waiting until the last moment to unnerve Brod, tacked, completing his manoeuvre with hardly more than ten feet to spare. He was now parallel with Brod. Neck and neck, Illich squeezed up to windward. Brod tried to ease upwind, but the gap closed. If Brod tacked now, he would lose a vital few feet of distance and lose the race. Illich kept squeezing up: Brod tried to inch away. The sides of the two boats kissed with a squeal of illicit pleasure. In any protest room, Illich would win, and he knew that Brod knew it too – a classic match-racing tactic. A few seconds later the two boats slid over the finishing line, centimetres between them, as decorously as paired dancers.

You would have thought, however, that Brod had been stung by a wasp. He stood up and roared: 'Son of a camel!'

Brod's Laser rocked. Illich thought he would topple into the water with rage.

*

Brod's wife Ilena served thick, black coffee. Their small house at Kecuk overlooked the sea, purple now with spring evening light.

The air was clear, free of the mosquitoes which plagued them in summer. The little garden, with its baskets of flowers, was peaceful. Offshore was the anchored, grey shape of a Sovremenny class destroyer – a series of cubistic surfaces. For Illich this was a typical image of the new political realities, a scene of great natural beauty with, in the background, the hovering presence of the armed forces. Just as the Russian State had become more refined, its controls more subtle, so it seemed to Illich that the military forms had become more streamlined, sculptural. The warship out there was like an abstract study in flat surfaces.

Brod said, a little stiffly perhaps, 'Congratulations, Ivan Ivanovitch, on your selection.'

Illich turned reluctantly from the ship anchored offshore. 'How did you know?'

Brod tapped his nose roguishly. 'Contacts. Besides, it was a foregone conclusion.'

'Was it?' asked Illich. 'You learned that too?'

'Who is the alternative?'

'Pilnyak won a gold medal at the Olympics in 2000 in the Soling class. Ogorov was second in the international Championship of Champions.'

The corners of Brod's mouth deflected downwards in an imitation of a street-vendor considering an offer. He rolled his head slowly from side to side, like a Georgian bargaining.

'Fifteen years younger than me, both of them,' Illich added.

'Fifteen years less experience.'

Offshore, a grey launch was approaching the warship. From this distance Illich could just see the shapes of three blue-uniformed officers in the stern. As the spring progressed into summer they would change into white uniforms, like the Mediterranean fleet. Illich turned away from these distractions to face Brod directly.

'We start training in a few weeks. Do you want to join us?'

Brod's reaction was not what he expected. He seemed to pause, suspended; his eyes flickered towards his wife. Ilena looked away. Illich glanced at her profile: her eyes were closed, as if against pain.

This reaction struck Illich suddenly with the force of a heavy blow. He realized his mistake too late.

'I'm sorry, I had no right to ask you that.' Illich glanced again at Ilena, who had raised a hand to her mouth, against her teeth. 'I think perhaps you would be a fool to accept.'

And of course he was right. Brod would return to cheerful alcoholism. Illich felt his guilt grow against him, suddenly vast.

'It's a difficult decision,' Brod said. 'We have discussed it often.'

Such lengthy discussions indicate a difference of view, thought Illich. He could see, out of the corner of his eye, that Ilena's physical position was unchanged. She would not, however, speak on Brod's behalf. Brod must tell Illich himself. Illich would not prolong his old friend's torture.

'If you can't make up your mind, Alexandre,' Illich said, 'I must make it up for you. I retract my offer.'

Ilena's head was still turned away. He asked himself, how could I introduce this unhappiness again, to this contented couple in this garden of Eden? Only the sinister, beautiful shape of the destroyer offshore put his guilt into perspective, demonstrating that there were other sources of tension in the world than himself.

Out of embarrassment for them both, he stared once again at the implacable profile of the warship. Ilena chose this moment to stand up and ask, in a muffled voice:

'More coffee?'

Turned away from the sun, her face was obscured by shadow, but he guessed she had been crying.

*

'Ivanya,' Brod said, while Ilena was making a fresh cup of coffee. 'Explain to me one thing.'

Illich waited. Far away, to the north, he fancied the coastline could just be discerned, a line of dark against the pallid evening sky. A northerly breeze had carried away to the south the cloud of smoke from the factories and dockyards of Sevastopol, leaving the light extraordinarily clear. Brod asked, 'Why did *New World* turn back at the finish line?'

The American helmsman's behaviour in the final race of the America's Cup might still haunt Illich's dreams. But it was almost a mundane subject here, away from all such matters, on a quiet evening overlooking the Black Sea.

Illich shrugged. A year after its occurrence, the matter was still a mystery.

'I read,' continued Brod, 'an account of it in a translated edition of the *Washington Post* newspaper. It said that Jim Shaw was under pressure from the US military, and deliberately lost the race to make an ideological point.'

'Ideology?' Illich asked out aloud. The ideology of a helmsman was to win. Jim Shaw had not been lacking in this ideology. Illich still remembered at an almost visceral level the unprecedented fury and power of Shaw's last four races. It was as if he drew upon unknown inner resources.

Brod was staring at him. It was a curious fact to Illich that, in the intervening year, none of his crew had raised the matter directly with him. It was as if each had tried to come to terms with this last act in the privacy of his own thoughts. Only Brod, who was retiring, sought clarification.

Ilena returned with the coffee. Illich waited while she poured.

'Frankly,' Illich said, 'I still do not understand.'

'The American article,' persisted Brod, 'stated that their helmsman Shaw was highly individualistic in his character. It said that he was in conflict with the American military authorities from the start.'

Is that sufficient reason to turn away from the greatest

triumph of his career, Illich asked himself? Do you really believe so? This would have been asked in a spirit of enquiry, had he wished to voice it out loud. Perhaps Brod did believe so, in which case he and Illich diverged.

'This paper said, in effect, that from Shaw's point of view he did not lose. Perhaps Shaw felt he gained, the article stated, a moral victory.'

Is there such a thing? Illich asked himself. Are medals awarded for 'moral victories'? Every race contained its crises, its turning points, where the issue was in the balance. The resolution of all these crises and balance points is who crosses the line first. Nevertheless, at moments during his triumphal tour of the Russian provinces, his mind had hovered uncomfortably over this question. He remembered the disconcerting nature of the spectators' response to Shaw's deliberate turn from the finish line. They had been silent at first, stunned. But as Shaw's boat had neared the shore during its return to base, they had started to cheer, hardly audibly at first, then louder. Did the spectators too believe in 'moral victories'?

Ilena was refilling their coffee cups, focused on her own thoughts.

Illich asked, 'Do you also believe in moral victories, Ilena?'

She shrugged. She now seemed fully recovered. He realized that her own crisis was over. Brod would not be racing in the America's Cup again. To her, that was all that mattered.

Ten

At Tallinn railway station the elderly porter Talun Kana was there again, puffing along the platform, his small blue eyes glinting with humour. Illich paused so that he could catch up with him.

'Where have you been this time, Ivan Ivanovitch? On another hero's tour?'

'Selfless devotion to the motherland,' Illich said. He knew this would inflame the old man's imagination.

'Disgraceful,' commented Comrade Kana. 'You were only doing your duty, of course.'

'Of course.'

At the turnstile, Kana cupped his hands and called after him. 'You brought tears of gratitude to the eyes of Russian womanhood.'

Several handsome Latvian matrons in the foyer turned to study Illich. He made his rapid escape into the street.

In the urban environment of the former Soviet Union, it was increasingly difficult to make simple distinctions between the roles of the inhabitants. In the last fifteen years, the years of Illich's adult memory, great changes had taken place. The old system of Communism was highly élitist. There had been a world of difference between the senior *apparatchik* in his chauffeur-driven limousine and the peasant newly arrived from the land, who trudged the streets as if still on the soil of his fathers. Between these two extremes were a series of recognizable gradations, the hierarchy of a centralized state.

The cumulative effect of *glaznost* and *perestroika* over many years had been the increasing growth of the middle class. Now, as in Western cities, it was difficult to tell, from appearances alone, the shop-girl from the daughter of one of the *vlasti*, since each had access to stores full of Western clothes and accessories. This was particularly the case in former Soviet republics such as Estonia, where economic autonomy had accelerated such changes. But the structure, too, had changed, the hierarchy had become more diluted, the gradations less clear.

In the old society there existed a clear line of precedence. In the new, how was one to differentiate between the owner of a small private building business and a trade delegate from one of the big worker-owned engineering companies seeking new orders in the city? Neither type had been present in the old regime.

Even the political vocabulary had changed beyond recognition. It followed that those who advocated adherence to the old Communist ways were the new conservatives, the élitists, the opposers of change. It was an irony of the new society that the Communists and conservatives were now one and the same.

To Illich, a colonel in the Russian Army, the proliferation of new social types, the dilution of the hierarchy and the clear chain of command which had existed in civilian life almost as much as military, all this seemed threatening. To Illich the half Estonian, the changes were a breath of fresh air, blowing away the cobwebs of the old, grey world of absolute Russian hegemony.

Across the face of the former USSR was a mosaic of ethnic groups, with separate traditions waiting to be released like the explosive energy stored in a molecule. Increasingly, the institutions of the old Communist empire appeared like the obtrusions of an alien culture from outer space. Its architectural monuments, for example, were inescapable in their physical expression but oddly outdated in their functions. In its architectural expression, the old Soviet culture suffered from gigantism: faceless apartment blocks, municipal administration centres, vast, impersonal, regional ministries. Even their attempts at entertainment and edification, the palaces of sport, the museums and national monuments of the revolution, exhibited a form of monumental clumsiness. In certain respects too these buildings, with their high, faceless walls, were turned within, secrecy defended by conditioned reflex.

In many cases the original buildings had been demolished to make way for these monstrosities. But equally often they had been built alongside the old culture. Now they seemed increasingly redundant, a line of old teeth in a mouth that was once again smiling.

The urbanization of the Estonian population, its increasing propensity to travel in and out of Estonia to either east or west, had returned to Tallinn some of its old cosmopolitan atmosphere. It was difficult to specify a particular Estonian physical type – perhaps a certain angularity of physique, a boniness of the face, a German or Scandinavian solidity – but now there was a complex mixture of Estonians, Russian immigrants, Georgians and Armenians who had followed the burgeoning commercial activities of the smallest and most liberal of former Soviet Republics.

The internal fabric of the society was changing even more rapidly than the buildings. He turned a corner on Saarema Street and came face to face with a little church. It had once been a Calvinist chapel. After the annexation of Estonia by the Soviet Union it had become a People's Hall, a meeting place of the Communist youth organization Komsomol, replete with a picture of Lenin haranguing an audience. Now it was a cinema for avant-garde films. The slogan 'Help the Motherland – Build Communism' had long since been replaced by the name of a film, this week *Naked Days* starring the Estonian actress Arla Vitnu. Where Lenin once stood in his greatcoat, the voluptuous curves of Arla Vitnu now emerged from a steaming forest spring.

Another film, showing simultaneously, exhibited a poster of an old woman walking along a road with buckets from a

58

communal well, a line of ducks parading behind her. This was the second harvest of freedom, Illich thought, a sentimental return to the old, simple days, when things were ordered by nature, a nostalgia for the country life of the little towns and villages.

In Saanen Street two drunken men in their mid-thirties passed him, supporting each other as they sang disjointed verses. Illich had the military's instinctive horror of such scenes of individual loss of control. As they passed, one of the men appeared to recognize him, halted, and called out: 'Ivan Illich.'

Illich turned. They were both standing, swaying, in the middle of the road. One of the men, the one who had called out, had long fair hair, which partly obscured his face. Bottle in hand, he swept the long strands away from his eyes.

It was something of a shock to recognize Jaan Pats, the poet, revealed behind the greasy curtain of hair. As children, they had been in the same class at school.

'Illich, come and talk to us.' Jaan Pats waved his hand in the direction of one of the street cafés that had sprung up in the city over the past few years.

Illich foresaw an absurd and perhaps tedious conversation with two drunks. But it was one of those times when one acts intuitively. He turned towards Jaan Pats, shook him and his companion by the hand, and the three of them walked over to one of the tables.

Pats sat down heavily. Illich recalled the times he had read of Pats' diatribes against Russia, his increasingly strident calls for the complete freedom of Estonia from remaining Russian military influence. He remembered a ferocious strength of character in his one-time schoolmate. Seated with his legs spread, hands on knees, Pats surveyed him through bloodshot eyes.

'Who would have guessed, Illich, that we would have found ourselves on different sides of the divide?'

'Pats,' Illich said gently, 'if you're about to denounce me as a Russian soldier, you should wait until you're sober.'

Pats appeared to consider this statement carefully.

'My friend,' Illich pressed on, 'I do not mind drunkenness. It is a condition which I enjoy myself. But I do not conduct my life in that state.'

Pats said simply, 'You are more pompous than I remember you.'

This was unexpected. Illich had braced himself against a wheedling, complaining criticism of him, to the effect that his service to the Russian Republic as a soldier was a service to the enemy of Estonia. He was ready to give as good as he got; hence the opening salvo on drunkenness. Russian army doctrine, he reflected, is based on striking first. Nevertheless, he could not help but smile at Pats' answer. Pats in turn started to smirk at Illich's response. Soon the three of them were laughing. Besides, a man who could deliver a reasonable retort was not entirely drunk.

Pats called the waiter and ordered two coffees for himself and his companion, and a vodka for his soldier comrade. This was, Illich reflected, a further nice touch.

While Pats ordered, Illich looked more closely at the third party. Bulky, dark-haired, dressed like Pats in the leather jacket and dungarees of the artist (we all have uniforms, thought Illich) he was clearly a man of few words. Pats turned away from the waiter.

'Permit me to introduce Johan Rudiger.'

Johan Rudiger; Illich tried to remember, his memory cells somewhat stretched: dissident film director, another of that small group of Estonian intelligentsia who recently had become increasingly vociferous in the political sphere. He couldn't remember the titles of the films, but he was pleased at least to have identified his background and occupation. Rudiger leaned over the table and shook hands with him. A powerful grasp, assured. In a flash of inspiration, Illich remembered that he had just seen Rudiger's name on a cinema poster. He said, '*Naked Days*.'

Rudiger's handsome, bear-like features froze.

Illich continued, 'A film which explores the new freedoms, I understand.'

'It is necessary sometimes to make commercial movies.'

Clearly, Rudiger was on the defensive. Pats came to his assistance.

'Nudity is a symbolic expression of freedom.'

More than merely symbolic, Illich reflected. Rudiger, in admitting the film was 'commercial', had clearly been caught off guard. Russian army doctrine recommends: once you have caught the enemy by surprise, press home your advantage. Illich said: 'Arla Vitnu's breasts symbolize the earth, the elemental mother soil?'

But there was no laughter this time. A dissident artist is less at ease with commercialism than a soldier with the nature of his profession.

The coffee arrived. And, with an extra flourish from the waiter, Illich's vodka – a final Parthian shot. Both sides had drawn blood. Honour, perhaps, was satisfied.

'So,' Pats said, 'you are here for some time?'

'Two years, more or less.'

'A military posting? Forgive my asking.'

There was no secrecy about Illich's role. In a day or two it would be announced in the press.

'To help prepare an America's Cup defence.'

Pats smiled: 'A veteran.'

Illich was all of thirty-eight. In the year of the defence, in 2003, he would be forty – for an international sportsman, a veteran indeed.

'You will be helmsman?'

'So it appears.'

There was genuine warmth at this.

'All Russia's best sailors are Estonians,' Rudiger said, with the national vanity of an Argentinian speaking of his country's football side.

'Not quite,' said Illich with due modesty.

'Somewhere, out there, there exists a Russian who can sail?' Pats asked.

'Let us drink to him, comrades, whoever he may be,' Rudiger announced. The two of them raised their coffee cups in deference to this unknown hero. Illich's vodka was like a Spetznaz force operating behind the lines. Whenever he felt safe, it reasserted its ironical presence.

On a more serious level, Illich knew that the authorities had become concerned with the virtual annexation of sailing talent in Estonia. They had set up a special training school on the Black Sea, a sufficient distance south of the holiday city of Odessa to avoid distraction. Here they had been giving intensive training to between forty and fifty promising young dinghy sailors, nearly all of Russian or Byelorussian extraction. He was expecting a contingent of such hopefuls to be sent along to Tallinn for training and assessment.

'Are you working on your next film?' Illich asked Rudiger politely.

'We are in the pre-production stage.' Rudiger changed the subject. 'Some day I would like to make a film about sailing.'

Illich had a not unpleasing vision of Rudiger's favourite actress, Arla Vitnu, as a figurehead on a sailing ship's prow with – a recurring motif – her bosom cleaving the water.

A few tables away some Georgians had gathered. They were dark, Turkish almost, in complexion. But it was their sociality which gave them away, a natural propensity to seek entertainment in groups. Bursts of loud laughter erupted as the drink flowed. The waiter hovered around their table, gathering fresh orders. Soon they would begin to sing maudlin songs . . .

Perhaps Rudiger, too, was lost in contemplation of this new sailing film.

Pats seemed restless. Had he had grown tired of the joke of drinking coffee while others all around them drank alcohol? Perhaps the irony had palled. Alternatively, there now appeared to be so little in common between them that nothing further could usefully be communicated. Whatever the reason, Pats said: 'We must not keep Russia's greatest sailor from his duties.'

'No,' agreed Rudiger.

They stood up. Pats embraced Illich. Rudiger shook hands.

Standing, the two artists exhibited once again their advanced stage of inebriation. Perhaps, being so unused to coffee, it had an unexpectedly severe toxic effect on their systems. This time Illich was not inclined to press his advantage.

He watched them walk, swaying, towards the old part of the city.

A few metres down the road, they turned round and shouted '*Haad aega!*' an Estonian goodbye, a sound which carried within it a ring of defiance, like one of those ancient Viking oaths which clash like swords in the air.

Eleven

The two hundred or so guests at the dance were largely drawn from the University of Tartu's faculty and leading academics. Illich found himself standing next to a statuesque Nordic beauty in the form of Lydia Teemant, a lecturer in child psychology. In the background her father, Professor Teemant, could be seen moving backwards and forwards between groups. Tartu University was, increasingly, a hotbed of student protest against the continuing Russian military presence in Estonia. It appeared that word had come through that several of Professor Teemant's own students had been arrested for disturbances of the peace, and arrangements were in progress with the university authorities to provide bail. Illich made polite conversation with his daughter.

'I wrote my thesis,' Lydia Teement said, 'on the psychology of slavery in recent Russian child-rearing and education.'

'Really?' Illich said cautiously. The music grew louder as the band picked up momentum. More couples joined those on the dance floor. The method of dancing was Western. The sexes did not touch, but danced separately like displaying birds. Nevertheless, the rhythm was infectious. On the perimeter the watchers tapped their feet.

'Do you think,' asked Illich, 'that Western dancing has marginalized the individual?'

Lydia Teemant gave him a quick glance, as if assessing whether his question was facetious, or actually based on interest.

'I'm sorry,' Illich said. 'What is the essence of your thesis to a layman such as myself?'

Having made his joke about Western dancing, he was forced to wait. Against the background of loud music, with pauses in the more obtrusive passages, Lydia Teemant said: 'Russian parents indulge their children. They appear to regard childhood as a golden world, a world, in short, of freedom from responsibility. To such people, to have children is not merely to rear future citizens, but also to return, via their children, to their own childhood.'

'To their own irresponsibility.'

Once again he was aware of her quick glance, as if assessing his interest.

'Precisely. Children are a means of psychological regression to that time of innocence, of, as you say, irresponsibility.'

'So,' asked Illich, 'what is wrong with that?'

'In itself, nothing. In its consequences, a great deal.'

Illich took another gulp of his vodka.

'What consequences would those be?'

'Imagine you are a Russian child, indulged at every opportunity. You associate your childhood with freedom and happiness. As you grow older, you become integrated into the adult world, a world of increasing restriction, increasing curtailment of the freedoms you had, as a child, taken for granted. What are the long term effects?'

'I don't know. Tell me.'

'Every Russian citizen who is the product of such a rearing process associates freedom with early childhood; therefore freedom is something he leaves behind with childhood. He associates adulthood with the loss of his personal freedom. In adulthood he is told what to do. The state does not indulge his freedoms. Thus he associates adulthood indelibly with slavery. This type of rearing process is perfectly suited to the production of adult slaves.'

Illich looked around him at the dance floor. Most people danced separately, Western style, moving arms and legs like marionettes. One couple were holding each other, moving round the dance floor, in that slow, circling sex-hunger which is more shocking because it is restrained.

'What is the antidote?'

'In psychology,' this serious young woman said, 'there is not necessarily an antidote.'

'But your thesis must lead you somewhere.'

'In my paper, I compared this type of upbringing with that of the bourgeois middle classes in the USA and in Britain, for example.'

'Oh?'

'There I found the upbringing to be very different.'

'In what way?'

'The children of the middle classes are highly restricted. They are not indulged to nearly the same extent. They are taught, from the earliest ages, strict codes of protocol and politeness. They are not allowed to intrude to nearly the same degree on adult activities.'

'I see.' He did not really see very much, however. The room was starting to sway slightly out of rhythm to the

65

band. He found he could more or less halt the process by staring at the floor. He sensed she was waiting for him to ask a further question. Above everything he wished her to continue, despite the fact that he felt she was indulging him, that she suspected his interest was peripheral. Now she was staring at the dancing couples in the centre of the room. He tried again.

'What happens as bourgeois children grow older?'

'As they grow older, they are allowed small but increasing amounts of freedom. Adulthood is associated with increasing personal liberty. The bourgeois parent rations this liberty, but the association is clear. In this respect, they are the opposite of Russian children. To someone reared in this bourgeois tradition, childhood is the time of restriction, of being removed from adult company, of being subservient to adults. As they grow older, they are allowed increasing dosages of the subtle drug of liberty.' The music grew louder and the dance more frenzied. 'The result,' continued Lydia Teemant, 'is that whereas the Russian individual associates adulthood with slavery, the child of bourgeois parents associates adulthood with freedom, freedom as a natural right of adulthood.'

It was difficult, now, to even make out the music above the stamping and rowdyism of those on the dance floor.

'Are you saying this is conscious?'

'No. But in each case, it is a self-perpetuating system. The Russian parent, by means of his upbringing, subtly inculcates the attitude of adult slavery, of subservience to authority. He thus generates model Russian citizens, citizens who understand, at the deepest psychological level, their role as mere accessories of the state. The bourgeois, on the other hand, believes that liberty is his prerogative as an adult, so he creates political institutions which allow him this liberty.'

Illich's mind was swimming. He wanted to ask Lydia Teemant to dance, but there was something highly inhibiting about the circumstances. Perhaps she would interpret any movements in this direction as a trivialization of what she had just said. Against the unbearable loudness of the music, he heard her say, 'The former British Prime Minister Mrs Thatcher, for example, is a classic example of this bourgeois upbringing. A fighter for freedom.'

So that was it, thought Illich. The bourgeois background was a perfect breeding ground for warrior queens. He might have known. Out of the corner of his eyes he caught a glimpse of Lydia Teemant's green eyes staring at the dancers gyrating over the wooden floor. They seemed to stare at no one in particular, but he had the feeling the dancing itself, the pattern of movement at least, was of some interest to her.

'Shall we dance?'

She paused. But after only a moment's hesitation she stood up easily and walked with him to the dance floor.

He was expecting someone a little stiffer. But she danced expertly, insofar as one could apply the word 'expertise' to so liberal a medium. He, on the other hand, was awkward. It was perhaps the military. More than that, his whole attitude was one of control, and this Western dancing was, in its 'expert' form at least, an abandonment of control. He felt out of place, even vulnerable. The alcohol came to his rescue, reducing his self-consciousness. If he made a fool of himself, he was some way towards being a full-blooded fool, and in this milieu of gyrating arms and legs, he had the small consolation that he was not entirely out of place.

The heat from the lights made him sweat. Lydia Teemant, on the other hand, seemed coolly to turn in upon herself, to dance almost as if in a form of trance. This was the key he suspected – to leave the body behind, to let it look after itself. The military officer stiff-backed on parade; the young dancer in a western-style discothèque. Equal and opposite faces, the one wholly misunderstood by the other. Perversely, the two images pleased him.

The music stopped. The band relaxed. Glancing at the musicians, he noticed that they slouched over their instruments now, smoking a hand-rolled cigarette, passing it between one another in conscious imitation of Western musicians handing around a marijuana 'reefer'. It was difficult to resist the thought that it would do them good to have their hair cut and be clapped into uniform. What sort of upbringing did they have, he wondered? He wanted to ask Lydia Teemant. Were they Russian children reverting to childhood, or new young bourgeoisie asserting their adult freedoms?

Their chairs had been taken. There was a bar at the other end of the hall, run by the student union.

'What would you like to drink?' he asked her.

'A Martini, please.'

Sure enough, the long-haired youth behind the counter could supply such a drink. Illich had a vodka.

'Tell me,' he said to her, 'Are you by any chance a descendant of Jaan Teemant?'

He noticed a flicker of amusement behind her eyes.

'The socialist leader,' he added stupidly.

'Yes,' she replied. 'He was a great-uncle.'

Prior to the Russian annexation, in the shifting coalitions between May 1919 and May 1933, Teemant, along with Pats and Tonisson, had each been *riigivanem*, parliamentary leader, no less than four times. It was a kind of golden period in Estonian history, a time of which most Estonians, whatever their political allegiance, were nostalgically conscious.

Three young men approached them. Students, he felt certain. They seemed to carry on their shoulders, almost in visible form, the traditional gravity of Estonian formal education, a typically Scandinavian scholastic heaviness. They introduced themselves formally and shook hands. He realized they were not students but lecturers, and with it came a realization of his own age.

Clearly, she knew them well. One, who had introduced himself as Artur Sirk, put an arm round her shoulders which he took to indicate some form of personal tie. He felt a sudden flash of jealousy, and then an equally rapid

68

realization of the absurdity of believing this young woman would not be attached.

In the unaccustomed role of benign uncle, he offered to buy them drinks. He watched Lydia Teement's face, hoping for some further sign of how she expected him to behave in this situation, but she gave no indication, at least that he could fathom.

He left them talking and went to get the drinks. The musicians had started to play again. On his way he looked at the dancers gyrating on the floor. A woman's eyes met his boldly, turned away. She had a shapely figure, leggy, attractive. Her eyes met his again, held his gaze insouciantly for several seconds.

He was both excited and ashamed. Excited, for reasons which were obvious, ashamed, because less than one minute after talking to Lydia Teemant, he was ready, if the opportunity arose, to pursue this sultry fox.

When he returned, the little group of four was in animated discussion. Although they welcomed him and the drinks, he felt like an intruder. They asked him questions, out of politeness it seemed, about sailing. Artur was at pains to let him know that he sailed himself. He was self-deprecatory, though Illich sensed that he was showing off his knowledge to her. He noticed how she would touch him occasionally, an almost instinctive possession, when she made a point, and this confirmed the relationship finally if it had not been obvious before.

The little band had picked up its momentum again and was pounding out the rhythm of another Western rock song. The lyrics sounded strange in Estonian. It was better with a nasal, American twang. Out of the corner of his eye he saw the girl in a blue dress leave the dance floor, accompanied by another man.

'Excuse me,' he said, deliberately addressing the group in general and not Lydia Teemant in particular, and made to leave. Again, if Lydia Teemant was surprised, she did not show it. He shook hands with them all, then walked quietly round the periphery of the hall, nodding at those who acknowledged him, shaking hands once or twice when called upon to do so, but determined to keep moving.

Navigating around a laughing group of students he saw the girl again, standing only ten feet away. Her male partner had disappeared. She was talking to a female friend, a short, fair girl like a small Brünnhilde. As a man who has prowled, he did not wish to approach her from her blind side. It was a little too sudden; it could put a girl on the defensive. So he moved casually but carefully into her field of view, turned, caught her eye, and smiled.

She smiled back. Then, perhaps because her friend would disapprove of too overt behaviour, she turned away. He walked up and introduced himself.

Twelve

He woke early. It was his military training. Some people tumble out of sleep and into waking with the confusion of immigrants entering a new land. He was one of those who, for whatever reason, snap awake as easily as if controlled by a switch. It was a useful, or perhaps fortunate, aspect of his constitution.

Today, however, he had a residual headache. Russians call drunkenness 'the white fever', and it was from this, rather than sleep, that he needed to recover.

Beside him in the bed, her face turned away, the clothes pulled over her full curves, was the shop manageress Vera. At least he could remember her name.

He raised himself carefully and moved on silent, bare feet across the pine floors to the bathroom. It was empty of implements. All the small accessories of a woman to which he had become accustomed had been removed by his wife. The bathroom contained merely a bar of soap, a shaver, a toothbrush and a tube of toothpaste. The toothpaste tube was another clue to her absence. It was squeezed from the tip and rolled from the bottom upwards with military care. Her own toothpaste tubes were squeezed at the centre, pressed into a shape like the hourglass figure of a woman, then pushed and pressed from all sides until they resembled a thin, battered old woman – an unconscious analogue of ageing, perhaps.

Electric shavers were still unreliable in Russia, and attachment points rare, except in the VIP hotels. On his travels he preferred the careful, sparse ceremony of applying soap to his cheeks, chin and neck, and carefully wiping through with a razor.

He was engaged in this when he heard the creak of the bed and, a little while later, the soft fall of a foot on the floor. He had left the bathroom door partly open. A shadow appeared there. He looked past his partly soaped cheeks in the mirror and noticed Vera was staring at him through the doorway, a half-smile on her face. Her expression indicated the shy pleasure of someone who is witness to some secret process. She had drawn a blanket round her body.

'Come in,' he said, facing sideways and grimacing while he completed shaving the other side of his face. But she merely smiled and continued to stand there, watching him. He rinsed his face and rubbed it down on a towel. At the door he put his arms round her but, though complaisant, she seemed to freeze slightly.

'Some coffee?' he asked.

She nodded.

He went through into the kitchen and put on the kettle. He heard the bathroom door close.

Outside it was already bright, with a clear sky. Staring out over the roofs of the houses, he could see signs of a small breeze furrowing the bay. It was still cold. Since arriving there a week before, he had not bothered to turn on the oil-fired central heating boiler which sat, in its enamelled box, in the cupboard beside the stove.

He poured two cups of coffee in the chipped, white cups that were all Anna had left him.

He called out, 'Your coffee's ready,' but he knew that it was a proven, statistical fact that no woman ever left a bathroom in less than half an hour. There was an answering call from the bathroom, an acknowledgement merely. He walked to the window.

Tallinn touched him with its human scale. The medieval hilled town at its centre was still intact, presiding over a port which, though prosperous in its time, had also been constructed on an intimate scale. Exclude, he thought idly, the ugly necklace of more recent Soviet buildings which disfigured its new shopping centres, and you have almost the perfect sized city, large enough to be impressive, small enough to recognize, if only by face, a high proportion of those beside whom you lived and worked.

Kropotkin, he remembered, had advocated the small city-state as the perfect model of a human community, for precisely these reasons. Somewhere he remembered reading a tract by the anarchist Prince against the concept of nations in which groups of cities, towns, were dominated by a single arbitrary centre, usually another great city. Such a capital city, Kropotkin had argued, was not a real city. It was a forced product of human ambition on a gigantic scale, no more organic than a block of administrative offices. That was the impression left upon Illich by Moscow. It was a willed, human ideal.

A rare few minutes of peace descended on him.

He glanced at the clock occasionally. He had time to reflect.

In the field of former Soviet science, because it was in constant and direct competition with Western science, there had been little room for dogma. In this it was unlike other aspects of Soviet culture. Rather, the practice of Soviet science was pragmatic. Hypotheses and theories were merely tools for understanding objects or processes, useful only if they are not falsified by practice. They could be created, amended, abandoned (if they do not prove useful) entirely on this principle. In the social field, such theories were extraordinarily difficult to find. However, certain areas, reflected Illich, showed promise. For example, careful sifting of the evidence regarding the time women spent in bathrooms generated an astonishing finding: not once had the hypothesis that no woman spends less than half an hour in the bathroom ever been falsified. Thus, he felt, the hypothesis, the Illich hypothesis, should surely now be advanced from its current status of speculative concept to that of a fully fledged theory.

When Vera emerged, some forty-three minutes later in conformity with the set patterns of womankind, he emptied the cold contents of her cup into the sink, reheated the kettle, and poured another cup of coffee.

She looked fresh and, if not classically beautiful, attractive. Her features still had a trace of puppy fat, her eyes were a trifle somnolent, but even so she glowed. An easy, almost casual self-awareness of this beauty only served to magnify it. He put aside, at least for the time being, the Illich theory of female behaviour.

Vera set about cooking breakfast. She made toast and, from the unused supplies of eggs that he had bought a week before, an omelette.

In the hallway they kissed. He asked her for her address. On the back of a card she wrote, with a ballpoint pen from her handbag, the number of her flat in Mustamae, one of the outlying modern districts. Her flat, she said proudly, even had a sauna. They descended the flights of stairs together. In the street he kissed her again and, walking in the other direction, glanced backward at her skirted figure.

It was only when he turned away that his thoughts returned to Lydia Teemant.

*

At least, he thought, his lack of faithfulness had the virtue of consistency. No sooner was one out of sight than he thought of another. But there were other more pressing matters to attend to. He was due to meet Major-General S. Vorolov at the training base. He looked forward once again to being in harness, to that physically exhausting schedule in which, merely by virtue of displacement, all emotional cares were banished. He caught a taxi and proceeded in the direction of the base camp.

Thirteen

So they began to arrive. Gustav Prem, Edvigs Tarku, Soren Gir were the first: bony, gaunt of frame, but a little flushed now, perhaps a little fatter as a result of the grace-and-favour jobs which had been granted to them all over Russia following the success of the *Leningrad* in winning the America's Cup. Like Brod, several of them had been granted jobs as 'professionals' in the outlying Russian sailing centres. As with the historical surge of tennis players in Sweden following the successes of Bjorn Borg, or the sudden flush of enthusiasm for football in West Germany after Beckenbauer, enthusiasm for sailing had exploded in Russia. New sailing clubs were being set up beside every piece of navigable water. To the local municipalities, major industries, or local government ministries who funded such developments, what greater privilege than to have, as its professional teacher, a member of the *Leningrad*?

Others of the crew, like Graf Ulder and Berol Baltir, had returned to their work – the first as a computer software designer, the second as an executive in the Estonian oil industry. One or two others had drifted, like disbanded soldiers from a war, relieved of tension but unable to find any commitment which would match the excitement of their previous regime.

Two or three would occasionally arrive at once, having arranged to meet previously. When they had assembled, however, the absence amongst them of Brod – their joker and mascot – was like a missing limb.

Illich did not need to explain Brod's absence. Even in a society as widely flung as Russia, the news of his retirement had spread.

The fierce routine of their training was begun immediately. Physical training at seven o'clock in the morning, in a little square cleared of builder's rubble outside the administration offices. Communal breakfast at half-past eight. Briefing at half-past nine. Sailing on the small fleet of 8-metres at ten. Lunch at one. More sailing from two-thirty until five approximately, meal at six, debriefing after the day's activities at seven. Exhaustion and collapse.

On the two 8-metres Illich took the helm of one, Gundar Arlof the other. Arlof was a fine helmsman, an Olympic silver medallist in Stars, and a worthy opponent. But he was, as a helmsman, more of a fleet-racing man, and Illich was ruthless in exploiting any weaknesses he might have in close-quarter duelling.

There were six men to a crew, a perfect split of the veterans. A pool of younger, less experienced but promising sailors was also being created. Four new winchgrinders – the winners of the People's Committee of Sport competition – joined them in the first three weeks.

The technicians and engineers, too, were starting to fill the halls with machinery, lathes, cutting equipment. A huge, raised wooden floor had been laid down, covering half the floor space of the second building, as a sailcutting loft. Bales of exotic sail-cloth began arriving on special grey 'high-security' delivery trucks, with darkened doors and windows of armoured glass, within which fierce dogs could sometimes be heard barking and growling. The association of high security with sail-cloth spawned a series of clumsy jokes. The affected belief that every bale of sail-cloth contained a KGB-trained Alsatian led to absurd cavortings and manoeuvres in the sail cutting loft. The jokes spread. In its increasing imitation of Western commercial freedoms, a new dogfood called *Droog Sobaka* (literally, 'dog's friend'), was being advertised extensively on Russian television. One joke went: How can you tell whether a bale of sail-cloth is dangerous? Answer: place a dish of *Droog Sobaka* in front of it. If it doesn't react, it's friendly.

Every group or institution which confronted the cold hand of security invented such jokes. As always, no one could tell from where they derived. They seemed to be precipitated out of the tension itself, like crystals in a copper sulphate solution.

In the administration building, the tall Major Archem was proving a gold-mine. No sooner was some item of equipment requested by the sailors or the machinery technicians, than he would be on the phone to his contacts in the Ministry of Machinery, ferreting out special supplies, inveighing against delayed delivery, casually invoking the name of Major-General Vorolov as a subliminal threat to the offending party. Vorolov himself was not above weighing in against some senior administration bureaucrat, invoking in his turn the names of General Chernavin and the Central Committee of the Armed Forces.

There had been a struggle, Illich knew, between Vorolov and the administrative bureaucracy in Moscow over who should man the security apparatus, the Ministry of the Interior (MVD) or the hated KGB. Sometimes, seated in his office, Illich could hear through the thin walls Vorolov's voice raised in argument, the snap of his threats; at other times, that singsong cajoling, the nasal vowels played like guitar strings, of which Russian is the mother-language. The battle proceeded for several weeks. Vorolov seemed preoccupied and intense, pondering the next stratagem in his battle for the control of the security apparatus. In the end, by means of his contacts, Vorolov had won. Accordingly, the final construction of the security fences was conducted under MVD supervision. Vorolov could be seen parading the building works with an MVD colonel, joking and laughing in a manner that would never have been possible with the more aloof KGB.

Illich had his own concerns. Just as the 'first crew', the veterans of the *Leningrad*, were Estonians, so the 'second crew', who would man the trial boat, were nearly all Russians, with the exception of a single Ukrainian. It was important to keep any underlying rivalry between the two crews on a friendly level.

It was difficult, too, not to assume that the uniformly Russian new crew-members were part of a deliberate attempt on the part of the authorities to generate a loyal, Slavic core. Certainly, Illich was aware that this assumption had festered in the minds of his own crew, and was responsible for some of the tension between the veterans and the new crew.

The Russians, for their part, were good-natured and hard-working. If the tension between the old and the new crews could be kept within limits, it had its beneficial side. During the physical exercises, both crews set about to outdo each other. In the deck-work on the boats, there was an extra snap. Every day that proceeded they became fitter. Illich too felt his mind lighten, the long winter burn slowly off him, along with the fat and the official parties and the memories of exhausting, apparently aimless travelling between this group of municipal officials and that group of earnest floor managers. This was a discipline into which he fitted. For six weeks prior to the delivery of the full-sized yachts, he was almost content.

Fourteen

As planned, the yacht *Leningrad* arrived by huge conveyor truck some six weeks after the start of training. In the same convoy, replete with four black Volga limousines filled with MVD security officials, and motor-cycle outriders, was the new yacht, the trial horse *Kirov*. The underwater appendages of both yachts were covered by security screens.

The convoy had travelled by night from Pskov, and by the time Illich and the crew had gathered for early morning training, the convoy was standing at the gates while security formalities were processed. At seven-thirty, General Vorolov and Major Archem stood by as the convoy rolled into the compound and the four MVD Volgas, their escort function completed, turned and disappeared down the bypass road to Tallinn.

A small crowd of spectators which had gathered outside the gates – early morning commuters, mostly, on their way to work in the city – was dispersed with unusual courtesy by the camp's own MVD. The huge tractor conveyors rumbled down to the dock area with the precious cargos, blue lights flashing, while the gates of the compound closed firmly behind them.

Illich was determined not to let the arrival of yachts intrude on his training regimen. He shouted sharply at anyone who paused during the exercises to study the convoy as it proceeded down to the dock area. When the exercises were over, however, he did not attempt to stem the rush of crew-members down to the docks to survey the two boats.

Major Archem appeared at his elbow.

'On schedule, Comrade Colonel?'

'Yes,' Illich agreed noncommittally.

Was Archem seeking praise for his part in the organization? He thought not. He liked Archem for his quiet ways, and was sufficiently familiar with him now to know that he would not fish for compliments.

No, Archem was saying something else. We have performed the first part of our function, perhaps. Now it is over to you.

Something about the second boat puzzled Illich. He had been led to understand it was merely a trial horse for *Leningrad*, a precise imitation. But as it passed him, he had a vague suspicion that the lines were subtly different. The stern, for example, was not quite as broad as *Leningrad*, he felt sure. And the angle of the deadrise – admittedly largely hidden by the security blanket – seemed shallower. Was he deceiving himself?

This threw his mind into some confusion over the matter. If the boats were not similar, then the new yacht was not a trial horse, but a new design. The implications of this were extraordinary. The so-called 'trial horse', to be crewed by Russian sailors, was in fact a new development yacht. But why, then, had this new development yacht been given to the second crew?

It was perplexing.

Major Archem stood beside him, silent. To allay his own fears, to displace his train of thought to another subject, no matter how trivial, Illich asked, 'What are the schedules for launch?'

Archem stirred uneasily, like a tree in the wind.

'*Leningrad* will be launched tomorrow.'

'And the second yacht?'

'The official launch of the second boat will be in three days' time.'

'Official . . .?' asked Illich. The notion took him by surprise.

'It has only just been arranged, sir.'

'An official launch?'

'Yes.'

'Is that what you were sent to tell me?'

'Yes, sir.' Major Archem's great height gave the impression of detachment. But in Illich's experience tall men were surprisingly sensitive. An urge to pull rank, to bully, overcame Illich. He waited for it to subside.

'Am I right in thinking the new yacht is a fresh design?'

'I believe so,' Major Archem said, somewhat hesitantly. It was, Illich reflected, a stupid question for him to have asked. It indicated to Archem how much he had been isolated in the decisions over the new boat. He experienced a sudden awareness of his own vulnerability.

'On the matter of the formal launch, sir,' Archem was continuing, 'General Vorolov requests the pleasure of your company. The yacht will be launched by Comrade Kerasnikov, Minister of the Interior.'

A senior government figure, a household name. Archem was surely mistaken about the recent nature of the arrangement. That must have been arranged months in advance. The degree to which he, Illich, had been left out of all decisions was now only too apparent.

'Thank you, Major Archem.'

Archem nodded, saluted, then walked away to the administration buildings.

Illich made his way to the changing room beside the dormitories, removed his tracksuit and physical exercise clothes. He showered, then changed into his uniform. It was his habit to join the crew at the communal breakfast at 8:30 a.m. He looked at his watch. 8:10.

Sometimes it is better to speak directly.

He walked over to the administration buildings. The MVD guards at the door stood by to let him in.

Vorolov's door was closed. He knocked on it and footsteps came to the door. Major Archem opened it.

'May I speak with General Vorolov?'

'Five minutes, sir,' Archem said, 'then he will see you.'

Illich went to his own office. Its walls were still bare. He withdrew a piece of paper from a drawer and wrote his resignation on it.

He read it through.

A short while afterwards, Major Archem knocked at his door.

'General Vorolov will be pleased to see you.' Illich folded the paper and placed it in his pocket. He walked the short distance to Vorolov's office, knocked, and heard him shout: 'Come in.'

Fifteen

'Please sit down, Ivan Ivanovitch,' Vorolov said, indicating a chair opposite.

'Thank you, sir.'

'You wished to speak to me?'

Vorolov folded his square fingers on the desk, and inclined his head to one side.

Illich took a deep breath and began: 'Having been involved in one America's Cup campaign, we followed normal precedent by building two identical yachts. This is considered by most experts to be crucial to the development of the campaign. With similar yachts, you can vary one feature at a time, and know that if there are any marked differences in performance between the two yachts, it will be due to this one feature which is different. This is analogous to the scientific method of model and control, where the "model" is what one is studying, and the control is a precise replica except in that thing which one is studying. If you have two dissimilar yachts, different in a number of respects, then it becomes far more difficult to ascertain what is causing the difference in performance between them. The first method is scientific, the second method . . .' Illich's throat went dry with suppressed rage.

'The second method is not scientific?' enquired Vorolov politely. Illich took several moments to recover.

'The second method, in my view, will produce certain failure.'

Illich waited again for his own anger to subside. Vorolov, for his part, waited for him to continue.

'When the two yachts were delivered this morning, I noticed that they were significantly different in hull form. While I have no doubt that both conform to the rule, it seems to me that a mistake has been made in building two such different boats.'

'Do you wish to write an official report and complaint?'

'Yes, sir.'

Vorolov nodded.

'I am sorry you feel as you do, Colonel.'

Why? thought Illich. Why sorry?

'In my report,' Illich continued, 'I will make the additional point that I should perhaps have been consulted on this matter. After all,' he added, 'I am in charge of the training and development programme, and the decision to build dissimilar boats severely curtails my ability to carry out my specific function.'

'I see.'

'In writing this report, I shall append my resignation from the programme for the reasons given.'

Vorolov became still. Carefully he opened a fresh packet of cigarettes. Extracting one, he tapped it on the desk several times. Outside, through the open office window, Illich could hear birds singing. A honey-coloured square of sunlight lay on the opposing wall.

Vorolov lit his cigarette, then threw the match expertly in the grey metal bin beside his desk.

'That would be a pity,' Vorolov said.

For several moments Illich waited for Vorolov to speak.

But Vorolov did not seem to be in any particular hurry. He inhaled thoughtfully, staring over Illich's head, exhaling out of the corner of his mouth. Finally he said: 'I have been engaged in this office for some six months now, Comrade Colonel, while you were fulfilling your obligations as a Hero of Russia. It has been an experience of considerable interest.

'As I taught my young officers of the College for Strategic Rocket Forces, it is necessary to undertake an appraisal of the situation in order to make clear, coherent decisions on strategy. It has been one of my functions to coordinate the activities of sailors on the one hand, and the design group on the other.'

Vorolov glanced at Illich, then continued: 'The design group, who have made an analysis of all historical aspects of the America's Cup, took pains to point out a particularly important area. In those challenges which had been successful, there was a conflict between the type of boat which the helmsman wanted, and the type of design which could best push forward the frontiers of speed. It is nearly always the case, they said, that the helmsman, whoever he may be, asks for a conventional boat, one which is similar to the best current boats. He argues that it is his own skill, and that of the crew, which will make the difference between winning and losing.' Vorolov paused to inhale and exhale. 'For example, in the classic case of *Australia 2* in 1983, the helmsman, John Bertrand, argued for the conventional boat *Challenge 12*, even after sailing for six months on the radical *Australia 2*. The syndicate overrode him in their final choice of the radical yacht.'

Vorolov paused, inhaled, waited several seconds as the smoke filled his lungs, breathed out unhurriedly. 'In the case of the British in the 1987 America's Cup, the designer David Hollom produced a major radical innovation in the form of *Crusader 2*, but the syndicate chose instead the conventional *Crusader 1*. They lost to more radical yachts.

'We studied the records of a number of such cases. Our

conclusion was that in the cases where the helmsman was able to influence the decision in favour of a conventional boat, the result was a loss. In those cases where a radical yacht was chosen, there was a far greater success rate.'

Vorolov brought his hands together on the table, and the line of his mouth became harder. 'That is why, Comrade Colonel, brilliant helmsman though you are, we did not wish you to influence the design of the second yacht in favour of a conventional boat.'

It was Vorolov's confidence, the blatancy of his reasoning, which struck Illich. They said Vorolov would one day be Chief of the General Staff. He saw now why Vorolov commanded such support.

'It is always reassuring,' Illich replied, 'to be given the reasons why you have been misled.'

'Ivan Ivanovitch,' Vorolov said with equanimity, 'I can tell by your remark that you have regained your sense of humour.'

'It is also a pleasure,' Illich added, 'to see a simple soldier display such unexpected virtue in politics.'

'Thank you, Colonel.' Vorolov stubbed out his cigarette in the ashtray. 'I take it you will not resign, for the time being at least.'

Illich paused. He had been outmanoeuvred by Vorolov, it was clear. Also, it was impossible to dislike the man. There was nothing for it but to admit defeat gracefully.

'For the time being,' Illich said. There were other aspects of the new boat which made him nervous, and which he required time to think about. Part of him remained angry, but he would let this work through his system in his own good time.

They stood up, and shook hands.

Sixteen

Major Archem studied Illich anxiously as he emerged from Vorolov's office.

'Perhaps you could accompany me to the boats,' Illich said. 'I will have a list of things to order.'

'Of course, Comrade Colonel.' Archem seemed relieved.

Archem's tall frame disappeared into his own office to pick up a clipboard on which to write. Illich and he made their way down to the two yachts.

Both yachts had been lifted off the conveyor trucks and placed on their own mobile cradles. The cradles, replete with boats, had been drawn into the main shed. MVD security men hovered at the doorway. They stood aside for Illich and Archem to enter.

Inside the shed, the security screens over the underbodies of the two yachts had been withdrawn. Leaving Archem standing in the doorway, Illich moved forward.

It was true that the new yacht *Kirov* had a significantly different hull. The untrained eye would detect little difference between them. But to the more expert witness the second boat had a narrower transom section, a slightly squarer shape. When one followed these lines through, as Illich now did with his hungry glance, one found that almost every aspect of *Kirov* was different, albeit only in some small degree. *Kirov*'s forefoot, for example, was deeper, the waterlines narrower. These divergences consisted of only tiny aspects, but in virtually no single respect were the two yachts absolutely similar. Taken collectively, they were two entirely different designs.

It was to be expected. A yacht linesplan was like a group

of planets; alter the orbit of one, and you alter subtly the motions of all others.

He walked from bow to stern. One of the most obvious differences was the keel. Two sweeping scythe shapes descended from the hull to the endplate, one directly behind the other. This configuration was rumoured to be one aspect of the design of the extraordinary American yacht *New World*.

He was temporarily lost in contemplation of the new yacht when he realized Archem was standing silently by his side. He concentrated on the task in hand.

'We need, Major, the following additional items of equipment against breakage. Beginning with the masts, two complete sets of standing rigging, enough ropes and running rigging for total replacement every week . . .'

Archem scribbled assiduously while Illich talked, walking round the two boats, until he had covered four full pages of immediate requirements.

Andre Vagir, the manager of the support operation, emerged from a small side-office to ask for a copy of the list so that he could arrange storage. Vagir was another old veteran of the *Leningrad* campaign. Short, red-haired, almost bald, the skin on his face and on the backs of his immensely strong hands was heavily freckled.

'What do you think of her?' Vagir indicated with his hand the new yacht.

'We will see how she performs.'

Vagir was a fine dinghy sailor, an Olympic competitor in Finns. Illich would have liked to ask him about the lines, but Major Archem's presence concentrated his mind on completing the list.

Seventeen

The Russian helmsman Petru Pilnyak arrived the day before the new boat was due to be launched.

A black Chaika was admitted through the compound gates and drew up at the administration buildings. Out stepped a smartly dressed captain of one of the Moscow ceremonial regiments, the ones which the average servicemen like to refer to as the 'toy soldiers'.

Illich had noticed the waiting Chaika outside the administration offices as he was returning to his office from the afternoon's training in the 8-metres. A military policeman emerged and spoke briefly to the chauffeur of the Chaika, which turned and left. Illich noticed that the number-plates were those of Vorolov's car and surmised that the general had ordered his car to the airport to pick up Pilnyak. It was a sign of Pilnyak's importance.

Inside the administration buildings, Vorolov's office door was closed. Illich went to his own office and began to fill out the day's progress reports and several forms itemizing equipment on the new boats. He had been engaged in this activity for an hour when he heard Vorolov's door open, and the general saying affably in the outside corridor: 'Come and meet Colonel Illich.'

There followed a knock on his office door, the blunt attack of Major-General Vorolov's square knuckles. Illich stood up and opened the door.

Vorolov was affability itself. 'Colonel Ivan Illich, this is Captain Petru Pilnyak.'

Pilnyak was tall, with the easy, slightly obsequious confidence of a young guards officer. His black hair was cut short. A pair of intelligent, quick eyes glanced back at Illich. Helming strengthens the hands, wrists, upper arms. Pilnyak's handshake was powerful.

'Would you have time, Colonel, to show the captain around the base. If not, Major Archem. . .'

'I have time,' Illich confirmed.

'Good,' Vorolov beamed. He said his goodbyes and returned to his office.

'This way,' Illich said to Pilnyak.

It was a relief to get out into the air again, even after only two hours of office work.

'May I congratulate you on your gold medal at the last Olympics, Captain.'

'Thank you,' Pilnyak said. 'I would not have the courage to congratulate you on your four golds.'

'They were some time ago,' said Illich. His training for the America's Cup during the year 2000 had meant that he could not participate in the Olympics of that date. He was filled with questions about the performances of international rivals at the last Olympics. There was an Englishman, Sinclair, who had won the Flying Dutchman class that year. Had Pilnyak met him?

'Several times,' Pilnyak replied. 'A brilliant helmsman. I watched his races whenever I had an opportunity.'

There were two groups of helmsmen at international level, those who had nothing but criticism for their rivals, and those – a smaller group – who admired their rivals and were keen to study their techniques. He was pleased to see that Pilnyak belonged to this second category.

'The British were often good in the Flying Dutchman class,' Illich said. 'Rodney Pattisson was the last great figure, perhaps, in the 1960s, but there have been one or two others since.'

'Rodney Pattisson,' Pilnyak said. 'Two golds and a silver. A lost opportunity in 1980, as a result of the Western boycott of the Olympic games.'

Knowledgeable, too, thought Illich. His liking for Pilnyak, and his fear of him as a rival, increased simultaneously.

There were upwards of fifty men working on the *Leningrad* and *Kirov* in the huge repair bays. Amongst them were at least a dozen crew-members, winchmen and trimmers particularly. Sheeting angles were being discussed. Faint, chalked lines were being drawn on the decks of both boats.

Activity on the two boats was at fever pitch. The hull of the *Kirov* was being given an extra polish before its official launching on the following day. Andre Vagir was directing operations, making urgent angles with his hands and forearms above the sound of power-drills to indicate the importance of completing their tasks within the next half hour.

Leningrad was due to be launched shortly so that the mast could be stepped. *Kirov*, after her official launch the following day, would lie side by side with her.

There is a saying, among sailing people, that the only boat that ever was launched on time was Noah's Ark; and that, they like to add, was a close thing. On the best organized racing yachts, however careful the preparation, there was always a last-minute rush.

Vagir was determined to launch *Leningrad* on schedule. His arm gestures were becoming more threatening. Several times he made the gesture of slitting his throat to the technicians on deck. Only when the tractor machine was actually connected up with the mobile cradle, and the lines were pulled taut so that the boat swayed, did the final army of workers descend via ropes and ladders like the mythical rats leaving the sinking ship.

The security screen was raised into place. With a whine of motors the huge doors were opened. The tractor pushed *Leningrad* out into the late afternoon sunlight. At the edge of the quay the tractor applied its brakes to the steel rails, then allowed the cradle carrying the yacht to ease forward under its own volition.

Down the slipway, into the water. Lines holding the

security screen were unfastened. A crane lifted the dripping screens from the water. The yacht floated, Illich noted, perfectly to her lines.

As always, *Leningrad* took his breath away with her beauty.

'Let me show you the rest of the base,' Illich said to Pilnyak.

Eighteen

On the day of the official launch of the *Kirov*, the training base was festooned with twinned Russian and Estonian flags. Officially, since the training base was part of Russian military territory, the flag which flew over the base was the Russian flag. However, it was felt that the local politicians and dignitaries should be placated. Therefore equivalence was the order of the day.

The two crews, main and reserve, were drawn up in two lines. A military band played the Russian anthem.

The Estonian President, Vajnen Aegu, stood beside the Minister of the Interior. Their respective wives stood behind them. A further party of Estonian dignitaries was placed on the right.

Major-General Vorolov stood up on the dais to give the opening speech.

Comrades, we are honoured today by the presence of the Minister for the Interior Yuri Kerasnikov, and President of the Estonian Republic Vajnen Aegu, and by numerous other honoured guests for the launching of a second yacht, Kirov, *which is part of our defence of the America's Cup.*

It is an occasion marked by sincere fraternal feelings between

Russia and the Republic of Estonia. Comrades, I am pleased to invite Interior Minister Kerasnikov to address us on this happy occasion.

The military band played the Russian anthem, followed by that of Estonia. The bulky, white-haired figure of Kerasnikov stepped up to the rostrum.

Fellow comrades, it is a pleasure to be called upon to address you, General Vorolov, and the dedicated men who will undertake the defence of the America's Cup. I do so on behalf of my distinguished colleagues in the Supreme Council and the Parliament of Peoples' Deputies.

My friends, I shall be brief. I do not sail myself. I have no experience of the sea. Yet this strange sport of sailing has excited the interest of our great country. In the year 2001 we witnessed, on television, the powerful challenge, led by Colonel Ivan Illich, and we joined in the victory of our country. It is sport, but sport conducted at a very intensive level. It involves a high degree of teamwork, the most advanced technology. In this sense it is not only a sport which enhances relations between countries, but also a trial of strength under international conditions which are mercifully free of overt aggression.

During recent years, in the conditions of increasing international stability which have obtained between ourselves and the West, we have dedicated our energies to building up our internal domestic economy. This has been a difficult process, beset with anguish and false starts. But we have persevered in our intention, and as a result the average citizen of Russia is now substantially better off in terms of the material necessities.

As Minister of the Interior, I have borne much of this responsibility on my shoulders. I pay tribute to my fellow members of the Supreme Council who have supported this task of reconstruction, and to my fellow members of the government, each of whom has contributed to this vision.

I come now to those honoured guests who are here as representatives of the Republic of Estonia. Comrades, I say to you that we have watched an unprecedented degree of economic liberty in this republic. We watch with interest your progress, your trials and your successes. Sometimes it is difficult, like a father watching his son play in a game of football, not to want to jump onto the pitch and help. But we have restrained ourselves. Sometimes, comrades, we hope that our restraint is recognized and appreciated. The forces of disorder are always present, and it is necessary to be permanently vigilant against them.

Now finally, I return to this scene in front of me, of cooperation between the Estonian Republic and Russia. It is with pleasure that I name this yacht Kirov. *I join with you in wishing our combined team success in its future defence of the America's Cup.*

Interior Minister Kerasnikov pressed a button. The tractor released tension on the hawsers holding the *Kirov*. Yacht and cradle slid down into the water. The band began to play a marching song. Illich noticed that amongst the stand of journalists many were still writing down Kerasnikov's speech. Several were whispering to one another, checking the contents. In the editorials tomorrow they would analyse the speech sentence by sentence. Did the passages on fraternal relations contain a warning? Was the Russian 'father' signalling that the Estonian 'son' must play according to the rules?

Whatever the status of Russian-Estonian relations, *Kirov* was now floating. The assembled dignitaries clapped somewhat distractedly, as if they too were pondering Kerasnikov's speech.

There was another aspect that was occupying Illich's mind, however. In the group of dignitaries in the second audience, standing beside a tall, gaunt man whom he recognized as her father, was Lydia Teemant.

Afterwards there was a cocktail party in a large tent which had been erected a short distance from the harbourside. The crews had been invited. General Vorolov was his sociable self. He gripped Illich by the arm and introduced him to several of the Minister's entourage. Out of the corner of his eye, Illich glimpsed Lydia Teemant standing on the other side of the room, talking to two middle-aged members of the Estonian Socialist Party. He waited as patiently as he could until Vorolov's introductions were over.

Having made his courteous departure, he was on his way to find Lydia Teemant when a square, powerful man tapped him on the shoulder.

'Ivan Illich?'

Illich recognized, from a hundred newspaper photographs, the features of the President of the Estonian Republic.

'Vajnen Aegu.' They shook hands.

Aegu asked, 'What do you think of the battleship *Kirov*?'

Illich was at a loss for a moment before he realized that the battleship was the new yacht.

'I look forward to the trials.'

Aegu surveyed him. 'Unlike my distinguished friend the Russian Interior Minister, I sailed a little in my youth. Enough,' Aegu continued, 'to appreciate that the trial yacht is a different design from the original.'

'You noticed?' Illich replied politely.

Aegu smiled.

'A diplomat, I see. I understand nevertheless that the *Kirov* is to be sailed by the second crew.'

'The reserve crew, that is correct.'

Aegu studied him again.

'When I was a student, I studied biology at the University of Tartu.' An expression almost of regret passed across Aegu's wide features. 'My thesis was written on the subject of the horned toad. I think perhaps I had a certain sympathy with the animal . . .' Aegu smiled self-deprecatingly, ' . . . half land creature, half water creature, like us Estonians.'

Aegu seemed to be staring past him, but Illich had the impression he was watching him closely.

'I have sympathy with all creatures whose life is divided

between two environments. I felt this particularly acutely when I worked within the Foreign Ministry of the USSR.'

Illich knew, as did virtually every Estonian, that prior to becoming First Secretary of the Estonian National Party, Aegu had served as Soviet ambassador in China.

'Sooner or later,' Aegu said, 'we human amphibians have to choose. The choice can be painful. Sometimes, however, we are lucky, it is made for us.'

An official approached Aegu, whispered in his ear.

'Forgive me, Colonel Illich. I am called elsewhere.'

They shook hands again. Aegu said: 'As a fellow Estonian, Colonel, I wouldn't be too concerned about the contents of Comrade Kerasnikov's speech this morning. By now we are used to Moscow's thunder. We have learned simply to sit tight and wait for better weather.'

He patted Illich on the shoulder and left.

Lydia Teemant was only a few feet away. He caught her eye and walked over.

She was wearing a blue dress with a black belt.

'Estonian colours,' Illich said. 'They suit you.'

'You know Vajnen Aegu?' she asked him.

'No,' Illich replied. 'I have never met him before today.'

'Strange. He seems to know you.'

'He is a very clever man. I am not sure I understood what he was saying.'

She laughed.

'Vajnen is a politician. He likes to speak in riddles.'

Vajnen? he thought. 'You know him?'

He noticed, for the first time, a sign of hesitancy, even evasiveness in her.

'He is a regular visitor at my father's house. They discuss Estonian history, particularly legal history.'

'The golden days of independence.'

She looked at him squarely, is if to say, this is not the time to joke. To cover his *faux pas*, he pressed on: 'I have been thinking about examples which disprove your theory about child-rearing.'

'Oh?' This clearly amused her.

'Georgians,' said Illich.

'Georgians?' she asked.

'Georgians are given every latitude in childhood. They are spoiled. Yet, as we know, every adult Georgian is an anarchist at heart.'

'An anarchist who is constantly looking for a dictator,' she said.

'A neurotic response?'

She ignored the remark, and replied instead: 'Look, for example, at the way the Georgians have sought democratic government. Not in any methodical sense, not through working towards it carefully, one step at a time. No, they riot in the streets, and invite the paternal response of the punishing father.'

'Are you sure,' he asked, 'that your theory is not like Freudianism or Marxism, one of those protected by its own structure from facts which negate it? Perhaps you have ambitions that it will become the reigning orthodoxy.'

For the first time, she laughed. A delightful laugh, crisp and musical, one which rewarded him for his clumsy sallies into the subject of psychology.

Nineteen

The flood-tide of history is unpredictable. It leaves certain individuals stranded. Others it drowns.

Tartu University stood, in true Estonian academic solemnity, somewhat at odds in the spring sunshine. Illich's lecture on the America's Cup was, unlike most of his other scheduled talks, open to the public. It was decided by the university authorities to tempt the weather and hold the talk in the open air within the walls of Tartu Castle.

Tartu was a sentimental occasion for Illich. He had studied engineering in the laboratories and lecture halls of the university's nineteenth-century classical buildings, had lain on the banks of the Emajogi River in the early evening sunlight, and had learned his initial sailing skills on Lake Peipus, about twenty miles away. The university's several new departments now spread through the town.

The expected audience for his talk was a few hundred sailing enthusiasts. Illich arrived early to set up his board, arrange his small number of slides, and to help set out the folding chairs for the open-air seating. The weather was increasingly overcast, but there was no immediate sign of rain. An hour before his talk was due to start, the expected audience of a few hundred was already exceeded. The numbers continued to increase. With forty minutes to go, it was standing room only. His host, Professor Arnold Kiivit of the Tartu Engineering Department, whispered in his ear that he had received a report that the crowds were extending through the town. The professor admitted that he had never seen such an audience. Police and militia were being rapidly assembled to cope with the numbers. Traffic in parts of the city had been stopped. Embarrassingly for Illich, his talk attracted an estimated seven thousand people, the bulk of whom appeared to be university students. (Later, the Russian papers would talk of 'agents provocateurs' and 'disorderly elements'.) Banners were raised and waved. In front of Illich, an area had been taken up by representatives of the Narva fishing cooperative behind a placard calling for an Estonia free of the Russian military. Illich's speech, which was tailored to a crisp forty minutes of discourse on the more abstruse aspects of racing tactics, with questions afterwards, lasted a full two hours, largely because it was continuously interrupted by outbreaks of patriotic singing. One group chanted passages from Eugen Kapp's opera *Avenging Flames*. Policemen

96

became involved in scuffles with largely well-tempered groups of students and young workers holding aloft the Estonian Tricolour.

The 'Tartu Riots', as they became known, achieved international media fame. A picture of Jaan Pats, the poet, standing on a nearby rooftop in the posture of an anthropoid ape, shaking his fists and hurling abuse at the forces of law and order, was pitched into the front pages of newspapers worldwide. Television screens were filled with scenes of 'violent insurrection' in Tartu, now widely reported as 'Estonia's second largest city'. Fainting girls, overcome by the crush, were photographed being helped onto makeshift stretchers hastily constructed of torn-up fence palings. An elderly widow, shouting 'Go home little boys', was televised belabouring a group of bemused militiamen with a rolled umbrella. Editorials pointed out that, more than a decade earlier, the national party had been formed by a white-haired female Professor of Journalism from Tartu University. Two months after the 'Tartu Riots', Rudiger's new cult film *Birth of a Republic* would be on cinemas worldwide. Using extensive footage from a hand-held camera in the thick of the student demonstration, punctuated by long, incomprehensible political statements from radical student leaders, it cemented the 'Tartu Riots mystic significance. Rudiger's second film celebrating the Tartu insurrection, to be called *The Earth Is Ours*, would be of a more mystical nature, consisting mainly of silent commentary between dry archive material of the historical Estonian Communist Party congresses intercut with close-ups of his favourite actress Arla Vitnu's magnificent nude figure.

Illich knew nothing of these repercussions when, after the talk, he gathered together the diagrams of the race course, the small magnetic arrows he used to indicate wind directions, and folded his box of slides of early America's Cup challengers. He had been almost deafened by the singing. Unable to move from the overcrowded spaces, it was half an hour before he could be escorted by university officials to a small hall beside the castle where a traditional May dance had been arranged by the University faculty. The band was a Finnish pop group, called by some strange coincidence (but coincidences were everywhere on 1 May) 'Angry Bear'. The doors were closed against those who had not been invited.

For Illich, it was as if history had descended upon him like a swarm of irate bees.

Twenty

Flying out of the airport at Tallinn, Illich felt no nervousness, so certain was he that his career was ended.

On his return to his office the day following his talk at Tartu, he had found on his desk a brown envelope. The telexed message it contained was brief:

Return to Ministry of Defence immediately.
Major-General V. Org

Several things passed through Illich's mind on reading it. The first was that not only was his career extinguished, but his life was in danger. Almost idly, a number of thoughts passed through his mind, including the possibility of escape. He could hide in Estonia, but he was not suited to a life of hiding. Alternatively, he could find some means of passage to Finland. This was not an insuperable problem to a sailor. Under nightfall, he could sail out in a small yacht such as a Dragon or even (taking a greater risk on the weather) a dinghy such as a Flying Dutchman or 505. They would be looking for him, but a small dinghy, particularly one which was fibreglass and without a radar reflector, would not be an easy target to find.

These were only peripheral distractions, however. A curious fatalism pervaded his thoughts. It was a legacy of the military. All his life he had lived in reasonable proximity to the view that, if his life were to be ended, it was useless to worry about it. To attempt to escape would have worked against a lifetime's attitude.

He knocked on Major-General Vorolov's office door and heard his abrupt 'Come in'.

Vorolov was writing a memo, his broad, square hand steadying the page. He indicated a chair.

'I have been summoned to Moscow,' Illich informed him.

Vorolov looked up and surveyed him dispassionately. 'Then you must go.'

Illich paused briefly, then continued: 'With respect to the yachts, I have left my report on my desk. The crew is working together well. Captain Pilnyak, though young, is well suited to take my place.'

Vorolov nodded. 'I wish you well, Comrade.'

Vorolov stood up. He shook hands with Illich, passing to him with his left hand a folded sheet of paper. Illich put this in his top pocket.

'I give you leave to prepare yourself for the flight to Moscow.'

Illich saluted, and left the office.

In the corridor, he almost ran into the tall figure of Major Archem. Archem's face carried no expression. Soldiers, Illich knew, often express their unease in formal gestures. Major Archem saluted. Illich appreciated this gesture of formal recognition of his rank. In the narrow array of gestures permitted to him, this was Archem's way of showing concern.

Major-General Vorolov's black Chaika was waiting at the doorway of the administration buildings to take him back to Tallinn. The chauffeur would have waited to take him to the airport, but Illich dismissed him outside his apartment block.

Only when he reached the safety of his flat did Illich take out the piece of folded paper which Vorolov had given him. It said simply. 'Comrade Vajnen Aegu phoned. He asks you to phone back.' Beside it was a telephone number.

He decided not to use the phone in his flat because it would be tapped. He packed his clothes, closed the flat, went downstairs, and knocked on the faded blue door of the janitor. Irkut, as though expecting him, opened the door cautiously. Illich informed him that he would be away indefinitely. Irkut, who had probably seen references to the Tartu incident on television, must have guessed something was wrong. He peered at Illich from behind the half-closed door, as if Illich were dangerous.

Outside, Illich walked to the town square and caught a taxi to the airport. The driver was jovial, recognizing him, bantering away about Estonian sailors. To this simple man, thought Illich, nothing is amiss.

The streets were quiet, but there were signs of troop and militia movements. In a sidestreet, several camouflaged lorries waited while soldiers gathered in line beside them. Before the airport, four lorries pulled out in convoy. Illich knew that they were full of troops.

It was 10 a.m. when he reached the airport. His flight was in thirty-five minutes. He telephoned Aegu.

A woman's voice answered.

'President Aegu is out. Who shall I say has called?'

Illich gave his name. There was a brief silence while the woman appeared to be consulting someone. Incongruously, the telephone began to play music, a folk song. Then the woman's voice returned suddenly, 'Can you phone another number? Tell the operator it is a reverse charge call.'

Illich took down the second number and did as instructed. Another woman's voice answered. He gave his name. Almost immediately, he heard Aegu's distinctive voice.

'Where are you phoning from?'

'The airport.'

'You have been summoned to Moscow?'

'Yes.'

'You should delay, do anything to delay. I can arrange with the civil authorities that for the time being, at least, you should stay in Estonia.'

'That would be considered disobedience. Desertion, in fact.'

'Tell them you were ordered to stay by me.'

'Unfortunately, Comrade President, I am a soldier. My first loyalty is to my military superiors.'

A moment for consideration. Aegu said, 'Then you go at your own risk.'

Illich was silent. Aegu continued, 'I can work on your behalf meanwhile. But it will be difficult. What do you expect to happen?'

'I expect a court martial, to be stripped of rank, perhaps a prison sentence.'

'At least you don't entertain any illusions.'

'No.'

'Delay one day only,' Aegu said. 'That should be sufficient to set up a process of negotiation.'

'It would be interpreted as a sign of guilt.'

'But,' said Aegu mildly, 'you have just said that you will be treated as guilty anyway.'

It was true, Illich thought. Logically, there was no point in behaving by the book. Nevertheless, he felt compelled to do so. Perhaps it was a matter of pride. In his own heart, he knew that he was not guilty of disloyalty. He would face the procedures with that certainty, even though the outcome was inevitable.

'As you wish,' Aegu said with a sigh. 'You remind me of Koestler's character Rubashov in the novel *Darkness at Noon*. Out of loyalty to the Party, he acquiesced in his own destruction. Use my name, invoke my authority if you feel it will do any good.'

'Thank you.'

'Goodbye.'

Illich made one other call, this time to Pridilenko's office. Pridilenko's receptionist answered. Illich gave his name.

'Just a moment.'

Several seconds later Pridilenko came on the line.

'Ivan Ivanovitch. I understand your lectures are dynamite.'

'I'm phoning to say that I have been recalled to the Ministry of Defence. With regard to the next meeting of the committee, I wish to inform you that I shall make every effort to attend. If I am unable to do so, it will be against my will.'

'You'll be placed under arrest?'

'That seems likely.'

'General Chernavin?'

Illich did not answer.

'It seems to me that this is a political matter,' remarked Pridilenko, 'not a military one.'

'I apologize in advance if I am unable to attend.'

'Thank you. Good luck.'

Illich replaced the receiver. In the airport lounge Aeroflot flight MS2302, the Moscow shuttle, was waiting. It would be full, he knew, of the *vlasti* and their wives who had enjoyed a weekend of shopping in the economic free zone of Estonia. The special privileges of the bureaucracy were still endemic to Russia, even after more than a decade of liberalization. He picked up his suitcase and made his way towards the flight clearance desk.

Twenty-One

On the aircraft the security procedures were tightened. Two plain-clothes members of the military police were standing beside the air hostess at the aircraft entrance. The shorter, darker of the two men, who was clearly the superior, said: 'Follow me, Colonel.'

Illich looked at him coldly, not moving. A sudden anger overcame him. Having voluntarily delivered himself to the flight, they appeared determined now to treat him as a prisoner.

The man became uncomfortable under his stare.

Illich pushed his way past. The two officials followed him.

'This way,' the man said, pointing to a batch of nine empty seats. Illich knew that important prisoners, criminals who have been apprehended, foreign spies, are isolated from the rest of the travellers by such means. The aircraft seats are generally in groups of three. The prisoner would sit in the middle between two security policemen, isolated at the front and rear by two rows of empty seats.

Disobeying the instructions of the security official, Illich sat in a seat near the window. The two officials crammed themselves into the two other seats on the row. They were forced to wait while the stewardess went through the safety procedures and the aircraft took off.

In the air, however, the two security officers seemed to relax. One, the older, senior figure of the two, offered him a cigarette, a new brand called *Dushaya*, which he refused.

After landing, the security officers and their charge were

waved through the Moscow customs screen. A black Volga was waiting outside, driven by another security man. In the back, he sat between the two security men who had accompanied him on the flight. They drove fast to the Ministry of Defence, cutting in from the Frunzenskaya Embankment on one of the unmarked delivery roads, heavily guarded by military police, which reached into the interior of the huge Ministry complex. Illich was escorted up the stairs to Chernavin's outer office. The security officers left, but not before a guard had been posted at the door.

For fully one and a half hours Illich was kept waiting, while senior officers moved in and out of Chernavin's office.

At 3:15 Major-General Org emerged from the inner office and walked over to Illich. It was the first time his presence had been acknowledged.

'Colonel Illich.'

Illich stood up and saluted.

'Come this way.'

Inside Chernavin's office were seated the same three officers who had interviewed him several months before. Generals Litski and Zholudev were, like Chernavin, seated.

Illich saluted. Major-General Org indicated a chair.

When Illich was seated, General Chernavin said without apparent irony, 'Thank you for returning so promptly.'

Did you arrange the security guard, thought Illich?

Chernavin, for all the apparent seriousness of the situation, seemed in a good mood. Illich suspected that this was because there were now serious matters which he could bring forward.

Chernavin said: 'Colonel Illich, you are here under grave circumstances. You gave a lecture at the University of Tartu which became, in the course of that lecture, a major riot and insurrection. What have you to say?'

'I gave a talk, which political elements used to generate a public controversy. I had nothing to do with the organization or encouragement of this demonstration.' Illich

104

looked at the other two generals. 'May I ask whether it is being suggested that I was involved in fomenting the riot?'

'You were present, Comrade Colonel,' Chernavin informed him crisply.

Illich glanced again at the faces of the other two. They gave away nothing.

'Clearly,' Illich replied, 'I am under suspicion. I therefore make a formal request to exercise my right that a record shall be made of the proceedings of this meeting.'

Chernavin paused. General Litski gestured with his hand, requesting permission to speak. Chernavin, with a glance at Litski, nodded. Litski said, 'Before we proceed to decide on the need for a formal investigation, perhaps I could ask you one question informally.' Litski reminded him of a clever elf, one of those strange peasant prodigies who emerge from some tiny village. He spoke with his head on one side, in the attitude of someone who listens intently. 'Let us say, merely for speculation, that it was accepted that you did not foment this riot. I emphasize that this is a hypothesis, and in no way prejudges the views of my colleagues or any investigation. If so, Colonel, why should your talk be chosen by the dissident elements as the scene of the riot?'

Illich was aware of the baleful stare of General Zholudev, who for the time being was silent.

'Merely as speculation, I suggest that any public meeting could be used as the excuse for a riot. I spoke entirely on the subject of yacht-racing tactics.'

'It was also reported that you could not be heard because of the cheering of the audience. Who could verify, then, that what you said was entirely concerned with yachting tactics?'

Illich felt again the intuition that Litski, the mildest one, was also the most dangerous.

'With due respect, sir, you are clearly engaged in an investigation of the issue, and I repeat my request that under the circumstances I am entitled to a formal record of the meeting.'

'If you insist on this, we will of course respect your request, Colonel. However, perhaps you will also understand that we three are in the position that we shall decide whether there is matter here for a formal court martial. In these circumstances your cooperation would be of assistance to us.'

'I have every intention to cooperate fully, sir, and answer all such questions. But I repeat that I am entitled to a formal record of all questions and answers which are part of an investigation.'

'You would seem to be a lawyer, as well as a helmsman,' Litski observed drily.

Chernavin glanced at General Zholudev, to see whether he wished to add anything to what had been said. Zholudev shook his head, hardly moving, his eyes fixed on Illich.

'Major-General Org,' General Chernavin said. 'Please escort the Colonel to the outer office, while we deliberate.'

Illich stood up, saluted, and followed Org out of the office.

Org indicated a seat in the outer office, then returned to the inner office and closed the door. Illich looked up at the metal clock on the wall opposite.

For one of the few times in his life, he had been unable to sleep the previous night. Now he was tired, not by the events themselves, but by their inevitability. It was, however, important to keep alert. The clock indicated 3:45. At 5:13 the door again opened.

'Colonel Illich.' Major-General Org was beckoning to him from the open door. Illich again went through the formalities of saluting, and sat down in front of the tribunal.

General Chernavin, as their spokesman, addressed him.

'We have decided that, in the circumstances, there is sufficient evidence to justify a court martial. The charges will be, firstly, that your lecture at Tartu University on 1 May was such as to generate disorder and riots. Secondly, you are charged generally that your loyalties to the Russian Army are secondary to your loyalties to the Estonian Republic, and this in itself is therefore treason. Do you understand?'

'Yes, sir.'

'Given the serious nature of the charges, you will be placed under arrest forthwith and held until the court martial. You will be informed of the date of the court martial in due course. Dismissed.'

Illich stood up and saluted. Major-General Vassily Org accompanied him once again to the outer office, where two armed military policemen were waiting.

They escorted him along what seemed to be an endless length of corridor, down several flights of stairs, into a basement which housed some of the vast records of the Ministry of Defence. At one end of the basement was the local headquarters of the military police who guarded the security of the building. The complex contained half a dozen cells. One such cell had been prepared for him. It contained a bed, a grey army blanket, and a metal wash-basin. At the foot of the bed were a set of grey prison overalls. He sat down on the bed. The reinforced steel door closed behind him.

Twenty-Two

Several days passed in solitary confinement.

To Illich, waking in the cell was the worst thing. His predicament poured in upon him; he felt prey to a mute terror. The cell had no barred window to the outside, merely a ventilation system from which stale air poured slowly, and he was unable to see genuine daylight. His gaolers turned out the lights at twelve, and turned them on at six in the morning with the morning shift.

Two meals a day were brought to him – officer's rations, not good, but better than those of the privates and non-commissioned officers. The courage and endurance of the average private he knew to be extraordinary. In similar circumstances, a private on a charge of treason would have been kept in continuous light twenty-four hours a day, woken if he slept, and perhaps casually beaten. Set about by privileges, he felt his courage drain and his morale fall. Even in those few days, the intrusion of the guards with food twice a day was a welcome break in the monotony of waiting.

Several more days went by. He heard nothing. A week passed. Two weeks. In one of his coat pockets he found a stub of pencil. He took to scratching a single numeral for each passing day on the wall adjacent his bed.

In his youth he had been told by a military pensioner who had suffered in the purges of the necessity of absorbing oneself in the daily routine. 'It is surprising how soon the mind becomes passive,' this old man said, 'how soon you enter a kind of living sleep.'

But it did not seem to be the case for him. He told himself he would soon be out, if only to face trial, but every day that passed his hopes grew more uncertain. Along the line of the bed, hidden from sight by the bed-frame itself, someone else had drawn a series of tiny vertical numerals, each designating a single day. He counted them. The total came to 103. One hundred and three days of solitary confinement!

In the first few days he had felt the desire to weep, but this had passed. His anguish gave way to torpor. The men who brought his meals did not talk, except to order him to swill out. He started to have headaches. It was difficult concentrating. Sometimes he felt weak and wondered whether it was the food.

As an exercise, he tried to imagine day and night outside.

He would calculate the time of day from the routine, and try to imagine the scene. Six o'clock in the evening, the dusk falling, white sky in the west, the desultory blue glow of the Moscow streetlights. Late shoppers, theatre-goers. He would imagine walking down a street, trying to remember the buildings on either side, the signs, even the numbers of certain buildings.

The river was nearby. He tried to reconstruct it in his mind from the various times he had made the passage on one of the Moscow hydrofoils. Upriver was the cantilevered Krasnoluzhkiy bridge; a little downriver the Setun River joined the Moskva. Further downstream still was the great sports centre of Luzhniki, site of the Olympics, where as he lay hundreds would be exercising in their physical freedom. When in training for his Olympic campaigns he had sometimes exercised there with other athletes.

The days passed slowly and then seemed to slide together in passive waiting.

On the twenty-sixth day, a Friday by his calculations, he heard footsteps outside the door at two o'clock in the afternoon, a key in the door. The bolts were drawn open.

Three plainclothes military security police stood in the doorway. Their superior said: 'You have a few minutes to dress and prepare yourself, Comrade Colonel. We will wait outside.' They left his uniform – trousers, jacket, boots, hat – on the chair.

Illich put on his coat and combed his hair. His trousers were rumpled but he could do nothing about it. He picked up his cap.

'Follow me,' the senior policeman said.

After solitary confinement, the sound of their boots on the tiled floor was loud. The older man led, the younger two officers brought up the rear.

Illich followed through a maze of corridors in the Ministry basement. There was a guarded exit by means of a large steel door which gave on to an underground carpark.

Waiting for them was a grey BMW with private number plates. As he passed from the open doorway to the car, he caught the dusty afternoon smell of Moscow.

One of the men drove. The officer and the other sat on either side of him in the back. They must have been on the east side of the Ministry buildings, because the car crossed the Komsomolskiy Prospekt and, keeping to the less-used thoroughfares, drove along the Frunzenskaya embankment, continued along the Kropotkinskaya embankment, leaving the Moskva swimming pool on the left.

They travelled north towards Red Square, turning right into Kuibyshev Street. It was a grey, overcast day.

A sudden torrent of rain hit them while they were driving along Kuibyshev Street. There was the usual traffic jam as drivers stopped and got out of their cars to replace the windscreen wipers they habitually stored in their dashboards as a protection against theft. Accordingly, they arrived at Pridilenko's office block at Novaya Place a few minutes late.

The military police accompanied Illich in the lift. At Pridilenko's office the receptionist looked somewhat nervously from one to the other. She knocked on the door of the committee room. A few moments later Pridilenko emerged. Ignoring the plain-clothes policemen, he shook Illich warmly by the hand.

'Natasha,' he said to his secretary. 'Take these men to reception.'

He ushered Illich through to the committee room.

Four members of the committee and Vera Ahktova stood to shake hands with him – all except for General Chernavin, who remained seated.

They sat down. There were a few seconds of awkward silence.

Pridilenko began, 'Comrades, as you may have read in the papers, or seen on television, when Colonel Illich gives a speech on sailing tactics, he draws several thousand people and causes a riot. Should he ever enter politics, may Heaven preserve us.'

There were a few smiles at this little speech. Illich glanced at Chernavin, whose face was stony.

Pridilenko turned to his right. 'Comrade Mamayev, as Chairman of the Committee of Sport Resources, I ask you to summarize progress.'

The Georgian placed his hands on the table and leaned forward: 'Members of the Committee, since our last meeting, some eighteen new crew-members have joined the training camp for the America's Cup. Each has been rigorously trained at the new People's Sailing School at Odessa. Future members of America's Cup crews will also no doubt be trained there.

'With regard to the siting of the America's Cup defence, it has been confirmed that the best such position will be west of St Petersburg, on the southern arm of the bay. While there are sensitive military installations on the northern shore, it is nevertheless clearly understood that the Army has given assurance of security . . .' Mamayev glanced at General Chernavin ' . . . in the necessary areas.'

Chernavin nodded.

Pridilenko interrupted: 'Forgive me, Comrade Mamayev. The position is that we are awaiting final ratification from the Supreme Council Secretariat as to the exact placement on the southern arm of the bay. It is noted that while General Chernavin believes security can be maintained in the region, the final decision is a political, not a military, one.'

'I understand, Comrade Chairman. Subject to Supreme Council ratification, then, the site will be west of St Petersburg.'

Pridilenko nodded.

'Thank you, Comrade Mamayev. I now turn to Comrade Osborov, Naval Intelligence.'

Osborov cleared his throat and leaned forward.

'My department was instructed to develop a successor to

111

the challenger *Leningrad*. We undertook this task over the last year, and the yacht *Kirov*, to this improved design, was delivered four weeks ago. The initial reports from the base camp at Tallinn are that the new yacht is outstanding.'

Pridilenko turned to Illich.

'Can you confirm this, Colonel?'

Illich said: 'It is impossible to tell. The new yacht has a concentration of new equipment and sails. Unless the new equipment is equally distributed between the two yachts one cannot tell which is better.'

'You do not agree, then, Colonel, that *Kirov* is a faster hull than *Leningrad*.'

'No, Comrade Chairman. A better procedure would have been to build an identical yacht, equip and tune the boats similarly, and then vary one aspect of design at a time. Otherwise we are in the dark.'

Pridilenko said: 'You were surely consulted on the design of the new yacht.'

'No, Comrade Chairman. Not at any stage.'

Pridilenko looked at Osborov. 'Who instructed you to build the second yacht *Kirov* to a different design?'

Osborov was clearly taken aback. He glanced down at his paper, looked up again, and was about to speak when he was interrupted.

'I did.'

The attention of the committee switched to General Chernavin.

It might have been expected to end there. But Pridilenko was relentless. He allowed several seconds to pass.

'You did so, Comrade General, without consulting Colonel Illich?'

'Comrade Chairman,' Chernavin was politeness itself, 'in the Army, we make our decisions without consulting our subordinates at every stage.'

'I see,' Pridilenko said mildly. 'Colonel Illich, have you anything to add?'

'No, Comrade Chairman.'

Pridilenko paused for several seconds, glanced down at his notes.

'Comrades, I thank you all for attending this meeting, particularly Colonel Illich, who is currently under arrest and had to interrupt a period of solitary confinement to join us.'

Illich saw Vera Ahktova's pencil inscribe her swift hieroglyphics. Pridilenko waited until she had finished. He began again slowly, with deliberation: 'As Chairman of this committee, and speaking entirely with respect to its proper function, I find it intolerable that our preparations for the America's Cup have been interrupted by the arrest of our chosen helmsman. The charges concern a riot which was started in the course of a speech on sailing given by Colonel Illich at the University of Tartu on 1 May. Although the civilian authorities have found no grounds to question the probity of Colonel Illich's behaviour in this matter, the military authorities have seen fit peremptorily to interrupt this critical programme by arresting and holding Colonel Illich on political charges.'

Pridilenko waited again until Vera Ahktova's pencil came to a halt.

Chernavin's face was impassive. Pridilenko paused again, so that his words would carry extra force: 'Comrades, I put to the vote that this committee expresses the view that Colonel Illich's arrest and detainment on political grounds by the military is a severe disruption of its work and aims.'

In the astonished silence, Illich heard the faintest shuffle of shoes under the table, as the minds of the committee worked on the implications of the vote. He himself could hardly believe Pridilenko's audacity, the audacity of a terrier before a lion. He glanced around at the others.

Arkady Virusk was effectively Pridilenko's opposite number in the Interior Ministry, a collaborator if not a subordinate. Slowly, he raised a hand. Illich watched the others. Chernavin's hand was as heavy as iron on the table.

Valentin Osborov, Second Secretary, Naval Intelligence, seemed to waver, but remained stationary. Andrey Veronin, of Directorate 3, Scientific Research, was one of those dry scientists who preferred to refrain from any overt political gesture. Illich's attention moved on to Sergei Mamayev, Chairman of the Committee of Sport Resources. Illich studied the little Georgian whose outward appearance reminded him of Stalin. Mamayev was looking around the table, as though deciding which was the stronger party. Chernavin turned towards Mamayev his intimidating stare. Mamayev seemed transfixed. Illich's hope wavered, sank.

Mamayev's sly, black, eyes turned towards Pridilenko.

Illich saw a line of Georgians stretching back through history – thieves, black marketeers, dictators. Then this man, who by rights should have been selling illegal carnations off a lorry in the back streets of Tibilisi, or liquidating millions in some vast purge, this person raised his hand. Never in the history of human relations has one racial stereotype been exchanged for another so rapidly as now occurred in Illich's mind. Josef Stalin and Lavrenti Beria moved into the background. Forward came happy, smiling men, descendants of poets, legislators and saints. Eduard Shevardnadze, the head of police who cleaned up the gangsters and criminals; selfless workers, agronomists, academicians. Illich silently promised himself that he would never make another joke about Georgians in his life. Every Georgian was, from henceforward, as pure as the driven snow.

Twenty-Three

Now Pridilenko was regarding him, Illich . . .

So used had Illich become to his existence as a prisoner, as a person in the path of events, as a passive witness to inexorable justice that, caught up in the unexpected and astonishing nature of Pridilenko's speech, he had forgotten entirely that he himself had a vote. He raised his hand.

Pridilenko looked around the table for signs of further support.

Vera Ahktova, as recordist and objective witness, did not exercise a vote. She made a verbal count.

'Three in favour out of six, Comrade Chairman,' declared Ahktova.

'As Chairman, ' said Pridilenko, 'I exercise my vote. I declare therefore that the vote is carried.'

Vera Ahktova's pencil made several quick, lucid manoeuvres. A light of graceful beauty soared in Illich's mind.

But now something was occurring at the end of the table. General Chernavin, his face white with rage, was rising. The force of his departure shook the table like an underground tremor, making the water glasses clink.

He said nothing as he strode past Pridilenko, opened the door, and slammed it behind him. They heard his footsteps echo down the corridor.

'At this point in the proceedings,' Pridilenko said quietly to Ahktova, 'General Chernavin left the room.' He looked around at the astonished faces, and raised his voice. 'As Chairman, I formally declare the meeting is over.'

Vera Ahktova inscribed these final notes into her pad.

*

A relief so profound affected Illich that for several moments he did not move. He knew it was a vain hope that his troubles were over. In due course he must face a court martial. Even so, it was enough that others were willing to stand up for him, that he was not alone in the world.

The others were now leaving, standing up and shaking hands with Pridilenko. Mamayev, that shining example of Georgian national virtue, patted Illich on the shoulder as he left. Illich, too, made his move to leave.

'Stay here,' Pridilenko said to Illich. He accompanied the others to the door.

'Natasha,' Illich heard Pridilenko say to his receptionist. 'Tell Colonel Illich's personal bodyguards that I shall be talking to him for another half-hour. Supply them with coffee.'

Pridilenko came back into the room, closing the door. There was a phone on a side-table in the committee room. Pridilenko dialled a single 8. 'Put me through to General Ivanov.'

'Lev,' Pridilenko said. 'The prisoner has arrived. Are your men ready? Quarter of an hour? Good. Your help is appreciated.'

Pridilenko sat down opposite Illich at the table. Illich noticed a barely suppressed excitement in his eyes. Pridilenko spoke precisely but rapidly.

'That was KGB General L. Ivanov. In a quarter of an hour some dozen of his men will be here to meet you. There is not much time. I must explain the background.

'There is a high-level row in progress, in which you are, unfortunately, the centre. Vajnen Aegu, President of Estonia, made a formal objection to the Council of Ministers that an Estonian national had been "abducted" by the military and was being placed on political trial. He argued that you had nothing to do with the riots at Tartu, that they were caused by disorderly elements using your open-air lecture as an excuse to foment trouble. He argued, further,

116

that the events took place in Estonia, and the civil authorities in Estonia see no reason to prosecute you.

'It appears that the Secretariat of the Council of Ministers passed this complaint through to the Supreme Council. The Supreme Council sent an official resolution to the Ministry of Defence questioning their decision to place you on trial by court martial on a matter which was political in nature rather than military.'

Pridilenko glanced rapidly at the clock on the opposite wall, hardly breaking his speech. 'However, the Defence Ministry were unrepentant. They argued that they had a right to order the court martial of any officer, and as part of a court martial they had the right to consider the evidence of political treason. They made it clear that they deeply resented outside interference in an internal matter of discipline.

'There was something of a stalemate. At this point, I made a formal request to the Defence Ministry, as Chairman of this committee, that you be allowed to fulfil your obligation to attend this committee while matters were pending. This permission was refused. I sent my letter and a copy of the letter of refusal to the Council of Ministers, who upheld my request and ratified the decision that you be allowed to attend the America's Cup Committee today. Reluctantly, the Defence Ministry acquiesced.

'In the meantime, President Aegu has filed a request that you be returned to Estonia as an Estonian national pending further enquiries, on the grounds that your proposed offence was committed in Estonia, and with the proviso that the Estonian authorities had found no reason to conduct any investigation into the probity of your actions. The Council of Ministers yesterday upheld this request.

'There remains the matter of your bodyguard. The necessary documentation has been passed to KGB General Ivanov, who has been charged with the task of ensuring your return to Estonia. His men will be here shortly.'

Pridilenko looked Illich directly in the eye. 'Do you understand?'

Illich nodded: 'But . . .'

'But,' said Pridilenko, 'you feel, nevertheless, as a soldier you should return to face the court martial.'

'Yes.'

'Unfortunately, Ivan Ivanovitch, you are now the centre of a trial of strength between the political and the military, which the military has initiated by arresting you. We cannot allow you to return to be court-martialled. It would mean that the military had won. I am afraid that your own preferences, however laudable, are somewhat secondary.'

Illich was only now beginning to understand the full implications of the row between the political and military establishments.

'You mean that, if necessary, I am to be put on a plane to Estonia against my will?'

'That is correct,' Pridilenko stated laconically. 'We have a State Deportation Order already signed and ready to be used in the event that you do not wish to return voluntarily. As I have said, I am afraid there are larger matters at stake than your own particular wishes.'

'I see.'

'I would ask you to consider other matters carefully. Firstly, if the military has its way, you will be court-martial-led and found guilty. Of that you should be certain. The consequences are that you would be stripped of your rank and equally certainly, Comrade, given the serious nature of the charges against you, this will be followed by a term of imprisonment. You have little to lose by not returning to the court martial.

'But,' Pridilenko continued, 'you must be aware of the other possibilities. If you return to Estonia, you will almost certainly be stripped of your rank by the military for not attending the court martial.'

'Even though I was forcibly removed against my will?'

'Even so. They may even try you *in absentia*. But we think,

118

having lost possession of the individual in question, they may be forced to think again. I therefore strongly recommend that you return to Estonia.'

There was a knock at the door. Natasha put her head round the door and said, speaking to Pridilenko: 'The bodyguards are getting restless. They asked to speak to you.'

'Tell them I will be with them in a few moments.'

'They say that it is urgent.'

'A few minutes.'

Pridilenko turned again to Illich: 'I should also caution you, Comrade, that given the delicacy of the situation, it would be wise to keep an eye behind you when in Estonia. I understand kidnappings are not unknown.'

Pridilenko referred to a recent case in which a Russian husband, after splitting up with his Estonian wife, had kidnapped the children from the Estonian town of Parnu. The message was clear.

'One further matter, Comrade,' Pridilenko said, and a certain irony entered his voice, 'I think you would be wise not to hold any more open lectures on the immensely political subject of racing tactics, for the time being at least.'

Illich nodded.

There was another knock at the door. Natasha said: 'There is another group of men who are asking for you.'

'How many?'

'About ten, maybe twelve.'

'Good,' said Pridilenko. Turning to Illich, he said, 'I understand that military theory recommends a ratio of at least three to one where offensive tactics are to be employed.'

Pridilenko left the room. Illich heard through the partly opened door several brief exchanges between Pridilenko and the military police bodyguards who had accompanied him to the meeting. Pridilenko was reading out a document, one which gave authority for the KGB to take over the prisoner from the military police. One man, who Illich guessed was the senior of his military police bodyguards, started to cavil and shout. There was the sound of a scuffle, a movement of heavy boots across a room, the thud of a falling body.

The door of the room was opened. Pridilenko stepped in. Behind him was an officer of the KGB.

'Captain Biryukov will escort you to the airport.'

'Follow me, please, Comrade Colonel.'

Outside, two KGB men were holding down the senior military police officer, who continued to thresh and shout face down on the floor. Four men had backed the remaining two military policemen into the furthest corner of the reception room. The KGB men were large, threatening, what the populace liked to call 'prime meat'.

Illich followed Captain Biryukov into the corridor. Six of Biryukov's KGB cohorts followed behind. In the lift there was a considerable press as eight crowded into the small space.

Through the foyer they walked rapidly, out into the evening air. Dusk was falling over Moscow; the streetlights were already on. A cavalcade of three limousines was waiting, two KGB Volgas and a Zil. Illich was escorted to the Zil. Biryukov sat on one side of Illich, a henchman on the other side. The remaining members of the KGB choir crowded into the forward and rear cars. The blue lights of the Volgas to front and rear were turned on. Sirens began to howl.

They drove fast down the centre lane, at the normal breakneck speed of a government member's cavalcade.

To Illich, still stunned by the rapid turn of events, Biryukov seemed a diffident young man. About a minute after their departure, Biryukov said: 'I hope you will forgive the drama, Colonel. General Ivanov has lent us his Zil for the purpose of taking you to the airport. It means no one will risk stopping us.'

They turned south-west to Vnukovo airport. Bypassing the normal entrance, the convoy drew up outside the VIP lounge. There was a special room for high-level officials.

The KGB guard at the entrance was clearly expecting them. They marched the prisoner into this area.

The KGB choir moved aside, standing in two groups of three at the other end. It was, Illich guessed, their 'unobtrusive' formation. Several of them gazed at the remarkable luxury of their surroundings. It was true that the lounge was plush. Pile carpets seemed an inch deep. The lighting was expensive German variety, the glass and steel tables Finnish, the hi-fi system, with its Western music, no doubt Japanese.

'Cigarette, Comrade Colonel?' Biryukov opened a leather cigarette case.

'No thanks.'

'Do you mind if I do?'

'Not at all, Captain.'

'Officially, we are not allowed to smoke on duty. But where it is necessary to blend, we are encouraged to adopt such postures.'

Biryukov placed a cigarette between his lips and reached into his pocket for his lighter. The offer of a cigarette reminded Illich of a joke about the KGB and their well-known Jesuitical cunning. At a seminar of security forces, a young officer of the MVD military police and another of a similar rank from the KGB met outside a lecture hall between lectures. The MVD man said 'Although we are officially on duty, do you think our superior would mind if we smoked while we study?' 'Let us ask him,' said the KGB officer. A day later they met in the same place outside the lecture theatre. 'I asked our superior whether I could smoke while I studied, and he refused,' the MVD officer said. 'How odd,' commented the KGB man. 'He gave me permission.' 'Really?' asked the astonished MVD man. 'Tell me, what did you say to him exactly?' 'Unlike you, Comrade,' replied the KGB officer, 'I rephrased my question. I asked him whether he would mind if I studied while I smoked.'

Beside him, Biryukov lit his cigarette, and turned his head to exhale at a respectful tangent to Illich.

Illich looked at the stalls. He wanted to buy something for Vera.

The flight information came up on a television screen. It was six-twenty. The announced flight time was six fifty-five.

'Do you mind, Captain, if I purchase a bottle of perfume for a girlfriend.'

Biryukov glanced at the flight times, then shrugged his shoulders diffidently.

Illich crossed the few yards to the counters at the perimeter of the lounge.

Twenty-Four

The Moscow cosmetics company Novaya Zarya had opened a plush stall among the Western-style goods counters. He approached the counter and peered through the frosted glass at the items on display. The names were confusing. Perfume brand-names included 'The Kremlin', 'Black Casket', 'Scent of the Motherland', and 'Success in Bratislava'. Were these, he wondered, coded erotic names? If so, their significance escaped him. What was 'Success in Bratislava', for example? It sounded like a chess championship. Mercifully, there was not yet one called 'Tartu Riot'.

The girl at the counter was helpful, however. She dabbed her wrists with several examples. One called 'May Day' seemed promising. But in the end he chose 'October Night'. This was a safe one, the girl said, not least because its price, which brought beads of sweat to his brow, gave it prestige.

Biryukov was standing politely at his shoulder.

'Your flight is waiting, Comrade Colonel.'

Biryukov and his men accompanied Illich to the aircraft. At the aircraft steps Biryukov shook hands with Illich. From his window seat Illich could see the group of them, Biryukov slightly apart, waiting for the gangway to be raised. Then the choir left, moving in a body over the tarmac towards the exits.

The engines started and the aircraft taxied to the runway, and took off. Before they reached cruising height, Illich sank into an exhausted sleep.

He woke as they were descending to Tallinn airport. His mind was accustomed now to waking in a solitary cell, and for several moments he was not sure where he was.

Having partially acclimatized, he found it was an opportunity, a fleeting one, to reflect on some of the events that had led to the present position.

The most intriguing was the function of Pridilenko. He had always liked Pridilenko, and the recent incidents had given him an insight into the method of operation of a high-level functionary. When Pridilenko carried the vote in the recent committee meeting, an elusive but discernible expression of fulfilment had come into his eyes. It was part of the game of power politics. And Illich confirmed another thing. He, Illich, was a solitary, and therefore unsuited to high-level political function. The successful *vlasti* were social, tribal animals, who took great care to build up contacts. Individuals did not function alone, but in wolf-packs. Thus, earlier in his career, Pridilenko would have curried favour with the rising KGB officer L. Ivanov, perhaps by supplying him with information which would help him to rise in the ranks. In return, one day he could call upon Ivanov to do him a favour, even to take a political risk in Pridilenko's favour. There would be other such contacts through the ministries. In this way certain groups of younger men moved upwards through the system. There was a word for it: 'mountaineering'. If Ivanov ever reached the exalted position of Head of the KGB, one could be

123

sure that he would put his weight behind the Ministerial candidature of a certain Pridilenko, the rising star of the Foreign Ministry. Moreover, this 'tribe' would protect itself from members of younger, more ambitious tribes while it enjoyed the exercise and perquisites of power. Thus it was clear that ultimate power would move from one tribe to another as a generational change. If one member of the younger tribe penetrated the upper levels, perhaps as a protégé of one of the existing figures, so in due course he would replace his colleagues with members drawn from his own tribal peer-group.

In the case of Illich, this younger tribe had begun to flex its muscles in his cause, not because it liked him, but because he represented a suitable object for its own self-aggrandizement. If it had expressed its confidence by defying the entrenched power of the military, this was because its members felt strong enough to do so, secure that each would protect the other in the event of repercussions.

In all this Illich was merely a pawn. He was grateful to Pridilenko for making this plain.

As the aircraft sank downwards through the night towards Tallinn, Illich reflected briefly on another aspect of his own future career. Up to the rank of colonel, it was possible to fulfil one's function as a soldier with most of the soldierly virtues – loyalty, discipline, courage. Above the rank of colonel, success or failure depended increasingly on political virtues, the same tribal virtues displayed by Pridilenko. He saw, more clearly than before, that he was unsuited for this type of manoeuvre. Made of more simple material, he did not foresee his future as a set of political battles, manipulations of committees in huge ministries. He recognized, in short, that whatever might now happen to him, his military career had reached its natural end. This realization did not help him with his immediate problems, but it did perhaps prepare him partially for the shocks that were to come.

*

At the airport he took a taxi back to the flat. It was eight-thirty in the evening and Tallinn was lively. Tourists crowded the streets, young people walked arm in arm, lovers kissed openly, once a rare sight in the former Soviet Union, with its traditional rigorous division between private and public life. Shops and restaurants lined the main thoroughfares. The windows were filled with luxury goods. Azerbaijanis and Georgians operated all-day privately owned shops and stalls, selling anything from vegetables to toothpaste.

His taxi driver, a Georgian, watched him staring at this panorama.

'You want a night-club, your excellency? I know the best.'

Illich shook his head.

A few minutes later the taxi driver tried again.

'I know beautiful girls; pretty faces, nice bottoms.'

Clearly, the man was a model of socialist probity. His life's wish was to distribute the benefits of pretty girls with nice bottoms as widely as possible.

'I am too tired.'

The old walled hill-town was lit up with lights for the tourists. They drove towards Laidoner Street.

Illich paid the taxi-driver and entered the hallway. As he climbed the stairs he noticed Irkut's door was open several inches. He unlocked the door of his apartment.

The flat was not as he had left it. It was a matter of small, subtle things. The pile of brown envelopes was more neatly arranged than he had left it. A drawer which he had left, from ancient habit, with a quarter of an inch of lip showing, was now fully closed. He switched on all the lights and conducted a thorough search of the flat. The kitchen and bathroom were undisturbed, as were both bedrooms. His search yielded no further signs of his mysterious visitor.

Despite this intrusion, tiredness and relief overcame him. He slid the bolt home on the inside of his door, removed his jacket and trousers, and lay on the bed. He had no sooner closed his eyes than he was asleep.

Twenty-Five

Despite his tiredness, he woke again at just before 5 a.m. White light filtered through his window on to the bare wooden floors.

The unexpected freedom of being able to move around at leisure in his own flat, the incredible luxury of a bath, filled him with a sense of well-being. Of such simple things is life made.

He dried himself and glanced at his face in the small mirror above the handbasin. Nearly four weeks in solitary confinement under artificial light had given him a pasty, unhealthy look. There were dark half moons under his eyes. Traces of dirt clung to his jawbone amongst the uneven stubble. But these small things could not touch the unalloyed delight of shaving at leisure with warm, fresh water, with a square of friendly sunlight lying on the floor at his feet, the scratching of doves' feet on the roof, the sound of early traffic stirring far away in the city.

The phone trilled in the bare apartment: 'Colonel Illich?' The voice was familiar, though he could not place it immediately.

'Speaking.'

'Vajnen Aegu. I trust you arrived home safely.'

'Yes.' Illich was guarded. Although grateful to Aegu for arranging his release, he did not relish his role as pawn between two warring political factions.

'Perhaps we could meet?' Aegu suggested.

It would have been churlish, nonetheless, for Illich to refuse. He owed it to Aegu as his protector. There was a pause. Aegu said: 'Perhaps you could come to my flat. 25 Keeman Street.'

'Now?'

'If you do not have anything more pressing,' Aegu answered politely.

Illich put on his jacket, closed the door of his flat, and walked down the entrance hall. Irkut's door was once again slightly ajar, as if to monitor the comings and goings of those on the stairs.

It was a matter of a few minutes' walk. Illich proceeded briskly, enjoying the sunshine on his face. There was a traffic jam in Tivol Street. A wedding party, it seemed; there had been a revival in religious attendance over the past several years, of which church weddings were only one expression. He arrived at Aegu's door twenty minutes later.

The flat was in an undistinguished neighbourhood. Aegu's official residence was one of the fine old houses in Kohtu Street not far from Toompea Palace. This flat was more in the nature of his private office and study. Aegu had the reputation of an ascetic in material possessions. Nevertheless, he was rumoured to be a womanizer, an aspect of his well-known charm.

Aegu himself opened the door. He was dressed in a jacket, as though ready to go out. He shook Illich's hand. Illich caught a glimpse of a tidy flat, smaller than expected, with very little furniture, except for a large, surprisingly ornate desk piled high with papers and reference books.

They shook hands. 'Shall we walk?' Aegu looked up at the sky, and smiled. 'All those committee meetings. I get so little chance to see the outside.'

They started to make their way along Keeman Street down towards the sea front, Aegu with brisk, strong strides. A black Toyota with two men drew out from the pavement fifty yards away, clearly following them.

'My security guards,' Aegu explained, with a brief shrug

of his shoulders. 'One of the unfortunate aspects of my office.' They crossed Tivol Street and walked down Irlat Square.

'Tell me,' Aegu asked as they walked. 'How does it feel for a Russian Army colonel to be rescued by a KGB choir?'

'A little strange,' Illich replied. Aegu clearly had a mischievous streak. He was prepared to play on the legendary animosity between the Army and the KGB.

'In order to keep the patriotic enthusiasm of the Army in check,' Aegu said drily, 'we are sometimes forced to rely upon unusual allies.'

This was something of an understatement. In the past decade, as the power of the armed services had declined, and their budgets had been trimmed, so the power of the KGB seemed to increase proportionately. It was a reformed, more sophisticated, more liberal KGB than in the bad old days, charged with security rather than suppression. Whereas Dzerzhinky's *Cheka* used the methods of torture and terror, his modern descendants were masters in the art of subtle pressure, of the hidden hand.

Aegu was walking fast, his short square frame pushing forward against the sea breeze.

At the corner of Satnu Square was an underground cellar. A small sign at the entrance said 'People's Art'. A wooden balustraded staircase led downwards to tiled stone floors. The basement area was large, subdivided by standing partitions. In the entrance area was a group of metal sculptures, tubular representations of human figures, standing, sitting, walking, lying in strange poses like Mayan goddesses. A number of the figures were representations of couples, highly suggestive. 'The police authorities,' Aegu commented drily, 'would like to prosecute these on obscenity charges, but one of the values of modern art is that the authorities cannot be certain precisely what the figures are doing. Now, of course, we do not bother. As long as it is somewhere off the streets, we have a policy of turning a blind eye.'

Aegu seemed to know his way through the exhibition. Illich followed him through groups of strangely dressed young people. Some were in sheets with shaved heads like Buddhists, others in extraordinary home-made confections; many of the women wore huge hats and veils revealing glimpses of white faces and flashes of red lipstick.

In a second screened area an audience of a few dozen were seated around a stage, on which an experimental band were playing; from it came vague Asiatic rumblings, screeches, the sudden howl of an electric guitar, punctuated by long silences. The players wore sheets and masks, and played with the oddly deliberate, disembodied movements of puppets.

Aegu did not pause. He was walking fast through an exhibition of modern paintings, many using religious symbols. Glancing at them, Illich was struck once again by the strangely ambiguous ambience of the exhibition. It was difficult to know whether the religious imagery arose from belief or merely a desire to shock.

The lights in the refectory at the other end of the huge basement were dimmed, but the furniture was pleasant; large, wooden pews like an old church, the wooden floors well swept, roughcast whitewashed walls in which light fittings had been cunningly placed. Aegu chose a secluded alcove. Several of the nearby tables were occupied, mostly by young couples. On one a family of four were eating. In the furthest corner a blonde Lithuanian girl was singing songs in a breathy voice.

Illich noticed Aegu's two security men enter, look around, and settle in a far corner. There was enough background noise to drown out their own voices. To overhear them, it would have been necessary to sit right at the table with them. Illich wondered whether this was the reason Aegu had chosen such a place.

They were seated opposite one another. Aegu chain-smoked. The unmistakable signs were there, the stained fingers, the automatic, almost subconscious movement of hands to cigarette packet, lighter, like a small production line. Even on the walk down, while he commented on the fresh air Aegu had taken a cigarette from his pocket and lit it, not pausing but striding forward forcefully. Illich had noticed that the majority of politicians smoked heavily, as if compensating for the tedium of committees; in this Aegu was no exception.

Aegu drew in and exhaled: 'Comrade Pridilenko is a courageous man, is he not?'

More than courageous, Illich reflected. Pridilenko was one of those who are not happy unless they are engaged in some battle, some crusade, against great odds. He remembered the excitement in Pridilenko's quick eyes as he arranged for Illich to be rescued by the KGB.

'He has set himself a difficult task,' Aegu added. But he was not inclined to elaborate on that task.

'And you now,' Aegu said kindly. 'You are facing a somewhat uncertain future.'

Illich could see, over Aegu's shoulder, the two security men stir uneasily, look around them. A waitress was serving them coffee. They paid her and drank morosely.

'Vodka,' said Aegu when the girl approached him. 'For you?'

'The same.' He was prepared to get drunk with Aegu if only because he wished to learn a little more about his own uncertain future.

'Two glasses.'

The girl, like many of the others here, was dressed in a home-made concoction, white, with the veils that seemed to be the fashion.

When the drinks arrived, and two glasses were filled, Aegu did not throw his at the back of his throat as the Russians did, but drank in occasional methodical gulps. Between gulps he drew on his cigarette and gazed around him. Illich waited patiently for him to speak.

Twenty-Six

'As you know,' Aegu began, 'I walk on a tightrope. On the one hand, there is the natural national aspiration of the Estonian people towards complete independence. On the other, the equally understandable wish of our Russian comrades to preserve strategic influence in the region. These must somehow be reconciled.

'It is fair to say, I believe, that although we do not have absolute self-determination, economically speaking we have effective autonomy. In cultural matters, too, Comrade Colonel, I think you will agree we have won for ourselves a free society.'

Illich merely nodded politely. It was necessary to get these preliminaries out of the way as soon as possible. Aegu averted his head and exhaled quietly.

'After the heady days in the early 1990s, when we declared formal independence, we negotiated our present relationship with Russia – a sovereign Republic in name, an independent nation in everything except collective military security.

'At the same time, we have a strong dissident element which wants to return to a completely independent nation state, guaranteeing its own security. Clearly, this presents us with a problem which is not easily overcome. On the one hand, one may have a limited sympathy with their aims. But on the other hand, the special privileges we have already gained have depended on a step-by-step approach, never moving faster than is necessary, while at the same time maintaining a constant pressure for reform.'

It was, Illich thought, like the two methods of drinking.

The Russians drank their vodka by downing fierce, whole glassfuls; large moves, five-year plans, big annual quota increases. The Estonians, on the other hand, drank patiently but relentlessly: steady reforms, always in a certain, fixed direction. It was like the hare and the tortoise. Of the two, generally, the Estonian reached oblivion first – hence the national reputation for alcoholism.

Aegu had fixed him with a speculative stare, and was addressing him directly. 'Now, Colonel, although I expended every effort to see that you were released from your confinement and returned to Estonia, I must say, frankly, that the riot at Tartu, at which you were present, was a considerable embarrassment to me and to those others like me who walk the tightrope. The riot showed the naked side of our nationalist ambition, in such a manner as to cause consternation amongst our Russian comrades.'

Aegu paused, gulped his vodka, stared for a moment at the pretty waitress as she went about her business.

'Two more glasses, please. No, bring a bottle.' Turning again to Illich, he continued: 'You see, in my usual role as tightrope walker, I found suddenly that someone was shaking the rope.

'And what is my position in all this?' Aegu paused for emphasis. 'Firstly, I am by inclination and belief a liberal socialist. I would like to see the supply services opened up to market forces, as is now the case. But I am not a fanatical nationalist. I do not believe in the inherent greatness of all things Estonian. Perhaps that shocks you? Frankly, I like the cosmopolitanism of this place . . .' Aegu waved an arm, indicating the refectory, the exhibition of art beyond, the city of Tallinn itself . . . 'I do not have to repeat the statistics in detail to you, Comrade, but as you know, some forty per cent of the Estonian population consists of Russian immigrants, nearly another ten per cent of immigrants from the other Republics – Byelorussians, Georgians Uzbeks, Azerbaijanis. The latest census statistics indicate that in a few years' time the Estonians will be in a minority. That

132

frightens our own extreme nationalist elements, who feel they are on the verge of being swamped by foreign nationals.'

The two security men cast occasional looks in Aegu's and his direction. Aegu was already on his fourth glass. Illich, attempting to keep pace with Aegu's measured but relentless intake, felt his head swimming.

'What they demand, therefore, is strict immigration laws, forced repatriation of the immigrants, in other words, the full panoply of measures associated with a fascist state.'

Aegu glanced at him, raised his eyebrows as if to say, 'Do you see how it is?' and when the waitress had returned with a bottle, poured two more glasses of vodka.

'So far, Comrade, I am doing all the talking,' Aegu smiled. 'As the kidnapper said to his gagged victim, I shall take your silence for agreement.'

Which would Aegu reach first, thought Illich, the conclusion of his argument, or inebriation? It was interesting – an aspect, perhaps, of performance art.

'The curious feature about these minorities in our Republic is that they do not represent obstructions on the path to full Estonian economic independence. On the contrary, the majority of our guest workers vote in favour of complete economic autonomy in Estonia. They, too, enjoy the special economic freedoms. That, after all, is why they immigrated here.

'And this returns me to you, Comrade Colonel. An amphibian, an Estonian nationalist, but with a Russian name and a Slavic father. Someone pulled in two directions, sometimes against his will.'

Illich nodded. 'It has been difficult for me being a counter between the Army and the political arm.'

'To be blunt,' Aegu replied, 'we didn't know how far the Army would go, whether it would really place you on trial. We could only find out in the course of time.'

Illich remembered his twenty-six days in solitary confinement and wondered if it was necessary.

As if anticipating his thoughts, Aegu said: 'Sometimes, one has to make sacrifices.' Aegu was thoughtful, pausing to stub out his cigarette and reach for his packet and lighter. 'There is a story about a blind man and his dog, standing at a bus stop. The dog is seated at the man's feet. For no apparent reason, the dog stands up and deliberately pisses on his master's leg. Without provocation. So what is he to do? He stands there with a wet leg, thinking. He reaches carefully into his pocket. He has stored a piece of chocolate there. Carefully, he takes it out and unwraps it. He holds it out and offers it to the dog. Another man sees him. "Comrade," this man says. "Your dog has just pissed over your leg. I saw it with my own eyes, and here you are offering him a piece of chocolate." "Don't worry," the blind man replies, "I am just finding out where his head is so I can kick him up the backside." '

Aegu lit another cigarette, then continued. 'This is how we deal with the Army. It pisses on our leg. We offer it a piece of chocolate and ascertain how we can kick it up the backside. Unfortunately,' Aegu added, 'in this case you are the piece of chocolate.'

'It is kind of you to explain,' Illich replied. He gulped the vodka, waiting for the stream to hit his stomach. 'Frankly, I feel more like the leg.'

'Such is life,' Aegu said philosophically, reaching forward with his free hand to refill his own and Illich's glass. 'We all have our turn at being the leg.'

A few moments later, Aegu said: 'I have gathered, from what others have said about you, that you are something of a reluctant hero. That is why your riot at Tartu is so ironical, if you do not mind my saying so.'

Aegu's face grew serious again.

'Now, with regard to your future. I understand that, as of several weeks ago, you were effectively dismissed from the Russian Republic's America's Cup defence?'

Illich nodded.

'I am afraid,' Aegu continued, 'I cannot help you there.

The Soviet authorities have the right to choose whomever they wish to represent them. However, we in Estonia also have a right to choose our own representatives, and this, Comrade, is the essence of the proposal I shall now put to you. Suppose, for the sake of argument, that we could, as the economically autonomous state of Estonia, place at your disposal funds to build a challenging America's Cup yacht. Let us say, further, that this yacht was entered as a challenger in the competition against the defending Russian Republic. Might you, as an Estonian and amphibian, be interested to helm such a challenger?'

It was a wholly unexpected question, one which threw Illich off balance. A whole tribe of emotions swam suddenly to the surface; elation, fear, and yes, a certain desire for revenge.

Behind these were a host of other questions of a more technical nature. Was there time to build one challenger, let alone a trial horse? And from which sector would the design experience come? Assuming the funds were available, who would build it? And the complex instrumentation, the computers derived from space programmes which both the Russians and the Americans would have available? Who would supply that?

Aegu was saying: 'I know enough of competition at this level to know that you cannot win against the huge resources of the USA or Russia. What I wish for, at the very least, is that we, a small, insignificant Baltic country with a population of only two million, may demonstrate that we are capable at least of organizing a contending yacht independently of our Russian comrades. If we could demonstrate this, it would strike a blow in favour of our status as an independent economic entity.'

Aegu regarded him slyly. He said softly: 'You know, your famous yacht *Leningrad* is not owned by the Russian Army. It is owned, to be precise, by the Estonian Trade Delegation. I have investigated the papers, and sought the advice of Professor Teemant on legal matters. The yacht is in the ownership of Estonia.'

Aegu took another gulp of his vodka. Illich's mind swam in a drunken haze. But there was one, overwhelming obstacle.

'The Army would not let it go.'

'Perhaps not, Comrade Colonel. On the other hand, suppose that it happened to leave the Army's jurisdiction.' This was outrageous. There was no way that the Army could be persuaded to part with *Leningrad*.

'After all,' Aegu said, and his broad face was full of mischief, 'Pridilenko released you from the jurisdiction of the Army.'

'Pridilenko would support it?'

'Comrade, in Estonia, what matters is whether I support it. And on that matter . . .' here Aegu hiccupped slightly, ' . . . I do.'

Aegu was starting to ramble. Illich watched him light another cigarette, then drain his glass again.

'They, the Russians, are liberalizing too. Their liberalization is slower than ours, of course, more cautious. They watch us and follow behind us, hoping not to make our mistakes. But it is there. There have always been jokes about the shortage of supplies, the gluts and starvations of a mixed economy. Some years ago they were no more than gripes, letting off steam. The assumption was that with a bit more tinkering, the system could be made to work.'

Aegu's eyes were unfocused; his voice, however, apart from the occasional slur, seemed unaffected. Illich was sure the two security men had moved to another table, but in his state it was difficult to be sure of anything.

'It is a strange thing,' Aegu was saying, 'but even the jokes in Moscow now express direct criticisms of the system. What is the definition of a queue? The Socialist approach to the counter. Not funny, but indicative. What is Socialism? The most difficult and arduous route to Capitalism. So it goes on.'

Aegu allowed himself a smile. 'Soon perhaps we will be hearing of the historical inevitability of Capitalism.' He glanced at Illich. 'You are not political, of course; you do not realize what a change these ideas represent.'

The bottle was empty. The waitress, used perhaps to the Estonian ways of drinking, replaced it with another full bottle.

'You know, it is a funny thing,' Aegu continued. 'Those of us who advocate the introduction of the free market almost invariably are not greatly concerned with material things, while those who advocate a forced social parsimony are invariably greedy and acquisitive of material things. Never believe a politician when he starts to preach morals, particularly a former Communist.'

In the advanced stage of inebriation, vodka strikes like a kick from behind. The face becomes numb. Illich could feel himself enter the final stages of intoxication.

'Do you know, Comrade,' Aegu said, 'that I have the distinct impression that as I get more drunk, so my security men get closer and closer.'

Illich glanced round. It was true. The security men were now only a table away, nonchalantly drinking their coffee.

They were half-way through their second bottle when Aegu tried to stand up, swayed, and was on the point of collapsing forward onto the table when the two security men caught him. One of the security men remarked, 'We were just in time again.' 'One learns by experience,' the other replied.

'Is it true,' asked Illich, 'that you move from table to table as he gets more drunk?'

'Yes,' said one. 'We find that if we move one table every three glasses, we usually get to the scene on time.'

One of the two security men paused to place a hundred-rouble note on the table. Then, putting each of Aegu's arms over their shoulders, they carried him away.

So used are Estonian café proprietors to drunkenness, that Illich was allowed to sleep at the table for several

137

hours. Some of the effects having worn off, he made his way gingerly to the exit, hailed a taxi, and was delivered in due course at his flat.

Twenty-Seven

Illich knew that in certain important respects Aegu was like himself. He had the stamp of Russia on him. Even though he was a pure-blood Estonian, there was some indelible mark of the larger neighbour, whose cause he had once served. What was it, exactly? One could see in small things, of course. In the choice of vodka to drink, against all the other alluring alcohols now freely available; in the Russian jokes that were not always funny but touched a bruise gently, affirming that the pain of living was not all one's own. But it was more than this. It was the terrible scale of Russia, the Russian love of the earthshaking concept and the giant programme. Leninism and the space programme were the political and physical expressions of the same thing, the same terrible presence. To a man without orthodox religious conviction, Russia was as big, as stern, as all-consuming as a God. It was a secondary consideration if you prospered or died. What mattered was to recognize that great presence.

All this Illich suspected of Aegu; like the religious everywhere, one could reach out and touch it if only because it was in oneself.

Nursing his hangover – not a headache but an eerie numbness of the face and upper head – he tried to phone his ex-wife in Charkov. As usual, the Soviet telephone system failed to respond.

He shaved, dressed, went out and bought himself a paper

and a bottle of milk from one of the corner stores that had sprung up in the last decade all over the city. He warmed the milk up on the stove, drank it, and then lay down again on the bed to read the newspaper. The news consisted of the usual chapter of disasters, massacres, political disorder. He fell into a heavy sleep.

At half-past ten he phoned Aegu's private number.

A woman answered. Aegu's wife? Almost certainly. Comrade Aegu was upstairs, working on his papers. Could it wait until tomorrow? It took courage to say that it couldn't wait – his brief, drunken intimacy with Aegu had increased, rather than decreased, his awe.

Aegu answered from an extension.

'Who is it?'

'Illich. Forgive my phoning.'

'*Tovarich*,' Aegu said. In this also, very Russian. He who drinks with me is my friend.

'You mentioned yesterday that a certain yacht is, formally speaking, the property of Estonia.'

'Yes.'

'Suppose that I was able to reclaim her? Would you be able to offer protection?'

'When are you thinking of . . . reclaiming this, er, property, Colonel?'

'Tomorrow.'

There was a brief silence.

'The element of surprise.'

'Precisely.'

He could sense the intensity of Aegu's concentration.

'Can you get her to Khiuma?' Aegu asked him. Khiuma was Estonia's second-largest island.

'Which part of Khiuma?'

'The harbour of Raferi.'

A fine place for a base; a small, newly constructed breakwater. Aegu was ranging ahead of him.

'I think we can reach it. But I'll need protection,' Illich said.

'We have local Customs patrol vessels. I can organize that now . . . You know the risks of entering the camp? Technically, the base is Soviet, not Estonian, territory. You come again under Army jurisdiction.'

Illich knew the risks. The odd lightness in his head helped him face them.

'I know.'

'Invoke Pridilenko. Raise my name. Try to intimidate them. When do you want the patrol vessel on hand?'

'From 10 a.m. tomorrow.'

'It will be there.'

'Thank you. There may be an incident.'

'If there is an incident, the Estonian authorities will take your side against the Army.'

How can you be so sure without consulting them, Illich wondered? But that was President Aegu's province. He had other things to worry about.

'Goodbye, Comrade,' Aegu said. 'Good luck.'

Illich hung up. Curiously, he felt a moment of elation. Now, he knew, he was committed to a course. There was no turning back.

Twenty-Eight

He was ravenously hungry when he woke up the following morning. There was no food in the flat. He walked fast towards the centre of the town, where he found an early morning café. Run by Azerbaijanis, it offered hot soup, rolls, a platter of bacon, liver, fried tomatoes. He washed it down with coffee, then caught a taxi to the base camp.

After an absence of four weeks, the guards checked his papers, but let him through without apparent fuss.

In the administration building all seemed normal. His office was untouched since he had left it. Five minutes later he heard, through his partly opened door, the sound of Vorolov's footsteps approach his suite of offices, and then the closing of Vorolov's door. It was important, he knew, to act fast, to apply continuous pressure. He knocked on the Major-General's door, heard his gruff 'Come in,' and entered.

Vorolov, seated at his desk, surveyed him for several seconds as he would a stranger. Then he said, 'Sit down, Colonel.'

Illich did so.

'I understand,' Vorolov said, 'that you are awaiting court martial.'

Illich nodded.

'Then what are you doing here, Comrade?'

'I was arrested by the KGB, and put on a plane to Estonia.'

'Then you should return to Moscow immediately.'

'An extradition warrant was prepared by the Ministry of the Interior. I am not permitted to enter Russia.'

'I do not know anything of this. I am simply informed that you have evaded a court martial, and that this makes you a deserter.'

Illich asked: 'Do you seriously believe I am a deserter?'

Perhaps it was the tone of his voice that made Vorolov hesitate.

'Beliefs, as you know, Comrade, do not influence what one is told. By rights I should arrest you.'

'If that is what you feel you should do, then my advice to you is that you should proceed.'

A pause.

'Why have you returned?' snapped Vorolov.

'Because it is my duty to report here, and to train the crew. Also, by returning here, it seems to me that I can disprove the theory that I am a deserter.'

'Nevertheless,' Vorolov insisted angrily, 'the General Staff demand your presence in Moscow for a court martial.'

'The court martial is on political grounds. The Army has no jurisdiction to undertake a court martial on such matters. Political matters are under the direct control of the civil authorities, and they have decided that no action will be taken. It was the civil authorities who decided to return me to Estonia. It was they, Comrade, who explained to me that in this respect, the General Staff is acting outside its jurisdiction. It is acting illegally.'

'Nevertheless,' insisted Vorolov, 'you are a deserter, and therefore it is my duty to arrest you. If you resist you will be shot.'

'If you arrest me, Comrade General, after I have informed you that such actions are, in this case, illegal, then you must bear the full consequences of your actions.'

For the first time, he saw hesitation enter Vorolov's eyes. Taking advantage of this momentary hesitation, Illich pressed ahead.

'My advice is to telephone Moscow, inform them that I have reported for duty as normal, and to avoid precipitate decisions until they have had time to consider the implications of their actions.'

'In the meantime,' Vorolov almost exploded, 'we will place you under arrest.'

'In the meantime, if you place me under arrest, you will bear full responsibility for your actions. Indeed, Comrade, if I am so much as impeded in my tasks, the authorities will press for the last reparation.'

Vorolov had started to sweat.

'Consider the wider situation,' Illich said. 'The authorities saw fit to remove me from the arrest of the Army. They spirited me out of Moscow and brought me safely to Estonia. What would be the consequences for you, Comrade, if the authorities discovered you had reversed their decision and, acting on your own responsibility, re-arrested me?'

This elaborate fencing was taking time. Illich was reasonably sure that General Chernavin would not arrive at his office before 10 a.m. It was now 8:30 in Tallinn, in Moscow 9:30. In half an hour Chernavin would be at the Ministry. Time was of the essence.

'If you will excuse me, Comrade General,' Illich said, rising, 'I will proceed to fulfil my duties.'

He stood up and saluted. Vorolov did not return his salute. Instead, he pressed a button on the intercom. 'Major Archem, could you come to my office immediately?'

In the corridor Illich passed Major Archem, who stared at him and saluted. Illich saluted in response and walked on. It was important to keep them off balance. He must show no personal warmth, no weakness.

Outside, in the little square beside the crew dormitory, the early morning training exercise had just been completed. The crew were standing about, breathing heavily. In a short while they would disperse to the changing rooms.

Gustav Prem saw him first: 'Illich!' Prem's shout was like an explosion. The rest of the two crews turned round. Prem and Soren Gir bounded towards him.

'Where have you been?'

'I was called away to Moscow. There is no time to talk. When are you scheduled to race?'

'Nine o' clock.'

It would be close.

'I will helm *Leningrad* today. Tell the crew to be a little early. I want to get out on the course as soon as possible. I will explain when we are on board.'

Illich looked back at the administration building. Vorolov's office overlooked them. Illich thought he saw a movement behind the grey glass.

He followed the others to the changing rooms. His sailing gear was as he had left it. They had preserved its pride of place in defiance of the Army authorities. He felt a brief stab of gratitude. But it was critical now to take the initiative, to keep the opposition off balance. He refused to answer

143

questions as he changed into the woollen underclothes that would protect him from the chill of the wind.

Gundar Arlof was changing close by. Illich said: 'How has it been going?'

'Pilnyak beats us almost every time.'

Illich made some calculations. Arlof was good. In addition, he had the veteran crew of *Leningrad*, on a boat they knew well. If Pilnyak could beat Arlof despite a relatively new crew on a relatively untried boat, then *Kirov* was fast, perhaps much faster than *Leningrad*.

'Where does he overtake you?'

'Upwind and downwind. It doesn't matter.'

'You think it's the boat?'

A rueful grin spread over Arlof's face, as if to say, 'What helmsman wouldn't?'

They finished changing and made their way to the shoreside. Illich refrained from glancing up at the administration buildings. They would be watching him while they waited to contact General Chernavin for orders. He imagined Major-General Vorolov, the MVD Colonel Ichurin and Major Archem in furious consultation over his sudden and unexpected re-appearance.

Kirov and *Leningrad* lay alongside the quay, *Kirov* ahead of *Leningrad*. It is a curious thing, Illich reflected, how one can tell at a glance which of two such yachts is receiving the main attention of the shore support teams. *Kirov* was immaculate. Her rigging and decks were neat, the installation of her systems beautifully finished. No expense or effort was being spared on her maintenance.

Leningrad, by contrast, looked almost dowdy. Admittedly, she was an older boat, but on such machines virtually all aspects of the working gear are renewable. The installations had been carried out with less care. On one side of her instrumentation box there was an egress of exposed wires. The normal dents and damage to the decks made by racing had merely been covered over with waterproof paint, so that the structure beneath was not penetrated with water.

As they worked to check the gear, Pilnyak and his crew appeared from their own changing rooms and walked down to the *Kirov*. They had the look of confidence of a pack of dominant dogs. Illich had no doubt that Pilnyak knew that he was back. Yet Pilnyak made no effort to approach him, despite the fact that Illich was his senior officer. This lack of civility indicated to Illich that he no longer had a place in the camp, and made him even more fiercely determined to carry out his plan.

The two towing launches were approaching the boats. Out of the corner of his eye he noticed a sudden movement in the direction of the administration buildings. Colonel Ichurin of the MVD strode out of the main doorway of the administration and over to the guard barracks situated some fifty feet away. Illich guessed that a telephone call had been made to the barracks. Some twenty MVD troops were gathering outside in a line, harried by a sergeant. Approaching them, Ichurin was now clearly giving orders to the lieutenant controlling the troop.

'Hurry,' said Illich to Victor Kingissep, the bowman. The towing rope was tied to the single ring on the bow. Colonel Ichurin had finished his orders and was leading his little troop down towards them now, striding ahead.

'Cast off!' Illich hissed. The bow rope tightened as the motor launch began to pull them out from the shoreside. It seemed to take ages, years. He could hear the footsteps of the approaching troops. He heard a shout from Ichurin or the lieutenant, saw the troops break into a run.

'Sing,' Illich said to the others. 'Something Russian. Gustav, for God's sake, sing!'

Prem, the amateur operatic singer, the former church choirmaster, began to sing from Mussorgsky's *Boris Godunov*. The others hesitated, then took him up. 'Soren, Berol, Graf,' hissed Illich, 'sing!' It was slow at first, a self-conscious cacophony of false starts. Then it seemed to gather force. Illich added his crow's voice to the proceedings.

Pilnyak and the other crew had turned round and were

watching them in astonishment. Their own launch was beginning to pull them out to sea.

Hardly more than twenty feet away, Ichurin's troop stood still on the dockside, uncertain. Illich noticed the troops had unshipped their submachine pistols, one or two were pointing them at *Leningrad*, at him in particular, but the lieutenant was waving the raised gunbarrels down. Colonel Ichurin walked up and down on the quay, hands on hips, like a caged animal.

It is one thing to shoot a Russian hero. It is another to shoot him when he is singing *Boris Godunov*.

The crew had surmised by now that the military police were intent on re-arresting Illich, and were singing lustily as they were drawn out to sea. Soren Gir's big baritone filled the air; the others tried to match him. It was like the song of the beasts in Aesop's fables, each contributing his own lion's roar or robin's contralto. Lions, crows, robins, wolves, elks; the entire singing bestiary was towed slowly out to sea.

Once started, it was difficult to stop. Estonia had a great choral tradition. A massed choir of thirty thousand gathered each spring in the Singer's Field in Tallinn.

Several hundred yards out they stopped. Naturally, they applauded their own superb efforts.

Then they moved to their gear, began the final check of lines, leads, winches, blocks, clips, outhauls, spinnaker pole attachments. The course had already been laid out. A starting launch formed one end of the line, a red buoy the other. The launches of both yachts were slowing, pulling them into wind.

'Mainsail up,' Illich shouted. Arlof was checking the instrumentation, feeding in the course distances.

The wind strength was about fifteen knots, though increased white horses to windward indicated some freshening of the breeze. Illich had to think fast. Unusually, the wind was from the west – 274 degrees, to be precise. This

146

meant that the first windward leg of the course was also almost due west, an unexpected blessing. It would take them several miles in the direction he wanted to go – to Khiuma.

Leningrad's mainsail was being hauled up, snaking and thundering slowly in the rising breeze.

He said to Soren Gir, the genoa trimmer: 'After the first leg, we'll break off the race, and then we'll sail to Khiuma. Tell the others. Don't gather in a group, or it will create suspicion.'

'Khiuma? The island?'

'Estonia owns the *Leningrad*. We'll set up our own challenge there.'

Soren Gir's big face seemed to contract, then open.

'You're joking.' Gir's grin spread from one side of his face to another while he stared at Illich. 'You're not, are you?'

'Tell the others, one by one. Tell them not to consult.'

In a fit of joy, Gir struck the genoa winch with the palm of his hand, making the winch ring.

'That's just the sort of behaviour I don't want.'

'I'm sorry. What happens if some of the others don't want to come?'

'Tell the ones who don't want to come they can leave now,' Illich said.

Soren Gir hit the winch a second time.

'I know, I know,' he said. He started to move forward. Several hundred yards away, on the other side of the starting box, *Kirov* had hauled up her mainsail. Illich could see, even from this distance, that it was brand new. He felt the anger start to rise inside him, the anger that always welled up in him at the beginning of a race.

Twenty-Nine

'Hoist genoa!'

Leningrad's genoa, too, had seen better days. He would worry about that later. With the headsail fully raised, he shouted: 'Cast off.' Two of the crew hauled in to take off the pressure on the bowrope while Stephan Migdal broke the back of the bowline and unleashed the rope. Illich swung the wheel over.

The power came on as they tightened in the sheets. He could feel the forces ride through the rigging, hear the sudden hiss of the bow-wave.

'Let's set her up to windward. Harden in sheets.' Graf Ulder and the huge Berol Baltir began to blast the coffee-grinders.

The boat seemed in reasonable shape. It wasn't as bad as he'd thought. It had been set up expertly by Arlof. When it went well – even though it was only a fraction of a knot faster – it had a curious cantering motion, difficult to explain, as if, metaphorically speaking, it was sitting on top of the water. Arlof said: 'Two minutes thirty seconds to the ten-minute gun.'

'Soren, the mainsail leech is a little tight,' Illich called. 'There is a swell today.'

Gir released pressure on the mainsheet. Illich watched the leech open a little.

'A fraction more.'

He was dealing with a crew who had tasted daily the bitterness of defeat. It was necessary to make changes, even changes which were ineffective, if only for psychological reasons.

'Edvigs!' Illich shouted forward to his port genoa trimmer. 'Open up the leech of the genoa in sympathy.'

'How much?'

'Two notches back on the track. Let's allow these old sails to breathe.'

Blame the sails, he thought. Blame anything except the human factor. Let's put some confidence back in the crew.

'Enough?'

'Enough.'

Actually, after another minute of tracking, allowing her to settle down, the boat did feel better.

'Speed is up one tenth of a knot,' announced Arlof. Illich felt once again the bonds of cooperation forming. Good. Let the crew know.

On the other side of the starting box, *Kirov* was wheeling powerfully. Her sails were setting perfectly. Pilnyak clearly had drilled his crew magnificently. It was a temptation, however, to become mesmerized by the other yacht.

'Forty seconds.'

'Bearing away.'

He swung the wheel. The sheets were eased. *Leningrad* picked up speed. They were closing on the starting box fast now.

'Twenty, nineteen, eighteen . . .'

The other boat, too was closing in on the starting box . . .

The explosion of cordite was like the start of a battle, one fought with ropes and sails, with blisters and overworked muscles.

The boats were closing fast, charging one another.

'He likes to go low and deep,' hissed Arlof, 'then strike upwards.'

They were close enough to hear the scream of *Kirov*'s eased sheets, the musical whine of her winches as she turned away in a loop.

'We won't turn with her. Keep full power.'

There was a point, on a two-sail reach, where *Leningrad* seemed to pick up an extra quarter of a knot of speed. He ignored the wheeling, charging *Kirov*, and rather than follow them into the circle, ordered sheets to be hardened slightly. Seventy degrees to the wind, her fastest course.

'Nine eight,' sang Orlof. 'Nine eight, nine nine. Ten zero!'

Kirov crossed the wake astern like an angry shark. Tacking, her boom crashed over. He saw her as she emerged on the new tack, chasing them.

'Gybe!' Illich shouted. He turned the wheel hard. The mainsheet squealed as Gustav Prem eased rope. Wheeling downwind, *Leningrad*'s boom seemed to hesitate once, like someone about to jump, then crashed across with a ferocious roar. The genoa was hauled in on the other side.

'Eight eight, eight nine, nine zero.'

They were approaching each other fast on parallel courses again. But *Kirov* had tacked to *Leningrad*'s gybe, and there must have been two knots difference in speed in favour of *Leningrad* . . .

'Wheel!' roared Illich.

Turning, they were like two stallions, neck against neck. Almost close enough to touch. With one difference. If you entered a turn with more speed, it could be translated into a faster turn rate. That was happening now. The turn was draining speed out of both boats, but *Kirov* had less speed to lose.

For the third time the boom thundered across, and they were on *Kirov*'s quarter . . .

'Keep away,' Arlof was shouting in Russian at the other boat. 'Our right of way!'

'Herding' was driving the other boat away, ruthlessly exercising right of way if the opponent tried to swing right or left. For the full remaining eight minutes to the start gun they herded *Kirov* away from the line.

Only when the starting gun went did they release their grip, turning rapidly towards the line. *Kirov* spun almost simultaneously, splitting tacks. Illich tacked to cover.

The crew were working well. *Leningrad*'s superiority in the start manoeuvres had put heart into them. It took several more tacks by each boat to reach the starting line.

'My advice is to keep a close cover,' Arlof said.

Illich glanced behind him at the other boat. Beyond *Kirov*, something caught his eye. A fast patrol vessel was setting out from the shore, almost certainly from the camp itself. They were going to arrest him on the water.

His inclination was to follow his instinct and seek out windshifts in an attempt to open up their short lead. But if the fast patrol vessel was aiming to intercept him, it would be more difficult if he were in a close duel with *Kirov*.

'He's tacking,' hissed Arlof.

The time to tack was just after the other boat had fully committed itself to the new tack. Sometimes the helmsman behind 'dummied', swinging back onto the original course, in the hope that the leading boat would commit itself to a tack. Illich waited until *Kirov* had swung through the wind, and roared out: 'Tack!'

Kirov's tack had been swift and efficient. Pilnyak's two winchgrinders, one a Siberian, the other a huge Ukrainian, were clearly a formidable combination. They pulled their genoa in on the other side with the smoothness of a watch spring.

Pilnyak was starting to press hard. A flurry of seven tacks followed. Each time *Kirov*'s bow seemed to move a little forward.

'Better acceleration out of the tack,' Illich whispered to to Arlof. 'Is it their keel?'

'We think so,' Arlof replied.

Six tacks later and *Kirov*'s bow was closer still, so close now that it almost seemed to ride over *Leningrad*'s transom.

Illich waited until Pilnyak had tacked to starboard, but did not cover this time by tacking with him. On port tack he separated, knowing that when they returned he would be on starboard, with right of way.

The fast patrol vessel had closed to half the distance. He could see its fluted bow wave.

'Eight one, eight one, eight two,' sang out Arlof.

Aside from the tacks, *Leningrad* was starting to go well. Opening up the leech a little had helped. What was lost in pointing was more than gained by a marginal increase in speed.

They caught a small advantageous lift in wind direction, pointing higher. Then the wind reduced a little.

'Tack!' shouted Illich.

It was a good one, as crisp as they could do. Several hundred yards away, *Kirov* tacked in response. Now they were closing with one another on converging courses.

The patrol vessel grew slowly like a tumour; same bearing, just larger.

'Nothing in it,' Arlof said.

Good.

'Give me a bearing to Khiuma.'

'Two hundred and seventy three degrees,' Arlof said.

It was ten-fifteen, no sign of the Customs boat Aegu had promised as escort. Illich allowed himself a brief flare of anger and frustration.

Kirov was almost on them.

'She's nearly a boat length up,' Arlof informed him. Enough to cross their bow? It was going to be a tight decision for Pilnyak.

'Fifty yards.'

Kirov's bow was slicing inexorably forward. The mark was riding up fast, too.

Now, Illich knew, Pilnyak would be making his decisions, living on fractions of a second, his body fearful but his mind cold.

'He's not bearing away,' said Arlof. 'He's crossing.'

Kirov sliced across their bow. It was so close that it was a wonder that two such huge machines could occupy the same space without touching, as if in violation of physics, as if the very intensity of their interaction was curving space itself. *Kirov* crossed with no more than two feet in it.

A sigh of relief and reluctant admiration from Arlof: 'He's got balls.'

Pilnyak tacked to place a close cover on them. Illich waited until Pilnyak was committed, and shouted: 'Tack!'

If the previous encounter was close, this time *Leningrad's* bow swung past *Kirov's* stern a matter of inches away.

Illich had split tacks. Pilnyak could not tack immediately to cover them for fear of losing too much speed. Brutal, simple; they had clear air for the crucial fifty yards before the buoy. . . .

The buoy had swelled into something enormous. Like a surreal act, the bridge of the fast patrol vessel expanded from it.

'Tack!' roared Illich.

Everything seemed louder, the thunder of the sails as they swept across, the blasting whine of the coffeegrinders.

Pilnyak had tacked too for the buoy. Three boats, *Kirov*, *Leningrad*, the patrol vessel, occupied the same small patch of water. *Kirov* crossed again, a few feet away.

Something cracked. He thought it was one of the running backstays. He turned to look behind him. Arlof was standing stupidly, holding his chest, sinking. An unexpected crimson flower appeared beneath his fingers. He's been shot, Illich thought. Merciful God!

'Tack!' he roared.

In the maelstrom of sails he prayed that there would be no easy targets for the marksman on the patrol vessel. His manoeuvre placed *Kirov* between him and the patrol vessel.

'Tighten in hard!' he shouted.

He was pressing Pilnyak close, using right of way, squeezing *Kirov* against the patrol boat. He could hear the patrol vessel's engines scream in reverse. Tighter.

Kirov caught the patrol vessel only a glancing blow, but it seemed enough to stop her. Illich saw why. *Kirov's* rigging had become tangled in the patrol vessel's bridge. Reversing, the patrol vessel was pulling the entangled yacht over towards her. *Kirov's* mast shook, the top section swinging

153

like a tree. As the patrol vessel reversed away a series of further cracks rang out, like further rifle shots, as *Kirov*'s lower shrouds snapped. With a squeal almost as high as a dog whistle, *Kirov*'s mast broke above the boom, and tumbled down on the bridge deck of the patrol vessel.

'Soren,' shouted Illich. 'Take the wheel.'

Arlof was lying on the floor, breathing slowly, wheezing. Jerking his jacket off, Illich propped it under Arlof's head. Pulling away Arlof's clothing was more difficult, without causing him further pain. Arlof's face screwed up.

'Murderers!' Soren Gir was screaming into the wind. *Kirov* and the patrol vessel were hopelessly entangled in sails and rigging. Pilnyak's crew were already working like ants to free them as the two craft ground together in the swell.

Gir was staring forward, pointing. Another boat had appeared about two hundred metres away. It was the Customs vessel promised by Aegu, fifteen minutes late.

The bullet had entered on Arlof's left side, an inch in from the pectoral, and then exited almost immediately. The blood was red, watery, not the thick, viscous blood of a lung wound.

Berol kneeled down beside him.

'Knife, cloth, binding tape, quickly,' Illich said.

'Soren,' he said. 'It's the Customs boat. They're here to escort us.'

'Fuck them!' Soren Gir shouted.

'Gundar's alive,' Illich said. He wanted to say, 'will live', but he did not wish to tempt fate.

'Lift him,' he said to Baltir, who had returned. Arlof gave a moan, another flower of blood emerged shyly from his mouth. Illich cut the splices of his clothing with the sharp knife, and pulled the pieces away.

Illich ripped the cloth into two pieces, folded them into staunches, taped one to Arlof's chest against the entry wound. He had to feel around the back for the other wound.

The exit wound was bigger. He could feel the hole with his fingers. Working as quickly as he could, he taped a staunch against it, wiping the bloody fulmus against his trousers.

'Wounded man!' Gir shouted at the incoming Customs launch. 'Do you have a stretcher?'

The boat shuddered as the Customs craft came alongside, and three men sprang onto the deck, one carrying a light stretcher under his arm.

The Customs boat hovered while they strapped Gundar Arlof to the stretcher.

'Thank you, Soren,' Illich said, taking the wheel. He swung the boat into wind, taking way off her while the sails shook and thundered. The Customs boat manoeuvred alongside again. Gir and Baltir helped to hand the stretcher across.

The captain came to the side. Dark glasses, a pale beard, angular, Nordic frame.

'He'll have to go ashore now,' Illich said. 'Leave us.'

'I've radioed for a replacement escort,' the captain replied.

'Have you any firearms?' Illich asked.

'Yes, two carbines. Under seal.'

'Break them, give them to us.'

'It's not permitted.'

'Captain, if they come after us, and shoot more of our unarmed crew, I swear to God I'll follow you and kill you.'

A few moments later two sealed cases were thrown onto the deck of the *Leningrad*.

'You break the seals,' the captain said, and disappeared into the bridge house.

The Customs vessel turned away, heading back for Tallinn. Illich swung *Leningrad* back on course.

'Soren, take the wheel again.'

'He'll live?' asked Soren. Gir's face was working; dried tears covered his cheeks. Large men tend to be emotional, thought Illich.

'The bastard will come back worse than before,' Illich

155

said to Gir. 'Take the wheel, keep heading towards Khiuma. We're not out of danger yet.'

Illich looked back. Now there were other boats around *Kirov*. They seemed to have appeared from nowhere. The two towing launches were helping to extricate her from the patrol vessel, using heavy wirecutters. With a wrenching scream the patrol vessel was finally free of the entangling rigging. It was circling backwards. Now the engines were being gunned into forward. It was starting after them again.

Illich used the blunt knife to break the seals. The guns were Kalashnikovs; the Army's old guns filtered through to the subsidiary services.

The best thing about a Kalashnikov was that you could load it with one hand on a dark night; the crudest, hardiest, most effective of semi-automatic rifles. Two full magazines came with each gun. He slammed into a magazine one of the guns, released the safety catch.

'Get down,' he shouted to the crew. 'Get down. Lie flat on the cockpit floor.'

After Arlof, there were no second thoughts.

'Soren, lie down too. There's nothing ahead. Sail by the wind.'

On the patrol vessel, they would assume there were no guns on board *Leningrad*.

A Kalashnikov with its crude sights, just unloaded from its storage case, was a primitive weapon, almost certainly wildly inaccurate. He knelt on the cockpit floor and steadied the gun on the side-decks.

Across the sights the patrol vessel loomed. He could see no figures. Illich wondered whether warning shots would be enough. Inside, a cold rage gripped him. He wanted blood for blood.

A figure was emerging from the bridge deck of the patrol vessel, a figure with a rifle. Casually the marksman steadied himself on the sidedecks, bracing himself against the boat's motion by placing a foot on the gunwale. The rifle came up. He was about to fire.

Illich aimed the Kalashnikov as best he could at the figure and squeezed the trigger. The bullet struck a tiny spark on the aluminium superstructure of the vessel high and to the left. If the figure was startled, he did not show it. He merely settled in to aim.

There was one chance to hit him. Illich aimed low and to the right, squeezing again. This time he could see no spark. The figure was standing still, unperturbed. Then, like a man lying down on a sundeck, the figure casually stretched out, and lay still. Illich guessed that he was dead.

His mind was numb to the thought of taking life. Like one of the deep bruises that the yacht gave to the human body, it would only emerge later as pain. What would shock him afterwards was that his desire for revenge was unquenched.

He turned the sights on the black glass of the bridge deck, aimed low and to the right, and began to squeeze off shots. He did not stop until he had emptied the entire magazine, until the white starcracks had spread across the windscreen like a weed. The patrol vessel began to career from side to side slowly, as if someone had released the wheel and then, hesitatingly, returned to it. Slowly the vessel turned and bore away.

Thirty

For a yacht race? Illich asked himself. We kill one another over a yacht race? A tremor spread from his chest to his arm and he began to shake.

There was a tradition in the former Soviet Union of treating a sport as a patriotic activity, a means of gaining international prestige; in this, an extension of foreign policy. But since when had sport become war?

He had known he was initiating some form of confrontation by asserting Estonia's right of ownership to the yacht *Leningrad*, but he had been fired on before he had departed, while he was still in the race. More, there had been no warning. He was certain that the bullet which found Gundar Arlof had been aimed at him. There was no attempt at arrest, no modulated threat of the use of force before its application. Who had given the order? Vorolov? Or had the MVD colonel Ichurin taken matters into his own hands? He knew, from his own experience, that the chain of command even in the Army is not as clear cut as one may believe. For example, the order 'Stop Illich at all costs' might conceivably be translated by an overzealous subordinate into an assassination. Thus are crises generated.

And his own actions? He and his crew were being fired upon, clearly with lethal intent. In such conditions, what else might he have done? Attempted to negotiate? But they had opened fire before any attempt at hailing or warning. How could one negotiate with assassins?

Thus, while he shook and trembled, he tried to justify his actions. It was too late to conduct any useful post-mortem. The crew were now beginning to stand up. Soren Gir, who had been lying on the cockpit floor, steering the wheel with one hand by the set of the sails, sat up and shaded his eye to stare after the retreating patrol boat.

Gir began to cheer. Ragged applause followed from the crew, then it ceased abruptly.

Far away, someone emerged from the wheelhouse of the departing motor patrol vessel and kneeled over the man who lay, still immobile, on the sidedecks.

Illich was determined not to let his shaking show. Still kneeling, he snapped on the safety catch of the Kalashnikov and removed the magazine clip. He replaced the gun and the magazine in the container.

'Are you all right?' Soren Gir was standing beside him. Illich rose to his feet, placing one hand on the wheel to steady himself. The yacht was still driving forward at a speed of seven knots. It was important not to allow the crew to slip into the despondency that sometimes follows a crisis. Illich said: 'We should get to Khiuma by nightfall if we push the boat. Let's get up speed.'

Soren Gir stood aside so that he could take over the wheel.

'Genoa in, mainsail tighter,' Illich ordered.

Somewhat slowly at first, the winchmen moved to their positions, spat on their hands and started to grind.

'Will they come back, do you think?' asked Gir.

'Not today, I imagine. They will stand off and watch us today.'

Forty minutes later, the promised second Customs vessel approached them, hailed them, and drew alongside with a turbulent wash.

'Is anyone hurt?' a voice called from the bridge deck.

'No one here,' Illich replied.

'We will escort you.'

The helmsman emerged; another bearded officer with dark glasses against the sun's glare.

'Colonel Illich?'

'Yes.'

'President Aegu is on the radio-telephone. Would you speak to him?'

The vessel closed the few remaining feet and Illich climbed on board. The interior of the Customs vessel was dark. It smelled of treated wood, stale tea, sweat. Several hats and extra protective coats hung beneath the sidedecks.

'Here,' the officer said, handing him the radio telephone.

'Colonel Illich?'

Aegu's voice was formal, the tone of a man who knows others are listening in. 'Can you tell me, as precisely as possible, about the events this morning?'

'Yes. The yachts *Leningrad* and *Kirov* went out to practise a race today, as is normal. I took the helm of the *Leningrad*. During the course of the race a motor patrol vessel, staffed by military police, approached the two yachts. Before we reached the first mark in the race, I heard a sound of a gunshot and saw that our tactician, Gundar Arlof, had been hit in the chest by a bullet. At the time, we were in a close tacking duel with *Kirov*. Exercising my rights of way as leeward boat, I pushed *Kirov* up to windward. *Kirov* collided with the motor patrol vessel. Her rigging became entangled with the bridgedeck of the patrol vessel, and her mast broke.

'Having been fired upon, we were able to use the resulting confusion to place as much distance between us and the patrol boat as possible. A Customs vessel approached us to give assistance and to take off the wounded man. At my own initiative, and against the advice of the Customs officer, I removed two sealed carbines from the Customs boat so that we could protect ourselves if the patrol vessel should attack us again.

'Once the patrol vessel had extricated itself from *Kirov*, it pursued us again. About a hundred metres away, a marksman on the patrol vessel again prepared to open fire on us. I returned fire against the patrol vessel. I believe my shots hit the marksman. I continued to fire at the vessel until it turned away.'

'Thank you, Colonel. You will testify to that sequence of events?'

'Yes.'

'You confirm that you were first fired on in the actual course of the race?'

'I do.'

'And you take personal responsibility for taking and using the firearms of the Customs vessel for the purposes of protecting yourself and your crew?'

'Yes.'

'Thank you, Colonel. Do you have anything further to add?'

'No.'

'I intend to see that the incident is properly investigated and that the guilty parties are punished.'

'Thank you.'

'Goodbye.'

Illich found himself shaking again. Curiously, now that he had reported the incident, his body suddenly felt cold. He sat down on one of the bunks while he recovered. His mind seemed reasonably clear. It was his body which continued to quiver, like a fish after it is dead.

Thirty-One

'Do you need any medical assistance?' asked the Customs officer. In the dark below deck, he had removed his dark glasses. Illich could see concern in his pale eyes.

'No, thank you. I must check the crew.'

The Customs vessel, which had stood off a few yards while Illich conducted his telephone conversation with President Aegu, now closed the distance with *Leningrad*. Illich crossed over to the yacht. The Customs vessel returned to its patrol.

It was about sixty miles from Tallinn to Khiuma, and they had covered nearly twelve miles. Soren Gir stepped aside for him at the wheel again. The wind had freed slightly, and strengthened. They were sailing at just under eight knots.

'Ease sheets slightly.'

He watched the speedometer numbers rise to eight point two.

During the course of the afternoon, an army helicopter, a Hind, flew above them at several thousand feet. The senior Customs officer shouted across to Illich. 'We have been ordered to return fire if necessary.' After a few minutes the helicopter turned away. Once, on the horizon, they saw the bridge-deck of another military patrol vessel.

'They are plotting our course on radar,' Illich confirmed to Gir.

At three forty-five in the afternoon, when they could just make out the outline of Khiuma ahead, the Customs officer shouted: 'Message from President Aegu's office. The emergency operation on Gundar Arlof was successful. He is in intensive care, but his condition is stable.'

The crew burst into applause.

The Customs officer continued: 'A second message, this one from my headquarters. There has been exceptionally heavy radio traffic on military radio frequencies all afternoon. Another Customs launch is being sent out as escort.'

'Thank you,' Illich said. The events of the morning would have stirred a wasps' nest in the local military bases. The visiting helicopter and the patrol boat offshore would be merely the tip of the iceberg.

At four twenty-three they were joined by the second Customs vessel, which passed across food and water for the crew, and then took up station on the other side of *Leningrad*.

Wind strength was steady at fifteen knots. Speed was now at eight and a half knots. At five forty the little convoy was drawing close to Khiuma.

The new fishing harbour at Raferi was almost empty. It had been the child of one of those planning decisions which are mysterious in their origins and which leave local communities bemused with their product. A decade before, a rise in the local fish stocks had been extrapolated into a sustained increase in local fishing activities. At the same time the Fishery Department had found itself with spare funding. Rather than report the surplus and risk a decrease in funds the following year, it had found an outlet for the spare capital in a fishing harbour for which no one had any use.

The harbour had twenty-two feet of water at low tide,

two large slipways, repair pens, and a complex of ancillary buildings on shore, including a large breeze-block shed of a size which could store, if suitably fitted, two America's Cup yachts. As they approached the harbour, Customs and local militia were already moving the fishing boats from their moorings. Private vessels bearing Finnish and Swedish flags had been politely advised to move down the coast.

Several civilian helicopters had landed on an open field beside the harbour. Their rotors were hardly stilled, their lights glowed in the fading dusk.

In the lee of Khiuma island the wind fell light. As they sailed into the harbour they dropped the genoa. Under mainsail alone they approached the quayside. Eighty metres away the crew dropped mainsail and let the boat's momentum carry them the final distance.

The two Customs vessels turned around for Tallinn.

They tied up and stepped ashore. A sergeant of militia approached Illich and asked him and the crew to follow him. Fifty yards from the harbour, through a small copse of trees, a dilapidated hall had been cleared for temporary dormitory use for the crew. The floors had been swept and mattresses laid out. Water was not yet on tap, but the sergeant pointed out that a well about seventy yards away nearby was supplied by a fresh underwater stream.

President Vajnen Aegu flew in by helicopter at last light.

Illich heard his approach in a bustle of accompanying militia. Out of the dusk Aegu burst, gripping Illich's shoulder and shaking his hand as if he were a war hero. Motioning the militia away, he drew Illich aside.

'While you have been engaged in hostilities, we have been working hard to prevent the Army from further action. It was necessary for the Secretariat of the Estonian Central Committee to issue a restraining order on any further activity by the Army. Were you expecting to be fired on directly?'

'No. Not without warning.'

163

Aegu's eyes were bright. He walked up and down, speaking as if to a larger audience.

'In news items of a controversial nature, it is our practice to clear aspects with the Russians first. In this case, we bypassed the procedure and transmitted your report directly to the news media. We said that while we cannot believe that the decision of the Army to open fire was other than an error, those who are responsible must be severely disciplined. We added that the action on the part of the Army against a yacht which is Estonian property is an outrage against the legality of the Estonian Republic. While I did not personally come under fire today, *tovarich*, I have been taking some unusual risks on your behalf.'

'Thank you.'

'We are flying in supplies tomorrow. Constructors will be building new temporary accommodation starting in two days' time. Please make a list of what you require to continue practice. I would suggest it is unsafe for you or your crew to leave the island for the next week, until the situation clarifies. Comrade Pridilenko sends his regards.'

Aegu looked towards the tall mast in the little harbour.

'Perhaps you will convey to your crew my warmest wishes. They must be tired and confused. Tell them your actions today have the full support of the Estonian people. Their relatives will be informed that they are safe. Leave any personal messages with Sergeant of Militia Rasa. They will be transmitted first thing tomorrow. One final thing.'

Behind Aegu, a small, bald man was signalling in the half-light. Aegu said: 'I promised Lars Brinsa, the editor of Radio Estonia News, that he could come with me, on the strict condition that he would only ask you one question.'

Aegu gestured. Lars Brinsa came forward out of the twilight. Brinsa's voice had the controlled modulation of a practised broadcaster. He held an outsize microphone towards Illich.

'Comrade Colonel, as a news editor, I am asked to give both sides of any story. The Russian America's Cup military camp issued a statement on the incident today. The statement said that you are, and I quote, "a trouble-maker, an agitator and a drunken immoralist". In addition, it said, you are "a mediocre helmsman". What answer have you to those assertions?'

Illich was outraged.

'To describe me as a trouble-maker, an agitator and a drunken immoralist is one thing,' Illich replied. 'But to call me a mediocre helmsman, well, that's positively insulting.'

'Spoken like a true Estonian,' Aegu's voice boomed approvingly out of the semi-darkness. To the stuttering Lars Brinsa he added: 'That's your question, Comrade.' Aegu winked at Illich. 'I bid you good-day, *tovarich*.'

Illich watched Aegu's square figure stride back towards the waiting helicopter, his arm over Brinsa's shoulder. Aegu's two faithful bodyguards followed at a respectful distance.

Thirty-Two

For several days afterwards the harbour at Raferi resembled a refugee camp. The weather was sultry, promising rain, but the rain did not break until the third day. They worked in the humidity to clear out the cattle stalls from the outlying farm buildings, and through the night, under open bulbs that attracted ghostly white swarms of insects. For the first week Aegu put at their disposal one of the state helicopters, so that supplies could be ferried from the mainland.

Vagir and the core of his works team left the camp at Tallinn and joined them, adding to their labour force, but placing a further strain on their rudimentary accommo-

165

dation. The local people were hospitable, supplying fresh milk, eggs, and meat, and accommodation for wives and families in the surrounding farmhouses. Vagir rapidly recruited other skilled labour. Within two weeks the camp had swelled to more than forty personnel and their families.

Leningrad remained in the water, and was repaired there, until a suitable lift was found at Parnu, and transported across on the Haapsalu ferry. It broke down at the second use, but within two days Vagir's engineers had stripped its engine and it was working again. Shortly afterwards, the first lathes and grinders were installed in the main repair building.

Illich insisted that they sail several hours each day. Without a trial boat they could not tune easily, and it was difficult sailing against one's own shadow. But they used the opportunity to calibrate the instruments against a measured mile, and to improve sail changes. Enforced activity was an antidote to the low morale that sometimes affects organizations after a crisis has receded.

It is a curious fact that the wear on the body during a sailing campaign is not as noticeable as a period of inactivity following it. During his solitary confinement, Illich was made painfully aware of the physical damage of his previous months of training. Now he plunged back into sailing with all the force of an addict returning to a drug.

Opportunities for other forms of solace were few. The evenings were reserved for administration. The problem of finding new sources of supply fell to him and Vagir. On an old typewriter supplied by the local militia, he tapped letters requesting information to various foreign manufacturers.

Within the Russian Republic, supplies dried up. It became increasingly clear that the Army had decided to place pressure on its civilian contractors not to supply the breakaway group. It was, Illich reflected, written in the military textbooks; cut the enemy's supply lines. His requests for replacement equipment were returned with mysterious excuses. Sometimes equipment was promised but never supplied. Spare parts and equipment essential in the ferocious wear and tear of a sailing campaign had to be sought elsewhere.

Vagir's native ingenuity came to his rescue. Lathes, cutters and grinders, spirited from nowhere, were installed in the network of sheds. An autoclave mysteriously appeared, Vagir refused to say from what source ('God provides', he commented to Illich, rolling his eyes towards Heaven). The workshops began to hum, grind, resound with the working of metal. In such physical matters they became self-sufficient. It was the complex electronic instrumentation which presented the most difficult problems. *Leningrad*'s onboard computer was a Russian model, a 'Krishin', one of the first copies of the American molecular or 'biological' computers. Its nervous system was astonishing, but there were constant flaws in the retrieval system which required extremely high-grade maintenance.

Jaan Paavelt, their port trimmer on *Leningrad*, was also a computer software designer. He struggled manfully with the problems imposed. But the unreliability of the central computer at sea suggested to Illich they should look to more basic instrumentation. An innate puritanism regarding the mechanics of sailing caused Illich to doubt the efficacy of hypersophisticated equipment, particularly in a harsh marine environment. Complex electronics were in large part accessories governed by fashion. He used the prevailing difficulties to force abandonment of the computer software during training, and returned to simpler, more reliable equipment. A dozen firms over the world sold accurate racing instrumentation – for boatspeed, and the basic software necessary to calculate real (as opposed to measured or apparent) windspeed and velocity made good in any given direction. He looked for reliability and service. In due course he bought an integrated package of instrumentation from Brookes and Gatehouse in England, and thought no more of biological computers.

Highly sophisticated instrumentation had another function, of which he was also aware. It pampered the egos of the crew, gave them the impression that no expense was being spared to help them win, and put them in a positive psychological frame of mind. In his view this was a more important advantage of sophisticated instrumentation than any practical advantage offered by the instruments themselves. To counterbalance it, he trained them even harder than before, providing no time for reflection. Slowly, after the dislocation of the voyage from Tallinn, the crew began to fall into the rhythm of training.

As always, Illich carried with him the internal bruises of sailing. Muscles, ligaments, tendons are stressed in subtle and wholly unnatural ways. Bracing against the heel of the yacht, ankles and knees take up postures never intended by nature. In addition, there is wear and tear, the myriad forgotten strikes and bumps, the sudden snap of knuckles against a winch, the glancing blow to the hip as the deck is crossed; strange crouches; odd, racking movements of the spine as the body turns with feet firmly on the deck. Finally there is the tension itself – for the yacht is 'highly-strung' in the strictest sense of that phrase – in the huge force loads carried by the rigging which seem to transmit directly to the nerves. Tension was present in the physical force of the crash of the boom, a square coffin of metal which the wind swings like an axe a foot above your head at every tack or gybe. A sailor's body is full of secret pains, pains laid in deep amongst the tissue; almost, it seems, inside the bones themselves.

After each strenuous practice Illich emerged drained, as if he had compressed several days into the tension of a few hours. And there was the sea air, richly nourishing, almost sickly, placing a bouquet of flowers on a body which feels like a grave. It was easy, at least, to sleep.

*

Several weeks passed. If his body suffered, the new regime suited his temperament. The reliance on simple instrumentation brought back the immediacy and pleasure of sailing. Apart from the problems of high maintenance, the devotion of precious manpower resources, and the diversion from the proper tasks of sailing, too-complex instrumentation tended to obfuscate, placing a miasma of figures between personnel and the direct experience of tuning. Now they learnt once more to trust to their intuition and physical sensation.

The best means of tuning was careful, laborious experimentation against another boat. With this in mind, several weeks after their departure he held a meeting with Andre Vagir, Gustav Prem and Soren Gir to discuss the possibility of building a new boat. Following their meeting, President Aegu was presented with budgets and was persuaded to agree to its funding.

In the meantime an official notification arrived from the Office of the Estonian State Prosecutor. Illich broke the official seal and opened it.

REPOSSESSION OF THE YACHT LENINGRAD ON BEHALF OF ESTONIA BY COLONEL IVAN ILLICH.

With regard to the above, an Enquiry was undertaken by three judges of the Estonian Court, whose decision was as follows:

1.   The ownership of the yacht Leningrad *was confirmed. The yacht and its equipment are the property of the Estonian Trade Delegation.*

2.   Colonel I. Illich was acting within his proper rights in establishing ownership of the said property on behalf of Estonia, and with the explicit permission of the office of President Aegu.

3.   The account of Colonel Illich, namely that he was fired on in the course of a race with the yacht Kirov, *prior to repossession, and acted in self-defence in returning fire, is accepted.*

4.   This account was corroborated by the Estonian Customs officers

R. Takule and L. Vare, who witnessed much of the incident in question, and whose evidence was submitted in written form.

5.　The Prosecutor's office therefore officially informs that no further action will be taken against Colonel Illich in this matter.

6.　In the meantime, however, the Office of Investigation will pursue the matter of the first shots being fired by the patrol vessel with the Legal Department of the Russian Armed Forces, Frunzenskaya Embankment, Moscow.

7.　To date the Armed Forces have declined to submit written evidence on the matter to an Enquiry or a civil court, on the proposed grounds that the incident in question is an internal matter between Colonel Illich and the Russian Armed Forces.

Illich read through the letter again. He was relieved to be exonerated by the Estonian civil authorities. But the Defence Ministry clearly intended to deal with him in its own good time. He was under no illusions as to what was meant by 'an internal matter between Colonel Illich and the Armed Forces'. He must submit himself for court martial, or face unspecified consequences.

Two days later a blue envelope arrived for Illich, containing a letter from Lydia Teemant, inviting him to lunch at her parents' house in Tartu the following Sunday. Partly out of deference to the island's strong Lutheran traditions, he and the crew had taken to observing a rest day on Sunday. He wrote to accept.

Thirty-Three

Professor Teemant carved the pork with precision, so that each slice fell gracefully in a neat pile. His wife stood by him like an assistant at a laboratory experiment, both amused and pleased by his expertise.

'Ivan,' Aetesta Teemant said: 'You clearly need fattening up.'

Seated opposite Lydia Teemant and her fiancé, Dr Artur Sirk, Illich said 'thank you' as a generous plate, heaped with pork, new potatoes and spinach, was placed in front of him.

'You see,' Sirk was saying, 'the concept of centralized control is an aspect of immature nineteenth-century science. It is founded on a belief in a single huge system, in which man – rational nineteenth-century man – occupies the centre like an omnipotent deity.'

'Artur. Another growing boy. A big helping?'

'Thank you. In the biology section we deal not with one system, but with a variety of systems which coexist. It is not so much the functioning of any one system which we study, but the relations between systems – these relations between systems we call meta-systems.'

Illich occasionally cast a glance at Lydia as this enthusiastic discourse developed. She seemed distant, locked in her own thoughts.

'You are aware of the scientific method of models and controls?'

Illich's ears pricked up. He nodded.

'Suppose one is studying a complex system, say a biological organism, and one wants to find out what happens if a particular input, a chemical or some stimulus, is introduced. Let us call the system the model. The model is so complex that it may change as the result of a number of other stimuli or conditions, or simply as part of some internal cycle. So in order to separate out the effects of the stimulus, it is necessary to have a "control" – that is, an organism preferably similar in every respect, but lacking the input or stimulus we want to study. If we do this, we know with much greater certainty that the difference in behaviour between the model and the control is caused by the stimulus.'

Professor Teemant sat down at the head of the table. His wife sat down next to him.

'Salt, please, Artur.'

'Certainly. Suppose we give our model a chemical which we believe will act as a sedative. It curls up and goes to sleep. We say. "Aha, clearly it is working." But we look at the control, which does not have the chemical, and the control also curls up and goes to sleep. We have to say that the chemical is not the cause of sleep. Some other factor, common to both, is the cause. If, however, the model goes to sleep, and the control remains highly active, we can say with more certainty that the chemical is the cause of the difference in behaviour between otherwise identical model and control.'

'Artur, I am sure you are boring the colonel.'

'Not at all,' Illich said truthfully. It was the essence of his own laborious method of improving a yacht. Make two yachts the same and change one thing at a time. Only in this way can one gauge the true effects of what one is doing.

Under the table Lydia Teemant had removed her shoe. Illich could tell because she had placed the warm sole of her foot against his instep. They deliberately averted their eyes from one another.

Sirk was saying: 'The model and control system is mandatory, as you know, in modern science. If you say "a factor A produces an effect B", one is asked "What is your control?" If you didn't include a control in your experiment, your results are simply not taken seriously.'

'Have you had gravy, Artur?' Aetesta Teemant asked.

'Thank you, not yet. If you transpose this central principle to economics, the idea of a single system, a "planned economy", runs counter to the fundamental method of modern science. An economist or politician with an understanding of modern science should instead ask, "If I say I shall change this or reform that, how do I know the true effect without a control?" '

The true effect of Lydia Teemant's sole on Illich's instep was difficult to gauge, except that if the activity in question was caused by her fiancé's monopoly of the conversation then clearly, working from cause to effect, it was to his advantage that Sirk continue. Illich therefore nodded vigorously.

'Don't let your food get cold,' Mrs Teemant said.

They started to eat, except Sirk, who continued: 'A true scientist would say: I must split the system into two identical units in order to establish model and control. Then, when I make a "reform" to my model, I can study its effects relative to the control. This is a revolutionary principle, if you don't mind my saying so. Economists argue that there are economies of scale, and this means one large organization is better than several smaller ones. But these are unimportant, short-term advantages. In the longer term, the quality of understanding of your system is more important to progress. You cannot begin to understand it unless you introduce the system of model and control. And you cannot introduce the concept of model and control unless you split the organization in question into two, or preferably more, smaller, identical units.'

Lydia Teemant's toes were now brushing gently back and forth on Illich's instep.

'If you will forgive me for saying so, this is why capitalism, or free enterprise, is more efficient than command economies, because it allows a number of similar systems to exist "in competition". In so doing it reproduces more closely the model and control system of science. Take, for example, two shops selling the same products in the same street. In a command system, that would be considered redundant. However, suppose one shop decides to improve its service by changing its management. If the numbers of products sold rises, you would say that is a good thing. But let us say that the shop across the street, in the same period, is selling even more. Clearly, it is not the change in management which caused the increase, but some change in the demand for the product. Comparing the other shop as a 'control', it becomes clear that the change in management has been a disadvantage. It would be better to change back to the original system.'

Illich nodded vigorously as the ever-active toes of Lydia Teemant's left foot began, tantalizingly, to climb towards his knee.

'The quality of information about your own system is immeasurably enhanced if you are in a position to compare it with other institutions of a similar nature operating in the same environment. Where several such systems are in competition with one another, each one uses the information about the performance of the others as a "control" in respect to his own affairs. It is generally done quite unconsciously. Thus, whereas planned economies claim to be "scientific" in nature, it is a fallacy based on an outdated nineteenth-century science. At the start of the twenty-first century, we must modernize our view. Capitalism, for all its numerous faults, is closer to the practice of modern science than scientific socialism.'

Unfortunately, this seemed to be the conclusion of Sirk's monologue. Lydia Teemant's toes had climbed to his knee and paused there, as if waiting. Clearly, it was of urgent importance to keep the conversation proceeding. Illich said: 'You are an advocate of capitalism?'

'Not as such. I believe the closer resemblance of a capitalist system to the scientific method of model and control is pure accident. If you listen to capitalists themselves, they also would prefer, as individuals, a monopoly. No, I believe in a conscious, sustained attack on the large, monopolistic economic structures using this method. This applies to both centralized socialism and capitalism. The government should split all its services into two or more similar elements, and advance on this front.'

This sally produced a movement of Lydia Teemant's toes several inches along Illich's inner thigh. He was encouraged to offer a further incentive to Sirk to continue his disquisition.

'Two armies, perhaps?'

'You may laugh, Colonel, but if the criterion is the efficiency of the army, its ability to organize itself in respect of its resources of manpower and development of equipment, then two independent branches would be a good thing. It is a fact, surely,' added Artur Sirk slyly, 'that in order to compete effectively, the armed forces are constrained to place in competition various design bureaus. Migoyan, Yakovlev . . .'

Illich was more than ever determined to keep the conversation in play. He replied: 'That is a cosy arrangement, as you are perhaps aware. They do not compete directly. One bureau undertakes a design competition for a fighter, while another does so for a bomber. The supply of different aspects of equipment is still largely a monopoly.'

'Precisely. And therefore its products lag behind America, which is always ahead – perhaps because it encourages fierce competition between several manufacturing sources.'

'Artur,' Mrs Teemant said, 'I think it is time you ate your food.'

'You are right, of course.'

Sirk began to cut up his pork, gulping down his food rapidly. Under the table, Lydia Teemant withdrew the erotic stormtroops of her advancing toes.

Thirty-Four

On Sundays, Illich allowed himself the luxury of returning to the flat at Tallinn. He could write his reports in quiet, catch up on paperwork, indulge for a few hours his reflective nature.

Tallinn is a city of bells. Orthodox, Lutheran and Catholic churches filled the city with their sound. The revival of religion in the aftermath of Communist repression was a sociological fact, a stolid statistic of social development. But the bells were its living expression; small bells which sounded like clear silver, heavier bells with a belly of bronze. In the clear evenings Illich would open the casement window and listen to them – flights of sounds in joyful or thoughtful cadences.

The Estonian composer Arvo Pärt, brought up in Tallinn, had infiltrated his great, spiritual compositions with the haunting purity of bells. Each assumed a different character, from explosive polyphony to a single haunting chime like a memory. Not far from Illich's flat a clock tower struck the hours in carefully measured tones. After solitary detention, when the minutes themselves had seemed to stop and institutional silence had invaded the soul, the bells were his second homecoming,

As the summer progressed, he had other reasons for returning occasionally to the flat at Tallinn.

Making love to Lydia Teemant he was again reminded of the physical punishment inflicted by sailing. She was a healthy young woman, as effective in love as she was in

176

dancing. Her mind seemed to detach itself, and her body followed its own instincts. Her passionate attentions disclosed the deep pains stored like sorrows in his body. Sometimes a caress was both a pleasure and torment.

Only when he spoke did she freeze. It was as if his speech brought her mind to active life, pulled her into human existence, and destroyed her animal balance. She preferred his silence.

Afterwards, too, she preferred to lie beside him without speaking, an expression of innocence and satiety on her face. He was reminded often of the duality of her nature, above the table the dutiful daughter, beneath the erotic nymph. By nature he was one of those introvert men who do not seek to dominate physically their women. He was fascinated by her nature, and it gave him pleasure to watch her express herself. He guessed that Sirk was more stereotyped in his responses, suspecting him of asserting the same male pomposity in bed as he did in conversation.

In discovering how a yacht behaves, at first it is necessary to let her have her head, and only slowly, when the helmsman begins to understand her virtues and strengths, her inclinations and responses, may he draw from her a deeper potential.

His lovers sometimes spoke affectionately of this trait in Illich, and in the grateful afterglow of lovemaking were not above attributing to him a greater humanity than he deserved. It was a subject about which he held no illusions. He knew he was filled with the harsh will to dominate, and it was merely his methods which were different. But it was typical of his attitude that if the illusion of his erotic altruism was a pleasure, he would not actively deny it.

In an unusual display of verbal communication after lovemaking, Lydia Teemant said, 'I love you because you are so light.'

'Lightweight?' asked Illich. 'Lacking in substance, perhaps?'

'No, light like air. Air above earth. And elusive.'

So his evasiveness, the evasiveness of most men in the face of female passion, was turned into a virtue, another benefit of his wish to please.

In his flat she would live happily without clothes, cooking his meal with only an apron while he worked on a report of racing.

'May I ask you a question?' Illich said.

She turned to look at him, opening her green eyes.

'You intend to marry Sirk?'

A curious set of expressions crossed her face: sudden surprise, as if she'd been pitched into another world, followed by a trace of anger; then a catlike indulgence, as if realizing the question had no malign intent behind it, was merely curious; all in less than a few seconds.

'Shouldn't I?'

'I don't know. I'm just curious.'

Her eyes seemed to be staring at a point behind him.

'You think I shouldn't?'

'It's not my business.'

She was quiet for a while.

'If it's not your business, then I do intend to marry him.'

Outside, on a Sunday morning, the city was quiet.

'Artur also has his pursuits.'

'Pursuits?'

She nodded.

'Other girls?'

She didn't reply.

'You don't mind?'

He could fathom no answer in her expression.

What was this, a species of Scandinavian tolerance? In his heart, he had hoped for a similar tolerance from his wife

Anna; and for a time at least he had received it. But the marriage on which it was based was a mirage, something his wife, out of realism more than disaffection, felt obliged to make clear to him.

That was when he began to dislike Artur Sirk. Previously, he had felt guilty about him. Now he disliked him not for his behaviour, but his illusions.

But what could he offer in return? It was difficult to explain to her that he had no future. The Army regarded him as a deserter. He had been *nash*, ours, and now he was not, for which the unspoken penalty was death. It might not arrive now, for several months, even perhaps a year or two. But it would come eventually.

At the same time, perhaps one had the right to plan one's life in the expectation of living. Perhaps that was a fundamental right which extended beyond the simple reality of the situation.

She must have realized something of what he was thinking, because she merely said: 'Don't worry. I won't interpret your interest as a proposal.'

I am the one with illusions, he thought, not Artur Sirk.

The janitor Irkut's attitude, now, was more predictable. He became more friendly, in his obsequious way. When he heard Illich's footsteps on the stairway, he would emerge from his door like a crab, with a respectful smile on his face, and an attitude which was almost one of nodding and bowing. An officer who was constantly accompanying beautiful women to his flat was clearly a man whose vices he could respect.

The attitude of such as Irkut towards their seniors was a complex one. Pondering the new tolerance of Irkut one day, Illich was reminded of the story of an NCO – the batman of a Russian Army General – who had retired from the Army and become a motor-cycle traffic policeman. The pay was better, and he and his family were not forever moving about the country. It became his duty, among other matters, to enforce the new, stringent laws about drunken driving which were modelled on Western counterparts. One evening he had flagged down a speeding grey sedan.

As he peered in through the window, and requested that the driver blow into the testing machine for alcohol, he recognized the features of his former master, the General – obviously retired now, and in civilian clothes, but still unmistakably his former master. It appeared, however, that the General, in a considerable state of inebriation, did not recognize him. The test was done, and the apparatus gruffly handed back. The reading indicated a truly astonishing level of alcohol in the blood.

'Good heavens, sir,' the former batman was heard to mutter admiringly. 'That's an absolute record.'

So, although Irkut had disliked Illich the cold, puritanical army colonel, and wished him no good, the stuck-up snob, he was positively pleased to do anything for the new Illich, the sacked army officer, the man he had heard described on the radio as a 'drunken immoralist'. This was clearly someone who knew something about the world, a man one could look up to.

Thirty-Five

Kalev Tammiste's small house was an A-frame in the forest outside Parnu.

With his loss of the perquisites of travel as a touring hero in Russia, Illich had bought an elderly BMW from one of the car dealers in Tallinn. Like most Russian officers, he was an admirer of German engineering. Now the car wobbled on the mud tracks leading up to Tammiste's house, past a tethered, whitetailed goat and a chicken-house.

Tammiste's wife Margarita was working in the vegetable garden. She stopped, leaning on her hoe, as Illich drove up the gravelled drive.

'Is Tammiste inside?'

'Somewhere,' answered Margarita. She indicated the house behind her. 'He's probably in his study.'

'Thank you.'

Margarita went back to her hoeing, using rhythmic, chopping strokes to break up the earth.

Illich tapped on the wooden front door, heard no response, and pressed the doorhandle. It opened soundlessly.

At the far end of the hall, through an open doorway, he caught sight of Tammiste balancing a folded piece of paper on a knife edge. Tammiste did not move. It was a delicate operation.

Beside him was a high-powered computer, an American model, a set of numbers glowing on the screen.

'Who is it?' asked Tammiste.

'Illich.'

'Sit down,' Tammiste said without moving. 'You catch me at an embarrassing moment. I am trying to work out the centroid of the profile of the underwater sections of a round-the-world racing yacht. It is something my computer can do in a fraction of a second. However, I do not trust it. So I have cut the shape in paper, and am finding the location of the centroid by balancing it on a knife-edge.'

'I will look the other way,' Illich said, 'if it embarrasses you.'

'I would appreciate it. Please,' Tammiste insisted, 'do sit down.'

A few minutes later, his measurements concluded, Tammiste was ready to talk. He sat down opposite Illich on a low wooden chair. His thin body had a classic Estonian angularity. His eyes were so pale they were almost colourless, surrounded by pale lashes. Wisps of red beard clung to his chin.

'I ask you,' Tammiste said, 'not to tell anyone you saw me doing what I just did. My reputation would be in shreds. What can I do for you?'

'An America's Cup yacht. You think you can help us?'

'How much time do I have?'

'To generate the shape? One month.'

A sharp intake of breath from Tammiste.

'Tank test facilities?'

'No time. And nearly all of the facilities are controlled by the military.'

'So I heard. You are something of an outcast. Tell me, do you want something similar to *Leningrad*?'

'Against all my instincts, I would prefer you to have a free hand in the new design. If you fail, which I happen to think is most likely because of the time and the lack of facilities, we will simply fall back on *Leningrad*.'

'Why are you prepared to take such a risk with the new boat?'

'Because Pilnyak's new yacht, *Kirov*, is already faster than *Leningrad*. For all I know, other challengers are also faster.'

'Who would build the new boat?'

'We will build it on Khiuma. Vagir will be in charge.'

Tammiste said: 'Vagir is good. If it fails, my reputation will suffer, of course.'

'Of course,' agreed Illich. 'And in addition I will probably shoot you.'

'Enough people seemed to have shot at you recently,' Tammiste commented drily. 'However, I like a client who is straightforward.' Tammiste paused, biting his lip, his pale eyes expressionless. 'The answer is "yes". But you must remember one thing, and I will write to confirm this. A radical design, however good, nearly always starts by being slower. That is because, being radical, it will require different sailing techniques, which will take time to learn. What you have to assess is its potential, its rate of improvement.

This requires patience. If in the first few races, the new boat is slower, and you decide to drop it, then I will shoot you.'

'Agreed.'

Tammiste went to a cupboard, and drew out a bottle of Georgian brandy. He held up the bottle to Illich's eyes. 'The wrong time of day, perhaps?'

'But an unusual agreement.'

Tammiste poured two glasses.

'Tell me,' Tamiste said, when he had seated himself again. 'Why do the new America's Cup rules specify wood construction?'

'The rules were proposed by Russia. The method of construction was aimed at eliminating the US superiority in exotic composite materials.'

'And the construction rules have now become formalized?'

'Yes.'

'A magnificent material, wood,' mused Tammiste. 'God's design. Extraordinary fatigue resistance. What method of construction? Laid over frames?'

'Yes.'

'The simplest. Another advantage. What do you want from me in the way of drawings?'

'A linesplan, with keel and rudder, and a sailplan.'

'That's all?''

'With all due respect, we know more about the construction from past experience than you. And the deck layout will be close to that of *Leningrad*, which we also know from experience works well.'

'That seems logical.' Tammiste paused. 'One other thing. Who designed *Leningrad*?'

'The naval research group.'

'Yes, but who?'

'No single individual.'

'A committee, then.'

'A committee backed by vast resources, by a huge network of computers.'

'Interesting. As you see, I prefer to design by balancing a piece of paper on a knife blade.'

'So I noticed.'

They drank, clinking glasses.

Two days later, Tammiste joined them at the camp to take measurements from *Leningrad* in order to use them as a comparison in his own design. At four in the afternoon, *Leningrad* was raised from the water. Tammiste took measurements from the hull, calling out figures to Vagir, who acted as his assistant.

Several hours later, with dusk already falling, he completed his measurements by floodlight.

Illich, passing by, asked, 'Do you have everything you need?'

'In terms of measurements, yes. May I ask you a couple of questions about the yacht's handling characteristics?'

'Go ahead.'

'As she heels, do you find quite a strong increase in weather helm?'

'Yes.'

'How do you counteract that?'

'By sliding the boom down to leeward, removing excess power from the mainsail. That in turn shifts the centre of effort of the sails forward.'

'That rebalances her?'

'Yes.'

Tammiste's pale eyes were thoughtful.

'Thank you.'

'That is all?'

'For the time being. Yes.'

'You remind me,' Illich observed, 'of one of those doctors who taps you on the chest and says "Aha", each time he does so. You suspect he knows what he is doing, but you can never be sure.'

'The mark of a true professional,' said Tammiste. 'Keep the client guessing.'

'You, on the other hand, balance a piece of paper on a knife blade, and say "Aha".'

Tammiste was pleased.

'Beneath your levity, Comrade, I detect a genuine apprehension.'

'As a designer, you would call this "creative tension"?'

'Precisely. It is important that the client should suffer. And now I am off to sharpen my knife.'

Three weeks later, Illich received a telephone call.

'Tammiste here. I have finished your linesplan. When could you come over?'

Illich restrained himself from saying that he would come over immediately.

'Tomorrow. Twelve o' clock?'

'I will be here all day,' Tammiste said.

The following day was overcast. Flurries of cloud came in from the west. Flowers of rain appeared in the water lying in draining ditches beside the road. By the time Illich reached the outskirts of Parnu the sky had cleared a little. Illich drove his aged BMW once again up the winding driveway to Tammiste's house.

Tammiste came to see him at the door this time. Illich noticed that his eyes were somewhat red-rimmed, though he was his usual insouciant self. Tammiste led Illich to a computer screen. After pressing several buttons on the keyboard, he resorted to a 'mouse', moving an arrow around the screen, selecting menus and codes. The computer paused for a moment, then projected a three-dimensional linesplan of a yacht onto the screen in white lines.

Tammiste said: 'This is the computer representation of *Leningrad*, taken from my measurements a few weeks ago.' He chose another menu, another symbol. The computer threw up a new linesplan, a bright blue line over the white.

Tammiste continued: 'This is a representation of *Kirov*'s lines, from information you and others have given me.

185

Notice that relative to *Leningrad Kirov* has a different-shaped stern, wider at the waterline and narrower at the deck line, giving an almost box-like shape . . .' Tammiste moved the mouse so that the arrow outlined the thin blue lines of *Kirov*'s stern. 'This shape, with its more vertical topsides in the region of the stern, is more closely associated with improved balance at differing angles of heel. Better balance means that less sail adjustment is required to set up the yacht at various angles of heel. It is an important advantage. It is immensely difficult to explain why this is so, but perhaps you will accept my prognosis.'

Tammiste selected another symbol and pressed the button on the mouse.

A third linesplan emerged, this time in green lines, overlaying those of *Leningrad* in white and *Kirov* in blue. At certain points on the hulls the lines were indistinguishable. But at the stern they diverged markedly.

'This,' Tammiste said, 'is the new boat.' Illich felt his heart grow still. Much though he distrusted designers, there was a curious magic in the beautiful shapes set out in front of him.

'Notice the new boat's stern. You see that as you move aft, the topsides actually begin to curve inwards. This shape creates even better balance than *Kirov*'s. As you heel, the balance of the boat relative to the sails is maintained. This is not merely theory. The shape was pioneered in radio control yachts in Britain. It received its strongest impetus in the designs of the English designer David Hollom.'

'It looks strange.'

'It looks strange until you see it working. Then it looks beautiful.'

Illich was both repelled and attracted by the shape. His wish for a known, conservative entity battled with his desire for an assay into a new, radical design.

Noticing Illich's hesitation, Tammiste smiled to himself. He said: 'I remember reading somewhere that when Dennis

Conner saw the new twelve-metre *Stars and Stripes*, the one that was to win the 1987 America's Cup, he said it looked like an ugly banana. When it began to win races against trial horses, it seemed to him like a rather good-looking banana. After it won some more races, it simply became beautiful.'

'I suspend my disbelief,' said Illich.

Tammiste unrolled a large sheet and spread it over a table top.

'This is a one-twentieth-scale linesplan of the new boat, with all the offset tables marked on the side. The offset measurements are computer calculated. The whole linesplan is computer-faired.'

A well-prepared linesplan has a magical flavour. Its faired surfaces, denoted by lines and filled by the imagination, reach out like the ghostly intuition of a perfect being – a blueprint from another planet, a cartoon by Leonardo da Vinci.

'Cognac or coffee?' asked Tammiste.

Illich emerged from his trance.

'Coffee, please.' Who needed alcohol when one had this in front of one?

'You like it?' enquired Tammiste courteously.

It was important to revert to type, or Tammiste would be disappointed.

'We'll see if it works,' Illich said gruffly. 'At the moment it still looks like a banana to me.'

Thirty-Six

Vagir set to work lofting the hull lines in the shed. During the previous month, an accurate engineering floor had been laid. Insulated walls had been built round the construction area. A heating and humidity regulation plant had been incorporated to optimize the conditions for the epoxy resins that would be used to bind the wood together. Part of this enclosed space included a dry storage shed for the numerous types of carefully selected wood – Western red cedar, spruce, highest grade marine ply, mahogany for the laminated frames and the central hog.

Vagir had scoured Estonia for the best wood-epoxy builders. A team of some fifteen craftsmen had been assembled and was ready to build by the time the design, carried carefully rolled under Illich's arm, reached them. Since arriving at the base six weeks earlier, new accommodation buildings, constructed using wooden A-frames for speed, were already nearing completion. An eight-foot security fence had been erected by the militia and local contract labour.

As soon as the linesplan for the new yacht was received, Vagir and his lieutenants began to work round the clock to loft the sections. A group was set to making up the central hog and laminated frames specified in the rules of construction. Once these were completed, the frames were set up carefully on the engineering floor. Following time-honoured precedent, the yacht would be constructed upside down. The frames formed the ribs. The laminated hog, too heavy to be carried by hand, was picked up by crane and carefully laid along the grooved centreline frames and fixed in position while the resins dried. Then two teams began laying the longitudinal cedar veneers. The entire inner skin layer of longitudinal cedar was laid up within the course of a single twenty-four hour period. A day was allowed for drying, then a diagonally aligned layer of mahogany veneer was laid over it. A second day was allowed for drying, and another diagonal layer was laid over that. Within ten days, the entire hull had been laid.

The laborious process of fairing the hull was begun.

In the rest days during drying, the crew laid up the deck and cockpit floor, bonding in the strengthening areas where winches, sheet block and genoa tracks would be placed. Sample bores were taken in the hull and deck to check that the constituents met the rule requirements. Then the hull was turned over.

It took several days to sand the interior down, vacuum out the dust, and paint the interior with several additional coats of epoxy to seal the wood. Further boreholes were made to check the hull construction conformed to the rule. Within a period of four weeks from start, the deck and cockpit structure was being lowered onto the hull.

Vagir moved through the workshops like a short, angry bull, organizing, exhorting, chastising. It took a week of fairing and painting before the hull and deck were ready to receive the deck equipment. Specialized winches had been flown out from England. The carbon-fibre mast, boom and spinnaker poles were made in a specialized plant in neighbouring Latvia. Highly engineered mainsheet cars came from Germany.

It was during this period of equipping the yacht that Illich noticed, in the crude pigeonholes set aside for correspondence from foreign suppliers, a note simply addressed to 'Ivan Illich, Tallinn, Estonia.' It bore an American stamp.

He folded the unopened letter, put it in his pocket, and forgot about it in the course of the day's frenetic activities.

That evening, before the communal meal in one of the outbuildings, he remembered it.

He glanced at the simple hand.

Dear Mr Illich,
I read that you had left the Russian America's Cup team. The incident had quite a lot of coverage here.

I'm going to be visiting Estonia with my wife Maria and my kid Jack on the 10th July. We'll be staying for a few days at Maria's aunt's flat at 14 Kidriv Street.

If you could spare a few minutes, I'd really like to meet you.

I understand if time is too precious, and I wish you luck with your Estonian challenge.

Yours sincerely,
Jim Shaw.

Illich's eyes filled with tears. To hide his emotion he coughed into his handkerchief. It was absurd. The Estonian in him watched the Slav cry. Gustav Prem patted him on the back.

Illich turned over the letter. A newspaper cutting had been enclosed. It was from the *New York Times*:

ERICSON SELECTED
John Ericson's selection for the US America's Cup team was announced officially this morning. His choice has long been considered a foregone conclusion. Ericson is regarded by most aficionados as the best big boat helmsman in the United States. His maxi yacht, Ghost Train 5, *has dominated international competition in this class for the past five years.*

Ericson was, however, beaten in the trials for the America's Cup in the last series by the brilliant but unpredictable Jim Shaw. Spokesmen from the Ericson camp have complained that it was an incorrect decision, and that a more consistent campaign could have been mounted by Ericson.

Following his extraordinary manoeuvre at the finish line of the last America's Cup, when Jim Shaw deliberately turned away only yards short of winning the series, Shaw has retired to a smallholding

*in his home state of Maine. He refuses to give interviews. Rumours
continue to circulate that he was reacting against extreme pressures
placed on him by the military administration, but these cannot be
confirmed.*

*John Ericson III could be described as the 'establishment choice'.
His father, John Ericson Junior, is a major industrialist, and a
key figure in what has sometimes been called the 'military industrial
oligarchy'. Advocates of John Ericson claim that this time the US
Challenge will be a cohesive unit, backed by the full weight of US
military and industrial technology. Ericson, the aggressive king of
the big boats, is well suited to spearhead the challenge.*

*A huge sponsorship budget, reported at over $100 million, has
been raised to bring the Cup back to the US. The challenge
syndicate is currently building its third development yacht. Informed
observers say this is the most determined and highly organized
America's Cup effort of all time.*

Illich folded the letter and the cutting and replaced them in
his pocket. The letter had taken a week to reach him. It was
only four days before the 10th. He would let Shaw and his
family settle in for a day or two, and see them on the 12th.

President Aegu flew in by helicopter the following day to
check the progress of the new yacht.

'Two weeks ahead of schedule,' Illich was able to report.
'Vagir and his men have been doing magnificent work.'

In the building shed the boat was swarming with men.
Illich's crew had taken the day off from sail-training to work
with the builders on the layout of the winches.

'We need to start practising as soon as possible,' Illich
said.

'What about a launching ceremony?'

Illich shrugged. To him launching ceremonies were need-
less delays.

'And a name,' Aegu insisted. 'I have been thinking about a
name. My staff and advisers have suggested Estonian
names. But I do not want this challenge to be a vehicle for

191

nationalism. Frankly, we have suffered enough from Russian chauvinism without falling into the same habits ourselves. The name I would prefer is *Novy Mir*, Russian for New World.' Aegu looked past Illich at the yacht. 'It would symbolize a new world of collaboration, yes? No bludgeoning national sentiment.'

Illich thought of the American boat that had beaten him. He suspected the name *Novy Mir* might please Jim Shaw.

'I will lend my support, Comrade President, to *Novy Mir* if we can have a quick naming ceremony and launch.'

'You drive a hard bargain, Comrade. As a politician, I was hoping to make heroic speeches, well publicized. However . . .'

Aegu shrugged. They shook hands. Aegu's two bodyguards followed him to his helicopter.

Two days afterwards, Illich crossed to the sheds where Vagir's men were completing the fit-out of the new yacht. He had cancelled sail practice on *Leningrad* so that the crew could collaborate with Vagir in the final, precise placement of winches, leads, genoa tracks about the deck and working cockpits.

The new yacht was swarming with personnel, covered by ladders, its shiny topsides muted by dust from the drills and saws which worked incessantly in the shed. Illich conducted his daily discussion with Vagir, then walked back to his office to finalize a spare equipment order. On his way back he noticed a figure standing on the harbourside, studying *Leningrad* as she floated in the water. The guards had let him in. Clearly he had a security pass.

At first Illich thought it was Aegu. Seen from behind, the figure had the same square shape. But the hair was darker. It took Illich several moments to recognize him.

'Brod!' he shouted.

Brod turned round, somewhat sheepishly. Illich walked, almost running, to meet him.

'What brings you here? A social visit? Want to check up on us?'

Brod was unusually reticent. 'Ilena sent me.'

Illich was nonplussed.

'We heard that you had broken away from the Russian team. She said that, as far as she was concerned, sailing for Estonia would be a different matter. If I wanted to, I could come and see you.'

It took Illich several moments to adjust.

'To sail with us?'

'I expect all the places are filled.'

He had never seen Brod so forlorn. It was so out of character he could not help but laugh.

Brod merely watched him.

The temptation to string Brod out had to be put behind him.

'Have you brought your gear?'

'As a matter of fact . . .'

'First signs of alcohol . . .' Illich drew his finger across his throat.

'I agree.'

'Loose women . . .' Illich drew his finger across his throat.

'I agree.'

'Loss of temper . . .'

Brod's eyes began to bulge.

'Bad behaviour . . . . Swearing . . . Rude gestures . . .' Illich drew his finger across his throat.

'Look here, ' Brod began to roar, 'what is this, a convent?'

From one of the open windows they heard Soren Gir say: 'Brod's back.' And another voice, almost certainly that of Prem, replied: 'God forgive us our sins.'

Thirty-Seven

Two days before *Novy Mir* was due to be launched, Illich crossed on the ferry from Khiuma to Haapsalu. He drove his aged BMW to Kidric Street in Tallinn. The house was in one of the older streets of the town, one which had been revived in the past five years by private contractors.

He knocked on the door of number 14, sending a flight of pigeons scuttering from the roofs of the neighbouring houses. A strikingly beautiful woman, dark, with wide green eyes, came to the door.

'Ivan Illich,' he said. 'I hope I am not inconveniencing you.'

'No, no.' Her Estonian was good, but with the trace of an American accent. 'Maria Shaw.' They shook hands formally. 'Come in.'

Inside it took several seconds for his eyes to adjust to the light. He followed her along the corridor.

A grey-haired woman, her hair drawn into a bun, appeared.

'Ivan Illich,' the young woman said. 'My aunt Liina.'

He shook hands with Aunt Liina.

In the kitchen Jim Shaw was seated across a table facing his small son, feeding him from a spoon.

Maria said, 'It's Ivan Illich.'

Jim Shaw spooned away a bubble of food from the child's mouth, and stood up.

Shaw was small for an American, light, strong in the arms and shoulders, with a powerful handshake. His eyes were swift, appraising. And absurdly young, a mere youth.

Illich remembered the demon that came at him in the last four races.

Maria lifted the child from its high chair.

'We'll leave you two to talk. Come on, Jack,' she said to the burbling child.

Jim Shaw indicated a seat in the small kitchen.

'You got my letter?' asked Shaw. 'With that stuff about Ericson?'

'Yes. Thank you for the information.'

'Your English is pretty good,' Shaw said.

Illich shrugged. 'So is your wife's Estonian.'

'Maria? Her family's Estonian. I sometimes think she's trying to persuade me to live here.'

In the interior of the house Illich heard the child shout something, and Auntie Liina answer in a chiding tone.

'You don't sail any more?' Illich asked.

Jim Shaw paused, then said slowly in Estonian, 'I'm not against it in principle. I just have other things to do.'

'Very impressive,' Illich said. He looked at Jim Shaw as if he had turned into a centaur.

Jim Shaw smiled sheepishly, a cracked student grin. 'Maria has been teaching me. She insists our son Jack should be bilingual. If you speak slowly, we can continue this discussion in Estonian.'

'Certainly,' Illich replied.

When Maria returned an hour later, they had managed to get along well enough in Estonian.

'Will you stay for lunch?' Maria asked Illich. 'I've just been out to buy food. We'd be disappointed if you didn't.'

They had lunch in Aunt Liina's small dining room, beneath the portrait of her late husband, a silver-haired, distinguished man with a long, Nordic face which reminded Illich of a photograph he had once seen of the writer August Jacobson. Her husband, Aunt Liina told him, had been Curator of the Estonian People's Museum. They had had a childless marriage. 'Too little time for anything else,' she said, and smiled. As if in compensation, on the walls were framed photographs of Aunt Liina's other nephews and nieces. Aunt Liina, it appeared, was a translator for the Estonian Trade Delegation.

'The Estonian Trade Delegation owns the yacht *Leningrad*,' Illich said. 'Which reminds me. Would you like to come to the launch of the new yacht the day after tomorrow? I am sure I can clear it with the authorities.'

Shaw glanced at Maria. Seeing his expression, Maria laughed.

'He'd like to,' she said to Illich.

'All of you, as my guests, please.'

Aunt Liina couldn't take a day off work, but the rest of the family could.

While in Tallinn, Illich took the opportunity to visit his flat and to pick up several spare sets of clothes. Someone had entered the flat again. Several drawers which had been left with a small lip open were now fully closed. Was it Irkut, he asked himself?

That day Irkut appeared to be out. The door of his flat was locked. He knew the janitor took a holiday with his family at this time of year on the Caspian Sea.

The flat was still uncomfortably full of the memories of his family. No doubt they would have heard news of his hijack of the *Leningrad*. He tried to phone his ex-wife. This time the call went through directly, but there was no answer. He imagined the telephone ringing in the empty flat, and experienced a sensation of a thousand sad telephones ringing in empty rooms.

The recent changes in his life had left his emotions curiously raw. Moving about the deserted flat, he was so overcome with gloom, with a sense of loss, that his jaw locked, and he was unable even to whistle or sing. He sat down in the kitchen. Perhaps it was the example of Shaw – his final choice of family, and his clear, unalloyed happiness – which threw his own empty life into such intolerable perspective.

He heard in the echoes of the flat the shouts of his own children. The windows in the kitchen faced north, but there was a small skylight on a west-facing roof. Through this opaque square a single beam of sunlight fell. He could see the dust whirling there, and for a short while he wondered whether his life had any more significance. A few minutes later, still in inexplicable gloom, he collected his clothes and prepared to drive back to the ferry at Haapsalu.

Thirty-Eight

It would be difficult to explain Jim Shaw to Aegu, Illich thought. In former Soviet society, even in a liberalized republic like Estonia, one retained the habit of looking over one's shoulder, always nervous that one was proceeding too far. Jim Shaw was as close to an independent being as Illich could imagine. He seemed to move by some self-contained system of reference, like a man with an internal compass.

Jim Shaw, Maria and their small child Jack arrived on the ferry from Haapsalu. Jim carried Jack on a backpack, striding alongside a line of disembarking cars. Illich waved them down and helped them into his car. Maria insisted on sitting in the back with the burbling Jack.

They drove to the base camp at Raferi over a narrow unmade track which ran between the grass meadows and shoreline.

Both the remoteness of the location, and the short notice given before the launching, meant that there was only a limited audience. Two helicopters brought senior Estonian officials. A television crew had been allowed. Some of the wives and families of the crew had arrived by mainland ferry. There was no band.

But the occasion, though sober, was not without its high-lights. *Novy Mir*'s green topsides could be seen shining above her security blanket, a perfect surface.

'Will you look at that?' Shaw said wonderingly. 'Think that stern will work?'

'We don't know. We asked the designer to give us a radical boat.'

'It's a risk. Who's the designer?'

'Kalev Tammiste,' Illich replied.

'Brilliant guy. He hasn't gone a bit crazy with this one though, has he?'

Illich laughed. Helmsmen's suspicions of designers were universal.

'Hey,' said Shaw, 'there's *Leningrad*.'

Maria smiled at Jim's disappearing back as he went over to look at his old rival.

Maria said: 'Is your wife here today?'

'My ex-wife. No,' Illich replied. 'She remarried. She lives in Kharkov now.'

'Do you have any children?'

'Two girls. Anna has custody.'

Maria swayed Jack about. Jack leaned over backwards.

'I do not have much time,' Illich said. 'I wanted to ask you a question.'

'Go ahead.'

'Would you mind if I asked Jim to join us and help us train. I have no idea whether he would wish to, of course, and I know what sailing does to family life.'

Maria stopped swaying Jack. She stood still. He could sense the strength of her determination. She said: 'I told Jim I wouldn't marry him unless he gave up sailing.'

'I understand,' Illich said. 'Then I won't ask him.'

Maria was silent, watching her husband staring at *Leningrad*, while her child, his blue eyes serious, placed his head against her cheek and regarded Illich.

There were some questions, he realized, which he had no right to ask. He had destroyed his family life by sailing, and yet blithely assumed others would make similar sacrifices. An oppressive sense of guilt invaded him.

Jim returned a few minutes later.

'Give the little brat to me,' Jim said to Maria.

He was oblivious to the silence.

'Please forgive me,' Illich said. 'I must attend to my duties.'

Aegu and his guests were assembling at the newly erected wooden stand. Vagir's men had built a small podium for Aegu to speak and make heroic gestures, if not to a huge audience, then to the camera. Gustav Prem, the choirmaster, had been given the task of acting as master of ceremonies. He was ushering people to their places.

'Prem,' Illich said. 'That man there with his family is Jim Shaw, the American helmsman. Give them front row seats.'

Prem turned to stare at Jim Shaw.

'That's Jim Shaw?' Prem was aghast. 'He's just a boy. He looks like a student.'

In the minds of the veteran crew of *Leningrad*, Shaw had become a monster, a figure of the imagination; more than flesh and blood.

'He's here with his wife and child. Don't stare. It isn't the ghost of Josef Stalin.'

'I was too young to be terrorized by Josef Stalin,' Prem said. 'The one who terrorized me was Jim Shaw.'

'His wife is an Estonian.'

'Then he can't be all bad.'

'In the front row,' repeated Illich.

'As you say, Comrade.'

Aegu made few heroic gestures. When he stood up on the small podium, his face had an unexpected calm.

Comrades,

In many areas of the world, great nations with highly developed economies have entered the strange contest of the America's Cup.

They have launched yachts like battleships, with national anthems playing and with huge cheering audiences waving national flags.

On one level, it is simply a sport, a competition between crews. But while the period of international military inactivity – an inactivity which is sometimes called peace – continues, so this strange sporting event has come to assume a peculiar importance. It is like a ritual war.

But there is something appealing in a war without guns, without engines, without smoke or devastated battlefields. And there is something even more attractive in the nature of the competition. Much of it is based on the understanding of nature, the movements of wind and water. While the competitiveness of great nations is sublimated into these complex, beautiful wind-driven machines, I believe there is a little hope for mankind.

It would have been tempting to call this boat by an Estonian name, perhaps the name of one of our historical battles. But our hope is that the condition which is called peace continues, and that something comes out of it which is more than mere military inactivity caused by a balance of terror. Perhaps it will be a world in which small nations can function effectively and independently, not as chauvinist replicas of their larger neighbours, not as petty nations obsessed with the desire to exclude all others, but in open contribution to a peaceful world order.

I name this yacht Novy Mir, *and dedicate her to a small country – not our country but to all small countries who find themselves arbitrarily on one side or another of an artificial divide.*

Novy Mir was launched. Vagir activated the winch, and she was lowered to the water slowly under her security screen. When she reached the water the security screen was withdrawn. Illich noticed that she floated several inches high in the bow, about level at the stern.

The audience, hardly more than two hundred people, applauded. To Illich, who loathed the razzmatazz of launchings, it was a good beginning – sober and tentative. Even Aegu's speech, though not without its share of high-flown rhetoric, had been mercifully brief.

It was shortly after the launch, a few minutes, that he saw the helicopter. It must have approached slowly, along the coast, because suddenly it was a hundred feet above them; in the strong sunlight, its military markings were plain. The little base was drenched in the thunder of its blades. Aegu had sat down, was looking up at it, expressionless.

Now the whole audience was staring upwards. Beyond the stand, Illich saw Aegu's two bodyguards moving backwards, as fluent as shadows, drawing handguns from beneath their bulky coats, edging sideways and backwards until they were propped against the shed, their guns raised.

At this distance, Illich could see every detail of the machine. It was an attack helicopter, the Russian Army's response to the United States AH-64; a purpose designed gunship. It had no fat underbody, merely a series of deflecting armoured surfaces concentrated around the pilot and gunner. The fuselage was as thin as the thorax of a wasp. Empty guided missile racks hung down like the ventral fins of a fish. Beneath its nose, almost directly under the gunner, was a remote-controlled 30 mm cannon, hooked upwards so that it seemed like the lower mandible of a predator.

The helicopter pivoted once, turning head to wind. Against the gusts of wind that whipped the couch grass into waves, it hung suspended for several seconds. Then it swung away. The barrels of Aegu's armed guards followed it unwaveringly. Then the guns came down, safety catches were punched on with the ball of the thumb. Once again the bodyguards became plump, middle-aged men.

Now the helicopter was no more than the size of a fly, moving back along the coast.

Aegu approached Illich.

'An illustration of my sermon, I think – of a somewhat negative kind.'

Aegu walked towards the buildings, followed by his bodyguards, explaining to his guests the peculiar advantages of the sailing camp, the extraordinary foresight of the fishing authorities in constructing the small harbour, as if they were guided by intuition as to its ultimate purpose. Illich returned to the newly launched *Novy Mir*.

He was still staring at *Novy Mir* in the water, assessing her flotation lines, when he became aware that Jim Shaw was standing beside him.

Maria stood a little way off, holding the baby. Shaw said, 'I understand you asked Maria whether I'd be interested in sailing again.'

Illich was ready to apologize.

'Well,' Shaw continued, 'we discussed it back there. It was a lively discussion, I have to admit. You see, she wouldn't marry me if I didn't give up sailing. Now, she's threatening to divorce me unless I join up with you.'

Illich looked at Maria, who turned away. His heart had exploded.

'We Americans are completely dominated by our women. Do you know that?' Shaw was saying. 'We have no defence against them. I told her I wasn't going to sail any more. . .'

'You will sail?'

'Have to. If you'll take me along. Just wanted to ask you one thing though. What's "*Novy Mir*" mean?'

'It's Russian for New World.'

There was a brief silence.

'I guess that settles it,' said Shaw in English.

Illich glanced at Maria again. She was staring along the coast, at the point where the helicopter had disappeared. Her face had the curious, almost empty expression of concentration. It occurred to him, unexpectedly, that what had triggered her response was the helicopter itself, the sudden thunderous presence of Russian military power. It had raised the atavistic fear of the great neighbour which had caused her family to emigrate. All this struck Illich with a peculiar lucidity. With this comprehension came a feeling of gratitude. In its heavy-handed way the Army had given

202

him, through this remarkable woman, a weapon of his own, the great American helmsman Jim Shaw.

Thirty-Nine

Aegu said: 'I need to walk. These days I am hardly ever outside my office. Perhaps you could accompany me? I must talk to a fellow amphibian.'

Outside the base camp gates the countryside rolled back in wide meadows. There were rutted wheeltracks, sometimes merely footpaths between small copses of wood. Away from the shore, there were only occasional farmhouses, mostly wooden, and small huts which wandering shepherds used.

Aegu walked fast, his hands clasped behind his back, his head low, as if addressing the earth.

About sixty yards behind them Aegu's two bodyguards shadowed them. In their crumpled suits they looked out of place in the country.

'Every day I struggle with the *vlasti* in Moscow, I have to remind myself that Russia has always been an autocratic country. Westerners believe that all reform is based on their model, on a liberal model, on increasing individual freedom and personal responsibility.' Aegu halted briefly to light a cigarette, cupping his hands around the flame. He threw the match aside, breathed smoke into his lungs, and began to walk again. 'Russia has never experienced any form of liberal structure, and it will take decades for them to understand it, even now that it is being encouraged to take root. "Reform" is equally likely to mean the kind of reform advocated by Solzhenitsyn, the return to a religious authoritarian state, one which is inward looking, irrational, mystical. Those who belong to that school of thought are as jealous of the so-called "purity" of Russia as the Nazis were of the so-called Aryan tradition. You know that Solzhenitsyn wrote an archaic form of Russian, in which the influences of all other languages and cultures were rigorously excluded? Increasingly, this way of thinking has support in the higher echelons of the authorities. As the belief in socialism decays, so nationalism becomes stronger, less reticent. And of course, as you know, in the Army it is the basic fuel of loyalty. The officer corps is now almost wholly Russian. Law-abiding on the skin, but nationalist beneath.'

They were leaving behind the foreshore, following a footpath through a huge meadow. Glancing behind them, Illich saw *Novy Mir* being raised again from the water by Vagir for final preparation work.

'Speaking for myself,' Aegu was saying, 'I prefer to see socialism becoming slightly more humane, introducing a reform here, a reform there. With regard to Russia at least, I am a gradualist. Those of us who advocate that our own preferred model of democracy is imposed on the Russian State are doing the Russians as great a disservice as they do to us when they assume that we would be best governed by their own model.'

They had reached the first of a series of small plateaus. At the side of the path a ring of old stones showed where a shepherd's shed had once stood. The sun was getting hotter, building up heat in a grey, glassy sky. Bees and flies worked feverishly in the vegetation.

Aegu was in the habit of changing a subject rapidly. 'You know why the Army hates you? Because you lack Russian loyalty? Nonsense; in that sense, the Army is pragmatic. No, it hates and fears you because you have another life, you are a sportsman, you have an existence outside their bounds. You are not their creature, and therefore they cannot abide you. A renegade is hated more deeply than any enemy. You lie awake and wonder what mistakes you made, what you did wrong. Perhaps you should have grovelled to your superiors, asked for time to put the record straight. But in your heart you know that would have resulted in only a partial reprieve.

'What I will say now has no meaning for you, but I will say it anyway. You are part of an old world, my friend, a world of self-reliance, bravery, individual heroism. You are an ancient and primitive being who, they suspect, has an inner soul that they have lost. As their world crumbles, so their suspicion of you grows. That is why they would like to sacrifice you. And your innocence is such that you do not even know what I am talking about.'

Illich did not answer. It was clear that Aegu expected none. Walking for a few moments in silence, Aegu continued: 'I too am caught in a dilemma. My parents were both prominent members of the Party. I lived more than half my life in the Soviet Union or in its employ as a diplomat. But I am also an Estonian. My loyalties are not to the Russian *Rodina*, but to a small state on the western fringes of the empire. In this way I also am no longer *nash*.'

When Aegu was not walking with his hands behind his back, he was smoking, lighting cigarette after cigarette. Once, he threw aside a packet and patted his pockets. He had run out. One of the two guards came forward with a fresh one. Aegu nodded, without exchanging a word, lit another cigarette, and the man dropped back again.

'But I do not believe that we can abandon Russia, declare ourselves disinterested, look inwards. As fervently as any Russian nationalist, I believe that Russia carries the fate of the world in its hands. It is like a huge adolescent, a giant who is at an unstable stage of development. It is enormously talented, but it holds within itself a terrible insecurity. It is above all a spiritual nation, fanatical and ascetic. It could provide a lead in literature, philosophy, in pure sciences, but its neurosis has led it to a sterile giganticism – the biggest dams, rockets, armaments, the largest number of men under arms. Scale is everything. A humane farmer judges his farm by the quality of its output, but

Russia viewed its agriculture in terms of the number of harvester machines. Its sciences should be absorbed in higher mathematics, in primary causes; but instead it preferred to see itself reflected in a gross arithmetic of size.'

The track they were following wound among a copse of trees. To the side of the track, in a grassy decline, a goat was tethered to pole, a healthy female; there were no humans in sight.

'On a purely pragmatic basis, if we do not understand this, we place ourselves in mortal danger. Our neighbour is one who is searching for a role in which he can fulfil himself. Like an animal, he thrashes against his cage. We hear him at night, howling in his room. An unfulfilled Russia is suspicious, powerful, dangerous. Am I boring you?'

Illich had been swept along by Aegu's obsessive intensity. Now he was surprised to find himself addressed personally. He merely shook his head. Aegu glanced at him for the briefest of moments, and then continued his monologue.

'It would be easier if Russia were a cynical, power-hungry empire. It would be less complex, easier to negotiate. But whatever punishments or hardships it has inflicted on its minorities, it inflicts as great or greater on itself. In most of the small republics the individual living standards have been higher than in the central Russian republic. This is not the structure of an exploitative empire. It is not a modern Carthage or Venice – rich and fat on the proceeds of its prudent, commercial manipulations. It cannot be understood in material terms.'

They had reached a kind of plateau. It was devoid of trees, and they could see down the gentle slope to the buildings of the sailing base, now several miles away to the east. The island of Vormi could just be discerned; behind that, the thin line of mainland.

Aegu remarked: 'Such clear air.' As if to celebrate, he lit another cigarette.

'Tell me,' Aegu said, throwing the match aside, and beginning to walk again, 'You must sometimes feel caught under the wheels. Here you are, a sailor, and, for no apparent reason, you have been arrested, put into solitary confinement, stripped of your rank, and publicly slandered. Yet you are not an agitator, and you seem to bear no conscious malice towards the military. If I may draw a parallel in my own case, I am forced to walk the tightrope of politics, but I am operating with known risks. With you, virtually every day brings fresh surprises.'

'What can I say?'

'Exactly. You can say nothing except, perhaps, continue your efforts to survive.'

'As a matter of fact, I do have a request.'

'A request?'

'Yes,' Illich said. 'It concerns the American helmsman Jim Shaw.'

'A remarkable man. The one who turned away at the finish line.'

'He is here with his wife, who is an Estonian. He is not part of any American effort. In fact, he has told me he would not represent them again. He had a disagreement with the American military over the running of the last campaign.'

'A dissident, then,' Aegu said, then added, 'A dangerous breed.'

'He is dangerous, I agree. That is why I wanted to ask you. We are desperately short of a powerful competitor to sharpen the crew. If he could steer the trial horse. . . His wife, as I say, is Estonian. They would like to live here. Shaw has told me today that he would like to join us.'

They were at the edge of a small wood. Birds were singing in the heat. A few miles away a stubble fire sent a trail of smoke into the cloudless sky.

'An American,' Aegu repeated. 'And a dangerous one.'

They walked on for several yards, Aegu with his hands clasped behind his back, a cigarette held between the second and third fingers of his right hand.

'Forgive me, Comrade President, but could we offer naturalization?' Illich asked.

'Naturalization is technically possible, even at short notice. What about the other implications? If we handled it carefully, I suppose that the naturalization of a prominent American sportsman might do us some good.'

'You said you didn't want a purely nationalist effort.'

'You should never quote a politician's words against him,' Aegu said. 'That is a shocking tactic. Nevertheless, I will consider it.'

'In the meantime, I have invited him as a guest helmsman, to sail the trial horse for the time being.'

'Which is now *Leningrad?*'

'Which is now *Leningrad.*'

'On that subject,' Aegu said, 'I have no objection.'

Forty

It was amusing introducing Jim Shaw to the rest of the crew. They stared at him wide-eyed, as if he were a dangerous animal. This was the terrible being who had all but destroyed their morale in the final races of the last America's Cup, who had managed to return from an impossible position to threaten them.

It was strange to them that he was held in no great respect by the American sailing establishment.

'A renegade,' Prem said. 'In his own country.' He shook his head in disbelief.

In the first race with Jim Shaw, the weather was moderate. A light breeze was filling from north of west. They moved the course offshore to remove themselves a little from the lee of the island. By the time they hoisted sail, the breeze was about ten knots, relatively steady.

After the ten-minute gun the two helmsmen kept their distance at the start line. Illich's first impression was that *Novy Mir* was light on the helm – too light. There seemed to be no grip on the rudder. Usually, when full sail was up, and the boat heeled, there was an increase in helm. In this case that bite was lacking.

'Fifteen, fourteen, thirteen, twelve . . .' Brod intoned. They were hardening up, striding towards the line, going well enough.

'Five, four, three . . .'

The starting gun exploded. At the other end *Leningrad* had burned across hardly a second after the gun, an almost perfect start.

They were on converging tacks, *Leningrad* with right of way. The helm felt light, nerveless.

'Prem,' Illich shouted, 'Tighten mainsail. I want more helm.'

The sheet came in. With it came some extra helm. But the boat still felt curiously lifeless.

Leningrad was ahead, only by a length and a half, but that was a bad sign so early in the race. They crossed under *Leningrad*'s stern.

Shaw did not tack to cover. On *Leningrad*'s deck Illich could see Shaw making hand-signals to the forward trimmer.

After a minute Illich roared: 'Tack.'

The tack was good. He couldn't fault it. Out on the left, Shaw tacked in response. Brod was watching the computer grid of the course. The two boats were starting to close fast. Brod said: 'She's three lengths ahead this time,' as *Leningrad* crossed their bows. Again Shaw did not cover.

'Prem,' Illich said. 'This isn't working. Let out mainsheet a little. Open up the leech.'

The light helm returned. It was almost lee helm.

When they crossed again, *Leningrad* was nearly five lengths ahead, and gaining steadily.

At the end of a week's racing the results were still the same. *Leningrad* was nearly always in front of *Novy Mir*. On the eighth day of racing, *Leningrad* reached the windward mark some sixty seconds ahead, the final straw.

Illich imagined his hands on Tammiste's throat, a friendly throttling; no noise, no flowers; just a simple, sober, quiet death.

'Tammiste!' he roared as he got out of the car at the familiar A-frame house.

Tammiste came to the door, leaning on the frame. Illich walked up to him. 'Your boat is no good.'

Tammiste's pale eyes were expressionless. He asked simply: 'Is it slow?'

'Slow.' Illich was lost for words. 'It's . . .'

'Come inside,' said Tammiste. In the study he turned to face Illich. 'What are the symptoms?'

'The symptoms are that we want to use it for firewood.'

'Those are your feelings. What are the symptoms?

'It feels no good and it's slow.'

'Light on the helm?'

'Yes.'

'You tighten the leech, and pick up some feel?'

'Yes, but –'

'But then it becomes even slower?'

'Yes.'

'So you try opening the leech, and you lose all feel on the helm. It develops lee helm. At this stage you find you can't point.'

'Yes!'

'That all sounds quite promising,' Tammiste said mildly.

'Promising?' Illich felt he must put a chair between himself and Tammiste for fear of losing control. He heard himself incredulously repeating: 'Promising!'

'Perhaps you'd care to sit down,' Tammiste suggested.

With an effort of will Illich controlled himself. He sat down carefully.

'Coffee?' suggested Tammiste. 'Perhaps some alcohol?'

'No thank you.'

Tammiste surveyed him quizzically.

'The problems that you describe derive from the fact that the boat is too well balanced – when it heels, there is no tendency to broach, and therefore little or no weather helm. The rudder is not contributing to the windward lift. It is an important factor.

'The best means of correcting this set of conditions,' Tammiste continued, 'is to move the keel forward. I would say about a foot. That will increase your weather helm.'

'That will make the boat faster?'

'Would you believe me if I told you it would?'

'No.'

'Then there is no point in my reassuring you.'

'We believe the boat is a hopeless case.'

'Then burn it,' replied Tammiste.

'We would prefer to burn you,' Illich said.

'I am afraid I would resist that.'

'If you know why it doesn't work, why didn't you design it right in the first place?'

'Because it is better to move one step at a time. The keel is in the same place relative to the hull as *Leningrad*. Now we know for sure that the stern does have an effect on the balance of the boat. If we had moved the keel we would not have been sure what was cause and effect, because we would have had two potential causes. The important thing in development,' said Tammiste, 'is not to be right first time, but to know how to put it right.'

'I don't want lectures. I want a boat that works.'

'Then move the keel forward.'

'A foot? Why not ten feet?'

'Ten feet if you wish,' said Tammiste, equably.

'And another thing. It is floating several inches high at the bow.'

'As I hoped,' said Tammiste.

Illich felt cold rage overtake him again.

'As you hoped?'

'Yes. If you move the keel forward by one foot, you will find the forward movement of the centre of gravity is such that the bow is depressed by several inches – precisely onto its marks, in fact. Are you sure you wouldn't like some coffee?'

Illich breathed a sigh, and nodded.

'Would you like anything with it? Milk? Sugar? A tranquillizer, perhaps?'

'Black. And no jokes, please.'

'I promise,' Tammiste said. 'No jokes.'

When Illich had left, Kalev Tammiste opened the back door and walked over to the vegetable garden. A late afternoon sun cast long shadows. It was a time of day Tammiste particularly liked. He could smell newly cut grass from his efforts the day before. The sun was a pale gold behind the birches.

In the vegetable garden he could see, over a hedge, the back of his wife Margarita as she worked to remove tufts of grass that had grown between the rows of runner beans. He stood beside her for a while, watching her beat the grass on the fork to remove the particles of soil; then she dropped the grass tussocks in a wheel-barrow. Without stopping, Margarita said: 'I heard Illich shouting for you.'

'Yes,' Tammiste replied. 'The boat is slow. He wanted to put a match to it. And to me as well.'

'They are all the same to begin with,' she said philosophically.

'I told him when I first agreed to do the design that the boat would be slow to start with, that in any radical yacht it takes time to understand how it works best.'

She continued to dig the grass tussocks with her fork,

212

beating them on the handle, throwing them into the wheel-barrow.

'By the way,' she said, remembering. 'There is a parcel for you. A case of champagne from Gunnar Ardstrom. I read the accompanying note. I hope you don't mind. He says the boat is performing particularly well.'

It was cheering news. It had been a boat which had often showed promise, but no real wins until this season.

'Tell me,' Margarita said. 'Wasn't he the one who threatened to bury you upside down in pigshit?'

'I don't think so. That was someone else.'

'I thought it was Ardstrom.'

'No, it wasn't Ardstrom.' Tammiste was embarrassed.

'How can you be sure?'

'Because Ardstrom threatened to hang me upside down by my testicles from a telephone pole.'

'Ah yes,' his wife said, knocking another tussock on the handle of the fork, and piling it in the wheelbarrow with the others. 'It all comes back now.'

Forty-One

It took Vagir and his men two days to change the keel position on *Novy Mir*. The keel proved difficult to detach, even after the keelbolts had been removed, because of the strength of the epoxy bonding. Once they had managed to prise it off, they had to rout out with grinders an additional recess for the new placement of the keel, and fill the twelve inches of recess in the aft section.

Jim Shaw, clucking his tongue, said to Illich: 'Designers.' Shaw shook his head. 'Afraid you've bought yourself a turkey.'

213

In expressions of emotion, Jim Shaw returned to the English. Illich found it hard to understand the colloquialisms.

'A turkey?'

'Something that doesn't work.'

'I see.'

'Radical boat, my ass.'

'Your ass?'

'Sure. My ass is all you're going to see with that boat.' Jim Shaw went back to the little house he shared with Maria.

Turkeys, asses, thought Illich. Inside every Russian, it was sometimes said, there lurked a canny, cautious peasant. So with Americans too, he suspected; their phrases were filled with the earthy, heroic language of the frontier farmer.

Novy Mir was launched early on the third day. Illich watched with interest as she settled in the water. Chill bubbles rose from the endplate on her keel. There was no sign of her former bow-up trim. Now she seemed almost exactly at her marks.

Once again it was blowing westerly. The two launches drew the two yachts out to sea the several miles necessary to clear the lee of the island. There was more wind than usual. Nearly twenty knots, and gusting. The two yachts were brought head to wind. When the breeze was fresh the sea looked green rather than blue. Whitecaps marched across the surface.

Novy Mir's mainsail began to thunder slowly as it was hauled up. It was important not to prolong such stress or it reduced the effective life of the sail.

'Cast off,' shouted Illich. The bow rope was released. He bore away so the sail could fill.

The genoa was hauled up immediately afterwards. Berol Baltir, the winchgrinder, powered in the genoa sheet. The boat heeled, picking up forward motion. As she built up speed, she seemed to heel less, to become more upright.

214

There was feel in the helm, not a great deal, but more than before.

Brod sang:'Seven two, seven three, seven five. . .'

You couldn't tell at first. Feel was only a part.

Leningrad in her new sails began to march up and down outside the starting box. Jim Shaw and the second crew had their tails up. Every day for eight consecutive days they had seen their first team trail behind at the finish line. They felt invincible and their responses were crisp.

'Twenty seconds to the ten-minute gun,' Brod said.

When the ten-minute gun went, the two boats entered a theoretical box and were physically engaged. But Illich kept to his corner, turning, trying to assess, to build into his nervous system the feel of *Novy Mir* in her new trim. He turned into wind as time moved towards the start gun.

'Thirty seconds,' Brod said.

'Harden up.'

In came the genoa.

'More,' Illich ordered.

It did feel better, but at this stage he didn't even want to believe it.

'Mainsail in a little.'

That wasn't right; the boat felt dead.

'Back out again.'

Better.

'Ten,' Brod sang, 'eight, seven, six . . .'

On parallel tacks, two hundred yards apart, an ostrich feather of smoke from the gun, and then the punch of the explosion.

Leningrad looked magnificent, with the Estonian tricolour on her red side, driven by an American individualist of the most extreme type. Crazy.

'Sing, Brod.'

'Seven nine, seven nine, eight zero, eight two.'

Green-hulled *Novy Mir*, pacing *Leningrad*, cantered fast over the swells.

'He's tacking,' hissed Brod.

And he has right of way, Illich thought. They were closing remarkably fast.

Prem, the mainsheet trimmer, was watching him.

'We'll duck their stern. Ease main.'

This was tense. As they bore off they were heading, for a few seconds, straight at *Leningrad*'s midships. It was where a helmsman showed his steel. Their bow missed *Leningrad*'s stern by two feet, no more, the hulls passing with a sound like a knife slicing a pillow.

In came the sheets again, the grinders punching fast, Prem's sure hands positioning the mainsail.

Leningrad tacked on top of them. A close cover. It was the first time Shaw had really come in close, eye to eye.

Leningrad's genoa came in two seconds slower than it should. Just enough to allow *Novy Mir* to squeeze out from under her lee. Now they were parallel, with hardly a boat length between them. No one seemed to breathe as they went about their tasks, treading the tightrope.

In a lull *Leningrad* seemed to draw ahead. In a gust, they seemed to draw a fraction better.

They were neck and neck for two minutes, the sound of the bow waves magnified between the hulls as in an echo chamber. The green sea sluiced between them like a river in a narrow gorge. Another gust; a few more inches; in concentration, the crew on both boats seemed like robots, like zombies.

'Tack!' roared Jim Shaw. The perfect moment, just before he was caught in *Novy Mir*'s backwind. But also a defeat. The concentration of time opened. In a matter of moments, *Leningrad* seemed a mile away.

There were no audible sounds of relief in *Novy Mir*'s crew; but shoulders opened, faces untightened.

'Concentrate!' Prem this time. Down in the bowels of the boat, the sewerman Herman Maask could be heard folding the coils of the spinnaker together ready for a hoist, humming to himself.

Novy Mir's lead was short-lived. *Leningrad* caught a

216

favourable wind-shift and drew ahead at the next mark, and it was all they could do to keep up with her until the finish line. But some metaphysical line between them had been crossed.

That evening, as the boats were hauled out of the water for overnight storage, Jim Shaw stood watching, as if trying to fathom *Novy Mir*'s strange stern.

Illich watched the slight figure, rapt, staring at *Novy Mir* rising out of the water, then walked back to the little office he had sectioned off in the building shed.

Kalev Tammiste put down the telephone.

His wife, Margarita, said: 'Who is it?'

He could see her seated in her chair through the doorway, writing a letter to her younger sister. She had an endearing myopia which made her lean over, her face close to the page.

'Illich,' Tammiste replied.

His wife waited patiently for him to speak.

'He said the boat is not quite so slow as he first thought. By means of heroic crew-work, et cetera, et cetera, they are now almost on a par with *Leningrad*.'

She did not look up, but continued at her careful writing, drawing out deliberate letters in long strokes. It was her preoccupation in the mundane things that he most appreciated, the assurance of her composure. He liked the way the light from the desk lamp illumined the crown of her hair.

'I think we are at phase two,' Tammiste said wryly.

'Phase two?'

'Phase one is when the helmsman threatens some dire physical retribution. At this stage the boat is always "your boat". "Your boat doesn't work." Phase two is when "your boat" becomes "*the* boat", that is to say, some more or less neutral entity.'

She continued to write. He leaned back against the wall, removed his glasses, rubbing them reflectively on his pullover, one lens and then the other.

'And phase three?'

'Phase three is when *the* boat becomes *our* boat. Due to our careful tuning, and despite your outrageous design, *our* boat is now working quite well.'

His wife did not ask about phase four. But there was such a phase, he knew. Phase four was when they turned up on your doorstep again, several years later, demanding a new design, but it better be a good one this time, not the horror you'd designed last time, or they'd bury you up to your neck in pigshit or hang you from a telephone pole by your balls . . .

Tammiste blew on the lenses of his glasses, and rubbed them again.

Finally, there was phase five. Phase five was when they reminisced with you about that wonderful boat you designed so many years ago – radical, yes, of course, a little ahead of its time, but any fool could see that it was going to be fast, as soon as it was launched – no sooner in the water than winning races. Ah yes, they didn't make boats like that any more.

Forty-Two

In the People's Hospital, an exclusive clinic built just outside Tallinn for the use of senior members of the Party (before the Party was dissolved), Illich was guided to Gundar Arlof's bed. Arlof looked pale. But there was life in his eyes. He had been walking that day, and in his face tiredness battled with exhilaration.

There had been complications. He had lost a great deal of blood and had been in a coma for twenty-four hours after the shooting.

Illich sat by his bedside.

Arlof said: 'I hear that Jim Shaw has joined you. Brod was here a few days ago. He told me.'

'You must meet him.'

'Brod said he is very young.'

Illich paused: 'He *is* young. He's twenty-six. What else does Brod say?'

'That of course Jim Shaw is a far better helmsman than you.'

'He does, does he?'

'Brod feels you're past it, of course.'

'Past it, I see.'

'Though he says you were good once.'

'Good once. How are you feeling?'

'I get tired so quickly. Otherwise, I'm improving.'

'Good', Illich said. 'And the nurses are treating you well?'

Arlof sighed: 'Exceptionally well.'

'They can make you very tired – while helping you to improve.'

In Estonia, as in Russia, the great majority of doctors are women. Arlof had moved from an all-male society into an all-female one.

'I heard some more news,' Arlof said: 'From an acquaintance in the army camp.'

Illich waited.

'*Kirov* was only superficially damaged in the incident. It took them a week to install a new mast.'

'Do they have a trial-horse, now that *Leningrad* is gone?'

'The Army has two new yachts. Both are reported to be faster than *Kirov*.'

Which is already faster than *Leningrad*, Illich thought. Arlof continued: 'They say that the spending on the Army's America's Cup effort has doubled now that you have broken away. The biggest increase is in design and technology resources.'

Illich was inclined to treat this as hearsay. Seeing Arlof

219

lying there, recovering slowly, Illich wondered again who had given the order for the boat to open fire, even prior to his leaving the race. He had tried several times to work out the sequence of discussions, from the base to headquarters, from headquarters to the base. Had they merely been panicked by his sudden, unexpected presence at the base? But in conditions of panic the Army tended to move cautiously. He tried to imagine a series of discussions in which an order was given to arrest him, Illich, at all costs. But there had been no preliminaries, no escalation of threats, no arrest, merely an attempt at assassination.

While he bantered with Arlof, one part of his mind tried to put himself in the position of the Army. They felt they were losing their grip on him. He had powerful protectors like Pridilenko and Aegu. He had an existence outside the Army, as a Russian sporting hero. And these protectors had spirited him out of the heart of the Defence Ministry, and had delivered him to his native country, Estonia, despite the charges brought against him. It must have been galling for the military authorities. Not content with these violations, this same man, a deserter in the eyes of the Army, had appeared unexpectedly at camp and exercised his right as chosen helmsman to practise on the *Leningrad* so that he could steal her. All this must have been an added goad, but it still did not add up to an assassination attempt, carried out in the open. That still seemed to him incautious, intemperate, inexplicable.

He bid Arlof goodbye and, since he was in Tallinn, returned to his flat.

In his flat the telephone rang. It was Aegu.

'I understand,' Aegu said, 'that the new boat is starting to do well.'

'It has some potential, I think.'

'Good. And how is your American guest?'

'A key part of our preparation. We needed a strong

opposing helmsman who could really test us. He has exceeded my expectations.'

'Excellent. Now, I have some news for you about the Russian America's Cup programme. It seems that the Army has taken over the programme entirely. It is being funded from their military research budget. The funding is lavish.'

So Arlof was right, Illich thought. It was extraordinary how fast rumours travelled. General Chernavin has had his way, Illich reflected. He has used my absence to consolidate the Army's position.

Aegu said: 'The extradition order against you has been lifted. Now you can return to Moscow if you wish.'

Forty-Three

They began the gruelling schedule of practice, the marathon of preparation, settling into a routine until the times of work and rest became like familiar grooves of wood.

Shaw was as quiet, as introvert as ever. Yet each day that he descended from the makeshift outhouses with his crew to *Leningrad*, they seemed to grow in confidence. More than ever, Illich watched and admired the cold dedication he brought to his art.

For the first weeks of training on two boats, neither helmsman made outrageous or dramatic sorties against the opposing boat. It was move and countermove, logical as chess. Illich began to see why Shaw had been such a formidable opponent. There was no aspect of his game that was weak. He was thorough, cautious, diligent. He possessed, moreover, that willingness to learn which is the humility of genius.

The crew of both boats became consumed in this even battle. They sharpened their expertise, forced one another to question the familiar wisdoms, relearnt the basic moves. In the evenings he and Jim Shaw would closet themselves with their tacticians, with Brod and Paavelt, and work through the moves of the day.

It was an exercise in revelation. In this atmosphere of professional enquiry, each man could express an intuition and subject it to scrutiny without risking the usual ignominy attached to failure. What did not work was simply put aside, a part of the learning process. They began to develop the closeness of a small scientific community in which all ideas are considered on their merits, irrespective of their authorship, and subjected to intensive analysis. Where there was doubt or disagreement, they would agree to rigorous procedures of testing them on the course.

Of these, the sail programme was the most intensive. Sometimes, great helmsmen could achieve equality with radically different sail cuts and shapes. With each shape came a different means of exploitation, a changed method of sailing, and a different optimization of the other sails that were used in combination. It was this constantly shifting ground of sail development for which there was no better procedure than direct boat-against-boat testing. They applied the time-honoured scientific method of changing one agreed aspect at a time, so that the subsequent effects were more apparent. To test them, individual egos and ambitions were ruthlessly subjugated. As the programme proceeded, the dominant intelligence became that of the group.

Neither helmsman had experienced this before. In his training for the earlier America's Cup, Jim Shaw had fought against the immensely powerful crew of John Ericson, a bitter battle without collaboration or compromise in the best interests of the final team. In Illich's own preparation for the last America's Cup, he had so dominated the rival helmsman that the training practices, though rigorous, never reached that level of competition in which the game itself becomes the dominating fact, and the individual players contained within it assume secondary importance.

This time it happened – two helmsmen so balanced in capability that every race became a closely fought battle. Both sides concentrated on eliminating errors. But Shaw's detachment allowed them to analyse each move in concert, to discuss with the measured objectivity of scientists the fury of the day's racing. Illich felt a lightness enter his life, the lightness of being airborne, moving.

The world closed to the small circle of racing, analysis, testing. At night, sometimes under the swinging paraffin lamps (the outer houses had not yet been supplied with electricity), they worked through until the small hours. The days of late summer carried with them the electric urgency of time.

Forty-Four

Their obsessive training drew them into autumn. The trees surrounding the camp grew golden. There were a series of frosts in early November, then the temperature became milder. Engaged in their duelling, the crew practiced in oilskins against the cold spray, but the return of milder weather meant that conditions were not uncomfortable.

Vagir had allocated some of his manpower to improving the camp for the winter. Now all the outlying houses had electricity and cold water. Built as summer residences, they were somewhat rudimentary. In preparation for winter, Vagir's men had installed insulation in the roofs. But as with all serious racing crews, physical discomfort was hardly unexpected.

Illich woke at half-past five in his small, cold room, pulled a blanket round him, and worked until seven on the correspondence that cluttered his battered metal desk. It was a time he liked, not because of the routine, but the relative silence. Sometimes, overhead, he could hear the flights of geese moving south.

At seven the crew gathered on the concreted area in front of the sheds where they exercised for half an hour to warm up before putting on oilskins and leaving in the boats. By eight the two yachts were engaged in combat.

When crews begin to train, they are generally noisy. Crews familiar with one another grow quiet. Their concentration feeds itself. They begin to take a pride in their calm efficiency. This was particularly true of the veteran crew of *Novy Mir*. The only sound became the slow, sliding hiss of the bow-wave, and the tactician feeding information to the helmsman.

There were often morning mists, not dense but enough to obscure visibility. Slowly they would be burned off by a winter sun which insinuated its warmth shyly. The boats would sometimes disappear from sight, appearing out of the cool whiteness at the next mark like ghosts.

Afterwards, towards mid-morning, when the crews were drained by concentration, the sails would be lowered and the towboats would return them to the quay.

Other factors impinged. The Russian camp had moved to Odessa for its winter programme. They were visited less by the observation helicopter from the other camp. A source of entertainment and tension was temporarily removed. But it meant that they entered the solipsistic trance of concentration more fully, only shaking themselves free when the race was over and the towboats lugged them towards the shore.

As the winter drew on Aegu, too, seemed to have forgotten them. He was engaged in that almost permanent, formalized war of nerves between Estonia and Moscow which had characterized their relationships since the 'thaw' in the

'90s. Illich saw newspaper photographs of Aegu shaking the hands of senior Russian politicians, engaged in discussions that the press described as 'direct' or 'an honest exchange of views', the terms of a conflict of interest.

Christmas came, and a skeleton staff remained at the camp until the New Year. The prospect of returning to the flat in Tallinn depressed Illich, and he was one of those who remained behind.

In the silent pre-dawn, Lydia Teemant breathed quietly beside him. In the cold of the little room they huddled for warmth. Even on Sundays when, in deference to the local community, the group did no physical labour or racing, Illich rose quietly to catch up on the correspondence, checking slowly through invoices and equipment lists by the light of a small table lamp. As he worked, he listened to the slow intake and exhalation of her breath, which seemed to fill the room until it was all around him. It was curious and pleasing, in the spartan environment of the camp, to see the physical evidence of a woman; spread over the single, high-backed chair were her long dress, her panties, the woollen pullovers, her warm fur boots.

To northerners, the exchange of warmth can seem more intimate than sex itself. In the darkness of the corner, he saw that she was turned away from him, facing the wall, and he could discern the high mountain of her hip. While he worked he fought off the ache to join her.

That morning she dressed in warm trousers and a heavy pullover and, their breaths freezing, they walked to the periphery of the camp and were let out by the militiaman on guard duty. Skirting a narrow creek that meandered inshore about a hundred yards, they made their way through the dewy grasses along the shore.

For a lecturer in child psychology, used to the deployment of words, she was a relatively silent companion, something he liked in her. Her visits, between those of family and other commitments, were fleeting. Illich sometimes thought of her relationship with Artur Sirk. He gained the impression that they were hardly lovers, though he deliberately refrained from thinking too deeply about the matter. If nothing else, the peripatetic nature of his life had taught him to live day by day. It was enough to have her company, to hear her breathing beside him as they walked.

At the small harbour at Tavere, amongst the old boarded houses there was a hotel, a converted nobleman's summer residence – all wood and gables – which offered breakfasts to the yachtsmen and tourists who visited the island in summer. In winter it stayed open for the odd, stray commercial travellers and minor bureaucrats who crossed on the ferry to Khiuma.

There were two other men in the dining room, businessmen waiting for the ferry later that morning. The owner, Mrs Sanu, made a fuss of Lydia Teemant. She so seldom had female guests, and gave them a table overlooking the nearby field and watermeadows. In the kitchen they could hear her husband singing as he cooked.

Illich noticed Lydia Teemant's eyes drift downwards to the table. After a while he said: 'I notice you look at my hands.'

He enjoyed the faint expression of surprise, almost of embarrassment, which crossed her face.

'So?' He enjoyed further her counter-attack.

'What men look at in women is quite stereotyped, don't you think?' Illich said. 'Breasts, legs, behinds. I often wonder what women look at in men.'

'Of course,' Lydia Teemant replied. 'And you think hands.'

'In your case, I suspect hands. More generally, I suspect woman's responses are much less stereotyped.'

'Do you?'

'I think so.'

'Tell me,' Lydia Teemant asked. 'Do you think of yourself as attractive?'

He was startled.

'No, not at all,' he answered truthfully. In the mirror when he caught sight of himself he saw a cold wolf's face, expressionless eyes. His mirror image often startled him, the sense of glimpsing a being utterly alien, some creature in a forest clearing.

'What about you?' he asked. 'Do you think of yourself as attractive?'

'I think so. What I mean is, I believe other people.'

'That seems reasonable enough.'

'Whereas you don't,' she observed.

'Don't what?'

'Believe other people.'

'What is there to believe?'

The breakfast came, toast, ham and eggs. There was no butter shortage on Khiuma. They were hungry. In the further corner the two businessmen were discussing rising prices from their different tables. Lydia Teemant ate well. Her appetite was good, in this as in other things.

Mrs Sanu brought coffee. When she left, Illich asked: 'How well do you know Aegu?'

Her expression was difficult to interpret. He thought he saw surprise, annoyance even, but not the embarrassment he had expected.

'You asked me that before.'

'Several months ago,' he agreed. 'You said he was a friend of your father.'

For a few moments they drank their coffee in silence. He paid for the meal and they left. They walked along the shore without talking.

As they approached the outer perimeter of the camp Lydia Teemant said: 'Why did you ask me about Aegu?'

'I suppose because he is a person who influences me.'

'I see. And of course, that makes you nervous of him.'

'I suppose so.' He shrugged. 'Also,' Illich continued, 'I wondered what you thought about his hands.'

She smiled to herself, but did not answer. He had let

227

jealousy raise its head, and it would get him nowhere. He had exhibited a vulnerability, a practice he could not afford.

Returning to the flat in Tallinn, he had been walking down the street when he felt a peculiar sense of anticipation, that odd floating feeling in the stomach which occurred before races. About fifty yards away, a group of four men crossed over from the other side of the street. There were at least fifty other people in sight, but several things disquieted him. The men were evidently Russian. They had the slight ill-fit of the clothes, the characteristic walk, slightly loping, of military men who almost make an effort not to march in step. As casually as he could, he turned left down Viru Street and then, almost immediately, turned right smartly into Sauna Street. In Sauna Street he entered a bookshop and proceeded to buy one of the newspapers that lay, carefully piled, beside the cash counter. Keeping a careful watch out of the corner of an eye at the street outside, he drew out a five rouble note. He was receiving his change when the group walked by on the other side. One of the men looked into the shop, but the morning sunshine was in his eyes and Illich doubted if he had been seen.

He walked out of the shop, crossed the road and followed the group, closing the distance gradually until he was only a few feet behind them. One of them, a burly blue-jawed man, turned to look behind him and Illich saw a look of careful recognition in his eye. They were talking quietly among themselves. A second man turned around casually. Illich looked each in the face, remembering the features, rehearsing to himself any peculiarities. Winter sunlight fell across the road. He was on a thoroughfare and there were people about. If the aim of the group was to jump him there would be witnesses. He closed up the distance until he was almost treading on their heels.

It is intimidating to find yourself followed by your victim – if that was what he was. In the long tradition of cat-and-mouse games between the former Soviet citizen and the secret police, he had been advised always to make it plain to your watchers that you have registered their presence. These were not KGB, he was certain, or MVD, but men from military intelligence, the GRU. At the junction at Valike-Karja the group hesitated for a moment, and turned right towards the Suur-Karja and the town centre. He waited until they had made their decision, then turned left. At Parnu Maantee he turned left again and made his way back to the flat, taking care not to look behind him, moving casually but with deceptive speed.

On reaching the flat he made himself a cup of coffee and as he lifted the cup, found to his surprise that he was shaking. Inside he felt calm. It was his body that reacted, exhibiting his tension and strain. The cup shook in his hands like a small seismograph of his feelings.

Sitting down at the kitchen table, he drafted a report of the incident, the time of the day, a description of each of the four men and the precise path he had walked while they followed him. He wrote down the name of the shop where he had bought the newspaper, and provided a detailed description of the girl who had served him. He placed it in an envelope and posted it to Aegu's office for the record. That was when he decided the area of Tallinn was potentially unsafe, even for brief visits, and he returned with relief to the relative security of the camp.

Forty-Five

Heavy frosts struck in late January, and for two weeks a skein of ice covered the sea. The sky was clear, and a cold sun flamed on its white surface. Snow turned the harbour white. For three weeks it was impossible to sail. The masts were unshipped from both yachts and they were drawn into the sheds. In an attempt to bring *Leningrad* up to *Novy Mir*'s standard, major surgery was undertaken on the older yacht's aft sections. With icicles hanging on the roofs outside, and the big blow heaters whirring almost constantly to maintain the temperature in the large shed, Vagir and his men removed *Leningrad*'s entire aft cockpit, sawed off nearly twelve feet of hull, and replaced it with aft sections to Tammiste's design.

It was Jim Shaw who pressed for the surgery, and Illich could not restrain himself from asking: 'So now you want a turkey too?'

'Yeah,' Shaw replied. 'I'm tired of looking at your ass.'

When Vagir and his men had finished, *Leningrad* lay newly painted on her cradle, exhibiting tumblehome like *Novy Mir*.

The ice melted in middle February. When they began to sail again, Shaw and his men hit back. It was even racing for the next month. The changes to the aft section of *Leningrad* had made a difference to her speed, particularly in the higher wind strengths which had previously been *Novy Mir*'s best sailing conditions. Shaw rallied his crew. A fresh cycle of duelling carried them through late winter and into early spring.

By then accounts were beginning to appear in the press on the progress of the challenger syndicates. According to reports, one syndicate had a remarkable secret weapon in new sail technology, another had a new rudder planform which gave extraordinary manoeuvrability. Shaw and Illich watched, partly concerned and partly amused, as each new revelation reached the newspapers.

It was a mild and passing interest. The exhaustive schedules of racing, repair, analysis, and a fresh day's racing, day after day, absorbed their full attention.

In early June the challenger eliminations would begin. Because they themselves were officially a part of the Russian defence, they would contest their own series against the

Army Group under Pilnyak. This was scheduled to take place in July. The winner of the defender eliminations would face the winner of the challenger eliminations to decide the outcome of the America's Cup. As in the America's Cup competition itself, the competition with the Army syndicate for the right to defend would constitute the best of seven races.

Their own training, which until spring had consisted of the largely staccato rhythm of starts followed by an upwind and downward leg, reached its final stages. Now they began to follow the formal round of full course racing. In April and May their training hit full stride.

It was in late May that Illich, during a temporary respite from training, timed a three-day crew rest period with a visit to Moscow.

Forty-Six

The aircraft which carried Illich, a short range Antonov, landed at Vnukovo airport, outside Moscow, at 8:45 a.m.

This time there was no sign of Pridilenko's Chaika. Illich was relieved. It was also, he noted with a certain ironic satisfaction, an indication of his changed status. Clearly, in the minds of Pridilenko and the committee, he was now an outsider.

He ordered a taxi and put his own luggage in the boot. His driver, a large Ukrainian, was morosely silent as they took the highway to central Moscow. Passing through the outer perimeters of Moscow, the tall blocks of flats for workers reminded him, in their blank impassivity, of the historic anti-tank defences on the northern road. In the bright sunlight, at a distance, they looked modern and efficient. Closer, they had started almost immediately to show signs of age.

In contrast, as they moved in towards the centre of the city, the apartment buildings began to take on an appearance of tidiness. They exhibited small landscaped gardens, parks, even fountains. This was the domain of the white collar workers, the minor bureaucrats and the new rising middle class. Legislation had been passed which bestowed private property rights on individual dwellings. These rights were not only assured for a lifetime, but could be passed from parents to children. Their tidiness was a physical fact in turn dependent upon a psychological insight. The new property rights had not only given the individual an incentive to maintain his property, perhaps even more importantly, they had tapped Russian familial closeness. Groups of residents had formed associations to look after communal areas. It had become the obsession of extended families to beautify their immediate surroundings.

Mozhayskoye Shosse, Marshala Grechko, Kutozovskiy Prospekt. Now they were passing through areas of shopping and offices. To Illich's eye, even since his last visit there were striking numbers of new cooperatives – capitalist enterprises in everything but name – a plethora of new brand labels for foodstores, clothing shops, and others selling televisions and hi-fis, cameras and videos, with prices and bargains ostentatiously displayed. There were still occasional billboards with injunctions and admonitions ('Build Socialism, Comrades'; 'Socialism is Peace') but these seemed part of an older culture, their fading messages and primitive graphics pushed aside by new economic forces.

They were crossing the Moskva River. In Kalinin Prospekt the changes were not so striking. It was the movement of the new economic forces spreading out through the suburbs that had been so remarkable.

Eventually the taxi passed Novaya Place and stopped

outside the smart white building in which Pridilenko's offices were housed.

Illich paid the diffident Ukrainian driver, removed his baggage while the driver watched, seemingly detached, and walked through the atrium, past the eyes of the remote control cameras, to the lifts.

The nuances of status in the new Russia were nevertheless still deeply ingrained. As Illich reached the lift, a security official stepped forward to ask for his identification. Illich gave him his Russian passport. The official studied it carefully, compared the photograph with Illich's face, handed it back, and turned towards his office, where a telephone was trilling. This was the self-same document which, emblazoned with Hero of Russia and the listing of four Olympic gold medals, had previously awed those in his path. Even the petty officials, it seemed, could sense, as if by some remote intuition, his fall from grace.

Pridilenko, however, was affability itself. At the entrance to his office, he drew Illich aside. His voice became serious.

'Sergei Mamayev has not been able to attend.'

Illich frowned.

'You are right to be concerned,' Pridilenko said. 'We are in the minority in this meeting.'

'Why couldn't Mamayev come?'

'An emergency meeting of the Committee of Sport Resources to discuss the Armed Services contribution at the next Olympics. It concerns a large part of his Committee's overall budget.'

Pridilenko made no further comment. Illich was left to draw his own conclusions. The most melancholy of these was that the Armed Services had threatened to withdraw part of their budget contribution to Mamayev's Committee of Sport resources. Mamayev was therefore under constraint to toe the line.

'The others are already here,' Pridilenko said. 'Let us go in.'

Arkady Virusk, Valentin Osborov, Andrey Veronin,

233

Vera Ahktova stood up to shake hands with Illich. General Chernavin, as was his habit, remained seated; he did not give Illich so much as a brief nod.

They sat down. Pridilenko brought the committee to order.

'Comrades, since our last meeting, events have occurred which require some discussion and clarification. The Estonian President gave his consent to an action to set up, unilaterally, a second defence syndicate for the America's Cup. Specifically, the Estonian State exercised its right, as formal owner of the yacht *Leningrad*, to take control of the said yacht. Estonia has begun its own separate base camp on the island of Khiuma, where it is now developing its programme of preparation. In the three months since this committee last met, a new yacht has been designed and built *in situ* and is currently undergoing sailing trials.

'In the meantime, the Russian sailing base at Tallinn has received a grant of an extra fifty million roubles from the Army to finance two further development yachts, in addition to the *Kirov*, and is also proceeding fast towards final preparations.'

Pridilenko paused, then continued: 'As you are aware, the base at Tallinn is effectively under Army control, and Colonel Illich functioned within the base as part of the military presence there. As it happens, when the Estonian state exercised its formal ownership over the yacht *Leningrad* by removing the yacht from the base, Colonel Illich was fired upon, and was forced to return fire. Because he acted in self-defence, a special hearing in Estonia found that he was not guilty of manslaughter. Colonel Illich did, however, find himself in conflict with his military superiors in this matter, and resigned his commission in the Army. The new legislation permits an officer to do so. To exercise this right at short notice entails no severance pay, and no pension. Comrade Illich is here today as a private citizen.'

Illich glanced at the impassive faces before him. Pridilenko folded his hands in front of him on the table before continuing.

'Clearly, there are difficulties and unforeseen complexities implicit in the current situation. What is urgently required now is to discuss these recent developments, establish a future *modus operandi*, and proceed with maximum efficiency towards the most effective defence.'

Pridilenko looked around the table. The faces were unyielding. A few moments passed, then General Chernavin raised his hand to speak.

'Comrade Chairman, I have some comments.'

'Please proceed.'

'Your account, no doubt put forward in good faith, is somewhat inaccurate. Colonel Illich . . .'

'Citizen Illich,' interjected Pridilenko.

Chernavin took no notice: ' . . . was at the time under arrest prior to a court martial charge. He eluded his guards and returned to his native Estonia. There he had the audacity to return to the base, and to commandeer the yacht *Leningrad* for a trial sail. In the process of stealing *Leningrad*, this deserter was fired upon by military police in a launch. He compounded his crimes by firing upon the launch, causing the death of one man and wounding another.

'Mistakenly, the Estonian People's Party have seen fit to give refuge to this criminal. A base has been set up on the Island of Khiuma. Facilities have been supplied by the civil authorities of Estonia.'

Chernavin looked around at the meeting.

'It is essential that these criminal activities be halted. I put it to this committee that a vote should be taken on the resolution to the effect that, following the theft of the *Leningrad*, the activities of those responsible should be suspended forthwith.'

Chernavin gazed impassively about the room, focusing on no one in particular but encompassing all.

Pridilenko turned towards Chernavin and said mildly: 'Comrade General, as Chairman it is my task to formulate

235

resolutions. Before we consider this matter further, it is important to air all sides of this matter. I therefore call upon Citizen Illich to comment.'

But Chernavin's face was coldly determined. 'Comrade Chairman,' he interposed, 'Colonel Illich no longer is a member of the defence, and therefore has no right to be represented on this committee.'

'Comrade General,' Pridilenko replied silkily, 'I must warn you officially, as a matter of record, that if you attempt to assume my role of Chairman once more, I will recommend that you are removed from this committee.' Pridilenko paused. 'I ask Citizen Illich to speak on behalf of himself and the current additional preparation camp at Khiuma.'

Illich felt the eyes of the committee turn towards him. It was an uncomfortable sensation.

'Thank you,' Illich said. 'I regret that there were a number of inaccuracies in the statement of General Chernavin. Firstly, my part in the riots at Tartu was a political matter. The Army authorities acted outside their jurisdiction in attempting to carry out a trial on a political charge which already had been investigated by the Estonian political authorities and found to be groundless.

'Since the charges against me were illegal, I had every right to return to Estonia and continue my duty to prepare for the defence of the America's Cup. It was clear, however, that I would not be allowed to continue this preparation in a camp in which I was likely to be re-arrested. I discussed the matter with President Aegu. Comrade Aegu reminded me that the formal ownership of *Leningrad* lay with the Estonian Trade Delegation, and was therefore in the ownership of the Estonian Republic. Comrade Aegu has authorized me to confirm to you that he issued formal authority to take possession of *Leningrad* on behalf of its rightful owners. This I did.'

Chernavin raised a hand.

'Comrade Chairman . . . .'

'Please allow the speaker to continue,' Pridilenko said. 'Continue, Citizen Illich.'

'I wish to comment on further inaccuracies in General Chernavin's statement. The military police launch did not open fire upon the *Leningrad* while I was engaged in abducting her, but during the course of a practice race with *Kirov*. At the time the crew of the *Leningrad* was unarmed. No attempt was made to hail us, or arrest us. As a result of opening fire, one of my crew, the tactician Gundar Arlof, was severely wounded, and required immediate hospital treatment. At a hearing which followed, my actions in acquiring firearms for the purposes of returning fire were deemed to be in self-defence.' Illich paused. 'Apart from the illegal charges brought against me by the Army, I am a free citizen cleared of all charges.'

Pridilenko asked: 'Is that all, Citizen?'

'Except for one more point, Comrade Chairman. General Chernavin described me as a criminal and deserter. That is slander. Perhaps I could say this in return. In bringing illegal charges against me, General Chernavin has violated the civil authority's rights to try all matters political. Comrade General Chernavin has acted against the authority of the state. I submit that it is General Chernavin who should be tried on charges of exceeding his authority, and who should now be brought to justice.'

'Is that all, Comrade?' Pridilenko asked smoothly.

'That is all, Comrade Chairman.'

Forty-Seven

The room seemed unnaturally calm. The only sound was Vera Ahktova's pen as it inscribed her rapid hieroglyphics on the page in front of her.

'Comrade General Chernavin?' said Pridilenko.

Illich watched General Chernavin's face. There was a suggestion of activity below the surface, but the surface itself registered nothing. Some earthquakes are deep, and take a long time to travel.

'Comrade Chairman,' Chernavin said at last. 'I do not wish to engage in polemics. May I suggest instead that we proceed to a vote? The committee has heard what has been said. Do we consider that the camp set up by the Estonians is a legitimate training camp?'

'Thank you,' Pridilenko said. 'An important question. Now that there exist, *de facto*, two training camps, and effectively two different defence organizations, how shall we decide between them? Comrade Illich is still the officially chosen helmsman of the defending yacht. I invite him to speak.'

Veronin and Osborov stared at Illich coldly. He was certain they would side with Chernavin. Arkady Virusk watched him with his customary expression of dry detachment. Without Mamayev to help counter the three votes of Veronin, Osborov and Chernavin, it was certain that any vote would go against him.

'Comrade Chairman,' Illich began. 'It is true that there are two separate defence organizations. In the history of the America's Cup that is not unusual. There is a time-honoured precedent. In other cases where two such defence

238

syndicates exist, it is normal to hold a competition, preferably one which is a replica of the competition in the America's Cup, between the yachts of these syndicates. The normal competition is the best of seven races. The yacht which achieves four wins automatically becomes the defender. This is the best means of insuring that the faster yacht shall prevail.'

'Thank you, Citizen.' Pridilenko turned to Chernavin. 'Comrade General?'

'The establishment of a second syndicate is a waste of resources.' Chernavin's mouth clamped off the words like a metal press. 'Effort is duplicated. It would be better if the defence were conducted within a single organization.'

'Even though that organization,' Pridilenko suggested quietly, 'that single command has already arrested the helmsman chosen by this committee, placed him in solitary confinement on an illegal charge, and fired upon him during a practice race? This hardly suggests efficiency.'

'Comrade Chairman,' Chernavin said, 'I am sorry to see that you, too, engage in polemics. I put it that we should vote on this subject. Should there be two camps?'

Chernavin, too, had experience of committees. Illich reflected that a senior soldier in peacetime is a bureaucrat in uniform. But the point that he had raised was one which must be considered, and which, in due course, must be voted upon. Chernavin obviously was confident that without Mamayev he would carry the day. He was clearly determined to deliver the final, crushing blow here in committee, under the formal gaze of Chairman Pridilenko. Illich saw why Chernavin had remained unmoved by his counter-attack. He had the means to finish Illich's involvement here. It was only necessary that he remain calm in order to deal the fatal blow. Pridilenko, skilled and courageous though he might be, would know, finally, that he could not avoid a vote on the issue.

'We will vote once the matter has been discussed,' said

Pridilenko. 'Before we do so, I ask Comrade Illich whether he accepts the necessity to vote on this matter.'

'I do, Comrade Chairman.'

'Then have you anything further to say?'

'Yes.'

He was aware of the stares of the others. He looked directly at Chernavin. Chernavin's expression was impassive, the face of a chess player who knows that the outcome is certain, that his opponent is merely prolonging the inevitable defeat. In this sense, Illich's brave words were so many gnats, to be swept aside in due course.

Illich produced from his top pocket an envelope. It was addressed to him and had been opened. He withdrew the letter and heard himself say: 'In view of the nature of the vote, I believe it is important that we are aware of the consequences of voting to prevent the Estonian syndicate from equal participation in defence trials. I should like to read out a message from the President of Estonia, Vajnen Aegu.'

'I object,' General Chernavin said suddenly, and his voice was harsh. 'Comrade Aegu is not a member of this committee. Therefore such a statement is an unwarranted intrusion.'

Pridilenko too was alerted. But his curiosity was aroused. Perhaps it was Chernavin's vehement note that surprised him, that awakened the predator in him. What did Chernavin suspect?

'Thank you, Comrade General. This committee, which I remind you is under my chairmanship, has the right to listen to, or take account of, any material evidence which is relevant to its area of operation and its decisions.'

'That is so, Comrade Chairman,' Chernavin said. 'But the opinion of an outsider, one with a vested interest, is not material evidence.'

'We cannot judge that until we have heard it, Comrade General.'

Pridilenko turned to Illich: 'Please continue.'

There was another pause. Illich said: 'The letter is addressed to the Committee for the Defence of the America's Cup. It reads as follows:

Dear Comrades,

For reasons which can be set out in detail if required, I gave authority for Comrade Illich to assert the legal Estonian ownership of the yacht Leningrad *by transferring it to another location.*

It is the Estonian Central Committee's view that we would like to contribute to the Russian defence of the America's Cup by participating in selection trials for the position of defender.

However, in the event that your Committee decides this is impossible, we shall register an independent Estonian challenge for the America's Cup. In this respect, we will join the other challengers against the Russian Republic.

We felt it was necessary and courteous to explain our future actions in this matter in the event that we are not permitted to function within the aegis of the Russian defence.'

Illich looked up: 'The letter is signed by President Aegu. I pass it to Chairman Pridilenko for confirmation.'

'Thank you, Citizen.' Pridilenko perused the letter for several seconds. 'I confirm that the letter is authentic. I pass it to Comrade Ahktova for direct transcription.'

Pridilenko waited several seconds to allow Aegu's message to sink home. He folded his long fingers and turned once again to the committee.

'We will now put this important matter to the vote. There would seem to be a choice. If we decide that the second defence syndicate is invalid, then Estonia will register its own, autonomous challenge and join the other challengers against Russia. If, however, we agree that the issue of the defender will be decided by open and fair sailing trials between the two existing camps, then the new syndicate will function within the Russian defence. Comrades, we each of us shall vote as we see fit. However, as Chairman I am prompted to say that it would be regrettable if Estonia were forced to abandon Russia in this matter, and to become one of the challengers instead of standing with us as a potential defender. I would add further, that in the event of this being the case, we must consider our own individual responsibilities in voting for such a course.'

Pridilenko paused for effect.

'I now put it to the vote. Those in favour of preventing the second syndicate from fair selection races for the defender, please raise your hand.'

Pridilenko looked around.

General Chernavin's hand was still on the table. Illich noted that his face was still remarkably composed. The others, he knew, would take their vote from the General.

Pridilenko lingered. As a predator, he hovered over the others' discomfort. Vera Ahktova waited, pen poised. Finally Pridilenko said: 'Comrades, the motion is defeated by a unanimous vote. Let us pass on to other business.'

The other business consisted almost entirely of arrangements for the venue of the America's Cup defence, the supply of facilities to thirty-one challenging syndicates, and the additional facilities required for two defence syndicates. Certain preparations were brought forward; others, difficult or impossible to achieve, were shelved.

Throughout this activity General Chernavin hardly participated at all. He stared in front of him. Once or twice, Illich caught the General studying him dispassionately across the table. It was the look of a man whose anger has become so deep that it no longer shows in any form of visible emotion. Hatred thus becomes sublime. Like love, it seems to live upon itself; detached, pure, constant. And Illich, the object of this devotion, experienced that sense of unworthiness which lovers sometimes feel at being the centre of such attention.

Forty-Eight

He had grown used to Khiuma. As summer drew on, a white heat lay on the land, through which walked the figures of farmers and their womenfolk, curiously reminiscent of the past. Most of the land was now privately owned. The people were fair and bony, angular, more Estonian than Estonians. They would sometimes lapse into an old dialect which was difficult to understand.

While they finalized preparations at Khiuma, the challenging syndicates had already set up their bases west of St Petersburg on the southern arm of the bay and had begun to duel. It was like the ceremonies of rutting stags. The official programme of selection trials had not yet begun, but the syndicates were already engaging in 'practice races'.

Jim Shaw read the English-language newspapers. Reports were emerging of individual strengths and weaknesses. The British, Germans and New Zealanders were considered the strongest of the new arrivals, the Japanese dark horses. The Americans were reported not to participate in practice matches. Their helmsman, John Ericson, gave a press conference in which he said, 'We believe we have little to learn from the others, and they have a lot to learn from us. So we're keeping a low profile.'

'That sounds like a pretty authentic quote,' Jim Shaw commented.

After their break for lunch, it became a custom of Illich and Shaw to walk for half an hour. It was an opportunity to discuss matters.

They were walking beside a dry ditch, only recently cleared, with a line of trees on one side. It had been a gruelling morning's racing. They would have another session starting at three-thirty, taking the boats out into the Soela Vain, where the sea breezes seemed to funnel through, increasing both strength and consistency.

Despite Jim Shaw's natural reticence, Illich used these walks to try to gain an impression of the great American adversary. Shaw said: 'Americans don't like losing. He's an American. You can bet he has the whole weight of the American military establishment behind him.'

But it was the personal information that Illich hungered for.

'Sure, I beat him,' Jim Shaw commented. 'But we were the chosen team. He came in late off his maxi, and really socked it to us. His crew are technically brilliant, and they've all been part of a team for the last ten years. They practically grew up together.'

It was the unknown aspect of Ericson that Illich found difficult. Nearly all the best big-boat helmsmen emerge from the dinghy classes. They have a track record, honing their skills on smaller boats and transferring them in due course to the larger yachts, gathering as they mature additional qualities of leadership and organization. One could ask their competitors about them, build up a picture of their evolution and background. But Ericson, almost as soon as he was able, was on his father's maxis, a big-boat helmsman from his youth.

'The thing you have to understand about that guy,' Jim Shaw said, 'is that he's not an individual so much as the sharp edge of an organization. It is going to be as if you're being attacked by a rollercoaster. That's what a maxi is, it's so big it's an organization. That's what he came out of.'

So Illich understood Ericson to be the quintessential corporate man, a man almost without individual reference points, except as part of a group.

A few days before Jim Shaw had shown him a newspaper cutting of John Ericson the Third with, beside him, his father John Ericson Jnr. Shaw had pointed to the white-haired figure of John Ericson Jnr, with his flawless shirt and deep tan, and had said, in a return to American colloquialism: 'Big bucks. I hate 'em.'

In his mind, Illich had translated 'big bucks' into 'large deer'. And these two might have had antlers, two confident stags gazing into the camera.

'It's tribal,' Shaw tried again. 'These guys are members of a dominant tribe.'

It was as much as Illich could gain.

They walked on through the white heat haze of Khiuma, the grit of the unmade roads sounding dry beneath their shoes, attempting to grasp a few straws about an opponent who, to Illich at least, appeared only to fade in the distance with the elusiveness of a mirage.

Forty-Nine

Illich called by his ex-wife's flat in Kharkov in the Ukrainian Republic, on the agreed date.

Professor Varilev came to the door. He was a tall man, with a white goatee beard and long fingers which fluttered about his distinguished person like disquieted birds. Anna was out, he said. He called inside: 'Livia, Natasha!'

The girls came out, still dressed in their school uniforms.

They kissed Illich, but as always they were subdued at these little ceremonies. Only when they were on the No 4 bus to Kharkov Square did he see a smile appear on Natasha's face. Livia, the five-year-old, sat on his knee and gazed out of the window.

Kharkov was a monument to Soviet giganticism. A big, powerful city of one and half million people, it was noted for its huge modern buildings, the scale of its great squares.

But Illich hardly noticed. Natasha, now almost nine, was tall, fair, and would be like her mother; already a beauty, she had that almost transparent skin of northerners. Livia was darker, livelier. Livia said now: 'Mama says you left the Army.'

'Yes.'

'Why?' asked Natasha. He had a vision of her, as wife, perplexed at her husband's actions.

How could one begin to explain?

'I had to choose between the Army and sailing.'

'Mama says you have no pension,' Livia insisted.

'That's right,' he said.

The two girls were silent, Natasha composed, Livia in almost unceasing motion on his knee, putting her face against him, only to spring forward to look at a peasant's wagon pulled by a horse in Dzerzinsky Square.

'How do you like school here?'

'It's all right.' It was Natasha who spoke for them.

No doubt helped by Professor Varilev's influence, they had been enrolled in the élite Gorky Institute, a training school for future scientists and administrators. It was an administrative adjunct of Gorky University, where Varilev was a professor of computer studies. A high proportion of children were the sons and daughters of the university staff and faculty. The education system identified promising children at a young age, and directed special facilities towards them. But the right connections also helped.

He wanted to ask 'How is mama? Is she happy?' But he exercised a rule that he did not extract personal information from the children about Anna, and he wished she would do the same.

He realised how little information he had. For example, what job did she now have? The great majority of Ukrainian mothers had jobs, particularly amongst the administrative classes. In Tallinn, Anna had worked for a publishing company, translating Russian into Estonian.

The bus arrived outside the Fine Arts Museum at 11

Sovnarkomovskaya Street. He held the two girls by their hands and together they walked into the museum, with its nineteen halls of art. Illich preferred pre-Revolutionary paintings. The social realism which had dominated the post-Revolutionary period had no attractions for him. And for him at least the avant-garde was too aware of its own beleaguered history, too self-conscious, to paint fluently. He preferred nineteenth-century art. The girls, too, seemed to like their realistic, clear paintings.

The museum had added to their collection of Repin paintings with a special exhibition. Illich, who had always like Repin, paused before *They Did Not Expect Him*, on the subject of a political exile returning. It was a theme which brought a slightly ironic smile. Beside it were the famous *The Volga Boatmen* and *Religious Procession in Kursk Province*. Alongside these acknowledged masterpieces were numerous portraits of famous men and women in the pre-Revolutionary period. Every face told its story, of struggle, fanaticism, venary, religious fervour, alcoholism, the panoply of idealistic and suffering humanity.

This was the best aspect of Kharkov, this rich reminder of Slavic history. It was delightful to stand with the two girls in front of the paintings. In doing so perhaps, somewhere there was a tinge of revenge against Anna. A highbrow in such matters, she affected to despise his taste for these 'bourgeois' paintings. He supposed all marriages were a battleground.

When they had exhausted themselves in watching, they sat down in the new cafeteria and he bought them pastries, *pirozhnaye*, ordering from a pretty, fat waitress who lavished motherly attention on the little girls.

The tables were sticky, the surroundings spartan, the ambience brutally modernist, but a wave of happiness filled his mind. Natasha, as always, began to tell him of their school, their routines, their little triumphs and defeats, the teachers they favoured or disliked. Livia, moving from side to side, would ask questions about him.

247

'Does daddy have a girlfriend?' she asked.

'Mummy is daddy's girlfriend.'

'No, she isn't,' Livia said sadly. 'Not any more.'

The waitress could tell he was divorced. He supposed she observed that only a man who felt guilty would be so tolerant, so attentive.

When they had finished tea, he took them back, catching the No 4 bus again.

One could see parts of the fortress that once formed the nucleus of the city in the triangle formed by Tevelev Square, Rosa Luxembourg Square and Proletarian Square. On a hill the great Uspensky cathedral overlooked them.

The bus was quicker than he expected. He was nearly ten minutes ahead of time when he returned the girls to the doorstep of their home (he had reconciled himself to referring to the flat in Kharkov as their home). He knocked on the door and heard a light tread.

She looked little different. Her face contained the expected components of alertness, detachment, and a hint of almost elfin humour.

'Bye-bye, daddy.' The girls kissed him and scuttled inside.

He looked up at her, standing in the doorway.

'Would you like to come inside?' she said.

An unexpected invitation, though he expected the worst.

Inside it was cool. The flat was spacious, the walls lined with books. A Bhokara rug covered the sitting-room floor. The flat had access to its own private garden. The sounds of birds and trilling insects came through the open patio doors. Clearly, the rewards of academic life, particularly in a field with an expanding future, were excellent.

The flat was big enough to absorb the girls entirely; they had disappeared to their rooms without a sound.

'Please sit down,' Anna gestured to a low sofa.

He sat down opposite her. She crossed her legs briskly, and folded her hands together, pointing downwards. He could tell from her attitude that this was to be a business talk.

'I understand you have been dismissed from the Army.'

'I resigned.'

'Without a pension.'

'So Livia tells me.'

That seemed to halt her for a moment.

'So you cannot pay maintenance.'

'It seems to me that you do not need maintenance.'

'Because of your behaviour, I have decided to apply that the girls are officially adopted by Stepan, and that you cease to become their official father. The new legislation permits it.'

'Therefore it is right.'

He had expected something like this, though not quite as immediate.

'As a matter of interest,' he continued, 'who told you I had resigned?'

'That's none of your business.'

'Your husband has contacts?'

Was he in the flat, thought Illich, perhaps listening?

Her face became tight with anger. He was tempted not to allow her too easy an action. But a premonition of his death, like a presence to which he had become accustomed, made him feel strangely light. Eventually he said: 'I won't oppose it.'

Curiously, this unhinged her grief. Perhaps she had been expecting a fight and this had shaken her assumptions. Tears appeared at the corner of her eyes. She managed a tight smile.

'You always knew how to hurt me.'

Wonderful, he thought. You do something good once in a while, and they say 'you always knew how to hurt me.' Perhaps I am also a little hurt, losing my daughters.

But no, having hurt her, he was forced to watch her cry, her shoulders shaking, in the elegant living-room of her new husband's flat.

Fifty

Lighter still.

At this time of year, the early morning breezes off the land proved some of the most consistent for practising in the prevailing hot weather. The two crews assembled at 6 a.m. by the boats. Their voices still held the almost imperceptible trace of sleep.

A wreath of fog obscured the island. It was warm, but their breaths seemed as heavy as liquid. The launches, grey shapes ahead of them, moved in and out of pockets of sea mist. They brought thermoses of warm tea, and spoke to one another in low voices.

The two yachts were towed for nearly an hour, seven miles out, until they could feel the land breeze coming off the mainland, a huge slice of slowly moving, cool air. Most of the fog had been dispersed. The towing launches released them and set out the pin end buoy for the start line. Then one anchored, acting as committee boat, and the other motored directly upwind to set up the top mark.

Mainsails first, then genoas. Both boats bore away a little to pick up speed; then they started to turn into wind. At first both boats seemed sluggish. The breeze was only a few miles an hour, hardly perceptible, just enough, perhaps, to stir a leaf. But as the boats started to pick up speed, the apparent windspeed across the deck increased. That was the magic, the curious power of these air-breathing machines. They seemed to make their own eerie energy. Behind Illich, Brod wound in the running backstays. The winchgrinders tightened in sheets. *Novy Mir* was strung like a violin. In the early morning, with only a trace of consistent landbreeze, *Novy Mir* and *Leningrad* made their smokeless way across the water, their bow-waves tumbling, heeling well.

'Five, four, three. . . . ' Brod intoned.

The ten-minute gun went. They wheeled and closed in on the starting box. At this advanced stage in preparations, the duels in the starting box were close and intense.

Brod said: 'Three more knots of breeze. Veering five degrees.'

Illich could feel it in the spring on the helm, the increased angle of heel, the steady climb of the instruments from six eight to seven nine.

At this speed you could hear the water tumbling from the counter. Even so, the impression was of owls, of ghosts moving across the surface.

Brod shifted uneasily beside him, staring into the instruments.

Leningrad was closing with them fast. They eased sheets and were both on a close reach, the apparent wind brought forward from midbeam by their own speed. On a quiet day, the sea-breeze hardly ruffling the water, their closing speed was almost sixteen knots.

He could feel his nerves tighten as they closed. Jim Shaw was a consummate duellist. Even now Shaw's intelligence would be reaching out across the water, studying his opponent for the faintest change of course that would provide a clue to his next move.

But today it was Shaw who moved first.

'He's going,' hissed Brod, working on intuition more than direct observation. A few seconds later, *Leningrad* swung downwind with a squeal of eased sheets.

Illich swung with her, hard. Brod roared out orders to the winchgrinders. There was a point of rudder turn above which it stalled; the resulting drag caused the speed to fall off. The point was to take it to that edge; fighting your nerves, you could hover above stall like a low flying aircraft.

The boom swung across, the winchgrinders exploded into

251

action to haul the sheets as they swung into wind; a fizz of release as they went through the wind. They were so close to *Leningrad* now as they ducked the swinging boom that Shaw and his tactician seemed in the same boat.

It was essential to remain calm, calculating the odds while everything that could move screamed, roared, crashed. The boom gybed and the mainsheets hissed by like a scythe. Caught in that rope a bone would be snapped like a toothpick.

'Even,' said Brod as they broke loose. It was true, neither side could find a weakness.

Now they circled each other loosely, at a distance.

Brod didn't take his eye off the other boat. The tactician's function is to find weakness. His is the eye of the vulture or carrion crow.

'Their grinders look tired,' commented Brod.

'Then let's hit them again.'

Aggression kept the adrenalin up. They swung in again, building up speed, stoking up the engines. *Leningrad* responded, but the few seconds between their manoeuvre and her response was the cause of almost a knot of difference in speed.

The crew felt this, and were exultant. Now in the swinging, crashing turns against the other boat they could feel their own edge, drive it home with their own renewed energy.

Brod was singing out the time to the start.

'Twenty-one, twenty, nineteen . . .'

They would be balked of their advantage by the start gun. Shaw was breaking off. Illich roared: 'Sheet in!'

The two boats were slicing together, neck and neck, towards the start line. *Novy Mir* was in the leeward position, and a little ahead.

'Nine, eight, seven . . .'

He was squeezing Shaw up, exercising right of way, forcing him up against the starting buoy. He heard an explosion of commands and a sudden squeal of sheets as Shaw luffed up to avoid the starting buoy.

'Four, three, two . . .'

The starting gun went and Shaw was having to re-round, approach the starting line again.

Novy Mir was at full speed, charging up the windward leg. The trimmers' concentration was unflagging. Brod said: 'He's turned, and he's approaching the line again. He's crossing, he's crossing . . . Now. Eighteen seconds behind.'

Eighteen seconds was all they needed. *Novy Mir*'s upwind speed was improving every day. Now they would crush the other boat. The crew's predatory instincts had taken over; she flew over the water. Brod sang: 'Seven eight, seven nine, eight zero, eight zero. True windspeed ten.'

Yet it had been close. Shaw had broken brilliantly for the start line, perfectly timed to get him out of trouble. If Illich had been half a second slower in responding, he would not have been able to force *Leningrad* to re-round the starting buoy. This was the advantage of duelling with a great helmsman. The crew had to fight him every inch of the way.

A crew which is falling behind, even a fine crew, begins to lose morale, imperceptibly at first. Shaw held the second crew together, imparting to them a sense of his own lethality, his own implacable will. They would work for him until exhausted, confident that if they sharpened the blade for him, he would drive it home against the other boat.

At the end of the second windward leg *Novy Mir* was sixty-eight seconds ahead, at the downwind buoy one minute twenty three seconds. But there was no letting up from Shaw. On the final upwind leg Shaw gambled by seeking wind on the port hand side of the course, found a lift, and from a position of over one and a half minutes behind, was closing fast on the finish line.

'Nothing in it now,' Brod said. 'The American is terrifying.'

They had to find every last fraction of speed to cross the line a few seconds ahead of *Leningrad*.

Fifty-One

The day always began with racing. Afterwards there was a thorough check of equipment throughout both boats, replacement of ropes, examination of winches, pulleys, spars, rigging.

Every night the sails were recut for both yachts. The huge sail floor was floodlit for ten permanent sailmakers. Prem, the mainsheet trimmer, was the key figure in coordinating with the sail loft. The heartbeat of the generator could be heard through the night supplying power to the laser cutting machine.

In every aspect of supply, from sails to masts to repairs, there was equality of access between the two boats. If *Novy Mir* was to be the lead boat, it must constantly prove itself against *Leningrad* in fair competition.

On shore, Vagir was all-pervasive. The workshops were filled with the sound of his repair and maintenance crews. The two boats were lifted out of the water every day under their security skirts. In sun or in rain, Vagir's men checked over the structure, the primary equipment, the hydraulics, winch attachments, and the spars. There was a programme to ascertain optimum rig balance which meant moving the mast of one boat several inches forward or back. Both *Leningrad* and *Novy Mir* were fitted with a hydraulic system beneath decks to haul the toe of the mast backward or forward a full two feet from one extension to the other. Vagir had installed this system. Several changes of keel had been instigated by the designer, first on one boat, then the other, in order to assess the results. Vagir's men had improved the time to change a keel down to a single day.

Masts and booms were subject to another improvement programme, both in terms of their flexibility and their lightness. To one side of Vagir's repair complex, in a sealed-off and tightly controlled workshop area in which all those who entered wore surgical gowns and masks, several new masts and booms were being made of carbon fibre composites. In the adjoining sheds, the repair crews worked in shifts, day and night. At night the floodlights filled the shed area of the base with powerful light.

To his amusement, the designer Kalev Tammiste was *persona grata* once more at the camp.

One day Illich said to him, 'How do we get more speed out of our boat upwind?'

'What is your programme for changing down sails in various wind strengths?'

Illich showed him the tables of sail changes relative to wind strengths.

'This is the same for *Leningrad*?' enquired Tammiste.

'Yes, both boats work from the same table. We put up similar sails in given wind strengths so that we can compare specific types of sails directly.'

'Perfectly logical. Presumably,' Tammiste added, 'these tables derive from *Leningrad* originally?'

'Yes.'

'I imagined so.' Tammiste was thoughtful. 'I am not criticizing you for the programme of sail evaluation, but *Novy Mir* is better balanced upwind because of her hull shape. The adjustments that were made to *Leningrad*'s stern closed the gap, but *Novy Mir*'s hull shape has other differences. Her improved balance means that she could be heeled further without ill effects. The mathematics are complex to explain, but why don't you try keeping up sail for two further knots of windstrength?'

'We'll try it. You think we'll get better speed?'

Tammiste was careful. His reputation was moving from the lowest of the low to almost tolerable. *Novy Mir* was improving faster than *Leningrad*, though both were subject

255

to the same intensive development programme. He didn't want to jeopardize his own improvement in reputation.

He shrugged his shoulders. 'Perhaps.'

For several days there were light winds, and neither boat operated at the limit of its ability to carry sail. A large high-pressure area guaranteed further light weather. Tammiste controlled his impatience. Thankfully, he had another project to work on, a 60-foot BOC yacht for a Finnish sailor. He buried himself in his work. Each morning he woke up and cursed the good weather.

On the fourth day, a stronger breeze filled in from the west. He could hear it in the night, rustling the leaves against the glass. He got up early, at half-past five, trying not to shake the double bed, and tiptoed past the sleeping Margarita. In the bluish glare of the bathroom's fluorescent light he shaved carefully, dressed as quietly as he could, and went down to the kitchen to pour himself a cup of coffee.

An hour later, Tammiste caught the early ferry from Haapsalu to Khiuma. It passed within two miles of the practice area habitually used by *Novy Mir* and *Leningrad*. At seven thirty-five he saw the two sails in the distance, and went out on the ferry's open upper deck to watch.

They were there. His heart jumped. The two boats were tangled in a close duel at the start. As they wheeled hard, their crossed sails formed a combined shape like the wings of a butterfly.

The ferry was wide, flat-bottomed and slow. It rolled with a friendly, almost lugubrious motion in the swell. From it he could see the two boats had broken for the start line, neck and neck. A helicopter, a military one, was hovering over them. Tammiste turned his attention back to the boats.

Now that a pocket of sea mist was clearing, he could distinguish the green hull of *Novy Mir* and the red hull of *Leningrad*.

Were his eyes deceiving him, or was *Leningrad* drawing

ahead? The ferry changed course, maddeningly, as the two boats were about to cross. He had to go over to the other side, which was crowded with sightseers.

'Excuse me,' he dug his elbow into the kidneys of a very large bearded man leaning over the rail.

'Excuse me.'

'What's your problem?' the man said.

'Who do you think you are?' asked a woman with white hair drawn back in a bun. She tapped the shoulder of her husband, another huge man. Why were there so many large people on the ferry this morning? Estonians are slow to anger, but once their blood is up, they like to see it through. There was a danger of a small riot starting here.

Luckily, the ferry changed course again. Tammiste himself changed tack and made a tactical withdrawal.

He went to the bow area. By squeezing past two talking women he got a clear sight. He wished, in a way, that he had not been able to do so. *Leningrad* was clearly ahead, pulling out a strong lead. His heart sank. He felt a sudden desire to throw himself overboard, and but for the fact that his fellow passengers would probably have cheered to see it, he might have done so.

He allowed himself one last glance before retreating to the fug of the ferry's passenger saloon. *Leningrad* was approaching the windward buoy, a good fifteen lengths ahead of *Novy Mir*. Above them the helicopter hovered.

The rest of the way his mind ran through a range of reasons as to why his predictions should prove wrong. None of them seemed particularly plausible. When the ferry disembarked, he caught one of the island's few taxis to the base.

Racing was continuing. Unfortunately, at a distance of three miles it was impossible to make out the different hulls in the slight sea-mist that still extended offshore.

Two hours later the two boats came in. He waited on the quay.

'Tammiste,' shouted Illich. 'I want to talk with you.'

The two boats tied up. Illich walked up the quay towards him. He was holding out his hand.

'Congratulations.'

Tammiste was completely off balance.

'But . . .'

'Brilliant advice. An extraordinary success.'

'But on the ferry . . .' Tammiste said miserably, 'I saw . . .'

'You watched from the ferry?'

Illich smiled. He called back to Jim Shaw: 'Tammiste watched us from the ferry . . . .'

Jim Shaw came up.

'He did?'

Illich and Shaw broke into smiles. They started to laugh. Tammiste felt like punching them.

'Did you see the helicopter above us?' Illich asked in the middle of his mirth.

'Yes.'

'It was a military helicopter, sent to survey us from the other camp. Whenever it appears we ease sheets slightly on *Novy Mir* and allow *Leningrad* to move ahead.'

'You do?'

'It's the only way *Leningrad* can win these days,' Jim Shaw explained ruefully.

'When the helicopter visits us, we do everything we can to give the impression *Novy Mir* is the slower boat.'

They looked at Tammiste's perplexed face.

'Jeez,' Jim Shaw said. 'I thought you designers were intelligent.'

'Naturally, we want to lull the other side into a false sense of security about the new boat. If it's slower than the old boat they'll be falsely confident.'

'Ah,' Tammiste said. But inside he seethed. He had always hated the psychological games that yachtsmen found it necessary to play against one another. It was the simple facts he thirsted after, the elemental data on performance. Illich continued: 'When the helicopter left, we restarted the race. We used an amount of sail on *Novy Mir* which would heel her more than normal relative to the wind conditions. It was an equal start. At the top mark, *Novy Mir* was forty-three seconds ahead. At the next windward mark she made up a similar time again. This was on pure boat-speed. The first trial is a success.'

Tammiste was relieved. But he had a nagging doubt.

'You're trying to give the impression to outsiders that *Novy Mir* is slow?'

'That's right,' Illich said.

'Real slow,' Jim Shaw affirmed.

'My reputation . . .' Tammiste could hardly keep himself from stammering.

'A typical designer,' Jim Shaw said, shaking his head in wonder.'Only thing he's worried about is his reputation. Everything else, the whole goddamn team effort, can go to hell.'

'Disgraceful,' Illich agreed.

'Back home, we lynch designers,' Shaw said. 'It's kind of traditional.'

Tammiste knew they were making fun of him again. But it was still annoying. One went through fire to provide a superior boat, and here they were telling everyone, for psychological reasons, that it was slow. He bit his tongue. He would have liked to scream.

'We have to go, I'm afraid,' Illich said. 'A meeting with the sailmakers. Congratulations.'

'Congratulations,' Shaw repeated.

Tammiste stepped aside to let them pass. Wait till Margarita hears about this one, he thought.

Fifty-Two

During those final months of preparation, in Illich's mind the outside world shrank to the decks of a racing yacht.

Though their late start in preparation would be against them, and the inferior resources of a small country would not match those of Russia or the United States, or indeed the powerful challenges from Britain or Germany or France, it was the constant improvement of *Novy Mir*'s performance that gave him hope that they would not disgrace themselves.

In the brisker winds, it had been axiomatic on *Leningrad* that the maximum heel angle was twenty-seven degrees; heeled beyond this the boat slowed. Sail changes were controlled to generate no more than this angle of heel. Consequently, Tammiste's suggestion that *Novy Mir* responded differently, though absurdly simple in its premise, had opened up a new line of investigation.

On the first day of brisk winds – the day Tammiste had observed them from the ferry – Illich had fought back his frustration as the helicopter hovered above them, and his trimmers subtly altered *Novy Mir*'s sails so that she slowed that quarter of a knot which would give *Leningrad* an advantage. Beneath the armoured topsides of the helicopter a sponson, just aft of the 30-mm cannon turret, held a remote-control camera. The machine sometimes came close enough for them to see its lens.

This blatant spying was also, no doubt, an intimidatory tactic, an aspect of the heavy hand of the Russian Army. Even Aegu had no official control over the matter. The fact was that Estonia, though economically almost wholly autonomous, fell within the Russian mutual defence orbit, and the Russian Armed Forces had a right to overfly all coastal waters.

All that remained was to attempt to turn this spying and intimidation to their own advantage, by giving them a false impression of the new boat's speed.

After half an hour of intrusive observation, the helicopter left. At the top mark, the two boats sailed back to the start line. Today they would forgo the pre-start manoeuvre battle in order to evaluate Tammiste's hypothesis.

The wind was twenty-two knots, kicking up a sharp swell with brilliant whitecaps. *Leningrad* maintained her sail area, full mainsail and No 3 jib. *Novy Mir* put up a heavy weather No 2, a bigger headsail that would heel her significantly more than *Leningrad*.

Illich said 'Ready' over the short-wave radio. The start controller on the anchored boat said 'Countdown one minute, starting . . . now.'

Leningrad and *Novy Mir* kept a respectable distance from each other.

'What speeds should we be getting under these conditions?' Illich asked.

Brod punched the enquiry into their small tactical computer.

'Eight point four knots average.'

A short while afterwards Brod began to sing down the seconds: 'Twelve, eleven, ten, nine, eight . . .'

They were heeling more, and it felt strange to his fingers. But it was true that the amount of helm had hardly increased at all, a measure of *Novy Mir*'s unusual balance.

Leningrad was magnificent, charging through the swells, her sails setting perfectly. They were approaching the start line neck and neck, fifty yards apart, *Novy Mir* to leeward.

The puff of the starting gun was followed by the punch of the explosion.

'Speed, Brod.'

'Eight two, eight two, eight two, eight three . . .'

'We'll stay on this tack.'

The swell was particularly sharp, exploding against the bow and sending jets of stinging water against their faces. He and Brod wore water-tight dark glasses coated with a film which caused water run-off. It made them look like Martians.

'Heel angle?' asked Illich.

'Thirty one point four.'

Four degrees over the theoretical optimum, thought Illich. A big difference. *Novy Mir*'s gunwale was sometimes in the water. In the short waves, the water was breaking in glassy sheets along the leeward side-decks. Usually, this was a sure sign of too much sail.

Illich concentrated on raising the figures. The trimmers alternatively eased sheets and hauled in, hunting for the right sail settings. It made only a marginal difference to the speed. They couldn't reach the predicted eight point four, and sometimes they were down to eight zero, even seven nine.

Illich kept running his eyes across the instrument panels, trying to will the figures up, steering with such concentration that he entered a trance.

'Not working,' he said to Brod.

Brod was silent. A few moments later Brod said: 'Look!'

In his concentration, Illich had almost forgotten *Leningrad*. She was still on the same tack, or Brod would have warned him. But he had not glanced at her in his obsession with the instruments.

'She's two lengths behind,' Brod said. 'And fading.'

A light filled Illich's mind. He was sure Jim Shaw would be driving her at speed.

'Fading,' Brod repeated. 'Fading. Three lengths now.'

'Why aren't we hitting the predicted figures?'

'The waves, I think,' Brod said. 'Unusually steep.'

Illich broke away from the instruments to look away at *Leningrad*.

Astonishing, he thought. It showed again that one

needed another boat, of known performance, before one could reach any useful conclusions. Even now a highly sophisticated computer could not simulate the full complexity of the environment within which the boat operated. On numbers alone the experiment had failed. But the true test was against *Leningrad*.

'Fading,' Brod said again. 'Four lengths in four minutes. Look.'

This was nothing short of remarkable. Compared to them, *Leningrad* was floundering.

At the top mark they were twenty lengths ahead. Both skippers had stayed as close to one another as possible without directly interfering with one another's wind. There was no possibility of a tactical advantage.

At the top mark they turned into wind, dropped the No 2 so that they didn't shorten its life unnecessarily, and waited for *Leningrad*. As Jim Shaw sliced past the buoy he turned parallel to them. Illich shouted to Shaw.

'What do you think?'

Jim Shaw held a thumb up.

Illich returned to the radio. On their frequency, he knew they could be overheard, and they agreed to keep instructions to a minimum.

'Chaseboat,' Illich said: 'Could you take our No 2 genoa over to *Leningrad*?'

On the chaseboat Lars Sund replied: 'Coming over now.'

'Jim,' Illich said.

'Roger, I read you.'

'You take the No 2 this time. We'll use your No 3.'

'Good thinking.'

Shaw understood immediately. To verify the assumption that *Novy Mir*'s superiority was due to her better balance, and not to a sail that might be intrinsically superior, they wanted to run the race again with *Leningrad* setting *Novy Mir*'s No 2, and *Novy Mir* setting *Leningrad*'s No 3.

With the foresails precisely reversed, they would be able to hunt down cause and effect, building up in due course a reliable picture. The support boat carried their No 2 to *Leningrad*, and brought back her No 3. Then the two yachts hauled up spinnakers and set off downwind to the start.

It was a curious and absorbing business. On their way back to the start Illich surveyed again the predictions that would come from Tammiste's hypothesis. This time *Leningrad*, pressed beyond her optimum heel angle by the big No 2, should be slower than normal. *Novy Mir*, carrying the usual size of foresail, should be as normal.

Brod counted down as the two yachts approached the start line.

On this race Shaw seemed to have a marginal advantage of three seconds at the start. They lined up again, on parallel starboard tack some fifty yards apart, and marched together across the short, steep swells.

'Eight zero, eight zero, seven nine . . .' Brod said.

At first there was little in it. But even this was a confirmation. They settled in to get the best out of the boat while Brod watched *Leningrad*.

Two minutes passed, three minutes.

'She's fading,' Brod confirmed. 'Two lengths behind. Holding steady with us now.'

In the gusts, it was noticeable that *Leningrad* suffered. As a gust struck, she broached into wind, and they could see Jim Shaw working the wheel hard to bring her back on course. In every gust *Leningrad* seemed to lose a little more. By the time they had tacked three times and reached the top mark, *Novy Mir* was four lengths ahead. Not as great as the spectacular distance last time, but enough to confirm that whereas *Novy Mir* was helped by a bigger sail, *Leningrad* was impeded by it. So far, Tammiste's predictions appeared correct.

But Illich wanted a further confirmation. *Novy Mir* had won twice. But perhaps the crew work was the factor in both her victories. He turned upwind and ordered the crew to drop the foresail. Then he contacted Jim Shaw on the agreed waveband.

'Would you like to change crews?'

'The hell I would!'

'Take down sail, lash the wheel, and the chase boat will change us over. Bring the No 2 back to *Novy Mir* with you. We'll take your No 3 back with us.'

'Roger.'

The chaseboat, which had listened in, came skipping across the water to them.

'Down sail,' shouted Illich. 'We're changing crews.'

It was a strange feeling, on the chaseboat, leaving *Novy Mir*'s green hull butting gently in the chop, like deserting a ship at sea. They clambered on board *Leningrad*.

Jim Shaw and the crew of *Leningrad* jumped on the chase boat.

Illich's crew set to work immediately to haul up the mainsail. Both boats were identical in their deck layouts. It was their policy to keep absolute similarity in all gear, so that neither boat had any obvious advantage except in the particular aspect they were currently testing.

An absurd emotion touched him as he watched Shaw's men haul up sail on *Novy Mir* – a distinct feeling of jealousy, of ownership. Tammiste would be amused at how attached he had become to *Novy Mir*. Even so, there was a satisfaction in being aboard the *Leningrad* again. The foresail followed the main up, and he bore off.

Under Jim Shaw's hands, the green hull of *Novy Mir*, with its tumblehome stern, swung towards them. It was the first time Illich had seen *Novy Mir* racing from another boat.

'Countdown,' Brod said. 'Twenty-three, twenty-two, twenty-one . . .'

Novy Mir swung parallel, and the two boats powered up to the line. Shaw was shouting: 'We're going to whip your ass.'

'This is serious, men,' Illich said. 'I want your best efforts.'

'Eleven, ten, nine, eight . . .'

'Let's show them who is the superior crew here.'

The gun produced its white feather; the explosion followed.

For a full minute, it seemed, they were holding off *Novy Mir*. But the other crew were learning how to set the sails – in particular that they didn't need to ease sheets when the gusts hit them.

In the fourth minute *Leningrad* was two boatlengths down. With a powerful effort, by means of extreme concentration, they managed to hang on for several more minutes, not gaining but not losing. The wind increased by two knots and then they started to slide back slowly but inexorably. More wind came in, and *Novy Mir* began to pour on the pressure. They tacked shortly after *Novy Mir*, keeping clear of her bad air, then tacked again.

At the top mark they were seven boatlengths behind *Novy Mir*. Illich was left with the impression of that smoking green hull, the curve of the tumblehome in the stern, the way she heeled easily to gusts, while *Leningrad* tried to spin into wind and he had to work the wheel and shout to Prem to ease mainsheet.

The crew of *Novy Mir* had already dropped their foresail by the time *Leningrad* reached the top mark, and were standing on the sidedecks watching them come in.

Jim Shaw had the good sense not to call out. Illich's crew were as angry as snakes.

They dropped sail and the towing launches approached them to attach towing ropes and take them in. They could have sailed as fast to base but, since the life of a first-class racing sail is measured in hours, they preferred to preserve their sails only for the race course.

Towed, the boats were like albatrosses, or those large winged insects that smaller workers hustle from the depths of nesting sites following rain. It was ten o' clock in the morning. They looked forward to a late breakfast, before the punishing schedule of afternoon debriefing, physical training, equipment maintenance and afternoon racing.

Fifty-Three

Directly after breakfast, with half an hour of recuperation before their physical exercise programme, Jim Shaw walked with Illich over to Illich's small office.

Illich closed the door and sat down at his desk opposite Shaw.

'I promised Gundar Arlof there would be a place for him as navigator. But he agreed with me he won't be in 100 per cent condition. And besides, he is engaged to a staff nurse Rana, a very pretty girl. We agreed that he should conserve his energy for the most important things.'

'He's got his priorities right,' Shaw commented. 'Guess that's why he's a good navigator.'

'That means' Illich persisted, 'we have a spare place in the afterguard.'

Jim Shaw was silent. Illich said: 'I have discussed this with Brod. He is as good a navigator as Arlof. We both wondered if you could join us as tactician.'

Shaw did not speak for several seconds. Partly to fill in the silence, Illich continued: 'I'm sorry to bring this up so late. You've helped us to train as much as possible right up to now, and without you in the other boat, we wouldn't be remotely as well prepared as we are now. But you saw what happened today. *Novy Mir* is now so far ahead that whatever crew takes her, she'll win. So the close competition is over. If it's over, then I'd prefer you on our boat.' Illich glanced at Shaw's face again. It was difficult to detect Shaw's thoughts. Illich said: 'I don't know how you'd feel about sailing on the yacht of a foreign country.'

'I'll have to think about that, sure.'

'You would like a few days, perhaps? To discuss it with Maria?'

'I already know what Maria would say. She'd say yes.'

'Forgive me for pressing you then. How long do you want to think about it?'

'About two minutes,' Jim Shaw said.

He stood up and leant against the wall. 'Three months ago, when I started here, it seemed to me exactly like the position I was used to at home. You wanted to conduct a good programme, and the military were getting in your way. That's exactly what happened to me. So I sympathized. Something else, just so you know. I will always think America is my country. But I don't necessarily like the people who are running the campaign there. They're the people that were screwing things up when I was part of the defence. Little people, people like me, don't matter to them. I happen to think those people are the real enemy.'

Shaw turned and looked out of the small window, to where the crew worked on the two yachts. 'I'd just love to get into action against the people that have taken over the American defence. That's much clearer to me now than it was. Screw the fact that this time I'm not on the American side. It's more important to identify the bad guys, see if we can't teach them a lesson.'

This was a long speech from a Maine man. Illich suspected they were like the northern Siberians. One grunt, yes; two grunts, no; three grunts – well, that more or less sums up the world.

'Are you sure Maria will support you?'

'Yes. She made up her mind the first few days. Her heart's behind this.'

'Yet,' Illich said gently, unable to restrain his curiosity, 'she opposed your involvement in the American effort.'

'Instinct. She didn't like the set-up. She likes this one. It's simple. I tend to agree with her.'

'Your two minutes are up,' said Illich.

'That's right. Count me in.'

A series of pieces fit together, like a jigsaw. One can only try to make up the final picture. Illich left the office in good heart. Shaw was on his team, and Tammiste's boat . . . well, that was different. Designers were fair game. Everyone knew that.

There were complications, but not insuperable ones. The America's Cup rules stated that crew must be nationals of the country from which the challenge derived. Dual nationality was, however, permitted.

Illich, exploiting his privileged position for once, telephoned Aegu's office: 'May I speak to Comrade Aegu?'

'Who's speaking?'

'Ivan Illich.'

There was a series of clicks.

'*Tovarich*,' Aegu's voice was crisp.

'A favour, Comrade President, regarding the American helmsman, Jim Shaw. He has helped us to train our crew to exceptional standards. I would like him as my tactician. However, we have a nationality problem.'

'How long has he been resident here?'

'Fourteen months.'

'We have a clause in our constitution which confers retrospective citizenship for exceptional services to the country.' A trace of irony entered Aegu's voice. 'It is a relic from the old Soviet constitution; it enables us to reward foreign spies working on our behalf.'

'Can it be used in this case?'

'I am almost certain. If you will write an affidavit confirming that he has provided a valuable service to your effort, we will do our best to see that it is granted. How soon do you require it?'

'As soon as possible.'

'A week?'

'A week.'

'Anything else?'

'No. And thank you.'

'My pleasure. Goodbye, Comrade.'

The phone went dead. Another problem solved.

'Look at this,' said Kalev Tammiste to Margarita. 'An invitation from those demons.'

She looked at the card. Headed 'Kalev Tammiste', it requested his attendance as guest of honour at a party to celebrate the selection of *Novy Mir* as the Estonian contender for the defence of the America's Cup.

'Is it a joke?' asked his wife. Was it, she wondered, part of their warped sense of humour?

'No,' Tammiste replied. 'It is something more frightening than that.' He paused for a moment. A look of intense worry crossed his features: 'I think it is genuine.'

Fifty-Four

Over the next two weeks they broke up camp and transported their equipment to the site of the defence, a bay just west of St Petersburg.

The position of the new camp had been approved by Illich several months earlier. A security perimeter fence had been installed. Vagir, their site manager, had been placed in charge of completing the facilities of the new camp. Loaders and lifters had already been installed. The buildings had been insulated for temperature and humidity control. Areas had been designated for storage of sensitive resins. Engineering floors had been laid. A large loft space for sail cutters with a raised wooden floor had been constructed. The accommodation and dormitory arrangements would still be rudimentary by the time they arrived, but they sufficed. An extra generating plant was incorporated in case of power cuts, which for some reason were notorious in that area.

Partly because their base camp at Khiuma had similar wind patterns to those expected at Leningrad, and partly because they wished to keep their boats an unknown quantity, they decided to move late, only a month before the races with the Army syndicate which would decide the defender of the America's Cup.

They waited two days for favourable weather, placed old, used sails aboard the boats for the journey, and fitted temporary navigation lights on both *Leningrad* and *Novy Mir*. Early on the third morning, they sailed the two yachts in convoy with the two launches from Khiuma, proceeding almost due east along the North Estonian coast in the direction of St Petersburg. Their course took them past Tallinn. Aegu had told them to expect a few local boats to cheer them on their way. They passed the small island of Osmussar, then Paldiski point. The wind shifted to the north, and increased to fifteen knots. It was almost perfect weather for a fast passage. As they approached Tallinn at midday, they observed a fleet so large that, at a distance, it blackened the sea. Drawing closer, they saw it consisted of many hundreds, if not thousands, of sailing vessels, power yachts, launches, dinghies under sail and outboard. It closed in on them, horns hooting. A huge and enthusiastic crowd began to sing the Estonian anthem. The two support vessels had to clear their path with hand-held loud hailers. Several incidents brought *Novy Mir* perilously close to being rammed. The two yachts were forced to reduce speed and dropped their foresails, proceeding under mainsails alone.

The huge fleet of motor vessels and yachts accompanied them for several hours along the coast, some as far as Viniistu, until forced to turn back before nightfall.

During the night the wind dropped to five knots from astern. They proceeded slowly. At dawn they could see the lights of Khotia-Jarve off their starboard bow, a pale meniscus of light reflected in the almost calm sea.

It took them the whole of the following day to complete the distance in the prevailing gentle Westerlies. At dawn the wind had fallen to nothing, and the two towing launches hauled them the rest of the way on a sea so smooth they floated on their own perfect reflections.

When the little convoy sailed into the bay in which their camp was situated, the sea was studded with the sails of the foreign challengers engaged in their selection trials. Some thirty-one foreign syndicates were participating in a series of selection races which had been proceeding for six weeks already. Along the line of the bay were dotted the shoreside facilities of the foreign syndicates, complete with advertising posters, support trucks, sponsors' entertainment centres, the whole panoply of international commercialism in a major sporting event. On the shore a huge new building, set above the bay, provided an information centre for some 1,400 accredited journalists. Five huge new hotels had been built on the hills overlooking the bay.

After the quiet island of Khiuma, this was something of a cultural shock. As they approached their own somewhat spartan camp a swarm of international press boats, who had been covering the day's racing, broke off to converge on them. For the second time in their journey they were surrounded by other boats. Television cameras were trained on them. With two-day growths of beard, they were towed in somewhat bemusedly. Long shadows already covered the quay when they finally docked.

Vagir was waiting for them, and twenty-five or so skilled shipwrights, support men, repairers, sail-makers. *Novy Mir, Leningrad* and the two launch boats tied up. A chain was hauled up behind them to prevent the more aggressive of the press launches from entering their compound area. They began the task of offloading the sails and equipment.

A quarter of an hour later Vagir was supervising the lifting of the two boats out of the water for a thorough checking and overhaul. The navigation lights were removed, the instruments and gear examined for damage in transit.

Onshore, Illich turned to study the bay. The challengers were still battling it out in pairs, each individual match race proceeding round the course half an hour behind the others. It was a course of approximately two hours, so there were always several pairs of boats on the course. Spread around the shore were the bases of the thirty-one challenging syndicates. The entire shoreside was a hive of activity. Some boats were being raised from the water, others were being lowered. In a nearby compound the British were testing the shape of a newly cut sail on a land mast. Launches and spectator craft ploughed backwards and forwards. At least a dozen helicopters and light aircraft, several carrying television cameras, hovered or flew above the course. It was a strange sight, no less so because it was situated in Russia. Along one shoreline, the horizon was dense with spectators. On this, a preliminary day, thousands had come to see the great yachts duelling in the bay.

'What do you think?' said Jim Shaw.

Illich could only shrug in reply. There was no answer that could describe the scene. It was eerie.

Illich studied the encampments more closely. About half a mile away, beneath a huge, fluttering Stars and Stripes, was the American *Eagle* syndicate. Several sleek power launches were drawn up in its private marina, strange capitalist sculptures, decked like wedding cakes. The hulls of no less than three individual racing yachts had been hauled up in in front of its huge white sheds. In a dome at the centre was a strange piece of equipment, a surveillance radar or sensor which provided detailed information on all the events in the bay.

It was shortly before eight o'clock. Early evening shadows were extending eastwards across the bay. They were themselves in shadow. The last of the two pairs racing that day was beating slowly to the finish line about two miles offshore.

Jim saw it first.

Before its sound reached them he pointed to the dark shape flashing along the shore. It was coming towards them fast, demonstrating its high speed. Soon it was overhead, its thundering blades producing an almost numinous shadow. The dark armoured glass threw off glints from the setting sun. Illich could see the lens of the remote control camera turning this way and that. He could make out only with difficulty the vague shape of the pilot and, behind him, the passenger. Only once, when the sun struck the side of the darkened armoured glass, he caught a glimpse of the passenger's face, and it seemed that for a brief moment he recognized, in a rhomboid shape of light, the heavy, angular features of Major-General Vorolov. Then the helicopter dipped its head and made off along the coastline, disappearing at remarkable speed.

'I knew this place was missing something,' Jim Shaw observed drily. 'Now I feel at home.'

Fifty-Five

It took two precious days fully to prepare the boats again for sailing.

But the crew and the support groups settled down well. Sailors and their technicians are travellers, as used as nomadic tribes to moving their location. Apart from their high degree of fitness, there were other resemblances to nomadic hunters. There was something ancient and primitively satisfying in belonging to a small group pitted against other groups. The sense of isolation only heightened this community.

President Aegu visited them on the second day. His

helicopter, with the Estonian tricolour emblazoned on its side, landed on an open space on the shorefront. Aegu emerged from beneath its drooping blades into the brisk sunlight of midmorning. They had begun their physical training, and had to move aside to give the helicopter space to land.

Aegu shook hands with Illich, Shaw, the sailors who had lined up to greet him. Standing with his arms hanging beside his short, bear-like body, he delivered a brief, impromptu address, pledging all support necessary from Estonia.

'A private word with you, *tovarich*,' he said to Illich afterwards. They walked over to the little office that had been partitioned off for Illich. Aegu seemed preoccupied. When Illich had closed the door, Aegu sat down heavily in the chair in the corner and was silent for several seconds. Finally he said: 'Pridilenko is dead.'

Illich was speechless. He leaned against the door. A sharp sense of loss invaded him. He had never known Pridilenko well, but he admired him.

'How?'

'A driving accident.'

Aegu remained slumped in the chair. Outside Illich could hear one of his two security guards move restlessly. Not far away from the open window was a flagpole on which the Estonian flag flapped like an unquiet sail.

Several things occurred to Illich. The casualties per driver in Russia are one of the highest in the world. The fears that rose in his mind were surely groundless. It was feasible that he had died as described.

Aegu said, voicing his own thoughts: 'They drive like gangsters, of course, the Moscow *vlasti*. The chauffeurs of the senior ones take pride in moving fast. He was crossing Kuznetsov Road in his Chaika when a supply lorry struck his car from the side and crushed it against a building. His own chauffeur was killed immediately. Pridilenko died in the ambulance on the way to the hospital. The

275

driver of the lorry, who was also injured by the way, claimed that the brake pedal had failed.'

'Was there an investigation?'

'Yes. And it seemed the man was telling the truth.'

Illich voiced his fear directly. 'But you think it might not be an accident?'

'I pulled strings to get someone to look over the case. Several coincidences. The first on the scene were several officers of the GRU. A group of four in plainclothes were passing by in a Volga. They must have been almost on the site of the accident. Secondly, in the Moscow district a traffic accident, even a bad one, is a matter for the militia. Yet the GRU men stepped in and took over. Their zeal was commendable. Apart from calling an ambulance for Pridilenko and his chauffeur – the normal contribution of a citizen to another in distress – they set up a roadblock to divert the traffic, and arranged for the truck to be towed away.'

'Who checked the brake cable?'

'Another coincidence. You would think the truck would be towed away to a local garage, or if there were suspicion, to the militia offices. But no, the truck was taken to an Army vehicle centre for checking.'

'They issued the report confirming the broken cable?'

'Yes.'

Illich felt his palms sweat. He leaned back against the closed door.

'What do you think?' Aegu asked.

It was not worth a reply, and Aegu was not expecting it. They thought the same thing. Beneath the apparently accidental surface detail, there was the heavy print of the Army. It was the lack of subtlety that was so shocking, the sign of an organization so sure of itself that it hardly needed to cover its tracks.

'Pridilenko was a powerful man . . .' Illich began. It was strange talking about him in the past. Pridilenko was one of those constants who he could not believe would simply cease to exist.

'And you think that his colleagues would protect him?' Aegu asked matter-of-factly. 'Pridilenko was a gladiator, a circus performer. When someone like that goes, it is not always in your interest to question the matter too closely. In these democratic days the civil authorities live in fear of scandal. To attempt to find out who is responsible is to show one's own position, to court unwelcome publicity.'

'But if there is evidence he was assassinated? And from the details of the case, it seems that the Army is implicated in it.'

'Perhaps, perhaps not,' Aegu said. 'Do you know how the politicians regard the Army? I will tell you. The Army is like a big, powerful watchdog, one which occasionally harms a passer by. It is part of the nature of the animal. Sharp words are spoken behind the scenes. Reprimands are issued, threats are made. Perhaps a senior subordinate is removed here or there as a cautionary warning. But the dog is necessary to its owner. Without him he cannot sleep at night. After a while all returns to normal.'

Illich could not hide his shock. Aegu watched him without amusement.

'The politicians condone this type of behaviour?'

'Indirectly. It mustn't get out of hand, of course. But what else can one do? Hold an investigation into the Army and risk losing your ally? Show the population a public split between themselves and their protector?'

'But if they suspect . . .?'

'So?' Aegu asked. 'And where does one point one's finger? It would be a very senior figure who authorized such a matter. Imagine conducting a normal criminal investigation, working from the crime outwards to the suspect, establishing a chain of cause and effect. From the lorry driver to the GRU to that hypothetical senior figure who ordered the "accident" is an impossible number of links. In that chain, subordinates would be sacrificed. One would never find him. And remember, these days the authorities are forced to prove the connection in a court of law.'

'But surely that is possible.'

Aegu had not ceased to smoke between sentences. Now he paused while he brought out a fresh cigarette, tapped it on the packet, lit it. 'Let us assume the full panoply of judicial investigation in a democratic state. How successful was the investigation into the assassination of President Kennedy. How successful, even now, in disinterring the vested interests that were involved? A couple of gunmen were tried, but they were merely pawns. Do you think that Russia, with its fledgling democratic institutions, its nervous judiciary, is capable of matching even that investigation?'

'What alternative is there?'

Aegu leaned back in his chair.

'You don't understand. In a reformist, former Communist state, the politicians are frightened. They are nervous at the increasing power of the people. They need the Army more than ever in case of civil disorder. The populace is the big grey wolf at the door. And the Army? Do you think it respects politicians who have lost the will to command? As the power of politicians decreases, so the restlessness of the Army grows. Pridilenko understood that more than anyone. That was why it was he who was in the forefront of the fight to control the Army. It was logical,' Aegu concluded simply, stubbing out his cigarette 'that the Army should seek to remove him.'

Somehow, offloading the details of the case seemed to release a tension in Aegu. It was like the presumed cathartic effect of discussing a neurosis. Now he reached into his pocket and felt for the cigarette packet. It was empty.

'Comrade,' Aegu said. 'Be so kind as to ask one of my men for a fresh packet of cigarettes.'

Illich opened the door. One of the men leaned against the partition wall. He was almost preternaturally relaxed, but his cold eyes studied Illich.

'Comrade Aegu has run out of cigarettes.'

The man smiled and came forward. He was the slightly smaller one of the two bodyguards, the older one. He approached with his comical penguin's walk. Withdrawing from his bulging inner coat pocket a packet of Duzba cigarettes, he handed it to Illich. Illich, an officer for most of his adult life, and used to judging men, looked casually into this man's eyes. Perhaps, he reflected, Pridilenko should have had a couple of bodyguards like this while the Army hunted him like a predator in the dark.

'Thank you, Comrade.' The man walked several yards away and leaned against the partition.

Inside again, with the door closed once more, Aegu extracted a cigarette and lit it. He changed the subject.

'You were impressed with the send-off from Tallinn?'

If it had not been for his thoughts about Pridilenko, Illich would have smiled.

'A precaution,' Aegu said.

'Precaution?'

'Yes.'

'The adversary, if I may call him that, is not averse to action of a drastic nature if he believes his victim is isolated. Of course,' Aegu said, 'we know that the authorities will be wholly fair in their treatment of the races. Even so, it is worth making clear that any hint of unfair treatment will be treated as an outrage by the entire Estonian population, if you understand me, and that this in turn would exacerbate an already delicate political position. The adversary is determined. But in the case of whole populations, he is somewhat more cautious than he is in the case of individuals.'

Aegu drew on his cigarette, exhaling smoke in the shape of a palm leaf, with curling fronds.

Illich heard a noise, a slight scraping, outside the window. Aegu watched his face freeze. Illich walked to the window and looked out. But it was only the second bodyguard. It explained his absence from the outside corridor. The two guards had moved, almost by intuition, to the two points of egress from the little office, the door and the window, and had taken up their positions accordingly, with the instincts of animals.

Aegu watched him return to his chair.

The ashtray was already full. Aegu squeezed the end of the cigarette between thumb and forefinger, another very Russian gesture. It reminded Illich of someone else . . . of Vorolov. Two men of similar type, professionals, but on different sides . . .

Aegu stood up.

'There is no harm in considering the unthinkable, and taking reasonable precautions. But one should not become obsessed.' He was his old, affable self again. He shook hands with Illich.

'Goodbye, *tovarich*. We must honour Pridilenko each in our own way. Good luck with the racing. No need to accompany me to the helicopter.'

Illich heard his receding footsteps, followed by the almost noiseless pad of the two bodyguards.

Fifty-Six

The next two weeks were frenetic with preparation.

Vagir once again was in full charge of the shore support, repair, overhaul. At all hours in the day there was some shift at work. The sailmakers worked through the night, only leaving their sodium-lit loft for an occasional smoke in the velvet darkness. The crew's sleep was lulled by the thump of the generator supplying extra power to the laser sail-cutting machine. In the early morning, at five, with the white dawn breaking and the water generally calm, a repair crew would burnish the underwater sections of both boats.

Because the bay was congested during the day, Illich decided to continue the practice of sailing early in the morning. At six the two boats were launched, at six-thirty the crew were assembled, and the towing launches would haul them out into the early morning sunlight.

Now that Jim Shaw was on *Novy Mir*, Gundar Arlof took the second boat. He was still pale and underweight from his hospitalization, but his mind and hands had not lost their touch. The second crew had been welded into a formidable force by Jim Shaw, and *Novy Mir*'s crew-work had to be flawless to beat them.

They made sure, however, that the subterfuge that the new boat was no faster than *Leningrad* was perpetuated by allowing her to win at least one race every day. By nine-thirty, when the other boats were beginning to emerge on the water, they had completed their main sailing practice.

They ate a late breakfast, debriefed the race, then did physical exercises until the midday meal. At three the two crews completed their overhaul.

The winds seemed to freshen in the afternoon, the effect of the heated land mass, and they practised later in the afternoon, at about four. It was important to practise in the fullest range of wind conditions. Between these activities they gathered intelligence about their opponents.

After the rigours of their early morning sailing practice, Illich and Shaw scanned the papers at breakfast each morning for amusement rather than edification. Almost every day there was a fresh rumour of some some newly-invented technology which would sweep aside all others – an underwater coating which was almost frictionless, an advanced sail-cloth which was half the weight of all rivals and which produced astonishingly precise and consistent shapes, and the perennial favourite – a keel of such beautiful and diabolical shape that it would devastate all opposition.

The great American yacht designer, Olin Stephens, who had dominated racing yacht design in the middle twentieth century, had once been asked what made his boats so fast. He had replied, 'Details; tiny grains of sand'. It was the level of overall preparation which was nearly always dominant, popular myths nothwithstanding.

By now, a clear pattern of dominance had been established amongst the challengers. Sailing is a sport with a long history, and there were four groups who, perhaps somewhat predictably, were showing formidable form; the Americans, Germans, British and New Zealanders. The French showed characteristic flashes of brilliance and the Japanese, exceptionally well organized, did not yet have the tradition to supply human talent in depth. Much play was being made in the press of the Japanese winchgrinders, two champion Sumo wrestlers who were able to put extraordinary bursts of power into their coffeegrinders.

The Americans were easily dominant. They had not lost a single race in the selection trials – an astonishing run of thirty-four wins. The Germans were their most significant opponents. The British syndicate was reckoned to have some of the best talent in the competition, but (so the press averred) their challenge had started late, underfunded, and was only now starting to hit its stride. The New Zealanders showed their characteristic panache and organization. Despite their tiny population, they had dominated sailing in its major forms in the past decade. Now it was only the sheer weight of technology in the other groups which had forced them out of their accustomed place at the centre.

It was widely agreed that the American dominance was due to professionalism and weight of effort. In the history of the sport, this had nearly always been the critical factor, just as weight of firepower decides most battles. The press loved stories of individual brilliance, but in the end it was the comprehensive nature of the effort which triumphed. The media referred to classic exceptions in the history of the sport. For example, the great win of *Australia II* in 1983, breaking 132 years of American supremacy in the event, was popularly thought to be due to a keel of mythical superiority. But they could just as easily, and perhaps with more reason, have pointed to the underlying statistics. In the long era of US dominance, the number of defending boats competing for the right to defend always exceeded the number of challengers – the latter almost always a single, lone yacht. The first time that the number of challenging syndicates exceeded the number of defence syndicates (seven to three respectively) was in 1983, the year of *Australia II*'s classic victory. The Australian victory was the sharp end of a huge and sustained challenging effort. Overall professionalism won the day. The famous winged keel (according to this argument at least) was a mere symptom of a comprehensive technological effort. In other respects the *Australia II* campaign was superior. It had been the crowning effort of three previous challenges over a twelve-year period. It carried the exclusive services of the greatest sailmaker of the time, Tom Schnackenberg. Its helmsman and crew surpassed all other previous challengers in training. And the fight with six other challenging syndicates sharpened its teeth for the final affray.

When Illich and Jim Shaw chortled over the marvels of technology, the devastating inventions that were sprung daily in the press, their cynicism had a certain justification. Popular history tends towards the anecdotal. But Illich had studied America's Cup history as closely as any general studied military strategy. When he looked out over the water at the challenger elimination races between no less than thirty-one national syndicates, he knew that overwhelming weight of firepower lay with the challengers. The winner of those races would be in a position which was almost unassailable.

Fifty-Seven

It was Pridilenko's death, and its threatening shadows, that sent Illich into his final tunnel of concentration.

The Russian base was round the headland, in a well-secluded position with fifty foot cliffs on one side and the sea on another. A security fence, patrolled by military police and guard dogs, had been erected along the lip of the cliff, so that it was impossible to look over and down into the camp. The Russians, like the Americans, reputedly had three racing yachts in full commission. Illich had heard that Pilnyak had taken to heart his own admonitions about the importance of step-by-step advances, changing only one feature at a time, proceeding cautiously to check all possible errors in assumptions.

Since Illich's departure, the official Russian defence had been scaled up extensively. It was as if the Army, in recovering from the wound of his leaving, had massively reinforced the tissue of its structure. It had also protected itself with secrecy. But secrecy, Illich knew, is a double-edged weapon. Secrecy limits communication in both directions. If the Russian camp had a flaw, it would be in the lost opportunities of learning by direct contact with the outside world. By contrast, Shaw had come in to help the Estonians, and had sharpened them immeasurably. In his rare reflective moments, Illich had wondered what the military would think of an American, a member of the former *glavnyi vrag*, the main enemy, as his prime ally. Perhaps there had been a few overloaded circuits in the higher command . . .

Returning from their early morning practice sail, they saw the two practising Russian yachts emerge from behind the headland, but their protective screen of patrol vessels would permit no close inspection. What was clear was that the chosen defence contender was *Kirov*. This was the most interesting information. It was clear that, rumours notwithstanding, the Russian camp had produced no revolutionary hulls which were clearly superior to their flagship. The other hulls which had been built were used merely as trial horses, to sharpen *Kirov*.

Their own tight security had at least held off the interest of the press. Effectively they had been written off as significant competitors. The huge material resources poured into the other syndicates, combined with the love of the media for high technology stories, had suggested to nearly all that the Estonian challenge was a mere gesture. Their late start, small population, and their low profile had all played their part.

It was helpful to them in the early stages. They attracted less attention than the other syndicates, and were able to practise quietly on their early morning training races without gross intrusion. It was only in the final four days before the forthcoming defender trials against *Kirov*, that a veteran reporter from the British *Independent* newspaper, John Herrick, identified Jim Shaw as a permanent part of the afterguard of *Novy Mir*.

If nothing else, the occasion of his identification caused Jim Shaw some amusement. They had just finished their early morning practice races and were returning to dock. The light offshore breeze had died completely. A sun-filled silence extended across the bay. The crew of *Novy Mir* were exhausted from two hours of tacking practice with *Leningrad*. They waited patiently for the towboats to pick up the buoys which they laid down for their practices. A small inflatable dinghy with outboard, which had been idling inshore several hundred yards away, surged forward suddenly through the screen of two support launches, scattering a group of floating seagulls. Kicking up a swift, curving wake, it powered towards *Novy Mir*. The two support launches gave quick pursuit, but no power on earth will hold back a journalist on the scent of a good story. Cutting its engines twenty feet out, the inflatable coasted in gently against the hull. Jim Shaw, checking the record of speed against wind strengths on the computer VDU, looked up into the beady, amused black eyes of the ace reporter. A large, grizzled hand was extended towards him. An English voice mellowed by innumerable pints of Guinness, honed to a fine, gravelly perfection by countless smoke-filled bar-room discussions, greeted Jim Shaw with the words 'Dr Livingstone, I presume.'

After a few seconds of silence, Shaw removed his dark glasses. 'John,' he said, 'you owe me two pints of Guinness.'

'One and a half, Jim,' Herrick replied curtly. There was protocol to be observed here. 'The other half if you beat *Kirov*.'

The ace reporter fired up his outboard engine and took off, neatly dodging the incoming, pursuing launch.

'A friend?' asked Illich.

'You could say that,' Shaw replied ruefully.

Herrick's article 'RENEGADE YANKEE' in the *Independent* began:

Imagine, if you will, approaching one of the defender candidates for the America's Cup, the green-hulled Novy Mir, *skippered by the great Ivan Illich, and seeing, in the stern, the face of an old American friend. As I peered over the topsides, Jim Shaw stared back through his dark glasses. For several seconds I experienced a sensation wholly new to me: I was lost for words.*

Jim Shaw had to laugh at that.

But media attention now became ferocious. That evening, the camp perimeters were crowded with press photographers recording every aspect of the camp's activities which was carried out in the open. Those who came and left the entrance were besieged by reporters with microphones and notepads. The following day, at their early morning practices, there were so many press boats hovering at the entrance that they were forced to abandon the practice session and return to their enclosed dock until mid-morning, when the security launches were once again in operation, and they were able to practice behind a screen of boats. Even so, occasional sorties by press boats prevented them from completing races. They resigned themselves for the last few days to merely tuning. There was, however, one sure advantage in their fragmented pattern. It was easy to preserve the myth that, of the two boats, there was no great difference between them, even that *Leningrad* was marginally faster.

In their final preparations, the sudden media hysteria precipitated by public knowledge of Shaw's inclusion only bothered them on the practice course. But there was one report that was more than mere speculation. It consisted of a quote on the inclusion of Jim Shaw on the Estonian boat from John Ericson the Third. The report was headed: 'TRAITOR ACCUSATION':

In an interview yesterday the skipper of the America's Cup Challenger, John Ericson, accused Jim Shaw, the loser of the America's Cup in 2001, of behaving as a traitor by joining the Estonian syndicate. Asked what he meant by his accusation, Ericson replied: 'You only have to look at his behaviour. Last time round he deliberately lost to the Russians. This time round he actually joined them.' Later in the interview, Ericson said it was well known that Shaw's father, Samuel Shaw, a Maine fisherman, was a former communist and agitator. John Ericson hinted that Shaw's selection in the previous America's Cup, during which John Ericson had been dropped, was a conspiracy.

In the interview, it was suggested to Ericson that his family firm, Ericson Traction, of which he was a senior Vice-President, was currently making profits out of selling computer software to Russia under the new 'open policies' scheme. Wasn't that collaborating with the Russians too? John Ericson's reply was that that was 'totally unrelated'.

Jim Shaw put down the paper. Maria watched him stand up and walk outside. Only she knew how angry he was.

Illich was largely untouched by the sudden increase in news coverage. In the last two days he was up at six in the morning with the crew preparing the two boats. Inevitably, the best equipment was now being concentrated on *Novy Mir*. Certain sails which were inexplicably fast now moved across into *Novy Mir*'s reserve wardrobe. All sheets and blocks on both boats were overhauled and replaced.

Illich and Shaw decided to allow a lay day the following day, a Wednesday, so that the crew could husband its energies. It was a somewhat nervous holiday. Some of the crew took part in light games, table tennis, an impromptu version of football. Others read or wrote letters. There was no contact with the outside. In the evening, Illich went into final conclave with Shaw over tactics. At the communal supper that evening, following Illich's permission, Prem stood up and read in the original Russian from an *Izvestia* article, headed 'RAGAMUFFIN GROUP MAKES FINAL PREPARATIONS'.

While the official Russian Defence makes its preparations for the defence races in the America's Cup, the Estonian Challenge, a renegade group which broke away from the united original Defence camp, is also preparing. Consisting of dissident elements, the group began its dubious existence by abducting the yacht Leningrad *from the Russian camp. Protected by Estonian security, the group has been granted the right to challenge. Experts believe it has little chance of success, despite the past record of its helmsman, Ivan Illich. In the view of the authorities, the group reinforced its pariah status by taking on the American helmsman Jim Shaw, who lost in the last America's Cup against the overwhelming Russian challenge.*

Despite the liberalization of the news media, the piece incorporated echoes right out of the Stalinist past. The two long tables burst into loud applause. There were calls for encores. Prem bowed, but modestly refused.

About twenty minutes later the lights went out. The entire camp electricity supply had failed. Out of the darkness Prem said, misquoting Lenin:

'Communism equals the power of the masses plus electrification.'

There was more laughter, though it had an uneasy edge. Out of their windows they could see the lights of the other camps were unaffected. It was clearly a very selective power failure.

Vagir and several of his men stood up and made their careful way out of the darkened room, leaving the door open to the welcome evening breeze. There were odd, eerie flashes of light like summer lightning, but it was the press photographers firing flashlights through the perimeter fences. A few minutes later they could hear, like a heartbeat, the sound of the reserve generator which Vagir had had the foresight to install a month earlier. The lights flickered and returned.

That night the sailcutters left the meal early so that they could use their laser cutting machines to make the final, precise adjustments to *Novy Mir*'s sail wardrobe.

Fifty-Eight

The breeze increased through the night. A low pressure system was moving east from the Atlantic. When they were woken up by their alarms at six the following morning, it was rattling the windows. They could hear it during the briefing called at six-thirty.

Illich addressed the crew. He would have liked to tell

them that, with age, his physical nervousness before the start had decreased. But if they could see his hands behind his back, the sweat dripping from his palms, and the flutter of his fingers if he tried to hold them steady, they would know otherwise. He did his best to maintain an impression of calm, and went through the procedures of the briefing like any other day.

They ate a good breakfast. It was customary for skippers to address their crews about the importance of the day, but he preferred to let his crew sink into their own thoughts. To him at least, the more nervousness that could be expended prior to the match, the better. And a crew too keyed up could make mistakes.

Some protocol was called for, however. Though his stomach seemed to have shrunk to a minus quantity, he ate a hearty meal with apparent relish. Shaw and Prem followed his example. As an act of bravado, he even called for a second helping. Outside the wind howled its baleful appreciation. He wondered idly if any of the crew would feel seasick. But the motion of a tuned yacht, moving fast, was not the queasy lurch of a slow-moving ferry or a yacht hove-to. Even in big seas, it was a purposeful glide, steadied by the stability of motion, the bows dealing crisply with the swells.

At nine-fifteen they were towed out of the harbour and into the sharp, five-foot seas, the other towboat at station on port side, the tender to starboard. Already the bay was crowded with launches and spectator craft. Many had travelled the previous days from Estonia. Two Army patrol vessels took up station ahead and astern. Illich, remembering the last contact with such a vessel, felt a trace of discomfort. Above them, more than a dozen helicopters hovered. Several hundred feet above them in turn, a number of light aircraft wheeled.

Another convoy was pulling out from the shore. At first, only the single tall mast protruding from the ranks of patrol vessels indicated that there was a sailing yacht at its centre.

Traditionally, the shepherding course patrol vessels had difficulty holding back spectator craft. But today the Army patrol vessels, their machine-guns mounted on the foredecks, were forbidding enough to cow such enthusiasm.

The two convoys slowly converged on the race course. Now they could easily see the huge Russian battleflag of white, blue and red on *Kirov*'s lower backstay.

As befits a contender for the Soviet defence, they carried their own red flag on a traditional ensign post at the stern.

When they were certain that *Kirov* could see them, Illich called forward to Prem and Gir. On *Novy Mir*'s deck they attached the main halyard to a twenty-foot Estonian tricolour and hauled it up. It coruscated in the breeze, snapping and thundering like a loose sail, dwarfing their own Russian flag.

The two yachts were parallel now, several hundred yards apart, their towboats carrying only enough way to hold them into wind.

This was the most difficult and nerve-racking time; relative inactivity while the blood sang with adrenalin, and the stomach churned in its own fear. No one was exempt. Each member of the crew knew of the condition of the others and was only concerned that, in his own case, it did not show too obviously. For ten minutes they checked equipment.

Jim Shaw read out the numbers: 'Wind twenty-five knots, steady, thirty-five degrees. Mild bias to port, almost nothing in it.'

'Sidestay tension twenty thousand kilograms,' Brod informed him.

'Higher,' Illich ordered: 'In this wind, take it to twenty two.'

On *Kirov* their superior instrumentation, based on a laser rangefinder, would be feeding into a *Chel* computer data on the wind speed and direction changes all around the course.

'Committee boat informs us course set,' Brod informed him. 'Twenty minutes to ten-minute gun.'

'Raise mainsail,' shouted Illich. The tiers were released

and the folds of their heavy air mainsail slid to the deck. Stephan Migdal and Herman Maask hauled up the main in quick, savage loops. When it was almost at the top of the mast, Illich raised his arm, palm forward, to signal that the bow rope should be cast off. For a few seconds they were in irons, while the main halyard was tightened to its appropriate tension. It was important not to let the sail flog needlessly. They were sliding backwards now. Illich reversed the helm so that the bow would pay off to starboard. About ten seconds later the mainsail filled, the boat heeled, and they felt a surge of forward power.

'Looking good,' said Shaw of the heavy main.

Illich was relieved. It was a sail with which he was less familiar. Twenty-five knots was an unusual wind strength, and their heavy weather mainsails were, for this reason, only occasionally used. But he had to agree with Shaw. Prem was putting it into good shape, tightening an outhaul here, applying more kicker tension there, changing mainsheet tension, moving the boom up and down the slide.

Out of the corner of his eye he could see *Kirov* raising mainsail and genoa simultaneously, her bow-rope rising in the air like a snake as it was cast off. Illich shouted: 'Hoist genoa.'

Short green seas marched towards them, a proliferation of white horses. Half-powered, under mainsail alone, their motion over the seas was slow, almost ponderous. But when the genoa was up and the winchgrinders powered in the sheet, *Novy Mir* seemed to come alive.

'Seven two, seven three, seven five,' Brod said.

The boat was starting to feel well strung, snapping through crests. The difference between a tuned yacht and an untuned yacht was that the untuned boat seemed passive, reacting to the swells, whereas the tuned yacht gave the impression of being active, imposing its own sliding motion on the seas. Every few seconds their bow exploded a crest and they were dowsed with stinging spray.

'Eight five,' Brod called: 'Eight five, eight four.'

'Twelve minutes before the ten-minute gun,' said Jim.

'Let's tune up on starboard.'

They tacked.

Abeam of them they could see *Kirov's* red hull slicing the waves.

Jim Shaw was watching the other boat, saying nothing, running his tactician's eye over the opposition. Illich was grateful for his silence while he and Prem and the port genoa trimmer sorted out the final windward tune.

'Eight four,' Brod said. 'Eight four.'

'Time?' asked Illich.

'Two minutes twenty-three.'

'Ease sheets,' Illich ordered.

They swung round in a slow loop, so that Brod could study boatspeed against the mean of the numbers in the computer. It did not give an accurate answer on final tune, but one could use it to tell if anything was drastically wrong.

'The numbers are good,' commented Brod.

On a reach in twenty-five knots, even under two sails, they were touching just under thirteen knots. A flat white wake boiled out behind them. Brod counted down the seconds to the ten-minute gun.

'Eleven, ten, nine, eight. . .'

The crew were working hard to raise speed, to spring into the starting box fast.

'Four, three, two, one. . .'

A puff of smoke from the starting launch, then the boom of the starting cannon carried suddenly loud on the wind.

Kirov was powering towards them, on a ramming course, her mast and sails huge, her bow sending two finely wrought plumes back almost level with her mast.

Now speed was close to fifteen knots. *Kirov* was doing the same. Their combined approach speed was a devastating thirty knots.

Kirov changed course two degrees downwind, a sharp, precise change in heading. Illich, almost automatically, prepared to turn upwind, steadied himself for the tack, when *Kirov* suddenly swung upwind. It threw Illich momentarily off balance. Now they were almost abreast, and *Kirov* was sweeping into a savage turn, her winches screaming, her huge winchgrinders pounding.

It was a time for rapid judgement. Pilnyak had caught him off guard. If he closed with them now he would be a fraction of a second behind *Kirov* in the turn. He steeled himself.

'Keep on course,' Illich shouted. 'Full power.'

'Jesus,' he heard Jim Shaw breathe behind him.

Kirov cut across their wake like an angry shark. But they were still driving at just under fifteen knots, and *Kirov*, coming through the wind, had slowed to eight. Their speed would take them outside *Kirov*'s range. Now Pilnyak would be forced laboriously to pick up acceleration. *Kirov*'s genoa thundered as it came through the wind, settled on the new tack, bore away after them in pursuit, as the crew frantically tried to regain speed.

'Bearing away!' shouted Illich. Downwind, the speed came down to thirteen knots. They gybed with a sudden explosion of the boom, and came out the other side on a reach, a touch above twelve knots.

'Twelve two, twelve three,' Brod said.

They were slicing past each other again, looking for one another's jugular. Now *Novy Mir* held a two-knot advantage in speed. Illich swung up to engage. But Pilnyak would not be drawn into a close turn, for precisely that reason. Instead *Kirov* was picking up acceleration. Illich, his mind full of changing patterns of speed, shouted: 'Bearing away.'

He spun the boat downwind.

'Gybe!'

The boom thundered across on its rails.

'Power reach,' roared Illich above the clattering winches.

The trap was sprung. They were bow to *Kirov*'s stern, less than two lengths away, the same speed, in the pole position. *Kirov* wheeled upwind to try to shake them off, but as Illich

294

swung to cut her off, Brod was roaring at *Kirov* for right of way.

'Got them,' Shaw breathed out. He had never seen anything like it. It was based on timings of a fraction of a second, no, nanoseconds.

The winchgrinders were powering up in the lulls, the trimmers were easing in the gusts, calling again for power in the lulls, as the two boats blasted along on a square reach.

They were driving *Kirov* away from the line, and while *Kirov* was within the few lengths of close engagement there was nothing she could do about it. Following boat exercised right of way.

For fully four minutes they drove *Kirov* away from the line, choosing their moment to swing suddenly and break back for the line.

'Gybe!' shouted Illich. By gybing they would emerge on the reciprocal course with greater speed than if they tacked.

It was a close reach back to the starting line. The starting gun went when they were still two minutes away, but that meant nothing. All that mattered was that they were ahead of *Kirov*.

They crossed the start line five lengths ahead.

'Cover?' Illich asked Shaw.

Pilnyak tacked away behind them to get out of their dirty wind.

They had discussed this over the past few days. To cover the other boat, placing yourself between him and the wind, was classic match-racing tactics. It was safe. It required a decision now.

'No,' Shaw said.

'I agree.'

So they let *Kirov* escape, and would deal with her on pure speed.

'Eight four,' Brod said. 'Rising slowly. Eight five.' The crew settled in. *Novy Mir* was heeled in the gusts, but instead of unbalancing, she struck more powerfully through the swells. The crew, sensing her power, were studies of concentration, easing a sheet here, tightening a leech line there. They squeezed speed.

'Eight six,' Brod called. 'Eight seven.'

Match-racing was strange. One moment you were toe-to-toe with the adversary, hardly able to hear your own shouts above his shouts inside the wail of tortured metal and the scream of his winches louder than your own. Thirty seconds later you were on your own, like monks at prayer, trying to ease tiny fractions of speed, and the only sound was the foam of the wake uncombing behind you.

'Eight eight,' Brod said. They could have been balanced on air, the figure was so magical. 'Wind direction steady, within two degrees.'

'*Kirov* is tacking,' Shaw informed Illich.

The other boat was spooked.

'Let's keep on another minute,' Shaw said.

A savage gust hit them. Illich could feel its blow through the boat, like a boxer taking the punch.

Heeled to the gunwales, *Novy Mir* was still balanced.

'Eight eight,' Brod said 'Eight nine.'

Now the boat seemed truly to be imposing its will on the seas, moving forward in a slow glide, pulverizing stray crests.

The gust reduced.

'Eight seven. Eight six. Wind is veering five degrees.'

'Tack,' shouted Illich.

They came through fast. The subdued thunder of the genoa quietened to nothing as the sheets were tightened in.

They had almost forgotten *Kirov*. It took Illich a fraction of a second to assess the situation. *Kirov* was between twelve and fifteen boat lengths behind. They crossed ahead of her and tacked again for the mark, rounding a minute and twenty seconds up.

On the downwind leg the positions were maintained, *Kirov* reducing the lead marginally by six seconds. On the second upwind leg they increased their lead by another fifty seconds, and on the final upwind leg they crossed the line three minutes fifteen seconds up.

Genoa down, idling under mainsail, they watched *Kirov* slice across the line behind them, while more than a hundred small Estonian craft charged towards them with blaring claxons over the turbulent waters of the bay.

Fifty-Nine

After the race, the first person to step aboard *Novy Mir* was President Vajnen Aegu. Illich had not noticed that, amongst the ubiquitous launches, there was one which bore the official Estonian insignia. The pilot of the launch placed the bow within a foot of the coasting *Novy Mir*, leaving not a scratch on the paintwork, and the square figure of Aegu stepped aboard.

On land his short, bowed legs gave him a slightly grotesque aspect in motion. On a vessel, he had a seaman's gait. He came towards Illich now with a smile which seemed almost as wide as his shoulders, and shook Illich's hand in his square paw until Illich felt numbness rising towards his wrist.

It was the first time Illich had seen Aegu rendered speechless with enthusiasm. It was eloquent testament to his emotion.

'We showed them today, *tovarich*.' Aegu tried to speak further, but he seemed to stumble and his voice was whipped away by the rising wind. He gathered himself and spoke again.

'It does not matter if you do not win a single further race. This is a triumph for our country.'

'You remember the American, Jim Shaw,' Illich said.

Shaw too was subjected to the powerful handshake.

The visit was remarkably brief. Aegu's launch hovered. Illich could see the faces of his two security men through the dark windows of the bridgedeck, watching blankly. The bow of the launch was edged forward again, with perfect positioning, within a few inches of *Novy Mir*'s topside. Aegu stepped back on board.

The course patrol vessels closed in to form a bastion against the gathering crowds of press and spectator launches. *Novy Mir* downed mainsail and was towed towards the shore. A pale sun, elusive during most of the race, now shone brightly on the wavecrests. They hoisted again the Russian flag at their stern and, from the backstay, the Estonian tricolour, which thundered above them like a great, loose sail.

Sixty

The following day, John Herrick's article in the British *Independent* ran:

Novy Mir, *the rival defender from Estonia, considered by experts to be an outsider, crushed the 'official' Russian yacht* Kirov *today. At the start of the race, the green-hulled Estonian yacht unfurled a huge Estonian tricolour from its backstay, and one could almost feel the tension between the two competitors as their respective crews surveyed each other across the three hundred yards of sea separating them.*

More than water separates the two teams. Rumours circulated among the sailing fraternity that tensions between the two camps started when Ivan Illich broke away from the official Army camp and, with government support from Estonia, set up a training compound on the remote island of Khiuma, off the Western seaboard of Estonia. The removal of the Leningrad from the Russian camp had a bizarre flavour of violence. The Army authorities fired upon Illich while he was in the process of reclaiming the former successful challenger, officially owned by the Estonian Trade Delegation. A gun-battle ensued, with casualties on both sides.

Since then, the Army authorities poured resources into their own camp in order to counter the 'upstart' Illich. They must have been further annoyed when Illich asked the American helmsman Jim Shaw to join him as training helmsman. Jim Shaw is the enigmatic American who lost the last America's Cup, turning away at the final mark. Theories abounded about that extraordinary episode, but Shaw has kept quiet about it ever since. Until he joined Illich's Estonian group, Shaw was living the life of a recluse on a smallholding in Maine.

I was the first to report to you that Jim Shaw is actually on board the Estonian yacht as tactician. Whatever Shaw may have contributed to the honing of Illich's effort (and I understand it was considerable), the final contribution must remain conjecture. Certainly today Novy Mir fell on Kirov like a bird of prey. In a brilliantly timed manoeuvre, Illich obtained the dominant or 'pole' position within the first five minutes of the pre-start manoeuvres. Having used this to cross the start line well ahead, he arrogantly abandoned close cover of the opponent and used superior speed and open water to widen the lead at the weather mark. In this heavy weather at least, it was no contest. The crew-work on Novy Mir appeared flawless. Estonians have a strong, seagoing tradition, and today's demonstration set a marker for the finals against the other challengers, among whom the American yacht is dominant.

The New York Times was more clipped. Its small headline was TWO RIVALS COMBINE.

The former America's Cup helmsman Jim Shaw, who lost to Ivan Illich in the last America's Cup, joined his former rival this time in the Estonian team competing for the Russian defence. Those who know Shaw also have a grudging respect for him as a fierce individualist. Something of a recluse, he was originally asked to help train the Illich squad, but later he proved to be sufficiently valuable that he was persuaded to join the team. Novy Mir, with Shaw on board as tactician, struck a devastating first blow against the highly trained and highly fancied Russian first team.

The British *Sun* reported the win under the banner headline '*GIVE IT TO THEM, IVAN!*'

Sailing superstar Ivan Illich, described by the Army authorities two years ago as a 'drunken immoralist' because of his success with the ladies, showed he could give it to the Russian giants as well. In a ferocious attack, he destroyed the official Soviet yacht Kirov *by a three minute fifteen second win, blazing a trail through the defender trials.*

Pravda was predictably cool.

The helmsman Ivan Illich, a former colonel in the Russian Army, is currently racing against the official defender Kirov. *Officials of the Russian Republic described the huge Estonian flag hoisted by Illich at the start of the match as 'unnecessarily provocative'. Illich was thought by some to be responsible a year ago for fomenting the Estonian nationalist riots at Tartu during the course of a lecture at Tartu University. A senior administrator in the Russian sailing squad described Illich as a 'known troublemaker'.*

Sixty-One

On the following day the wind had changed direction, but it was still strong. As the low pressure system moved east the winds gave their final, northerly kick.

At the start, when their towing launch swung into wind, they raised the huge Estonian tricolour. As it sighed and thundered above them they checked through their equipment. Several hundred yards away *Kirov* also swung to her towing launch. Today the spectator fleets were even greater. Loudhailer systems had to be used by the course patrol vessels to push them back from the racing area.

Twenty minutes before the ten-minute gun they pulled down their flag, hoisted sail and set about their final tuning. Illich, bearing away to close with the starting box, noticed *Kirov* had a new mainsail, one of fuller cut. Was it an imitation of their own, he wondered? The previous day Shaw had commented on the unusual flatness of *Kirov*'s heavy weather main.

It was the only sign of the panic that would have taken hold of the *Kirov* camp the previous evening. They would be fighting to find the explanation for the huge disparity in upwind boatspeed. For the first time, they would be concerned about *Novy Mir*'s unusual aft lines.

He put these thoughts out of his mind. After a victory like that of the previous day, his own crew, so effective under pressure, would be subject to the subtle narcotic of overconfidence.

'Thirty seconds,' Brod warned, and started the countdown to the ten-minute gun.

Three, two, one ... A white feather appeared in the mouth of the starting gun, then the shock of the cordite charge. Both boats punched into the starting box and reached towards one another fast.

Illich could see Pilnyak high on the weather side of *Kirov*, one hand on the wheel, gripping the cockpit side with the other. They were close enough now to hear the clatter of *Kirov*'s winches as they drove towards one another, head-on.

Kirov swung low. It was a swift and decisive move, and Illich was forced to react within an instant. This time he would close with them. He swept high and then swung downwind, chasing *Kirov*'s stern. Now they were as close as battleships preparing to board, with the crewbosses shouting, the sails battering, and the scream of tortured gear. In the second of the circles the genoa sheet jammed. Brod, roaring like a bull, was at the shrouds; it took him three seconds to kick it free.

But it was enough to give *Kirov* the margin Pilynak required. When they broke out, *Kirov* was on their stern, and they were now in the invidious position of being herded away from the line.

'Look at them . . .' Jim Shaw hissed. 'Don't they just love it?'

Pilynak's tactician had come forward to the mast to shout at them, enforcing right of way. A good number of insults were thrown in for good measure, along with some friendly, free-wheeling abuse. 'Estonian boneheads' was one. 'Yankee rat' was another.

'Parachute?' Jim asked.

In close-quarter manoeuvres before the start, the boats stuck to the highly flexible genoa and mainsail. The great ballooning spinnakers were only used on the course, during reaches or runs downwind. But as part of their tactical discussions, Illich and Shaw had raised the question of whether a spinnaker might be suddenly sprung to haul the driven boat out of reach of the driver. It needed surprise, and luck, and a strong wind. They had the strong wind, and they could work on the others.

'Brod,' Illich ordered. 'Get the men to prepare the heavy spinnaker. Set it up beneath decks. Tell me when you're ready.'

Brod nodded, moving forward until he could drop down the hatchway.

Kirov kept driving them away. *Kirov*'s tactician had moved from racial slurs and was exploring more general areas of abuse. 'Where's your navigator?' He shouted in his heavy Siberian accent. 'Gone to change his underpants?' There was a roar of laughter from *Kirov*'s winchgrinders.

Surreptitiously, Victor Kingissep the bowman passed the spinnaker halyards, guys and sheets through the hatchway so they could be fixed to the corners of the spinnaker below decks.

Brod appeared in the hatchway and raised his thumb.

Illich nodded. 'Raise spinnaker.'

Then, to cause a distraction, he swung *Novy Mir* to port, forcing *Kirov* to drive upwind and cut him off. In the course of this diversion the foredeck crew, with Brod helping, swung out the spinnaker pole. At the same time the spinnaker in its bag, with halyard, sheets, guys already attached to it, was hurled upwards through the hatch and dragged forward by the bowman.

Kirov's big Siberian tactician had spotted the ploy and had run aft. On *Novy Mir*, Maask and Migdal were hauling up the spinnaker in quick, alternative pulls. Illich bore away. With a clatter the boom was raised. In twenty-three knots of true wind, the spinnaker opened out with a punch that went through the ship.

Jim Shaw was reading speed.

'Twelve three, twelve four, thirteen five, fourteen two, fourteen eight, fifteen six, sixteen . . . Hell, look at that.'

They were semi-planing, four knots faster than *Kirov*. Behind them the other boat was in pandemonium. There was a flurry of foredeck activity. *Kirov*'s crew had now raised the spinnaker pole. A heavy weather spinnaker was being dragged forward, but had not yet been attached.

'Three boat lengths,' Shaw said. 'Four.'

The recovery on the other boat was commendable. But unexpected manoeuvres are the bane of all crews, even great ones. *Kirov*'s spinnaker, when launched, had an hourglass twist in it.

'Six lengths. We're out of range.'

Now they could turn freely without being subject to *Kirov*'s rights of way.

'Prepare to drop spinnaker.'

Behind them, the hourglass twist in *Kirov*'s spinnaker rose up the sail and fell out. Only now was it fully set.

'Drop!' shouted Illich.

Victor Kingissep, the bowman, was already out on the pole. With a single strong tug, he withdrew the pin from the snap shackle, and the foot of the spinnaker burst free. All power in the sail was now gone. Flapping, the huge spinnaker was gathered in, arm over arm, by Migdal.

'Pole down!' roared Brod. 'Ready to tack!'

The pole, released from its topping lift, swung down and was rapidly unclipped.

Already Illich was turning up into wind, the winchgrinders powering in the sails. Behind them there were shouts on the other boat.

'Tack!'

Illich swung *Novy Mir* through the wind, with sails thundering, turning back, facing the other boat now on starboard tack, with right of way. Illich drove towards them. This was cruel.

With spinnaker flapping uncontrollably, *Kirov* was forced to turn downwind to avoid them. Brod was already up by the mast, shouting at the other boat for right of way.

Novy Mir sailed past them and back towards the start line. *Kirov*, her spinnaker still being gathered in, swung upwind behind them. They could hear fresh shouts and angry orders as *Kirov*'s pole fouled the tacking genoa.

Now it was *Novy Mir* who had a three lengths lead back to the start line.

'Thirty-two seconds,' Shaw said.

It would take them at least fifty to get to the start line. This too was good. They would not need to delay before crossing while *Kirov* caught up behind them.

They closed with the start line. They would skirt the starting launch closely.

'Five, four, three, two . . .'

Twenty-two seconds after the gun they were over. With a lead of three boatlengths on *Kirov*, they slid across the starting line, leaving ten feet between themselves and the starting launch.

This time they placed a loose cover on *Kirov* up the first

304

beat. It was a conservative tactic, but safe. At the top mark they were forty-eight seconds ahead, enough to hold off the other boat without great difficulty on the downwind leg.

After that the race held no special incidents. They kept their lead in the offwind legs, and increased it upwind. At the finish *Novy Mir* was two minutes five seconds ahead. They turned into wind and shot the finishing line in traditional manner. The fleet of Estonian launches hooted and trumpeted, and nearly nine hundred wakes converged towards them like an imploding star.

Sixty-Two

'Hallo, hallo, hallo.'

'Who is speaking, please?' asked Tammiste.

'Is that the, uh, world-famous Kalev Tammiste?'

'Tammiste here. Who is speaking please?'

'James O'Grundy, *Connecticut Enquirer*.'

'Can I help you?'

'You sure can, Kalip. What's with this brilliant boat you have designed?'

'Forgive me. Which boat?'

'*Novy Mir*.'

'Yes, I designed it.'

'I hear that it just whips everything in sight.'

'Whip?'

'Heh, heh. Excuse me. I mean beats.'

'It seems to be quite fast.'

'Fast? I hear any idiot's just got to touch the helm, and the race is just about won.'

'Not quite.'

'Think you'll stand a chance against the Americans?'

'The Americans are very good . . .'

'You bet they are, Kalip. They're just sweeping the board.'

'As I say. . .'

'Now what exactly makes your boat so special? Got some kind of weird keel on it?'

'No . . .'

'I hear some syndicates have put on a special underwater coating. Frictionless, they tell me. You got some of that?'

'No, I think . . .'

'Hell, you're not being very helpful here, Tulip. I've got column inches to fill.'

'If you'd let me finish . . .'

'Well, it's been good talking to you. Pity you don't have anything I can use. Guess I'll have to check some other sources.'

The phone went dead.

Margarita said from the kitchen: 'Who was it?'

'A journalist.'

'Another one?'

'It's Illich and Shaw. They've discovered a new way to persecute me.'

Margarita appeared in his study with a cup of coffee.

'How?'

'They keep telling journalists I'm a genius.'

'But that's very nice of them.'

'It's not nice. It's another sign of their diabolical cunning.'

'Kalev, my dear,' Margarita said. 'That really is absurd. If I didn't know and love you, I would say that you have a persecution complex. I can see you're not in a good mood.'

Margarita put the coffee down and swept out, imperious. For some reason he always felt a quickening of desire for her at such moments. Through the window he watched as she walked, straight backed, towards the vegetable garden.

Perhaps she was right. He was still smarting, several weeks afterwards, from the memory of being thrown in the water three times during the celebration of *Novy Mir*'s selection at Khiuma. There at least his fears had been genuine.

No, not even they would be so diabolical as to persecute him through journalists. They had enough troubles of their own.

Sixty-Three

Now the camp was truly under siege. The defender eliminations had been timed to coincide with a break in the trials of the challenger yachts. *Novy Mir*'s two victories eclipsed the other news as the final four challengers prepared for their knockout eliminations.

Throughout the day, helicopters hovered overhead, filming their camp, the exercising men, the repair crews working on the decks of *Novy Mir*. Reporters shouted questions through the wire security fences.

Illich, subject to the Army's instinctive distrust of the excesses of reportage, kept himself to himself. He had a reputation for silence. The main target of the reporters' attentions was Jim Shaw.

Failing to gain access to Illich or Shaw, the reporters fell on Tammiste. Tammiste, the recipient of ingenious threats from owners and helmsman, the butt of criticism, emerged cautiously and somewhat owlishly into the full glare of his fame. In the crew's rest room was a television set. They watched the media transform Tammiste from a quiet recluse into the fêted international genius of yacht design. Superlatives were heaped upon him. Tammiste, looking like a man suspecting a trap, watched with careful amusement.

The other media star was Estonia herself. What, the

media asked, was this strange, small country from the former Soviet bloc that could produce such savage victories in sailing? Reporters were sent scurrying to examine its identity, the background to its sporting valour. Was it a lost part of Finland or a former province of Sweden? Would it now take its place among the nations of the world? The pink walls and red tiled roofs of Toompea Palace, housing the Council of Ministers, made their appearance on television screens. The multitudes of the world, bored by politics, were intrigued by sporting success. Film footage appeared from obscure stocks of the patron of the Estonian sailing syndicate, the short square figure of President Aegu, treading the delicate boundary between Estonia's Soviet past and her increasingly independent future. Slowly, an impression of a small Baltic state emerged, talented and eccentric, self-righteous and nationalistic, attempting to square its expanding, increasingly capitalist economy with the puritan influences of Luther and Marx.

Vagir organized an overnight guard on *Novy Mir*, changing shifts every three hours through the night. There had been a second power cut (once again a surprisingly local failure), and the spare generator beat out through the night.

In the full song of the defence eliminations, the sailmakers had become almost wholly nocturnal, emerging from the cutting room floors white-faced in the early hours to pile the recut, folded sails outside the crew quarters, before turning to their own bunks for well-earned rest.

On the third day of the races the wind fell quiet, *Novy Mir* was towed out amongst grey banks of acrid-smelling diesel fumes from the surrounding launches and spectator craft. It was extraordinary how many Estonian craft had emerged. In addition to the sleek, spectator motor yachts, there were old wooden clinker-built hulls with tall chimneys, fishing boats gone on holiday, open workboats, official launches for the senior politicians and bureaucrats. From the Western Scandinavian states – Sweden, Denmark, Finland – sailing and motor yachts had crossed the Baltic to attend. A huge convoy moved forward with *Novy Mir* at its centre towards the race course, swinging in behind the tall mast with the Estonian tricolour.

Amongst this fleet the official patrol vessels appeared oddly out of place. Despite the liberalization of the political system, the movement towards open markets, the patrol boats seemed discomforted in the noisy chaos of an international forum.

'A lottery,' said Jim Shaw about the weather. In truth, however, they relished the slow intricacies of light weather duelling, when tactical sharpness, the instinct for better breeze, each played a more prominent part.

Stationary, facing up into breeze, there was hardly enough wind to stir the flag. But once sails were up, the slightest breeze would cause the boats to move forward, generating their own 'apparent' wind. The sails would stretch, and the two crews, their boats heeling to their own generated breeze, would try with patient concentration to stoke up the engines of their speed. Although heavy weather is spectacular, to the aficionados it is two-dimensional compared to light weather racing.

With hardly a breath of wind, the crew went through the pre-match routine of checking equipment. The direction of the top mark was radioed from the committee boat to both yachts, then changed, then altered again as the wind continued its erratic movements.

Around them the course patrol craft drove back the spectator fleet, making short rushes like sheep dogs. Slowly the clouds of diesel fumes receded until they were sitting in their own reflection, rising faintly to each swell. The sun beat down on water which was so unblemished it was almost oily. Occasional fluky breezes disturbed its surface.

Until the wind direction settled, however, the committee boat postponed a start. It grew hotter.

Another factor raised their concentration. Heavy weather and light weather races favour different types of boat. In the heavy winds of Fremantle in 1986, the dominant *Stars and Stripes* was a design optimized for heavy weather. In the 1987 World Championships in the light winds of Porto Cervo in the Mediterranean, the same invincible *Stars and Stripes* was consistently last, behind a fleet of comparative mediocrities. Her full-ended, high prismatic hull, even helmed by the great Dennis Conner, was like a fish out of water.

So they watched *Kirov* with renewed interest as she waited, like them, for the breeze to settle, and the race committee to lay the course and start. On hot days such as this, the likelihood was a westerly breeze as the great land mass to the east heated up and the wind flowed off the cold Baltic surface to take its place. At 11:45 the first signs of a new breeze caused a ripple on the water. At first it was from the northwest. But slowly it swung west. By 12:10 it seemed to have settled, a little north of due west. The course was laid to provide the traditional first leg directly upwind. A radio message from the committee boat announced the ten minute gun at twelve thirty.

With only twenty minutes to tune, both yachts cast off from their respective towing boats and hoisted sail. Their long wait was over.

There was another worry in Illich's mind. In the hurly-burly of strong wind racing, crew ability and the speed of the hull are predominant factors. In the surreal, phantas-magoric conditions of light winds, with 'real' and 'apparent' winds in which wind directions alter radically as a result of boat speed, and in which a distant point can be reached by sailing faster along obtuse vectors, in such conditions computational facilities are critical.

Kirov, they had heard, had a *Chel* tactical supercomputer. The 'open policy' between Japan and Russia had produced a new generation of Soviet military computers, of which the *Chel* was only one. Looking across at *Kirov* now, heeling beneath its apparent wind, its light wind sails setting perfectly, they perceived a different enemy, an enemy reborn as an angel.

They set up *Novy Mir* on port and starboard tacks, then swung her slowly through 360 degrees to check hull speed against predicted speeds for the points of the compass.

'Two minutes to ten-minute gun,' Shaw called.

Illich tacked. *Novy Mir* reached slowly towards the starting box. In light winds, with the prospect of the wind fading at any moment, calculations tended to be conservative.

'True wind, five knots,' Brod announced. 'Appears to be steady. Slight bias to pin end of start line. About three degrees.'

'Thirty seconds,' Shaw said.

A slight chill entered their clipped instructions as they began to manoeuvre at the edge of the starting box. *Kirov*'s laser rangefinder would be firing at points around the course, measuring the movement of dust particles. This information would be processed into the central tactical computer, and the wind pattern over the entire course would be collected, analysed and displayed on a CRT screen in flowing lines. On a second screen, course options would be displayed, with figures of predicted real speeds and (more importantly) velocity made good to any given mark. Armed with this strategic information, *Kirov* would be approaching them now.

'Seven, six, five . . .' Shaw called out the seconds.

Without the wind to whip away the sound, the ten minute starting cannon was inordinately loud. The smoke hung heavily on the air as they crossed into the starting box and moved towards *Kirov*.

But *Kirov* appeared to have no intention of moving towards them. It hovered at the other end of the starting box. Then it began to move on a semicircular path at right angles to them.

They continued to close slowly. But whereas in the big winds the two yachts had charged each other with a combined closing speed of thirty knots, now *Novy Mir*'s six-knot reaching speed drew them towards their opponent only gradually.

Kirov was elusive. Drawing them out downwind, the Russian yacht continued to sail in a slow semicircle until they were a similar distance from the start line. They felt the chill of being outmanoeuvered, and abandoned their slow-motion pursuit to return to the line, keeping a wary eye on their opponent.

'Fifty seconds . . .'

Upwind to the line, sailing parallel, their apparent wind speed increased and they made reasonable time. But *Kirov*'s tactics for the race were clear.

'Action at a distance,' commented Shaw.

'True windspeed four knots, occasionally five,' Brod informed him. 'Direction constant. Unbiased line.'

Prem was slowly massaging the great lightweather mainsail with kicker, halyard tension, cunningham, sheet, outhaul. They were firing on all cylinders as the two boats crossed the line.

'Port side has more wind.'

They kept to port, slicing at seven knots into the long swell. *Kirov* too was moving fast. But why was she on the other side of the course? What had she seen there, or rather, what had the computer told them?

They concentrated on their speed. After three minutes they tacked. *Kirov*, on the other side of the course, tacked twenty seconds later.

Converging, the two boats seemed neck and neck. A minute went by, then another. The relative positions seemed unchanged.

'Damn,' Shaw said. 'There she goes.'

Kirov had caught an advantageous change in local wind direction, a 'lift'. She was sailing higher.

'We're being knocked down,' Brod said. 'Four degrees.' Orthodox opinion would have advised them to tack in order to minimize damage. But Illich made no such move.

Kirov crossed their bow two boatlengths up. Would she

312

tack and cover them? Illich was curious. The answer was no. *Kirov* continued on her careful path, picking her way. Illich felt a certain admiration for Pilnyak in keeping to his course, looking for wind. His 'action-at-a-distance' had worked up till now. Why should he not continue to pursue it?

At the top mark *Kirov* was four and half lengths up. She slid round easily and launched a perfectly timed spinnaker. They followed her around. Pilnyak was tacking downwind, gybing through eighty-degree angles. To sail directly downwind was slow, even though it was the shortest line to the mark. As one moved away from the wind, the apparent windspeed decreased, as did speed. By moving at carefully calculated angles down the course, the speed of the boat brought the wind forward, and increased the 'apparent' wind. Boat speed increased proportionately. Sailed this way, along ghostly vectors, the boat reached the downwind mark more quickly.

Tactically, sailing through such large angles was also beneficial for the leading boat. It made it far more difficult for Illich to place *Novy Mir* between the wind and *Kirov* in an attempt to slow down the lead boat. They had to bide their time, make careful sail changes, watch.

On the second upwind leg, *Kirov* continued to sail freely, without placing a cover, looking for advantageous shifts and corridors of wind. It was like sailing against a perfectly tuned robot.

At the top mark *Kirov* was six boatlengths up. On the second downwind leg they managed to pull back a boatlength, but *Kirov* was in a dominant position.

'What now?' Illich asked Shaw.

He knew the answer in principle. In match-racing, it is often said, there is no second. There is simply the winner and the loser. If they sailed conservatively, they would almost certainly lose. As the almost certain loser, therefore, they had nothing further to lose by being adventurous.

Kirov had detected advantageous wind to port.

'Let's split tacks.'

'I agree.'

The wind is not homogeneous. There are shifts within shifts, holes within holes. Not even a supercomputer, stitching together the wind directions over the course, could predict every aspect. Between each line there would be whorls, changes . . .

'Forget the other boat,' Illich said to the crew.

'The other boat is Medusa,' Prem the crewboss said. 'He who looks will die.'

The boat became quiet as they concentrated. Only the gentle slicing of the bow as it cut the lazy swells, the sigh of sheets being eased.

'Two degree shift, knock,' Brod was in a trance over the display screen.

'Tack.'

They took it carefully, coming out the other side cleanly, tightening in the genoa as *Novy Mir* picked up speed.

'Lifting two degrees, three degrees.'

'Dark patch of water to port.'

A flurry of faster wind was moving over the water, darkening its surface like a shoal of fish.

'Shall we take it?' Illich asked Shaw. 'We'll lose this lift.'

Shaw was silent, judging its extent.

'Let it go.'

They remained on this tack for another two minutes, feathering up a little into each tiny gust, easing off in the lulls to maintain speed. Shaw studied Illich's technique at the wheel. Certain helmsmen moved the wheel or tiller quite considerably, aligning the boat with each wave, each tiny change in wind. Illich, on the other hand, was a minimalist. It was something Shaw agreed with. Instinctively, he felt that any movement of the rudder caused drag. There was enough difference between top helmsmen to make it a lively issue. Illich's hands moved only occasionally on the wheel. When they did so, it was with the care of a surgeon.

314

'Another patch of wind to port,' Shaw informed, 'Looks bigger.'

'Brod?'

'One degree knock,' Brod cut in crisply. 'Two degrees. More.'

'Prepare to tack.' Illich could see the patch now. It seemed to have depth. 'Tack.'

They felt their way through, drew in sail quietly on the other side, tightened in harder as the speed came on.

'Fifty yards away,' Shaw said. 'We're on intercept.'

The boat nodded, raised itself, nodded to a new gust, held there. The crew held their breath.

With an increase in boatspeed came more apparent wind. The boat heeled more.

'Seven one, seven one, seven three, seven four, seven five . . . Steady seven five.'

Beyond analysis, beyond training, experience, there was luck. Sometimes the boat felt good. It did now, not working against the water but with it, the bow parting the small crests with an easy deference.

'Knock,' Brod intoned. 'Bad one. Three, four, five, six degrees.'

'Tack!'

On the other tack it was still changing, but this time lifting. Somewhere a fresh breeze was coming in. On the new tack it was all to the good.

'Lift, two degrees, two degrees. More coming now. Four, six, seven.'

And speed, too. *Novy Mir* heeled more. Power came from her submersed shoulder. Illich allowed himself the first glance at *Kirov*.

He could have cried out for joy. *Kirov* was clearly in the old wind, moving forward doggedly, hardly heeling. Tacking now, she came through and was heading towards them. Had they seen on their computer screens the wind-corridor on this side of the course?

Positionally, however, it was difficult to tell.

315

They were converging on the line at opposite ends. It was a knife edge. He prayed that no one on *Novy Mir* would look and freeze. They did look; it would have been inhuman not to. But their concentration held. The two bows sliced towards the line. He could sense the held breath aboard a thousand spectator boats. The gun went. They had done it by a hair.

For the first time the Estonian crew really went wild. Prem was bouncing up and down like a kangaroo. There was enough hugging to embarrass even a Slav.

Over the shortwave radio, the committee boat announced: '*Novy Mir*, by two point three seconds.'

They ran up the huge Estonian tricolour on the backstay as the spectator fleet, breaking in like a football crowd at a match final, cascaded towards them.

At their quay the press of journalists and other media was the most intense they had seen.

As they docked, casting off the tow rope and gliding the last few feet under their own momentum, it seemed the camp was under siege. In certain areas the perimeter fence was bowing inward as a result of pressure. Microphones were pushed through the wire meshing. Flashlights exploded.

They were begged to stand still while the photographers clicked and the flashbulbs snickered. A West German television commentator asked in heavily accented English: 'One question, please. To what do you owe your victories?'

'To the designer, Kalev Tammiste.' Illich had to raise his voice above the hubbub. A quietness descended as this exotic name went down on a hundred notepads.

'He is responsible?'

'A genius,' Illich said.

Shaw was standing beside Illich, hands on hips.

'And you, Mr Shaw, you agree with this?'

'One hundred per cent,' Shaw said.

'You think he is a genius, too?'

316

Shaw shrugged. 'I couldn't even begin to describe what I feel.'

The pencils moved. For a moment there was silence.

'Thank you, gentlemen,' Illich said, moving away.

That evening, after the break, they would turn on the television and watch Tammiste, blinking like an owl, emerge once again into the full glare of his fame.

Sixty-Four

During the night an alarm was raised by the guard on *Novy Mir*. Artur Kriis, one of Vagir's right-hand men, had heard a stealthy movement of a ladder being placed against the hull. Hearing his shout and his footsteps, the intruder had dropped to the ground and slipped out of the door of the shed. Kriis, a large man carrying not a small amount of additional weight, had pursued him over the lawn, through the scattered storage buildings at the back of the site, following which he had disappeared. There was a large hole in the perimeter fence severed by wire-cutters.

The sailcutters, working through the night, were the first on the scene. Illich, woken by Kriis's angry shouts, joined them at the opening in the fence. Shaw was there a few moments later.

'Did you actually see him go through here?' Illich asked Kriis.

Artur Kriis shook his head.

'So he could still be in the camp?'

It was possible.

Others, Vagir and several of his men, were approaching them now, rubbing the sleep out of their eyes.

'You did well, Kriis,' Illich said. In his haste to get to the

317

scene of the break-in, Illich had left his watch behind. One of the sailmakers gave him the time.

'Three twenty-three.'

'Vagir, could you spare two extra men to guard the two boats?'

Vagir nodded.

'I'll put another one at the hole here.'

'Good.' Illich turned to Kriis again.

'Did you get a look at him?'

Kriis shook his head. He took it as a personal failing that he hadn't managed to catch the man and change his looks permanently.

Vagir turned to Illich: 'We'll check all the outhouses and make sure that nothing has been touched. You should get some sleep, Colonel. Tomorrow's the final race.'

Illich could not prevent Vagir calling him 'Colonel', even though, technically speaking, he had been stripped of his rank. And he had a morbid superstition of talking about races that were not yet won. He could see, however, that as regards security, they were in capable hands.

He, Shaw, and the others of the crew who had been woken, returned to their respective beds to catch a couple of further hours of precious sleep.

On his way back Illich looked at the sky. There was more wind than yesterday. A small low-pressure system was moving in. Looking up, he could see clouds scudding against the moon. That, at least, was a good sign for the following day.

In the morning it was bright, angry. They checked the weather patterns provided hourly by the Climatological Institute at Tartu. Eighteen to twenty-two knots south, becoming south-westerly.

It was Illich's custom to say a few words at breakfast about the day's forthcoming race. This morning he stood up.

'Medium strong winds south, not much sea, at least to

318

begin with. Code 13 genoas. What we must remember is this. We have had three wins, and some would say the first two in stronger winds were decisive. But you know that it is precisely when you are confident that you lose your edge and become careless. One should be ruthless about any sign of this in oneself.' He looked around at the steady, confident faces, the faces of men who believed in him, perhaps too much.

'*Kirov* is a fast boat. She is faster than *Leningrad*, and they have a fine team. I warn you not to tempt fate.'

It was a peculiarly sombre speech. One or two at the back shouted 'bravo, Colonel', but he suspected the message went home. If there was one thing Illich loathed, it was bravado when in a winning position. It offended his professionalism. He was determined to savage anyone who showed it today.

Afterwards they went to the boat to load the sails and prepare the gear. Additional sails were placed aboard the support boat for windstrengths both above and below that predicted. Although it was strictly forbidden to load sails while the race was in progress, if the weather seemed to be changing unpredictably, one could load additional sails at any point prior to the ten-minute gun.

It was chill for summer. Although the wind was brisk, there was hardly any swell on the southerly shore. At ten-thirty the towing boat pulled them out. A convoy of hooting spectator boats accompanied them the five miles out to the course.

Kirov's convoy emerged from the headland about a mile away, on a converging course. Illich struggled against his own natural assumptions of superiority against *Kirov*. It was tempting to believe that this would be the final race, that in this weather they had proved invincible. The crew were quiet on *Novy Mir*. Taking their cue from him, they prepared for this as if it were their first race against an unknown quantity. If bravado was present, it was in the cheering crowds which clustered the sides of the larger spectator craft, causing them to heel under their human loads.

At the starting box the towboats of the two yachts swung into wind while the course patrol vessels disciplined the unruly fleets, driving and hectoring them behind the lines. As they did so the water opened up between the two boats. When the wall of spectator craft receded only two great sailing yachts were left, facing parallel, waiting.

It was always an eerie time. The spectator fleet was a dark wall. Within that wall was a mass of engine exhausts, frenetic manoeuvre, churning wakes. But from this distance they were almost an abstract quantity. Their combined noise was like the faint hubbub of geese on a marsh. Sailors tend to be obsessed with their sport, and wonder why outsiders do not share their enthusiasm and awe for its manifold complexities. But occasionally the positions are reversed. It was at this time, waiting for a race to begin, that Illich was afflicted by the notion of the almost cosmic triviality of the event in which he was participating, and the absurd importance attached to it.

The mechanics of preparation held such nervous thoughts at bay. While the waves beat slowly against *Novy Mir*'s hull, they completed their second check of gear and sails. The intruder the previous evening had caused, if anything, an increase in the thoroughness of their preparation.

Illich had noticed a special reticence in Jim Shaw over the event. In the early hours Shaw, staring at the gaping hole caused by the intruder, had not said a word. He seemed lost in his own thoughts. It was something that could easily be explained by other things; the hour itself, at the quietest time of night, when humans were at their most vulnerable and least communicative, the traditional hour at which secret policemen had knocked on doors. In this sense it was unremarkable.

In the silence of waiting, however, while the crew went

through their operations, and after the prevailing wind conditions, direction and velocity, had been programmed in to their computer, Shaw said unexpectedly: 'That guy last night was an American.'

It was a somewhat distracting statement.

'Why do you say that?'

'I heard a shout and I got up. I went to the window and caught a glimpse of someone running across the lawn, about fifty feet away.'

Brod, focused on the computer instrumentation, gave a course reading from the short-wave radio. 'One hundred and thirty-eight degrees.'

Shaw paused to punch this information into the tactical computer.

'How could you tell he was American?' persisted Illich.

'I've been trying to work that out. I just can't find an answer. If you're walking down a street in a foreign town, and someone walks towards you, you sometimes know that guy's nationality on a gut level. You can't explain why.'

'It was dark,' Illich said. Now he was concerned that Shaw was in the grip of an obsession.

'That doesn't matter. That guy was an American.'

Brod had removed the headphones: 'What American?'

'Thank you for telling me,' Illich said. He knew that Shaw was, on his own quiet level, intensely proud of his nationality, and it was a painful matter to make such a statement.

'For telling you what?' asked Brod.

'Mind your own business,' Illich said to Brod. 'Bonehead.'

'Forgive me for even asking,' Brod replied. 'I apologize if my humble question has offended you. The course, by the way, is confirmed. The committee boat says the wind is now steady. Twenty minutes to the ten-minute gun.'

'Down flag,' Illich ordered. 'Mainsail up.'

Brod moved forward to pass instructions to the bowman and the sewerman who was packing sails below decks, checking every aspect prior to their use. The tow-rope was cast off.

'Thank you for the information,' Illich repeated to Shaw. Shaw shrugged; he started to draw data from the tactical computer. Illich suspected that the mere admission of his suspicion had exercised a cathartic effect. He hoped so.

When the ten-minute gun went, *Kirov* broke into the starting box with a bone in her teeth and aggression in every perfect curve of her sails. *Novy Mir*, on the other hand, deliberately loitered.

It was part of his and Shaw's policy of behaving unpredictably. The crew on *Kirov* were younger and did not have the experience of the veterans of *Novy Mir*. In unexpected situations they would be at a disadvantage. That, at least, was their theory.

When *Kirov* had covered half the distance between them, Illich turned *Novy Mir* away and reached away from the line and *Kirov*. *Kirov* followed them aggressively, but she was still sixty yards away when Pilnyak and his tactician began to grow nervous about returning to the line in time. *Novy Mir*, pursuing a tactic similar to Pilnyak's on the previous day, had moved in an avoiding semicircle and was now positioned at about the same distance from the line. Now *Novy Mir* swung hard towards the line and began to power fast towards it on a close reach. That was the end of *Kirov*'s hopes of close pre-start manoeuvres. She swung back too.

The 'timed run' to the line was said to have been devised by Vanderbilt in the era of the great J-Class racers, and had been used by numerous helmsmen in the past. It had reached a high level in the hands of Dennis Conner, who had used it extensively with his winning twelve-metre *Stars and Stripes*, big and fast in a straight line, but slow at manoeuvre. It was a nerve-wracking strategy. If the wind fell, the boat which used it could be left floundering after the start gun.

Pilnyak would also be nervous, and Illich used Pilnyak's

nervousness deliberately to drive further distance between them. Each was closer to a different part of the line. In his fear of losing vital seconds, Pilnyak aimed *Kirov* towards the pin end of the line, leaving *Novy Mir* free to power towards the committee boat end.

The outcome was that *Kirov* was driven to one side of the course out of *force majeure*, whatever its tactical supercomputer might say about the respective advantages of one end of the line or the other.

'Twenty-three seconds,' Shaw informed Illich. They were, Illich calculated, only ten seconds away from the start line and if they continued on this tack they would cross ahead of the gun.

'Bearing away,' Illich warned.

They eased sheets, powering parallel to the line.

'Eleven two knots,' Brod said. 'Eleven four, Eleven four steady.'

'Seven, six, five, four . . . .'

'Tighten in hard,' shouted Illich. He swung the wheel and, with the momentum of their reaching speed, they rushed the line at ten knots.

The cannon went.

Three seconds behind the gun. A good enough start. Illich glanced towards *Kirov*. They too had started on time, and were now converging with *Novy Mir* on starboard tack.

He held port tack for another twenty seconds, then tacked.

On parallel tacks, the distance of a hundred and fifty yards between the boats was maintained.

There is a fine but crucial edge between a crew in perfect working order and one which is working at only marginally less proficiency. Their tack had been slightly short of those perfect timings. Now the boat felt ragged to Illich. Other helmsmen would have ranted and raved. Certain isolated incidents had passed in racing folklore. Nearly twenty years earlier, the fiery Irish skipper of the British America's Cup yacht *Crusader I* had felt a similar frustration at the off-peak

323

performance of his crew in one of their contender races. Shouts and imprecations had no effect. In a fit of rage, Cudmore stepped forward and kicked the mainsheet trimmer, Chris Mason, on the backside. There was a pause while the victim, with an icy self-discipline, waited for the pain to dissipate. Then six foot three of burly mainsheet trimmer turned round with that slow menace which is a prelude to fisticuffs. 'What was that for, Harold?' 'Nothing,' hissed Cudmore. 'Just pass it on.'

Terror tactics were of questionable value. Outside their peak performance, the strategy of standing off and relying on boat speed now seemed to Illich to be suspect. Such fine judgements form the essence of match-racing.

'This is looking dicey,' Jim Shaw said. 'I think we should go and get 'em.'

'I agree,' Illich replied. 'Prepare to tack.'

They would move in on *Kirov*, engage in a close-quarter duel, shake the complacency of *Novy Mir*'s crew.

'Tack!'

For the second time Illich felt the tiny hesitation which comes from slightly less than perfect timing. And a second aspect now became clearer. *Kirov* was ahead.

It is surprising how fast yachts on converging tacks came closer. Although pointing obliquely towards one another, their combined vector closing speed may be greater than the speed of either yacht. They could assess the damage as *Kirov* drew closer.

'Two and half lengths,' Shaw noted.

Kirov crossed ahead, moving well, and threw a perfectly timed tack, aimed at bringing them on to the same course and taking their wind.

'Tack!' shouted Illich.

The loosened genoa thundered. *Novy Mir*'s winchgrinders hit a frenzied, driving roll. Eight seconds later *Kirov* tacked, determined to hold them under close cover. *Novy Mir* sprang upright and heeled in the turbulence of *Kirov*'s backwind.

'Tack!' roared Illich.

Fourteen tacks, in brutal succession, until the winchgrinders were exhausted, heaving for breath between each burst of winching, and the trimmers, shaking with adrenalin, tensed themselves for the next manoeuvre.

Kirov was still ahead. Her crew was superbly fit. But her boatspeed, sapped by fifteen consecutive tacks, was now low. Illich would try once more to escape the effects of her damaging backwind.

'Tack!' *Novy Mir*, with her own speed down to four knots, came through slowly, the grinders in furious motion. On the other tack he bore off to pick up speed, then feathered *Novy Mir* into wind, treading the delicate line between pointing 'low' and 'high'. *Kirov* continued to recover her own speed on her current tack.

The two boats diverged, each entering that strange hyper-silence which follows the deafening panic of a tacking duel.

Less than a minute later, *Kirov* rounded the top mark a good three lengths up.

They followed her round and sprung the spinnaker. The next decision too was a psychological one. Many helmsmen, their blood up, would have engaged in a downwind tacking duel with the lead boat, trying to take her wind as she zigzagged out of danger. This leg Illich was content to let the crew recover. The tacking duel had blown away the cobwebs. Their trailing position would add to their aggression. Other factors impinged. If they caught up on this leg, the other boat would be tempted, on rounding the lower mark, to place a close cover. With a lead maintained, her willingness to enter a second savage tacking duel would be less.

There was a second fine calculation of Pilnyak's psychological state. Pilnyak had proved to himself that *Kirov* was capable of overcoming *Novy Mir* in fast conditions. Illich felt instinctively that, given an opportunity, Pilnyak would like to prove this more fully. Placing a close cover on an opponent is, after all, a sign of fear, an implicit admission of inferiority. He would place temptation in Pilnyak's way, play on his arrogance, counter his own impatience, and wait his opportunity.

They rounded the mark four lengths behind *Kirov*. Illich tacked away. *Kirov* waited ten seconds and tacked with them. Illich tacked again and waited. After twenty seconds he was beginning to be convinced that *Kirov* would not tack, but as he settled down to concentrate on speed, Shaw said: 'He's tacked. Loose cover.'

'Loose cover' was a compromise between the grinding tacking duel that developed from a 'close cover', and allowing your opponent free range. Although it lacked the destructive characteristics of backwinding the opponent, it ensured that the leading boat stayed in the same area of the course, leaving open the option of placing a close cover if the opponent seemed to be gaining.

It was logical, it was safe, and for this leg at least, it worked for *Kirov*. She rounded the top mark just over three lengths ahead.

On the next downwind leg *Novy Mir* held on, rounding the mark five lengths behind. It was a difficult position. The windstrength had dropped to eighteen knots. They raised their largest heavy genoa.

At first *Novy Mir* heeled too much, even for Illich. Her gunwales went under, the waves began sliding back along the deck.

'Eight two, eight three, eight three steady . . .' Brod intoned. The speed was still good.

By feathering slightly, he could raise the gunwales above the water. Even so, they were still heeled five degrees further than *Kirov*.

'Speed rising,' Brod said. 'Eight four, eight five, eight five, eight six.'

'*Kirov* tacks,' Jim Shaw cut in. 'Loose cover.'

At least there was no backwind, Illich consoled himself.

'We're pointing one and a half degrees higher,' Brod said. 'Speed eight six, eight six, eight seven.'

Now the crew were concentrating fully. The mind may be willing but the body can be slow. Now at last their position in the race had shaken them into tune.

Kirov was also moving fast, sliding gracefully to the seas on their starboard beam.

'*Kirov* ahead by two and half boatlengths,' Shaw confirmed.

Pilnyak would sense it too, Illich suspected. If *Novy Mir* tacked now, Pilnyak would place them under close cover. They kept on the same course, bringing the loosely covering *Kirov* with them.

They had to shake *Kirov* off. It was difficult, perhaps impossible against a determined opponent who was willing where necessary to place a ruthless close cover.

With less experienced opponents, it was possible sometimes to 'dummy-tack', to undertake a half-tack, induce the opponent to tack with you, and then fall back on the original course. It was too crude, too unlikely to succeed . . . Besides, the Siberian tactician on *Kirov* watched them like a hawk, preferring not to take his eyes off *Novy Mir* for a second. They were close enough now for Illich to clearly see his face, even his expression.

Occasionally, however, the Siberian would turn away for about ten seconds to study his instrumentation. These ten-second bursts were becoming more obvious now that the two boats were nearing the 'lay-line', the point at which they could tack for the line and reach it on the next tack.

'Two lengths,' Shaw said.

Kirov would stick to them like a limpet now. But a thought began to tempt Illich. This same Siberian had been very free with his phrases about Estonian boneheads and Yankee rats. What could they lose? He said to Shaw: 'What about a double-tack?'

'Crazy,' Shaw said.

Illich was not entirely certain about the provenance of

the word 'crazy' – that is to say, used on its own, without a clear context. The literal meaning, yes, but the actual implication in this case . . .?

'That's one hell of a good idea,' Shaw added.

Ah.

'Prem,' Illich called softly. 'Double-tack. Tell the men. Five second interval.'

He heard Prem pass the word forward.

The pale eyes of the Siberian were fixed on him.

'Tack!' roared Illich, loud enough for it to be heard easily on *Kirov*. *Novy Mir* blasted through the wind, genoa thundering, the winches screaming as the genoa was hauled in.

'Tack!' he heard the Siberian call. *Kirov* came about. The Siberian paused two seconds, and then turned away to check the course to the lay-line on his computer.

Without speaking, Illich swung *Novy Mir* back through the tack. Edvigs Tarku, the port trimmer, waited until the genoa was almost backwinded before he released it, so that it would flap only slightly in transit. The winchgrinders moved like giant, silent mice. It was a comical enough sight. The genoa was quietly hauled in.

'Six knots, six four, six seven.'

They had lost considerable speed, but it would build up rapidly. Illich bore away before feathering up into wind.

The Siberian was still crouched over his computer screen. Several seconds later he turned round and his eyes nearly started out of his head. It was a moment to remember. Pilnyak, alerted, swung around wide-eyed. There was a rapid exchange, carried away by the wind between the parting boats.

'Lay-line about a hundred yards ahead,' Shaw informed him. 'Did you see that bastard's face?'

'We'll keep going another fifty yards,' Illich said.

Brod intoned: 'Eight two, eight three, eight three, eight four, eight five.'

'Windshift,' Shaw said. 'Two degrees. Lay-line moves out fifty extra yards.'

It was tempting to keep on this tack. But the wind could as easily shift back in direction, and they would be at a disadvantage. There was already enough distance between boats to be free of *Kirov*'s backwind.

'Tack!' Illich shouted.

It was the best tack of the race, as close to perfection as it was possible to be.

'Seven eight,' Brod said. 'Eight zero, eight two, eight two, eight three.'

They settled down. In the gusts Illich feathered up. The genoa, relatively heavy but designed for lighter winds than this, had stood up well, though undoubtedly it would have stretched. He prayed that the wind direction would stay constant. If it did, it would mean that *Kirov* would have to tack before the line. Feathering up in the gusts, he might be able to make it in one . . .

It was a calculated gamble.

Kirov tacked and now sliced in towards the line.

A distraction appeared. Helicopters were forbidden during racing to fly below five hundred feet over the course, because the wash of the rotor blades could disturb the sails of the yachts. But a small black dot, moving fast, was approaching them at relatively low level.

Illich did not have to look too closely to see what it was. The military deflections of the armour were now obvious. Beneath the chin turret, the 30-mm cannon was like the lower mandible of an insect.

They were forty yards from the line. Part of him wanted to shout. But his sudden fears were no more than a silent scream. It was impossible. Still, it came towards him, growing larger. Jim Shaw had seen it, too, and was turning to point towards it as it hurtled towards them at masthead height.

It thundered over the mast at nearly two hundred knots. The downwash of the rotors struck with such force that *Novy*

Mir heeled to forty degrees, gunwales deep in the water, the mast complaining. Illich saw, like a line of madness, a split run from the foot of the genoa to its head. In less than two seconds the genoa was flapping tatters.

He swung the wheel to bring the boat into wind. *Novy Mir* seemed to hesitate, recover, then its momentum carried it across the line.

Sixty-Five

'Goddamn.' Shaw stared after the disappearing blip.

Then the crew burst into loud cheering. In their concentration they had not seen the helicopter until it was past them. What remained in their minds, as *Novy Mir* heeled, spun into wind, and drifted over the line, was the memory of *Kirov*'s own hungry bow crossing the line a hundred yards away and several seconds afterwards. The committee boat announced: '*Novy Mir*, three point seven seconds.'

Illich felt a lightness in the head, and was forced to lean against the cockpit side for support. Shaw turned away from the horizon in which the helicopter had disappeared.

'Friends of yours?'

'An expression of military displeasure, I think,' Illich replied.

The crew hauled down the rags of the genoa.

In what seemed a matter of seconds they were hemmed in so closely by the spectator fleet that they had to pull down the main, take off speed and drift for fear of hitting someone. Their own towing launch hurried through the crowds, turned alongside, and flung them a tow-rope. They were hauled forward through the lines of yachts. Two course patrol vessels took up station on either side. Ahead of the convoy, a launch with the livery of Estonia cleared a path through the milling craft.

Vagir and the shore support team were lined up on the quayside to congratulate them. Generally speaking, Vagir and his men regarded the crew of *Novy Mir* as amateurs, playboys, and essentially trivial elements. They felt themselves to be at the heart of the programme. Today it was something of a pleasure to see them line up to congratulate the crew and shake hands as they stepped off. These useless drones, irresponsible *prima donnas* and adepts at self-glorification could, after all, occasionally do something useful.

And for Illich, what could be a greater pleasure afterwards than to go to the crew rest room with a cup of coffee, turn on the old television set and, settling back into one of the ageing armchairs, to watch the genius Tammiste, his eyes blinking in alarm, struggle, float, and finally disappear beneath a flood of inane questions about yacht design?

Life had its compensations.

Before he could relax in that armchair, however, Aegu telephoned to congratulate him. Aegu had been doing 'missionary work' in Moscow, and would fly back the following day, making a detour to the sailing site just west of St Petersburg on his way to Tallinn. Out of long habit, Aegu avoided detail on the telephone.

There was a final incident in the day. Illich left the main building for the workshops to hold a post-race briefing with Vagir over any possible damage that might have occurred when the helicopter downwash had punched into their sails. He was crossing the exercise courtyard when he heard the familiar whine of a turbine. When he looked up the whirring blades were set against the sun. A flood of anger went through him. The machine thundered above him, its rotors like smoke-shadows. Although he couldn't see clearly into the armoured glass of the cockpit, it was as if whoever was there addressed him personally. He felt certain it was Vorolov, as sure as he could be without proof. Turning to face directly into the sun and the helicopter's rotors, he raised his fist in a clenched fist salute like a freedom fighter. Was there a change in the frequency, the sound of the blades? Perhaps he imagined it. Certainly the power of the turbines increased, like a howl of anger. In hardly more than a few seconds it had grown small, swinging inland and disappearing over a group of low hills to the south.

Shaking with anger, he opened the door to Vagir's workshop.

Inside it was cool and dark. To keep a balanced temperature for resins, an efficient air-conditioner had been installed. It could be heard humming in the background. For several seconds he could see nothing except the ingress of light from skylights ranged across the roof. Several men were working in the gloom. Vagir's workshops always reminded him of some infernal region. A figure was approaching him, features clarifying as his eyes adjusted to the light. It was Artur Kriis.

'Is Vagir here?'

'I think so. I'll call him.' Artur Kriis had half-turned away when he said: 'Oh, I forgot.' Kriis withdrew from his pocket a small, blue object, a cigarette lighter.

'One of the men found it. Lying on the ground at the back of the outbuildings.'

Illich took it. It had the emblem 'Lucky Strike' on its semi-transparent plastic holder. American. Illich flicked it with his thumb. A small flame appeared.

'Sorry, when Hav picked it up, he didn't think about the fingerprints. Then it occurred to us it might have been dropped by our visitor last night.'

'Thank you,' Illich said. He took out a handkerchief and wrapped it. No one apart from himself, as far as he knew, was aware of Jim Shaw's intuition that it was an American. In such matters, it was important not to jump to conclusions. The lighter might have been dropped by someone else. If it was the property of the intruder, then its American origin might be pure coincidence. The intruder could have bought it up in a *beriozka* store, among the display of other items. Even newsagents would have them. He put it in his pocket.

'I'll find Vagir,' Kriis said.

Presently Vagir's short, bull-like figure emerged from his inner office.

Vagir was affable. Not for the first time, it struck Illich how much *Novy Mir* depended on the men who worked selflessly in these workshops, away from the light, patiently, and whose only reward, apart from a working wage, was a certain cynicism regarding the contributions of those out on the water.

'Come to my office,' Vagir said.

It was surprisingly spacious, lit by a quiet, green-filtered skylight. As on the other occasions he had visited, Illich was struck by its quietness. Vagir pulled up a chair for Illich and leaned on the metal desk.

'Kriis gave me the cigarette lighter,' Illich said. 'Was there any other sign left by our night visitor?'

'No,' Vagir shook his head. 'This morning we went over the base with a fine tooth comb. No sign of disturbance anywhere.'

'What was he after, do you think?'

Vagir shrugged. Illich did not press him. Vagir said: 'We've remade the fence, and installed a light on that part of the perimeter. Our visitor chose a night when there was no one working. Usually a shift is working into the early hours.'

'Will you check the mast and rig after today's incident with the helicopter?'

'Certainly. Do you think that was deliberate?' Vagir was offhand, but Illich sensed the depth of his interest.

'I think it was intended as a warning.'

'Warnings mean nothing,' Vagir replied, 'unless followed by action.'

Robust words, thought Illich. Vagir too was irritated by the attentions of the helicopter.

'When you've checked for damage,' Illich suggested, 'you and your men should take a rest. It's two weeks before the races against the challenger. You should take forty-eight hours off.'

'Is that an order, Colonel?'

'You may take it as such,' Illich replied.

Illich stood up. He had stayed longer than intended. As he opened the door to leave, Vagir said: 'Congratulations.'

'Thank you.' Illich closed the door and stepped into the humidity-controlled atmosphere of the workshop, which reminded him again of a quiet hell, though he could not say why.

Sixty-Six

Aegu seemed tired. His face was whiter than usual, his cheeks drawn. There were red flecks in his eyes. Apart from these physical manifestations of overwork, he seemed in reasonable spirits.

He was strangely exultant over a meeting with Chernavin. Following Pridilenko's death, the chairmanship of the committee overseeing the defence of the America's Cup had been taken over by Sergei Mamayev. Aegu had been asked to sit on the newly constituted committee.

'It was a somewhat unusual meeting,' Aegu said. 'Chernavin could not bring himself to look directly at me. He merely glowered in my general direction from the other end of the table.'

It was still Illich's habit not to criticize senior officers, a habit he found difficult to break, even now that he was outside the Army.

Aegu was seated in a chair in Illich's office, chain-smoking.

'Chernavin managed, after considerable effort, to acknowledge the fact that the Army's defending yacht had been beaten. He even put forward the proposal that it was clear *Novy Mir* was the superior boat. I thought this was further progress. Then I saw what he was leading towards. Chernavin stated that it was in the best interests of the defence to combine Pilnyak and his crew with the boat *Novy Mir*. If this formula were accepted, the challenge would eliminate its anti-social elements, namely you and Jim Shaw. "Anti-social elements".' Aegu smiled at the recollection. 'It is a phrase out of the past, preserved like a dinosaur in the mind of this man.'

Aegu shook his head. 'I thought to myself: this is someone who would drive tanks into a free country and describe opposition as anti-social.' He drew on his cigarette. 'What is frightening is not that it is an individual madness, but that it represents the old collective madness of the Party. The only difference is that whereas the old Party faithfuls would have ordered the tanks in on behalf of the proletariat, this type of military mind would do so in the name of order.'

'I agree that General Chernavin is not a special case,' Illich said. He remembered the troika of Chernavin, Zholudev and Litski who had intended to court martial him.

Aegu breathed out a plume of smoke from the corner of his mouth. He stubbed out the cigarette in a metal dish now littered with cigarette ends. Finally he said: 'I replied that this suggestion was out of the question. Chernavin said it should be put to the vote. I argued that, with due respect, it was not up to him to suggest the means of continuing the defence. The Army group had lost.' Aegu tapped another cigarette on the packet, and placed it in his mouth. He had run out of matches. Illich remembered the lighter in his own pocket. He took it out, removed the handkerchief, and lit Aegu's cigarette.

'Thank you. An American lighter, I see.' Aegu settled

back. 'I thought Chernavin would explode. When people are that angry, I find, they reach a kind of plateau and can get no angrier, and so one can do other things with impunity. I said that I wished to express my deep anger at the harassment of the Estonian syndicate by Russian Army helicopters. I suggested that a motion condemning this should be put to the vote. Mamayev agreed. A vote condemning the practice was carried by one. Mamayev had to exercise his Chairman's vote in favour.'

A breeze was blowing outside, drawing the plumes of Aegu's cigarette smoke through the open window. Illich felt a deep foreboding. He wanted to say to Aegu: 'Be careful, you are now in the firing line.' He could not formulate the words without sounding portentous. There was a brief silence, and then the moment had gone.

Aegu liked his coffee black. One of his two guards knocked on the door, having made two cups in the nearby rudimentary kitchen. It was only natural that Aegu and his men should help themselves to the facilities and, in offering Illich a cup of coffee, Aegu should act as gracious host.

'Thank you, Comrade,' Illich said to Aegu's guard. The door was closed silently.

Aegu sipped his coffee, grimaced as if he had swallowed poison, and pronounced: 'Excellent.' He sat back in his chair, his tie undone, his square left hand laid out on the table, his brown-stained right hand holding a cigarette wedged between second and third fingers.

Illich returned his thoughts to the subject of Aegu's safety. He himself was curiously devoid of fear. It was perhaps one of the few beneficial consequences of effectively having lost his family. But unlike him, Aegu was important, one of those figures on whom history turns. Most Estonians would have felt similarly, he thought. In this matter, however, Aegu appeared to pre-empt him.

'I can see you are concerned for me, *tovarich*. You are thinking perhaps that I could follow in Pridilenko's footsteps.'

336

'I assumed Pridilenko was invulnerable.'

'I am chastened. Your concern is appreciated. I do not say there is no danger. In this world, virtually every politician, every public figure, is in some form of danger. You learn simply to ignore it, apart from a few sleepless nights.'

'You have antagonized Chernavin personally.'

Aegu smiled.

'And you, of course, you lead by example, always taking the least contentious course.'

'I think like a soldier. Risk is part of my work.'

'Ah yes, a soldier. And as a soldier, you are asking me not to antagonize the military. You understand their mentality. You know what they can do.'

'Yes.'

'What could Chernavin do?' Aegu asked with almost shy interest. 'If he arranged for my demise, for example, there would be major upheaval and anger in Estonia against the Russian state, not out of affection for me, but at the interference of a foreign power in Estonian affairs.'

'Chernavin might see those riots as an excuse to re-occupy the country militarily.'

Aegu halted now. He regarded Illich with detached interest, drawing on his cigarette, waiting for him to speak. Illich, taking advantage of this halt in the one-sided flow from Aegu, continued: 'In all political matters, I listen to you. But in this, I know the military better than you. As you said previously, this is a man who would drive tanks into a free country.'

'Granted,' Aegu stated. 'But he would have to contend with his own politicians first.'

Though no politician, Illich was capable of following through a line of reason. He had a suspicion that Aegu was encouraging him to do so. 'If he is in the process of eliminating the effective opposition, like Pridilenko, perhaps he would see an outbreak of disorder in a satellite state as an opportunity to take power.'

He knew that this was not new to Aegu; rather, that Aegu was using him as a sounding board for his own nightmares.

'It is a nice thesis,' said Aegu. 'He arranges to dispose of the Estonian President, rioting breaks out, Estonia threatens to sever all military links with Russia, to move out from its theatre of influence. Then he uses the disorder to occupy the country, to overthrow evolving democratic institutions and re-establish order.'

'The Chinese generals re-established order in June 1989,' Illich said.

'They did not, as far as we know, foment the students' revolution that preceded their action. However, that may be a detail. The point is they reacted in a certain way. Is that what you are saying?'

'Yes.'

'It is all very interesting. As an outsider, I try to place myself in the mind of the Russian military. They sit in their offices with their enormous physical firepower; with tanks, guns, rockets, intercontinental missiles. And the democratic procedures are pushing them aside. They are treated as pariahs, as relics of the old order. They see politicians playing to the masses.

'For nearly two decades there have been continuous improvements in relations between Russia and America. They are lost. They see the old order dissolving, the theatre of confrontation breaking down.'

Aegu continued to smoke.

'Do you know what you have done with this absurd yacht race? Estonia may produce some of the finest academies in the world in certain disciplines, we may be one of the greatest producers of oil shale, over the past two decades we have been in the process of successfully extricating ourself from the Russian sphere. Our past is full of tragedy, our history is as rich as the Baltic itself, but until now the country was a little known entity, an area on a map. And now, having defeated Russia in a yacht race, we are suddenly on everyone's lips. If you will forgive me, *tovarich*, I feel a certain irritation over this matter. I work on the political stage, making decisions, coaxing, pushing, driving. You, on the other hand, cross the finish line in a yacht, and suddenly everything I have struggled for has arrived. The world regards us as a sovereign nation at last. We are no longer on a level with mythical fairy-tale kingdoms, but a modern state, with all its idiosyncracies.'

Aegu inhaled, breathing out slowly.

'And now,' Aegu continued, 'we have to face America. Do we have it in ourselves to defeat not one military super-power, but two?'

'It is unlikely,' Illich said.

'You have beaten the Americans before.'

This was still a sensitive point. Illich felt his mind go cloudy.

'The American helmsman turned away. I lost.' So, he had said it at last.

Aegu regarded him carefully.

'There are two rival defenders in this series,' Illich continued, 'and thirty-one rival challengers.'

'Ah, the military mind again,' Aegu said kindly. 'Or a touch of personal modesty, perhaps.'

'I am not modest, merely a realist.'

'A realist, of course. And as a realist you are also warning me to be on guard against General Chernavin.'

Aegu stood up. Illich heard one of Aegu's guards moving in the corridor. They reminded him again of faithful dogs, stirred by an almost telepathic sympathy with their master. When he thought of Chernavin, these two men at least gave him confidence that Aegu was not wholly unprotected.

Sixty-Seven

The crew were given two days' leave. Most – the unmarried ones – went to St Petersburg to drink and to pick up girls. Out of time-honoured military habit, Illich read them the lesson on diseases, and the importance of keeping in groups in some of St Petersburg's low dives. They laughed and cheered.

The entire camp had followed Vagir's example and taken to calling him 'Colonel'. From his own point of view, it was a scandal and an outrage. The new ones, hardly more than half his age, made him feel like some retired White Russian general.

Several of the older ones, Prem included, visited their wives and families and girlfriends, driving back to Estonia through the night. The following day the camp was almost deserted, except for a couple of guards, and several of the married couples. Jim Shaw and Maria asked Illich to supper that evening with Brod and Ilena.

Maria had converted the outbuilding, with its primitive facilities, into a charming little residence. It had been scrubbed and whitewashed on the inner walls. A partition had been set up for their son Jack.

One of Vagir's carpenters had run them up a table. This evening its scrubbed boards groaned with dishes. As they were on Russian soil, Maria and Ilena had collaborated to prepare a meal *à la Russe*.

They began with vodka and *bliny*, small buckwheat cakes with black Beluga caviare which Ilena had bought in Leningrad. Seated around the room on old sailbags scattered about the floorboards, they might have been in some modern architect's house, except that necessity, rather than aesthetics, had dictated the décor.

Afterwards they settled on wooden stools around the table, and ate *borsch*, with ham and cabbage added to the basic beetroot, and *pirozhki*.

There were toasts to Illich by Shaw and Brod. He was, said Brod, a bit past his prime in his steering ability, of course, but he was more or less adequate. Shaw nodded and they drank. Then Shaw's turn came. Illich's tactics, said Shaw, were a little rusty, but with more practice he could be helped back to form. They drank again.

But Illich, who had waited for this occasion long enough, raised his glass and toasted two strongminded women, without whose influence on their menfolk their victory over *Kirov* would have been impossible.

During the main meal, *kulebiaka*, a flaky pastry loaf stuffed with salmon, more toasts were made, to the absent members, to Vagir and his men, to the sailmakers, and to the Siberian tactician on *Kirov* whose loss of concentration for a few seconds had let them through in the final race.

Then they ate, for desert, *vareniky*, sweet dumplings filled with fruit, and made more toasts, to the helicopters of the Russian Armed Forces for their deep interest in the syndicate affairs, to the journalists who by day still crowded the perimeter fence, and not forgetting Kalev Tammiste, the greatest genius of yacht design perhaps for all time.

Maria said she thought Tammiste was 'sweet', and they toasted him again. The facilities were somewhat cramped, the three men went outside to relieve themselves in the darkness. Behind the little bungalow was a telephone post. The three of them were urinating on the post when a flash of light announced the presence of hitherto hidden cadres of the press photographer corps behind the nearby fence.

The photograph, of the three afterguard of *Novy Mir*, taken from behind, became a classic of the tabloids. The British *Sun*, leading the fray, had the caption, 'Now for the Americans'. Vagir and his men, over the next few days, pinned the newspaper cutout of the picture on their notice-board. In case anyone should miss the point, Vagir had written in biro underneath, 'A typical working day in the life of those for whom we work.'

Apart from the embarrassing incident of the photograph, it was a very good evening. When Illich, Brod and Ilena left at three in the morning, not even the press were present to see them manoeuvre unsteadily across the lawn to their respective residences.

Before retiring to sleep, Illich called by the main building to check on *Novy Mir*. The two men Vagir had left were on station, playing cards to while the time away. They shone a light on his face as he opened the door, recognized him, and said 'Excuse me, Colonel.'

Tonight at least he was beyond caring about being called 'Colonel', and found his way to his bedroom in the main residential quarters. He did not wake until just after nine in the morning.

He had a prodigious hangover – the result of, among other things, the excellent Armenian brandy they had drunk in the early hours.

It was the first time for months that he had time to think about himself. Perhaps it was the emptiness of the camp, perhaps his isolation, which caused the memory of his lost family to strike him so forcibly. He realized, with melancholy hindsight, that he would give up everything to be with them. There was not much affection remaining between him and Anna, but with an effort they could have made it tolerable. He went through his memories of the two girls, of their last meeting in Kharkov; memories laid out like small, bright threads.

Half an hour later, he stood up to wash and shave. From his window he could see, past the sprawling sheds of the encampment, two sails in the bay.

Water had not yet been laid to the building in which he resided. He had to fill a bowl from a tap on the side of the building shed. He lathered and washed himself carefully in the chipped enamel bowl, studying progress in a mirror propped against the whitewashed wall.

The face that stared back at him in the mirror was never one that he had easily identified with. It seemed cold, inhuman, wolfish. He had even distrusted women who were drawn to that face. His father, from whom he had inherited his bony features and pale, expressionless eyes, had quoted to him the words of the missionary Pertsov: 'Inside the eyes of every demon there lives a fallen angel'. Somehow, on this late summer morning, with only the sounds of birds for company, he hoped that it was true.

After shaving he dressed in shirt and sweater and, ignoring the entreaties of the press for comments, picked up the pile of newspapers that had been delivered to the gate of the compound, retreating once again to his office.

He, Jim Shaw, Brod and Prem had all watched with fascination as the American steamroller advanced through the challenging fleet. Every day that they had sailed, they had taken advantage of any opportunity to study the American boat sailing. Illich's private view of the merits of the American effort was formed by direct observation. It was seldom that he read accounts in newspapers, except occasionally to remind himself of their inaccuracy, but for the first time in what seemed ages he had time to kill.

He opened the papers. A typical article was headed 'ESTONIAN SAILING GENIUS OVERCOMES OPPOSITION.'

Yesterday the Estonian sailing genius Ivan Illich effortlessly outmanoeuvred the highly drilled Russian sailing team on Kirov, *reaching a four-nil lead, an overwhelming victory in the defender trials.*

What did that explain? The victory was used to deduce that Illich was a 'genius', which in turn was used to explain the victory. It was an empty, circular process. The further assumption that 'genius' is 'effortless' added nothing to the picture.

In the matter of assessment of the Americans, he preferred a non-partisan view. The British *Times* was of marginally more interest.

The American predominance over the other challengers occurs not just in one set of weather conditions, but in all. Classic winners of the race have generally exhibited weaknesses. Australia II, *for example, was known to 'wobble' in a choppy sea with little wind, conditions in which she could be beaten by almost any of her rivals. Dennis Conner's* Stars and Stripes *was known to be vulnerable in light weather conditions. The professionalism of the Americans is evidenced in an apparent lack of weaknesses, a characteristic which must currently be exercising the mind of the defending helmsman, Ivan Illich.*

It was always gratifying to know what was exercising one's mind. But at least the summary supplied information which was of potential use.

Illich turned to John Herrick and read the following.

There is here a curious conjunction. The American effort has no apparent weaknesses. In virtually every respect, in organization, crewing, sail technology, boat design, their yacht Eagle *is marginally but significantly ahead of her rivals. In most respects* Novy Mir *seems rather similar to her rivals; her sail technology is not out of the ordinary, her crew-work is confident and effective, but it does not have the bloodthirsty efficiency of the American squad. The organisation behind her is loyal, but lacks the single-minded drive of the American challenge team. But she does have the odd taint of genius. Her helmsman is perhaps the greatest living sailor; her tactician is a man of almost comparable talent, and her unusual hull, with its oddly shaped aft sections, may hold the promise of speed.*

Those of us who have speculated about the protagonists' respective merits will be watching this coming contest with special interest. Paradoxically, the USA is the land of the individual, and she has

produced a machine. Estonia, that small, calm state, has produced
a team of individualists. One would like to say the outcome looks
uncertain. But that would be inaccurate. Regrettably, in this case,
the machine will win.

Illich felt the blood rise to his head. In his mind he knew Herrick was right. All the odds were on the side of the American juggernaut. But journalism had another function. It could anger and provoke. It could even sharpen, in a participant who is forced to recognize a palpable truth, a growing anger, a determination to win.

Sixty-Eight

He called by the rough wooden pigeonholes where the letters were delivered. In the pigeonhole reserved for him there were several telegrams of congratulation, one from the University of Tartu, invitations to lecture, some bills for equipment, a handful of messages from individuals. One, in a blue envelope, caught his eye. He opened it with his thumb and stared at the writing with its long upstrokes and neat lines.

Dear Ivan,
    Am in St Petersburg, staying at the Pribaltiyskaya Hotel, at U1.
Korablestroitely, on the West part of Vasil'yevskiy Island. I am
attending a conference here on child psychology. It lasts for two
weeks.
    I read that you won the defender trials. Wonderful news.
    Artur arrives here next week. In the meantime, I would give
anything for some non-academic company!
    Yours
    Lydia

It was written on the headed paper of the Pribaltiyskaya. At the bottom right hand corner, written by hand, there was a room number: 233.

He went to his small office, which housed the only telephone in the camp, and rang the number on the letterhead. A girl's voice answered, with the slightly clipped accent of St Petersburgers. He asked for room 233. The telephone rang for some time. He was about to put down the phone when it was picked up at the other end.

'Lydia?'

'Who is it?'

'Illich.'

She had always disliked him using his surname, and replied: 'Teemant here.'

'The crew are all away for two days. Could I meet you this evening?'

A moment of reticence. She was seeing someone else?

'Yes. I didn't expect you to phone so soon.'

'Your letter just arrived.'

'I have to go to the conference in an hour's time. I'm just making some notes now. I'll be back at about six. If you could give me an hour to bathe and get ready.'

'Seven?' he asked.

'Seven.'

'Goodbye, Illich,' she said, chiding him again.

Afterwards, he went through the letters and drafted out replies for Ilena to type when the work began again.

There was no communication from the Russian camp. It is a custom in the America's Cup competition that the team who has been beaten in the defender trials offers his facilities to the successful party, so that their strengths are combined against the challenger. If he had been of more belligerent disposition, he would have written a letter of complaint. It amused him for a few seconds to compose in his mind such a letter.

Dear General Vorolov,
   It has come my notice that, as the defeated team

346

*in the defender selection trials of the America's Cup, you have not
seen fit to offer your camp's facilities to us so that jointly, in
true military spirit, we may go on to strive for Russian
victory against the challengers. In this respect you have broken with
the tradition of mutual assistance. Your action, in this case lack of
action, has weakened our effort against the common enemy.*

Your fraternal comrade,
Ivan Ivanovich Illich
(formerly of the Russian Army)

The taxi which came to collect him was driven by a Byelorussian driver. Taped against the dashboard beside his
large, powerful hands, like an icon whose face he could
touch, was an image of Stalin in half profile, smiling with an
almost vulpine expression. Even from that angle Stalin's
cheeks were fat. Illich wondered whether it was taken in
the late period, the period of gluttony, when his wife had
committed suicide. He found the image so offensive that he
was inclined to ask the driver why he displayed it. However,
the Byelorussian looked aggressive and – what was perhaps
more threatening – entirely humourless. So, as with the
letter he had composed in his mind to Vorolov, he desisted.
Instead, as they travelled the coastal road, he gazed out
across the water of the bay, lit by that crystal light of the
north which is curiously tolerant of all objects, expressing a
kind of lucid indifference. A large grey warship was moving
majestically across the bay. It was close enough to identify.
A Tibilisi-class aircraft carrier, recently commissioned, the
Boris Yeltsin. Lacking overt guns, it was nevertheless replete
with the sinister shapes of missile housings. On its aft deck
he could see clearly a helicopter and the sleeker shape of one
of its upgraded Forger V/STOL aircraft. As he watched, a
fresh white wake spewed aft as it turned on the full power of
its four steam turbines. Seagulls turned in its wake, falling
like snowflakes. It reminded him of the time he, Brod and
Ilena had sat in their garden last year overlooking the Black

Sea. In the foreground, the German and American teams were practising separately before their match the following day. Beyond them, the great warship moved carefully on its track, oblivious.

The lounge of the Pribaltiyskaya Hotel was full of business-men with a sprinkling of academics. There had been less traffic on the journey into St Petersburg than he expected and he was several minutes early. A group of smartly dressed Siberians discussed the opening of a chain of fresh produce shops, their cigarette smoke rolling in ecstatic waves across the foyer. This was an almost certain means of distinguishing between Russian businessmen and their health- and ecology-conscious Western counterparts. The Russians, still at the stage of conspicuous consumption, smoked heavily. There was a joke that the best means of bringing a Swedish or American businessman to clinch a deal was patiently to breathe cigarette smoke into his face until his fear for his health overcame his fear for his bank balance. Apart from the Siberians, there were no other Russian citizens in the foyer. Westerners dominated in this hotel.

At five minutes past seven he asked the desk clerk to ring up to room 233 and inform Dr Teemant he was in the foyer. The desk clerk had to go inside the office to ring. A short while later he emerged: 'Doctor Teemant will be down in a little while, sir.'

She surprised him by arriving a few minutes afterwards. It was part of her directness. He watched her walk across the foyer with that self-possession which he found both alluring and slightly intimidating.

They embraced. Her cheeks were smooth, almost cool. In public greetings she seemed distant.

'I don't know the local restaurants,' Illich said. 'Do you have a favourite?'

348

'The Kadorski.' She did not hesitate. 'Just round the corner. We can walk.'

Arm in arm they crossed the street, turning down the new International Friendship Boulevard. St Petersburg was, if anything, in advance of Moscow. The shops, particularly the clothes and shoe shops, were full of products. Large international stores proliferated. The new boulevard was an aggregation of fashionable brand names. The residents were as well dressed as any European city – perhaps like those who have newly acquired prosperity, a little over-dressed.

The Kadorski was in a small sidestreet. It had a modest exterior, a pale blue door without signs. Inside, however, was an extensive floorspace, strong wooden tables, chairs as thick and heavy as church pews, low ceiling lights. Though unadvertised, off the tourist track, it seemed to be well patronized.

The maître seemed to recognize her and ushered them to a secluded alcove on the far side of the room. Illich, who needed a clear head for the following morning, ordered a bottle of Georgian white Tsinandali wine, promising himself that he would drink only sparely. After the maître had left, Illich said: 'He seems to know you.'

'It's my favourite place.'

They were silent for several seconds. At a nearby table, a man was saying in a voice that sounded both listless and pedantic: 'In the old days, a great deal of the official menu was not available. Reading a menu then was a surreal act, an act of the imagination. Today all the charm has been removed. It is now a mundane fact. What is there can no longer be caressed by the imagination. No – horror of horrors – it is actually here to be eaten.'

He guessed that the author of this remark must be some kind of artist.

'Frankly,' his companion said, 'the international market is no good for fiction. Satire is no longer fashionable. Voino-vich did all that.'

349

Lydia Teemant smiled at him, the smile of a lover who shares a secret. The maître returned with a bottle of wine and two food menus. All through the previous weeks, it seemed to Illich, he had issued a stream of orders, exhortations. Now, with her in front of him, he did not wish to speak again. He was content to study her as the conversation at the next table continued.

'So, what is left?' the first man asked. 'What do you think of the report of a resurgence of reading in the young?'

'Frankly, if it's true, it hasn't affected us. The motive has gone out of the intelligentsia. Repressive liberalism has had its effect. It is no longer dangerous to write. Now all writers do is produce soft porn and argue about contracts.'

'It's a sorry state,' the other agreed. 'In the old days young writers used to deliver their manuscripts personally, because they were frightened of sending it by post, in case it fell into the wrong hands. They used to come into my office, trembling with ecstatic fear. They had written something tender and truthful, and they would have to suffer. Do the KGB know what they've done to the quality of writing? They used to be so reliable.'

'A lawsuit, perhaps, for offences against the state of literature.' This must have been a joke, but the other did not laugh.

'A public show-trial, I think, would be more appropriate, preferably with the verdict worked out in advance.'

It was clearly something they had been through before, a joke worn smooth with retelling, perhaps embellished here and there.

It made Illich laugh. Lydia Teemant merely smiled, as if it were simply part of the entertainment of the place. At neighbouring tables other couples were laughing. Lydia Teemant whispered: 'Semyov and Barushnikov, a comedy team. They practise their routines here. The maître gives them a free meal, as much as they can eat, in return for attracting customers.'

This was indeed surreal. Illich raised his head surreptitiously so that his eyes were at a sufficient elevation to look over the wooden partition dividing them and the satirists. The one called Semyov was a white-bearded man in his forties. Barushnikov was short, plump, bald. Illich lowered his eyes. Lydia Teemant whispered: 'They're on television, they're famous.'

Semyov said: 'One is struck by a certain nostalgia for the old days, of course. The KGB was bad and you knew where you were. You were unsafe in your bed at night, and all things were constant.'

'You look thin and fit,' Lydia Teemant said to him, 'but not healthy.'

'Is that a compliment or a criticism?'

'Neither,' she whispered, then: 'Both.'

Part of him was still listening to their neighbours' comments about the sorry state of modern liberalism, the weakness of the KGB. For so many years he had been living underground, like a mole, and only now was emerging into this strange new world, with its subtle but profound shifts in emphasis. St Petersburgers prided themselves on their modernity, and this was hardly typical of Russia as a whole, but it was nevertheless a jolt.

Lydia Teemant's knees touched his under the table.

'Ready to order?' asked the maître. 'Starters?'

'Zalyvnaya ryba,' Lydia Teemant said. 'Then Baranina.'

'And you, sir?'

'Silyotka. Main course Svinina. And another bottle of the Tsinandali.'

'Thank you.'

The maître left for the table of Semyov and Barushnikov. 'Messieurs?'

Listening to the two comedians was a pleasant drug.

'What do you *not* have today?' Semyov asked.

'Only the gavyadina. We have everything else.'

'The gavyadina! My mouth was watering over the gavyadina!'

'Leave him alone,' Barushnikov said. 'He's not an ideal-ist like you.'

'But it was probably the best gavyadina he never had!'

'Literary gavyadina. Good for the soul but bad for the stomach. Let him be.'

The two comedians were not so funny now that Illich knew who they were. Good humour was like snuff; you teetered on the edge of surprise. Lydia Teemant folded her hands and looked across the table at him.

'Are you pleased to have won?'

Curiously enough, no. He merely looked ahead to the next problem. It was difficult to say this, however, because it invariably disappointed his listener. A helmsman's mind is not satisfied by success. If it were, one meal would be enough.

Semyov came to his rescue: 'Give me an egg then,' he said to the maitre. 'A KGB egg.'

'A KGB egg?'

'Hard on the outside,' Semyov explained, 'soft on the inside.'

As with a number of satirists, the KGB had played cat-and-mouse with Semyov during his earlier, struggling years, and he lost no opportunity in baiting it now as far as he could go.

'And how has your conference been?' asked Illich.

'Busy. One uses these occasions to establish contact with the people in the same field overseas. I beg them to send me papers and periodicals we still find difficult to get here.'

'I am still trying to think up refutations of your theory that repressed children make better adult citizens.'

'And have you?'

'Take myself, for instance. I had a strict, disciplinarian father, and yet I am conformist in all things.'

'You were arrested for causing a riot at Tartu, and then expelled from the Army for commandeering the yacht *Lenin-grad*. Hardly conformist.'

'Circumstances,' pleaded Illich. 'Small things.'

'Naturally. Martin Luther also thought of himself as a conformist. And I didn't say children should be repressed. I said they should not be over-indulged.'

On the other table, Barushnikov was saying: 'You better bring the chicken along as well.'

'Chicken Kiev,' Semyov added. 'For two.'

'Anything else?'

'Yes. Why does the KGB remind me of my grandfather?'

'I don't know,' said the put-upon maître.

'Because his teeth have fallen out and he can't screw anyone any more.'

'Anything else, sir?'

The maître disappeared. Semyov and Barushnikov appeared to have satisfied their consciences in the matter of entertaining their fellow customers. They no longer raised their voices. In the silence Illich stared into the unwavering green eyes of Lydia Teemant.

It was a good meal, though Illich was no gourmet. Talking with her relaxed him.

In bed with her afterwards she commented again on the surface damage to his body, the bruises, cuts, contusions, half-healed scars, which covered his skin. He had no vanity about his looks. His body had a peculiar Nordic boniness, at an opposite pole to the bronzed, somewhat fleshy beauty of classical Greek statues. In his own eyes at least, it had all the aesthetic appeal of a forklift truck.

Lydia Teemant commented mischievously on his physical characteristics, deflecting attention from her own. He wondered whether it was her form of feminism. At the sight of her naked, stepping across the room, her gently swinging breasts, he was silent, feeling such comment intrusive.

In bed, however, he could not arouse her. She lay against him passively, and he drifted off to sleep. In the early hours he felt her move and, cautiously, slide a leg across him. She felt him stir and whispered 'Don't speak' as she knelt astride him, encouraging him into her.

He left her sleeping, dressed and left quietly at five-thirty.

The doorman was tolerant. With the extra conciliation of a five rouble note, he tapped the sleeping desk clerk on the shoulder so that Illich could use a telephone to call a taxi. During the time that the taxi took to arrive, the old doorman talked to him of his life in the Army. As he opened the glass door and allowed Illich out, the old man was weeping for no apparent reason. Age, he explained, made one sentimental.

Sixty-Nine

'Move, you scum!'

Prem it was who took the exercise classes, a majordomo of considerable talent and malevolence. A former paratrooper, and the oldest of them all, the others claimed it gave him an excuse to cease exercising himself in order to strut about and instruct the others.

The crew had returned in ones, twos and threes the previous evening from St Petersburg, two with blackened eyes from a waterfront fight. Mercifully, there were no broken limbs or split skulls. They were asleep shortly after dark like, Prem commented, a pack of wolves after a hard day's hunting. Prem liked to quote from an Estonian fairy tale in which it is said that the wicked elves sleep best of all. At six they gathered on the exercise ground where, wicked elves or not, Prem mercilessly played on their hangovers.

After seventy-five minutes of relentless physical punishment they were allowed to leave for the boats.

In their sail-training programme, they were subject to the ebb and flow of media interest. The American yacht *Eagle* had just beaten the British in the semi-finals, and was due to face the Germans in the finals. The press seemed elsewhere, at the American and German camps. Illich decided that, this morning at least, it would be possible to take an early morning practice. Vagir and his men were in the process of lowering both yachts into the water for the day. At seven, the crew broke off from exercising on Illich's command to pile sails on the yachts and prepare for racing.

Shortly before they were due to set off, there was a commotion at the gates. At first Illich thought that a particularly obstreperous section of the press corps was trying to force entry.

A young man with long, fair hair seemed to be at the centre of it. The guards at the gate were answering his own imprecations with ones of their own. Illich looked again. He was vaguely familiar.

Brod, standing at his elbow, said: 'Ian Sinclair.'

A light dawned. The British challenge helmsman, the Flying Dutchman Olympic Gold medallist in 2000, when he was absent; the crown prince of his class.

He walked up to the guards.

'Sinclair?'

'Illich.'

'Let him in,' Illich said to the guards.

They shook hands. Sinclair wore jeans and a teeshirt. He had the usual bonebreaking handshake of the helmsman.

'I wondered whether you could do with a practice helmsman,' Sinclair said, 'someone who knows the Americans.'

It was an offer which struck home. The second crew on *Leningrad* were not a close match. If, on the other hand, he split up the first crew, allowing say Jim Shaw to take the second boat, they would lose their team cohesion.

'Can you sail now?'

'Of course.'

The British had, against all expectations, won the first race in the best of seven races against the Americans.

'You did well in the first race,' Illich said. 'What happened?'

'They just seemed to go up a gear, and rolled right over us. They won the next four races in succession.'

'Where are they strong?' Illich asked.

'Everywhere,' Sinclair confirmed. 'A completely professional effort.'

'Jim Shaw,' Illich introduced them.

'An honour,' Sinclair said.

'Going to teach us a lesson?' Shaw asked slyly.

At the boats, Illich introduced him to the second crew. Their helmsman, Gundar Arlof, was not too put out to be replaced by an international star.

Towards *Leningrad*, a good-natured enthusiasm flowed out of Sinclair. He examined the cockpit layout carefully, enquiring here, nodding his approval there.

By seven thirty-five they were being towed out, past the group of early, waiting press boats, into the quiet waters of the bay.

The winds were light at this time of the morning, hardly ruffling the water. Flowing offshore, they generated sufficient force to fill the sails of the two boats.

The support launch laid down the buoys that would mark the course.

Even to Illich, it was a useful experience to be reminded of the power of a world class helmsman. *Leningrad* recently had seemed to their eyes lacklustre. The practice races with the second crew were tepid affairs, slow waltzes with a maiden aunt. With Sinclair aboard, *Leningrad* descended upon them in the prestart manoeuvres like the hand of God. They found themselves fighting for their lives.

Caught unawares, they were trounced in the first race. The second crew, smelling blood, started to gain confidence. Gundar Arlof, as tactician, could be seen explaining to Sinclair Illich's special manoeuvres. It was clear that Sinclair was not awed by the toughness of the experienced Estonian first crew, or the mental firepower of *Novy Mir*'s afterguard.

By midmorning the score was two all in the short practice

races. Illich, Shaw, Brod and Prem stepped back on shore as angry as bears. Sinclair shook hands with them, and asked cheerfully 'Same time tomorrow?'

'That would be good of you,' Illich said through his teeth. They watched Sinclair saunter back to his camp a few hundred yards down the road. Illich had an unpleasant vision of Sinclair saying to his British companions 'Nice people, those Estonians. Had to teach them how to sail of course. A bit more training and they could be quite good.'

It was Illich's custom after practice races to hold a debriefing session. Usually, with the benefit of easy victory over the second team, he could lecture and harangue the other crew with impunity, request better performances from them the following day, and set out some of the other goals of tomorrow's racing practice. Today, however, Gundar Arlof, now apparently fully recovered from his wound, rubbed salt in Illich's by suggesting that several of *Novy Mir*'s tactical ploys needed practice if they were to work 'against a really expert crew, Colonel'.

The 'Colonel' restrained himself only with difficulty.

His afternoon was spent in administration, an almost soothing occupation after the humiliations of the morning. The following morning he waited for Sinclair to appear. He was ten minutes late, another factor which threw Illich into a quiet rage. Unruffled, Sinclair stepped onto *Leningrad* and the towboats drew both yachts away into the wry morning sunlight.

There was more breeze today, about ten knots, but not consistent. On board *Leningrad* there was a shout of laughter from Gundar Arlof at a joke by Sinclair. They hauled up respective mainsails and cast off from their towing launch.

'He's really got you worked up, hasn't he?' Jim Shaw said laconically.

'Nonsense. I am calmness itself.'

'Sure.' Shaw was sympathetic. 'What about trying to unclench your fingers from the wheel.'

Illich glanced down at his white knuckles.

'Just thinking of the wheel,' Shaw said.

Illich smiled stiffly.

'What about your jaw now?' Shaw suggested. 'It helps to try opening your mouth when you speak.'

Brod was guffawing to himself as he studied the instrumentation. Illich shouted: 'Raise genoa.'

Prem was joining in the others' mirth. Illich was shocked. Prem, his crew-boss, the disciplinarian, the dedicated mainsheet trimmer, now was laughing out loud.

To restrain himself, Illich studied the other yacht. The foresail had been raised. Sinclair had seated himself to windward and, with one hand on the wheel, was bearing away slightly to pick up speed.

'Two minutes to the gun,' Shaw said. 'Unless you explode first.'

Brod was weeping with laughter in the cockpit, rubbing the tears from his eyes.

'Shall we start sailing now?' Illich suggested. He would have to give up hope of beating Sinclair today. Tomorrow perhaps.

But the sail went up in reasonable order, and by the time the ten-minute gun went *Novy Mir* was moving tolerably well through the water. *Leningrad* closed in with them. There was a flurry of turns as the two boats battled like stallions for predominance.

This time *Novy Mir* got the better of *Leningrad*, and began to drive her away from the line. While the other yacht bullies him away from the start, cutting off retreat, it is usually a humiliating time for the loser. But in this case Sinclair seemed unconcerned. With one hand on the wheel, he was explaining a point to Gundar Arlof. Neither took much interest in the boat following. For a little over two minutes *Leningrad* sailed away from the line. Then, almost casually, without looking back, Sinclair must have spun the wheel one-handed on the lower rim, without apparent movement. *Leningrad* sprung up into wind. Illich shouted 'coming up', and swung to cut off *Leningrad*. But in the turmoil and thunder of swinging *Novy Mir* into wind, *Leningrad* had spun downwind, Sinclair surreptitiously moving the wheel by deft wrist movements below the line of sight. *Leningrad* gybed while they were still pointing up. Illich swung to follow, but *Leningrad* was too far ahead in her manoeuvre now to be cut off. Suddenly she was facing them, on starboard tack, with right of way, and driving back towards the start line. Sinclair was perched up to windward, driving her fast, forcing right of way. Illich had been completely wrong-footed.

He followed *Leningrad* round, and tacked to free his wind. *Leningrad* tacked on top of him. Illich shouted: 'Tack!' and they came through the wind again. *Leningrad* followed suit. Fifteen tacks followed before the start line was reached.

'Look at that doggy go,' Shaw said.

'Tack!' roared Illich.

Twenty-five consecutive tacks later, and *Leningrad* was almost stopped in the water, her winchmen flailing for breath. Only *Novy Mir*'s more experienced grinders saved her from defeat. As a result of their efforts, *Novy Mir* slid past her opponent with one and a half knots more boatspeed.

This time they won three out of four short races against *Leningrad*. But every one was close. Each one required that Sinclair be watched like a hawk.

'Tomorrow, same time?' Sinclair asked.

'Please,' Illich replied.

He watched Sinclair walked casually away, and shook his head. Shaw said: 'No wonder that guy took the first race off *Eagle*.'

'No wonder,' Illich agreed.

Seventy

'Our friend John Ericson is at it again,' Jim Shaw said.

He placed a newspaper in front of Illich at the breakfast table. It was headed *US SKIPPER OBJECTS*.

John Ericson III, the skipper of the US America's Cup challenger Eagle, *held a press conference to complain today about the way in which the skipper and helmsman of the British challenger, Ian Sinclair, was helping the Estonians to prepare their defence. Ericson claimed that it was traditional that defeated challengers helped the winning challenger against the defender. He called the action on the part of the British skipper 'outright treachery'.*

Ian Sinclair, answering the charge, said that he had offered to help the American syndicate in their training, but they had 'turned his offer down out of hand'. He therefore felt free to go elsewhere. Mr Sinclair added that the defender, Novy Mir, *in fact derived from the small country of Estonia, a state effectively independent of the Russians. He felt they were the 'underdogs' and merited any help he could give them. Ericson, informed of his reply, said that the defence consisted largely of American and British turncoats. He was clearly referring to Jim Shaw, the former US America's Cup helmsman who has been involved in Ivan Illich's Estonian group.*

Illich said: 'He sounds charming.'

'Oh, he is,' replied Shaw. 'He's just the sort of guy to give America a good name.'

'Why is he so worried about Sinclair?'

'Sinclair's an intuitive helmsman, seat of the pants. Ericson's an organization man. Natural opposites. Wish we could use Sinclair to our advantage.'

Illich drank his coffee and turned over the page. There was some further comment of interest:

Today is the first round of the challenger selection finals between the US yacht Eagle *and the German yacht* Unification. *The Germans have produced a magnificent technical effort. Their yacht had always been the favourite to reach the challenger finals against the outstanding US team. The German helmsman Gustav Zimmer was an Olympic medallist in the Flying Dutchman class, one of that select group, including Jim Shaw and Ivan Illich, who dominated international yachting.*

Excellent though the German effort may be, the US are clear favourites to win. In all previous encounters, eight in all, the Americans won. The reason is that the two teams are very similar, both wholly professional. In this case, however, the Eagle *group is simply more so.*

Illich finished his coffee. They stood up and left the refectory on their way to the administration office. Shaw said: 'There's a rule in the revised constitution that says you can add an extra crew member in the form of an international "witness" or "adviser". The man has to be of a different nationality from the crew, and take no physical part in the race. Positionally, he has to stay aft of the helmsman throughout the entire course of the race.'

'I had forgotten that. The witness can give evidence in the case of protests, and he can advise the crew.'

'That's the idea.'

They walked a little further.

'I was thinking,' Shaw said. 'If Ericson is so spooked by Sinclair, why don't we take Sinclair on board as our "witness"?'

'An interesting concept.'

'Just a thought.'

They paused to look out to sea. It was nine-thirty and the Germans and Americans were practising.

'Do you think Sinclair would accept?'

Shaw shrugged: 'Let's ask.'

*

That afternoon Illich, Shaw and Brod went out in the support launch to watch the American yacht *Eagle* in action against the German team.

In a moderate breeze the two yachts manoeuvred cautiously, neither committing itself to a direct attack. They hit the line at the same time, two seconds behind the gun, and each began to slice to windward, about a hundred yards apart. *Eagle* drew ahead slowly but inexorably, turning the top mark four lengths ahead of her rival. Zimmer, the German helmsman, tried to break back in the downwind leg but *Eagle*'s cross tacks made it difficult, if not impossible. The American lead had doubled by the lower mark. After that it became processional. Zimmer managed to restrain the lead over the next two legs, but in the final windward leg, *Eagle* had drawn out a finish of one and a half minutes, a convincing win.

Illich carried away the impression of a heartless race, won by superlative technical proficiency. Shaw said: 'Ericson seems to have changed a lot. He used to come out every day and try and bludgeon me in the start manoeuvres. I just suspect that underneath that outer shell it's the same guy.'

But it was the same the following day. Zimmer tried to engage this time during the pre-start manoeuvres, but *Eagle* moved carefully out of reach and then did a 'timed run' to the line. There was more breeze than the previous day, but *Eagle* showed the same technical edge. To the Germans, who had beaten the other challengers by exactly such means, it must have been heartrending.

The following morning, Sinclair arrived at his usual time for a practice. Before they went on board the boat, Illich drew him aside.

'Do you know the international witness rule?'

'Vaguely.'

'A yacht is allowed to take on board a non-national as a witness. The witness can't participate physically in the crew work but he can offer advice.'

Sinclair smiled.

'What are you suggesting?'

'Perhaps you'd care to join us? That is, if it wouldn't jeopardize your position further.'

'With Ericson?' Sinclair laughed. 'I'd give anything to be there.'

'He'll criticize you in the press.'

'Sticks and stones may break my bones,' Sinclair replied. 'But bullshit doesn't do a lot to me.'

They shook hands. Then Sinclair beat them three–two in the practice races.

'Try and loosen that jaw up some,' Shaw suggested to Illich afterwards.

'Very amusing.'

Shaw tried again. 'As you're not much good at losing, have you thought of ventriloquism as a career? You wouldn't have to move your lips at all.'

'Ha, ha.'

'Look,' persisted Shaw, 'if I could just get a monkey wrench on those knuckles of yours, I might be able to prise them apart . . .'

Illich went to the administration offices. Shaw went to brief the sailmakers over recutting the sails.

The third race between *Eagle* and *Unification*, in light winds, followed the same pattern as the two previous races, except that this time the margin of win was a full three and a half minutes. The newspaper accounts were relentless:

Not since Dennis Conner in Stars and Stripes *beat* Kookaburra III *in 1987 in four straight races has there been such relentless domination as is currently being demonstrated here in the challenger finals. The two boats, magnificent technical products both of them, proceed about their business as if in an ancient ritual. It is a heartless slaughter. Each day the American tender, a shining piece of naval sculpture with a high bridge, and two powerful engines, tows back the victorious yacht to her palace by the water's edge. Rumour has it that the two other practice yachts in* Eagle's

entourage are each as fast as Eagle *herself. The same sources say
that Ericson could beat the opposition in any one of these three boats
if he chose.*

*Meanwhile, the British sailor Ian Sinclair continues to break
precedent by helming the practice yacht* Leningrad *against the
defender* Novy Mir. *The blood-and-guts battles between Illich and
Sinclair, conducted in the early morning offshore breezes, make
anything seen in the challenger eliminations seemed quiet by
comparison.*

The following day, *Novy Mir* beat *Leningrad* four-one in their
early-morning short practice races. In the second race,
during the pre-start manoeuvres, the two crews became
so tired during the fierce infighting that the two main
winchgrinders on each boat had to sit helplessly by, heaving
for breath, while the reserve winchmen took over.

In the later morning they took the launch out to view the
fourth race of the Challenger elimination finals. It was a
brisk breeze of eighteen knots, gusting twenty. Again the
German yacht *Unification* attempted to engage. This time
Eagle responded. The fur started to fly. Unlike the other
challengers, the superbly maintained American challenger
had experienced no significant gear failure throughout the
challenger trials. But in the pre-start mêlée the main halyard snapped with a sharp report. Ericson turned away,
with *Unification* chasing him hard. Within a few seconds of
the failure, the American bowman was being hauled up the
mast. Under full sail, the boat heeling to gusts, they
watched him ascend ninety feet in the air, above the loose,
flapping mainsail.

Unification was merciless in pressing her advantage. The
bowman rethreaded the halyard, and the mast crew hauled
up the mainsail again. The bowman abseiled down in great
loops. Now *Eagle* had full power again, but was being
pursued remorselessly away from the line.

Capitalizing on its position, the German yacht swung
back rapidly to the line. In a fast loop *Eagle* followed. Now

she was three boat lengths behind. The start gun issued its feather of smoke and the dull gong of its explosion. Twenty seconds later *Unification* crossed the line, followed by *Eagle*. *Eagle* tacked away. The German yacht tacked with her to provide close cover. There was a flurry of tacks and counter-tacks.

Illich could sense the pressure *Eagle* was placing on *Unification*. On the eighteenth tack the German yacht did not have the speed to tack again without the risk of stalling. *Eagle* broke free.

At the top mark, Ericson had sliced in on port tack across *Unification*'s bows, one and a half boat lengths up. It was the end of the German boat's only respite. At the finish *Eagle* powered its way across the line one minute seven seconds ahead, the winner in the best of seven by four victories to nil.

An American warship, the *Annapolis*, set off its great siren in the distance. A fire-launch, hired in confident expectation of a victory that day, dutifully fired its twenty fountains into the air.

Seventy-One

'Look at those fat cats,' Jim Shaw said.

The newspapers were full of pictures of the men of *Eagle*, bursting champagne corks on the flying bridge and afterdecks on board their huge support vessel. In another photograph Ericson's father, John Ericson Junior, grasped his son's hand in his own large paw. In another, he could be seen leaning sideways, speaking to Senator Cartright and General Marcus Walters. The male guests had expensive wrist watches and their women had even tans that could be created, so the press averred, only by Cap d'Antibes sun.

'Are you sure you aren't motivated by jealousy?' asked Illich.

'Sure I'm motivated by jealousy,' Jim Shaw said. 'Every one of those guys has led a completely pure and blameless life. Not one of them ever made a sharp deal and they always looked after their business associates. Their wives are happy and their children are unspoiled. You can take it from me they all have clean consciences and can sleep soundly at night. Sure I'm jealous.'

'Beneath your sarcasm, nevertheless,' persisted Illich, 'there lurks a certain . . . admiration?'

Banter aside, Illich knew Jim Shaw had as much right to his views as anyone. He had, after all, turned his back on the life of a hero by bearing away from the finish line in the final of the previous America's Cup races. And apart from a slightly morbid interest in his case by the odd journalist as an example of an eccentric recluse, he had faded from the national consciousness.

Beneath the photographs, there were further quotes from John Ericson the Third on his opponents.

Ericson repeated his accusations that Jim Shaw is a traitor. As someone used to living in a highly litigious society, and to operating on the fine line between truth and slander, he asked the rhetorical question: 'Isn't someone who goes over to the other side a traitor? His father was a known communist. I would say what he's doing is un-American.'

Illich looked at Jim Shaw and saw suddenly that he was shaking. He had never seen Shaw show any sign of uncontrolled emotion. Horrified, Illich lightly touched his elbow: 'I apologize for what I have just said.'

Shaw was wound up like a spring. Illich could sense the charge running through him.

'It's not you,' Shaw replied after a few moments. 'It's the nerve of that guy, someone without integrity, without morals, who just can't stand to lose because he's an empty shell.'

Shaw stood there trembling, Illich helplessly standing by.

'I'll be all right,' Shaw said after a little while. 'What really pisses me off, you know, is that I should get affected by anything that asshole says.'

That sentiment, at least, seemed to help to calm him down. Illich watched his shaking gradually ease off. After a few more minutes they could move on to other things.

Seventy-Two

Under a sky scorching and unclouded, enveloped in a white mist of late summer heat, *Novy Mir* left the anchorage and was towed out towards the course buoys five miles offshore. She was shepherded between two motor patrol vessels of the Ministry of the Interior in which could be seen the red flashings and shoulder boards of the MVD police. Leading the convoy was the state launch of the President of Estonia. At *Novy Mir*'s stern was the Russian flag, with its white, blue and red. From her main halyard fluttered the huge tricolour of the Estonian Republic. Outside this ring a fleet of smaller patrol vessels kept the massive spectator fleet at a distance.

The sky above them was filled with aircraft. In the lower air, a few hundred feet up, helicopters darted like dragonflies. At three hundred feet and above, small fixed wing aircraft proceeded in slow anti-clockwise circles. Above them were the sleek cigar shapes of modern airships, many painted grey for military usage. Higher still, a pike among minnows, its eighteen shrouded, ducted turbofans holding it steady against the southerly breeze, the huge Russian airship *St Petersburg* shone silver. In the cupola beneath its belly twelve hundred guests of the Russian Republic were served champagne and ate finest black Beluga caviar.

Novy Mir was towed between two islets of rafted pleasure craft, crossed obliquely the anchorage ground of the great sail-training ships, swung through half a circle where the America's Cup base camps of thirty-one nations lay sprawled beneath the shadow of the hills, and north towards the open waters of the course.

Behind the course was a circle of grey warships, the representatives of numerous navies. Military helicopters moved between them. There was a shuttle of political and diplomatic activity from the shore, fast launches moving constantly between the quays of St Petersburg and the anchored ships.

In the past few days the spectator fleets had trebled. Three huge new marinas at St Petersburg hardly coped with the influx from the Scandinavian states, and more distant travellers from Britain, Germany, France were still arriving.

On *Novy Mir* the crew waved to the Estonian and Russian convoy of launches and pleasure craft that surrounded them. Only one man on the yacht was not able physically to participate. Beneath decks, sitting on a sailbag, the British helmsman Ian Sinclair was out of the way, unobserved. Because of his non-participating status, he couldn't make himself useful by helping to check the sails. That morning they had, as the rules specified, notified the course authorities that one Ian Sinclair would be aboard as an international witness. It had been carefully timed until the last moment to give minimum warning to the US camp. The likelihood was that, the crew of both yachts being well known in advance, no additional check would be made on the final morning in the rush of last-minute preparations.

They could see the other convoy now, about a mile inshore of them, a phalanx of expensive power boats, grey tinted glass, flying bridges, their throttles held back. With

Eagle's single tall mast at the centre, the convoy progressed at a steady eight knots towards the racing course.

There must have been close to eighty of them, the yachts of the great industrialists of the United States and Western Europe. The vessels had travelled from the Mediterranean and the Caribbean with their uniformed captains and professional crew. The yachts' owners, having flown in from New York, Los Angeles, from Chicago and Pittsburgh, London and Paris, from Dusseldorf and Rome and Osaka, could join them here and enjoy, in the territorial waters of Russia, the style of living to which they were accustomed. It was an opportunity, too, to speak with a second secretary at the Russian Interior Ministry on the possibility of a new automobile production plant in Sverdlovsk, milling machinery for Kazan, a network of superstores across the former Soviet republics. Or, since individual republics showed increasing economic independence, a political chieftain from Moldavia or Azerbaijan would be wooed for a five-year international marketing monopoly on wool, oil, dairy produce, wines.

No medieval tournament between the kings and nobles of Europe carried so much wealth and power in its train. Adding a slightly more controversial note to the proceedings was a light aircraft, flown from Finland by a pilot of the burgeoning European Green movement. Taking care to keep within easy reaching distance of international waters, it trailed a long, gently fluttering message behind it in the form of a deliberate misquote from Marx: CAPITALISM IS THE OPIUM OF THE MASSES.

On *Novy Mir* they were again subjected to the surreal experience of waiting, as the waters around them were emptied of craft, and the spectator fleet became a bank of indistinguishable bulk behind the blue traces of diesel fumes.

The forecast was of a north-westerly sea breeze, beginning during the mid morning and building up to eighteen knots in the afternoon. It meant that they had to carry on

369

board a range of sails from light to brisk breezes. The sewerman Herman Maask went below to make his final check on the sails neatly laid out below decks. The open hatch, combined with the forward speed of the boat, produced a welcome draft through the interior of the boat as he repacked spinnakers and checked that the sails would run up free of tangles. Opposite him Sinclair sat on a spare heavy weather spinnaker bag, his elbows on his knees, his face in his hands, staring forward into the slow, golden fires of the epoxied wooden hull.

The last of the big power-yachts, the flagship of the Ericson Traction Corporation, with its cargo of crew wives and relations, drew away from *Eagle*. Now only the two yachts, with their towboats holding them into wind in slow forward gear, occupied the heated, empty spaces.

For almost the first time, Illich was able to study *Eagle* at relatively close quarters, without the distraction of intervening launches. She was painted gunsmoke blue. The perfect fairness of her topsides shone in the reflecting water surface. Above her the Stars and Stripes moved languidly in the slowly gathering breeze.

'Wind has settled down,' Jim Shaw said.

A short while later Brod, listening to the instructions of the committee boat on the radio, said: 'Committee boat. Course is set. Ten-minute gun in twenty minutes.'

'Mainsail up,' ordered Illich.

The lethargy was broken. It was always a relief when the waiting was over, when sweating anxiety gave way to the first pellet of adrenalin into the bloodstream.

On *Eagle* too the mainsail was being hauled up in quick, powerful surges.

'Cast off!'

The towing launch hauled in the loosened tow-rope and moved away to give *Novy Mir* sea-room.

'Genoa up!'

The crew were moving fast to trim the mainsail, standing

370

by on the genoa sheets. Jim Shaw gave a final check to the rigging tensions on the plate of dials in front of him.

'Brod,' Illich said, 'go forward and tell our secret weapon that we expect him on deck immediately after the ten-minute gun.'

Brod went forward to repeat the message to Sinclair. In the darkness below, all Brod could see were the Englishman's upturned eyes.

In these early manoeuvres the adrenalin made Illich feel nauseous for several minutes, hardly able to stand. Then slowly his body would accustom to its charge of violent chemicals. His fear and anger, in which at first he seemed to drown, would become solid, an indistinguishable background constant, a surface on which, in the fullness of time, his mind could move as smoothly as a skater. Apprehension, terror, cold aggression; three different psychological states, three wholly different characters, an entire play in the course of a few minutes. It was as well he knew the characters by heart.

It was also the stage at which, outwardly at least, he appeared most calm. While his system transformed him from trembling sheep to cunning wolf, he did not speak for fear of showing his cracked voice, the tremor of indecision, the pallor of his fear.

With the genoa sheeted in, Illich pointed *Novy Mir* slowly upwind. The crew trimmed her sails and slowly began to edge up the speed.

'Six five, six six, six seven, six seven.'

Illich was settling down and could afford now to look at the other boat. It was generally agreed that of all *Eagle*'s strengths, her sails were perhaps the greatest. A new plastic substrate had been produced, immensely strong, highly resistant to changes in shape. Embedded in it were high tensile fibres which followed the exact stress lines of the sails. The shimmering, perfect presence of these sails was commented upon by many of the numerous crews which she had beaten. Sinclair too had ruefully cited them.

Illich's mind was becoming clearer; the final traces of fear were leaving. He felt cold and light.

'Let's set her up on the other tack.'

Having tacked, they proceeded on starboard for several minutes, edging the speed upwards, sheeting in the foresail an inch here, easing the main a fraction there, working on cunningham, kicker, halyard tension, outhaul, until they could feel the boat begin to hum.

'Breeze increasing steadily,' Brod confirmed. 'Up a knot and a half on average in the last ten minutes. Eight minutes to ten-minute gun.'

Eagle did three rapid tacks in succession, as perfectly as clockwork; an exercise aimed partly at practice, partly at demoralizing the opposing crew.

'What happens,' Illich had asked Jim Shaw earlier that morning, before they set out, 'when Ericson recognizes Sinclair?'

'The guy is almost pathologically aggressive. All his life, he's been used to getting his own way. OK, recently he seems to have learned how to hold his temper. You saw what he did to the Germans. Maybe he's matured, I don't know. Knowing what he's like, that's impressive control. But his first reaction will be to raise a stink. That's what we want to do, shake his complacency, right?'

Generally speaking, Illich was not an exponent of the 'psychological' school of racing. But every helmsman has a more than academic interest in the mental characteristics of his opponent.

'Two minutes,' Brod said.

'Bearing away,' Illich warned the crew.

Novy Mir eased sheets and they began closing on the starting box.

A little later, Brod began the countdown.

'Twenty, nineteen, eighteen, seventeen . . .'

Now they began to work up full power, to reach what they called 'ramming' speed, as they accelerated towards the box.

'Five, four, three, two . . .'

Cordite rolled across the water.

Eagle had also entered at the charge, and was bearing down on them fast.

Sinclair appeared from the hatchway and carefully made his way to the stern, standing well behind the three after-guard, in the aft section of the boat sometimes referred to as the 'owners' enclosure'.

'A cup of tea, Mr Sinclair?' Jim Shaw asked in his poshest accent.

'Frightfully kind, but no thanks,' replied Sinclair.

This infantile exchange, in English, had no effect on the crew, but it cheered up Illich and Shaw.

'Eight four, eight five, eight five,' Brod intoned.

Closing speed about seventeen knots.

'He's going low,' snapped Shaw. *Eagle* was on an unchanged collision course, but Shaw had seen her genoa trimmer stand back a few inches preparatory to letting out sheets – a slight, but telling movement.

Well before time, too, *Eagle* starting to swing deep. It was not an engagement tactic but a wide circle.

'My advice is to stand off,' Shaw said. 'Let him take a look.'

They swung in a wide circle around *Eagle*.

Ericson was saying something to his tactician. The tactician moved towards the stern, and unfurled their red protest flag. Then *Eagle* bore away.

'That wasn't much of an explosion,' Illich said.

'Don't worry,' Jim assured him. 'Inside, the solids have hit the fan. The acid is starting to work. Every time he looks around, he'll be reminded of that protest flag, and he'll just get madder and madder.'

'I think you have a very rich imagination.'

They gave chase to *Eagle*, but she slipped out of their reach.

'Action at a distance,' Illich said to Shaw.

'Wind continues to fill in slowly,' Brod commented. 'Slight bias to port end of line. Nothing in it, though.'

'If Ericson won't engage, let's get the good side,' Illich replied. 'Bearing away to port.'

Seventy-Three

'Six, five, four, three . . .'

The report of the gun was so close that, for several moments afterwards, it rang in their ears. An acrid cloud of cordite smoke rolled across their decks like fire on an old battleship.

Eagle had sliced across the line on parallel tack at the other end, about a second ahead.

'Wind steady, eight knots true. Speed seven two, seven two, seven three.'

There was a short, unpleasant swell, in part the confused residue of the fleet of spectator craft. Water retains the memory of a boat's passage for some time afterwards, moving it backwards and forwards like thought.

They took advantage of each tiny change of wind direction, tacking as it shifted. The boat seemed to settle into its own rhythm. As *Novy Mir* came through the wind, the genoa thundered for a few seconds, incoherent, and then settled into silent converse with itself.

They entered a trance of concentration, in which the background sounds were the slice of the waves, the slight creaks and squeals of sheets being eased and hauled in, crisp requests from the trimmers to the grinders for a bite of power, the intonation of the speed readings by Brod. Like a counterpoint, there were occasional warnings of changes in wind direction, and the running conversation between helmsman and tactician about the other boat.

'Tack!' shouted Illich.

On the final run in to the top buoy on starboard tack, the bow sliced the short swells precisely.

'*Eagle*'s ahead,' Shaw remarked, 'but not by much. Maybe a boatlength.'

It was an interesting situation. They had right of way on starboard. If the other boat was to cross ahead of them, it must be sure to be clear.

Eagle closed steadily. Would she try it?

The answer was no. With a thunder of sails, she tacked some distance out; precisely, conservatively.

'It's just eating him up inside,' Shaw said. 'Frankly, I feel sorry for the guy.'

'Your imagination is extraordinary.'

'Seven six, seven five, seven five, seven four.'

'We're in her backwind now,' Shaw warned.

But this close to the buoy there was little they could do that wouldn't make things worse. They had to follow *Eagle* meekly around the mark, losing almost another boatlength in the process. *Eagle* set a perfect spinnaker. They followed suit. Two boatlengths behind, however, was close enough to strike back, to begin the hunt.

Illich struck first by placing *Novy Mir* between *Eagle* and the source of the wind.

Ericson bore up sharply to shake them off. Illich followed suit. Ericson bore up more, almost square reaching now. Illich hung on for grim death.

'Wind has increased two knots,' Brod said.

For the time being, *Eagle* was holding them off.

Move and countermove, gybe and gybe, they fought until the lower buoy was reached. *Eagle* was still two lengths ahead. But the closeness in speed must have surprised Ericson.

'Down spinnaker!' shouted Illich. In spinnaker drops he was conservatively early. Better a foot or two of distance

375

lost than the strong possibility of a foul-up. The snap shackle was pulled and the huge sail collapsed. Migdal and Maask gathered in the folds frantically as *Novy Mir* rounded the lower mark, her winches grinding.

'Will he place a close cover on us?' Illich asked Shaw.

'If he does, he's spooked,' Shaw replied.

Instead, Ericson tacked away.

'Impressive,' said Shaw. 'Maybe he *has* grown up.'

As the two boats closed in on the top buoy again, *Eagle* was four lengths ahead.

'Mr Sinclair?' Illich asked.

'You called, sir.'

'What do you think of the cut of *Eagle*'s spinnaker?'

'Deep cut. They use superior sail technology to sail deep.'

'Jim?'

'I agree. What are you thinking?'

'Windspeed's twelve knots. Let's put up a flat spinnaker and push fast.'

It was a complicated matter. If you sailed 'deep' downwind, the apparent wind – the wind felt in the sails – decreased. If you sailed at a closer angle to the wind, the boat's speed changed the direction of the apparent wind, increasing its speed, and the boat moved faster. The question was, did the speed towards the buoy increase as a result? Modern instruments calculated the actual speed, called the 'velocity made good'. But even now, no expert sailor entirely trusted the instruments. There was an area of doubt, a penumbra, in which the final choice was a matter of intuition.

There was a second consideration. *Eagle* had nearly always beaten her opponents to the upwind mark. In the downwind legs she was hardly ever 'pressed' by the opposing boat. Illich had a suspicion that this lack of severe competition in the downwind legs might mask a weakness.

There were no objections, so Illich said: 'Tell Victor.'

Jim went forward. In the gloom of the interior, he could only see the whites of Victor Kingissep's eyes.

'Prepare the flatcut spinnaker.'

'Sure.'

Eagle crossed ahead of them. They were three lengths behind round the top mark. *Eagle's* spinnaker launch was perfect. They followed suit.

This time Illich did not press Ericson, but gybed onto a separate tack.

'True wind constant twelve knots,' Brod called. 'Boatspeed eight nine, eight nine, nine zero, nine zero, nine one . . .'

Reaching fast, they could ride the steep, short waves for several seconds, pushing the speed to ten, sometimes eleven knots.

'Water's darker ahead,' Shaw said. About fifty yards forward the water was a deeper blue as if a cloud-shadow were passing across its surface. Slowly they were acquiring a rhythm, feeling their way with the waves. As the boat's stern lifted, the spinnaker trimmers gave a shout for more power. The grinders gave a burst of frenzied turning, bringing the spinnaker aft, increasing the forces on the big sail. Illich waited for the surge of power and speed, then peeled the hull downwave, prolonging the surf as much as he could. It was engrossing.

'One and a half knots more windspeed,' Brod informed him. 'Gusting now.'

Eagle seemed aeons away, running parallel, a distant shape.

'Gybe!'

They swung downwind. The spinnaker was tripped and reset. On the new tack, Illich flat-reached to pick up speed, using accumulated momentum to surge downwind on the waves. No primitive dance, no voodoo ceremony, could hold the mind in such a trance as these delicate, complicated rhythms.

He held his breath as they began to close with *Eagle*. It looked promising, but a five degree wind change could put the other boat a hundred yards ahead . . .

Power on, build up speed, peel down the wave face.

Behind him, Shaw breathed out slowly. No one spoke. It was a superstition not to comment too early.

Two minutes later they cut across *Eagle*'s bow, gybed, sailed ahead of her for forty yards, dropped spinnaker, and rounded the buoy two boatlengths in front.

'Close cover,' shouted Illich.

In this, the final leg, there would be no quarter given.

Eagle, rounding, tacked away. Illich roared 'Tack!' and dumped bad air on the other boat. *Eagle* tacked again.

Now it was the brutal, close-quarter struggle of winch-grinders. Berol Baltir and Graf Ulder, their shoulders bunching with the strain, flung their power into the handles. Eight tacks later, they were showing signs of acute pain, their brows hunched, their eyes screwed tight. Twelve tacks later and their faces were relaxing as they started to 'clear'. After fifteen tacks they were 'coasting', high on the body's opiates.

Caught in *Novy Mir*'s disturbed wind, *Eagle* had slipped back a further one and a half boatlengths. At this distance they could afford to place *Eagle* under loose cover. When Ericson tacked again, Illich kept on course, winding up speed. Forty seconds later, he shouted 'Tack!' Over the next ten minutes, *Eagle* closed up a boatlength. But they were heading for the line now, with that superstitious terror that any sound, however small, will cause the mast to fall like tumbling confetti, the boat to sink mysteriously without trace. No-one made so much as a sign. Even when Illich swung her into wind to 'shoot' the line, the crew were silent. The finish gun erupted into their trance. In the two seconds of gravid disbelief before they broke into loud cheers, a laconic voice behind them said:

'I'll take my tea now, please, Mr Shaw.'

Seventy-Four

If a yacht could have been lifted on the shoulders of its fans, it would surely have happened to *Novy Mir*. The moment of severest apprehension to Illich occurred when the spectator fleet, breaking out of its enclosures, raced towards them from every angle. They were the centre of an implosion, the point at which a thousand collision courses converged.

It was an occasion for genuine fear. It is one thing to be rushed by a crowd of cheering, back-thumping supporters, but another when the hysterical fan is gunning towards you at forty knots with his hand forward on the throttle of a few hundred horsepower of turbo-diesel. There was one glancing collision as a television craft, power off, tried to swing away in the last few final yards and struck sideways on, leaving a deep gash in *Novy Mir*'s shining green topsides.

Brod, stepping forward lightly, pointed towards the gash, then unleashed a thunderous blow into the face of a photographer, watching him collapse on the lifelines while his falling camera flashed once, hit the water with a hiss and pirouetted away below the surface. Still apparently composed, Brod walked to the other side of the craft to reason with a second press boat which seemed on the point of unloading photographers onto *Novy Mir*. It backed off apprehensively.

For a minute there was an ugly mood as the crew of *Novy Mir* lined the sidedecks, facing outwards. They could hear the occasional impact and grinding of hulls as the late arrivals came in behind the first wave. A patrol vessel, klaxons blaring, loudspeakers haranguing, eventually restored some inner space by circling *Novy Mir* and deflecting, with its rubber-lined bows, any boat which intervened. Like an old, slow sheepdog, their towboat eventually reached them, casting a line. As they were towed away to clearer water, the mood lightened again.

After its initial moments, the fleet became well behaved and orderly. They moved away in a huge convoy towards the base camp. In this lighter atmosphere, they gazed about them, at a sky filled with circling aircraft, the ranks of larger spectator craft, the tall sail training ships in the shore anchorage and, out to sea, the grey ramparts of the encircling warships. Illich was again afflicted with the absurd thought that a yacht race could be the centre of such an aggregation of physical might, of earthly power.

On their way back, there was a brief aerial entertainment. The little Finnish Cessna flying the banner message CAPITALISM IS THE OPIUM OF THE MASSES, perhaps emboldened by the win of the Estonians against the American giant, flew over the returning fleet. Its action brought it deeper into Russian waters and, technically speaking, into Russian airspace. The precise cause of what followed was never clear. Perhaps some senior St Petersburg bureaucrat had felt the banner cast a slur on the enthusiastic party between capitalism and the early stages of post-communism. Perhaps in the mind of this hypothetical bureaucrat, dark memories were stirred of 1987, when another Cessna light aircraft flown from Finland, piloted by the German teenager Matthias Rust, had passed undetected through the central air defence region of the Soviet Union, landing unannounced in the middle of Red Square. Perhaps this same hypothetical bureaucrat interpreted the message as an insult to his capitalist guests. Whatever the precise sequence, a neighbouring Army base was informed of the invasion of airspace, and given instructions to expel the intruder.

Several minutes later, looking up, they noticed that a black military attack helicopter was following the light aircraft and its message. The pursuer continued to close the distance. It was an unremarkable sight until the blades of the advancing helicopter began to dismember the message. Like the fins of a Siamese fighting fish, letters began to float down, a recognizable S, a mutilated E, two more hissing Ss. There was something comical about the sight. The watching multitudes burst into laughter. For some time the pilot of the light aircraft seemed unaware that he was being pursued by the equivalent of an aerial lawnmower. His message had been shortened to the more existential CAPI-TALISM IS THE OPIATE when, suddenly alerted, he started to weave and turn. But this only made the pursuit more comi-cal. Violent and angry manoeuvres, imparted to a message still nearly seventy yards long, do not have much energy when they reach the serenely floating tail. The helicopter continued with its determined shearing. Only when the message had been reduced to the terser, epigrammatic statement CAPITALISM IS did the light aircraft manage to break away. Shorn of its peacock tail, it flew towards the open sea and the safety of Finland. The incident became a *cause célèbre*. The Russian satirist Semyov called the incident a 'true example of aerial dialogue', carried out, moreover, 'in the full view of the masses' , and advocated a return match. There was considerable speculation that the heli-copter had been given precise instructions at which point to stop in its shearing. Others suggested that to fly out with the witty Eco-message CAPITALISM IS THE OPIUM OF THE MASSES and return, with the full force of a conversion, CAPITALISM IS, would be punishment enough to the offending pilot.

Who is Ivan Illich? asked the British *Independent* newspaper.

The physical impression is of a somewhat thin man of medium height in his late thirties. His face has the lines of his calling etched into it. He does not smile often, and when he does it is hardly more than a quizzical lightening of expression. He seems constantly on guard. He strikes the world as reticent, and certainly a press hungry for information regards him as publicity shy, indeed

*reclusive. Yet against all the odds, after a bitter expulsion from the
Army-controlled Russian defence syndicate, he has proceeded to
build up an Estonian challenge in a small, Baltic country without
great resources except in the quality of its manpower. He has
emerged from this background to destroy Russia's official defender,
and challenge on an equal footing the might of American technical
and professional sailing supremacy. It is interesting to speak to his
sailing rivals. Those who no longer have an axe to grind in this
competition bear towards him none of the grudges reserved for the
mighty. Several have described his personality as retiring, almost
colourless. In a crowd he does not stand out. In company he does not
shine. He is not especially charismatic or assertive. But when the
talk moves to Ivan Illich as a sailor, to Illich at the helm of a racing
yacht, then they might not be speaking of a human being – a
creature of flesh and blood – at all, but of a demon or an angel.*

'They write a lot of crap about me, too,' said Jim Shaw.

Seventy-Five

Golden sunshine illuminated the second day. But the winds
were stronger, indicating the first signs of a low pressure
system that was approaching from the west. Gusting out of
the blue Baltic, a colour now reminiscent of the eyes of
Scandinavians, it was strong enough to enliven the surface
of the bay with whitecaps.

It was strong enough too, to blow away the torpor of the
heat. It freshened through the training camps, stiffening the
flags of the various national teams who, though they might
place their defeated yachts in storage ready for shipping to
their own countries, remained behind in person to watch
the finals.

If anything, the spectator fleets had grown. News of *Novy Mir*'s win the previous day had indicated that the result was not yet a foregone conclusion. Illich, standing on the terrace overlooking the bay, watched them stream outwards in their hundreds from St Petersburg, reinforced by further arrivals from the west, from Narva, Kohtia-Jarve, from Tallinn and Helsinki. Of all the Baltic nations, the Finns were the closest to the Estonians in outlook, language and culture, and they came in force to view the final races. Many had travelled overnight.

Two great United States warships, the nuclear carrier *Gettysburg* and the battleship *Ohio*, swelled the ranks of naval grey at anchor.

Aegu telephoned Illich that morning to congratulate the Estonian team on yesterday's race.

'The British did the same,' Illich replied. 'Then the Americans won every single race.'

'Never mind. We have done far better than I ever expected. I have read more about Estonia now than I ever have in the past.'

This was Aegu the politician's criterion of success, and Illich owed Aegu too much to resent it.

Aegu continued: 'In Moscow yesterday we had a meeting of the Presidents of the Republics to discuss Western trade concessions. There is a great deal of commercial negotiation while the Westerners are gathered here for the America's Cup races. Prestige is a strange thing. You would have thought I was the President of the United States himself by the reactions. A curious matter that a yacht race can so affect political relations. By the way, if you should wish to call me, I am in St Petersburg for the time being, at the Pribaltiyskaya Hotel. Phone reception, give your name, and they will put you through. Good luck.'

Aegu rang off.

Illich put the phone down thoughtfully. A curious coincidence. Lydia Teemant was at the same hotel.

Someone was knocking on the door of the little office. Shaw put his head around the door.

'Time to go, skipper.'

Illich picked up his sailing bag, carrying his oilskins, dark glasses, hat, salve against the burning heat.

They walked down the path together.

'Some good news,' Shaw said. 'The protest committee threw out Ericson's objection that Sinclair was on board illegally. They said the authorities had been properly notified in advance, and that his presence on board as a physically non-participating witness or adviser was perfectly legal.'

Vagir overtook them with a fax of the hourly summary of the weather from Tartu.

'Thanks.' Jim Shaw glanced at the summary. The important figure was the wind strength, which was as earlier predicted. He folded the sheet for further reference on the way out to the course.

Sinclair approached them across the lawn, walking quickly, extending his hand.

'You won't be needing me today. Just wanted to wish you good luck.'

Shaw turned towards Illich.

'If it's all right with you, skipper, as tactician I'd really like this guy aboard. If he steps off today, Ericson will think he's intimidated us.'

'Shall I leave while you discuss this?' Sinclair asked.

'No,' Illich replied. 'Stay here. You also helped with the decision to fast-reach yesterday. We'd like you on board again, please.'

The crew was waiting for them at the dock. Baltir was piling the last of the sails on board. Light and heavy weather sails were being loaded on the support vessel. It was illegal to bring sails on board after the ten-minute gun, but if the wind changed unexpectedly before the ten-minute gun, it was reassuring to know that they could load appropriate extra sails from the tender. Too many extra sails were

384

added weight, too few entailed a risk that if the wind changed strength, the sails carried would be inappropriate. Sinclair was a case in point. He weighed the equivalent of three sails. This had to be counterbalanced against the psychological advantage of putting the opposing helmsman off his stroke. There is no more 'logic' in such decisions than the aesthetic comparison of apples and pears. Yet out of such fine considerations, both absurd and crucial, are America's Cup races made.

Lying beneath psychological justification, another reason also played its part. Men who are keyed up for a race, who are operating on the limit of their nerves, are prone to superstition. In yesterday's race they had won. Disturb any one element, the superstitious mind says, and the whole constellation changes. If only as a mascot, then, Illich would have kept Sinclair aboard.

Small, fleecy clouds were approaching from the south-west as the convoy made their way out of the harbour. Setting course for the racing grounds, they crossed a quartering swell; the yacht rolled queasily without the steadying influence of sail. The effects of motion at sea are somewhat unpredictable. A single-handed sailor had circumnavigated the world in a tiny nineteen feet sailing yacht. The only time he was seasick was on the Sydney Harbour ferry. It seemed the motion on his little passage-maker was short and crisp, whereas the motion of the ferry was slower but more nauseous. On *Novy Mir* the man most likely to be affected was the sewerman Herman Maask, packing sails in the dark recesses of the hull. Illich was sufficiently concerned to order him temporarily up on deck, into the bright sunlight and distractions of the spectator fleet.

The bay was dark with traffic of boats. It seemed astonishing that a course some four miles square could be cleared in this mêlée. As the American yacht emerged, the nuclear carrier *Gettysburg* blasted out a salute on its foghorns. The other warships followed. After the glancing collision the

385

previous day, security had been tightened, and they now had a screen of ten course patrol vessels, a ring of protecting hulls through which hardly a dinghy could have squeezed.

Above the forest of bridge-decks the clouds closest to the sun took on a fiery tinge. A consistently brisk wind blew away the diesel smoke. Visibility was remarkably clear. On the hills overlooking the bay, every vantage point was black with spectators. Occasional reflections bounced off the shiny roofs of more than two hundred thousand cars, parked in huge temporary lots on the green hillsides. The shadows of aircraft crossed and recrossed like birds.

They reached the area of the starting line and turned into wind and sea. The motion of the yacht became quieter. Herman Maask disappeared below decks to make his final check on the sails. *Eagle*, surrounded still by her phalanx of great motor-yachts, took up parallel station. The course patrol vessels were driving back the spectator fleet, chasing stragglers.

'Radio from committee boat,' Brod called. 'Course is laid. One hundred and fifteen degrees. Twenty minutes to ten-minute gun.'

Parts of the course were still cluttered with spectator boats. Even so, it was important to tune the yacht in the short time available. Illich shouted for sail and the bowman prepared to cast off the towline.

Brod, standing in the stern, gave two sweeping waves to the tender to signal that the wind was steady and they would take on no further sails.

Migdal and Maask hauled up the mainsail. Looking towards *Eagle*, Illich saw the single tall mast still locked inside a phalanx of power craft.

Shaw, catching his glance, commented: 'A big pow-wow's going on there. You can bet Ericson's father will be giving their guy a pep talk.'

Novy Mir's tow-rope was cast off and snaked away. Prem sheeted in the thundering mainsail to generate power. Illich bore off to increase speed. At the mast, Migdal and Maask were hauling up the genoa now in huge alternative sweeps, Kingissep taking up slack on the halyard winch.

Illich was forced to look for clear water before they could settle down on port tack and begin to put the yacht into final tune.

Only now was *Eagle's* blue hull discernible as the Ericson power flagship drew away, a dazzling rhomboid of shining white sculpture. Moving backwards with a punch from her turbo-charged diesels, the wash of the reversed propellers slid forward like two snakes along her topsides.

'Eight two,' Brod intoned, 'eight three, eight three steady.'

Illich put thoughts of the other boat out of his mind and concentrated on the tuning of *Novy Mir*.

The streamers on the genoa indicated a perfect flow, but the boat felt slightly choked. It was hardly perceptible, merely an intuition. Another of those hairline judgements presented itself to Illich. If he expressed dissatisfaction with the set of the sails, it would subtly undermine the confidence of his superb crew. If he allowed it to be, then they would enter the starting box with psychological confidence.

Illich was determined to pursue the point, however. There was his own confidence to consider, and he wanted the yacht in perfect tune.

'Eight three, steady,' Brod repeated.

'Tarku,' Illich called to the genoa trimmer. 'Open the leech of the genoa.'

He could see that Tarku didn't like it, though he obediently adjusted the sheetlead backward.

'Eight three,' Brod said. 'Eight three.' Perhaps, Illich thought, he was chasing a ghost, but the boat felt better.

'Eight four,' Brod said.

Looking up at the sail, the top tell-tale was stalling, indicating an imperfect flow. Nevertheless the boat felt better through the wheel in his hands. This was another of those strange aspects of sailing. Perhaps the genoa, in its current configuration, was reacting beneficially with the main, so that the part might be wrong, but the whole improved. Tarku still didn't like it, and shook his head again.

'Eight five,' Brod said.

It was clearly better. But now he had a disbelieving trimmer, an unhappy sailor, and Tarku's attitude would subtly affect the others.

'What do you think?' he asked Shaw.

'Speed says it all,' Shaw replied. 'I'll go and talk with Tarku.'

Shaw went forward. Tarku was one of the two crew whom Jim had brought with him from *Leningrad*. He was a protégé of Shaw's, and as such would listen to him more readily than Illich.

Illich looked towards *Eagle*. Only now were her sails setting as she started to move.

'Twelve minutes to the ten-minute gun,' Brod said.

Illich strained to hear what Shaw was saying to Tarku, but Shaw was speaking in carefully modulated, low tones. Perhaps it was just as well.

'He's OK, I think,' Shaw whispered. 'I had to strike a bargain with him, though.'

'What bargain?'

'Well, I told him that in both our views the boat was going faster with the genoa set like it is now.'

'Yes.'

'I said if he wanted to, he could set it as he wished. But if we lost, I'd feed him to the sharks.'

'A firm directive,' said Illich, approvingly. 'How did he respond?'

'He said, if he set it as you want it, and we lost, he wanted a categorical assurance that you would be fed to the sharks.'

'And?'

'Well, naturally, I agreed.'

'I am not entirely sure about your methods,' Illich said.

'Eight six,' Brod interrupted their earnest, whispered discussion. It was time to set up on the other tack.

*

The same, strange alchemy showed itself on the other tack. When the leech of the genoa was opened, and the top tell-tale flew high, indicating an imperfect flow, *Novy Mir* became faster. Later they would work out why. In sailing, however, theory followed practice. For the time being, all that mattered was performance.

This time there was no need to explain the point to the veteran Soren Gir. If Illich said the boat went faster, he would set the genoa upside down and inside out if necessary.

'Two minutes to the ten-minute gun,' Brod called.

Illich bore off and reached towards the starting box.

Eagle's tender still hovered on the outer perimeter of the starting box, a pure abstraction of sharp angles, masculine straight lines.

'Sixteen, fifteen, fourteen. . .'

They were accelerating fast on a reach. *Eagle* had swung onto course and was approaching the starting box from the other end.

Would *Eagle* charge them, looking for a fight? Illich and Shaw had held a discussion on it the previous evening. Shaw had argued that Ericson's psychological response to the previous day's defeat would be to come out swinging. On the other hand, Ericson's logic would tell him that, until the last running leg, his tactic of standing off had worked, and he should try it again. Illich had needled Shaw about the accuracy of his other predictions – for example, that Ericson would flip when he saw Sinclair. Now he watched *Eagle* with interest as Brod counted down the final seconds and the starting gun produced its petrified tree of white smoke.

Eagle was driving on towards them; heading unchanged, collision course. He knew that if he turned now to look at Jim Shaw, there would be a satisfied smile – not broad, but discernible nevertheless – on his tactician's face.

Eagle accelerated towards them, heeling to a gust, her bow slicing a twelve-foot flute.

And what then, he had asked Shaw?

If his heart is set on a fight, Shaw replied, then frustrate it. Back off, move out of range. Keep him off guard. Just don't give the bastard what he wants. So:

'Harden in!' Illich shouted.

He swung *Novy Mir* upwind. As he did so he noted *Eagle* change course towards him.

'Tack!'

Now they were sailing almost directly away. Ericson was giving chase.

In his mind Jim Shaw could hear Ericson say to his tactician, so that all the Ra-Ra college boys forward with their deep tans could hear: 'Look at those sonofabitches hightailing it out of here.' The tactician, adjusting his four-hundred dollar shades, would be replying 'Yeah, they know when it's time to be screwed.' And the winchgrinders, two prize Ivy League jocks with Che Guevara headbands, would push their big shoulders out an extra couple of inches, and they'd growl 'Yeah man, let's go and get the motherfuckers.' Motherfuckers, pronounced muthuh-fuckuhs, being just a single word for a jock, not two.

'Eight minutes,' Brod notified.

Dancing ahead of them would be *Novy Mir*, full of Estonian boneheads, American traitors and Limey fruits. It was enough to set a bunch of Ivy Leaguers afire with righteous rage.

The Estonian grinders didn't like running away, either. Ulder and Baltir had detected a weakness in the American grinding the day before. It was a matter of pain threshold. There was a just perceptible sluggishness on the American boat after the twelfth or thirteenth tack.

Whatever the grinders felt, *Novy Mir* kept retreating, climbing upwind, constantly evaporating.

'Ready spinnaker,' Illich said. 'Clip it on below decks. Leave the pole until the last moment.'

'Four minutes,' Brod called softly. It was a critical time. It would take nearly as long for them to reach the line.

The distance between them had shrunk to two boat lengths. 'Spinnaker,' Illich called softly.

Several things happened at once. The spinnaker bag came out of the forward hatch, its leads attached. Kingissep the bowman ran forward. Stefan Migdal and Herman Maask were swigging up the spinnaker pole. Migdal was already starting the first haul of the spinnaker halyard when a sound like a collective howl of rage came from the other boat.

Illich swung away. Within eight seconds of his order, the spinnaker was up, not yet setting, but on the point of exploding its elastic bands.

'Bearing away,' shouted Illich.

On *Eagle*, once the threat had been identified, they were working remarkably fast. Ericson had swung parallel to cut them off. *Eagle*'s spinnaker pole already was in place. The spinnaker was streaming up. But before it could open out, *Novy Mir*'s own spinnaker set with a satisfying punch, a sound like a collapsing mineshaft.

'Ten two,' Brod said. 'Ten five, ten eight . . .'

Shaw's throat locked.

They marvelled, nevertheless, at the disciplined frenzy of the American recovery. Ivy Leaguers they may have been, but each had almost lived on big racing yachts for the last ten years; each was saturated in racing culture. In a crisis it showed. But it was not fast enough. As *Novy Mir*'s spinnaker set, she started to roll over *Eagle* upwind, accelerating to twelve knots. Starved of wind by *Novy Mir*, *Eagle*'s spinnaker collapsed, recovered briefly, collapsed again. They could hear *Eagle*'s crewboss screaming like a cat on a hot tin roof. In a final, desperate effort to prevent *Novy Mir* passing her, Ericson luffed up, exercising right of way. But *Eagle* lacked speed. Her bow sliced past *Novy Mir*'s stern, missing by a full eight feet. Now the difference in speed was four knots rising to nearly five knots. A distance of one boatlength between them became two, then three as the Estonians hit full stride.

Seventy-Six

The start gun fired when they were still forty seconds away from the line. With *Eagle* in hot pursuit, they swung below it, turned a tight half-circle into wind, and began their beat up the windward leg.

Behind them, *Eagle* followed suit and tacked away.

'Cover?' Illich asked Shaw.

'I suggest we go for speed,' Shaw replied. 'Let's show them our contempt.'

'I agree.'

Whatever Edvigs Tarku's misgivings about setting the genoa, he held to his promise, opening the leech until the top tell-tale ceased fluttering. Perhaps it was the prospect of feeding Illich to the sharks.

'Eight four,' Brod intoned. 'Eight four, eight five . . .'

Prem was crouched over the mainsheet winch, on high gearing, taking in an inch here, letting out half an inch there. Eleven minds concentrated on speed.

Some of the swells were short, striking the bow with a heavy punch; others exploded crisply, inexplicably causing no noise, but dowsing the crew with a fine, stinging spray.

'We're being headed two degrees,' Brod said.

'Tack!'

In the rhythm of the tack he sensed the nerves of the crew. The difference between a good tack and a bad one was mysterious, but at the same time unmistakable. Now Soren Gir set up the genoa with the top tell-tale stalled.

Following air currents, they hunted their way upwind, as sensitive as any bird dog.

As they approached the top mark they closed with *Eagle*.

'Eight lengths up,' Shaw commented.

On the first downwind leg *Eagle* caught up two lengths. On the second upward leg *Novy Mir* stretched the lead to almost ten lengths, then held this lead virtually unchanged in the second downwind leg.

In the final leg they ignored the other boat completely and concentrated entirely on speed. When *Novy Mir* sliced the line, and the horns of more than a thousand spectator craft produced their hoarse response, they were fifteen lengths up and (as Shaw would say to his son years later) still climbing.

The genoa was hauled down, and they moved slowly ahead under mainsail alone. Shaw turned to say something to their mascot, witness, adviser and *doppelgänger*. There was no one there. For half a second of consternation, his eyes traversed empty space. Then Shaw's eyes travelled downwards. Sinclair lay sprawled in the sun of the aft cockpit, wedged into a corner, his sunhat tipped forward over his face, snoring quietly.

Seventy-Seven

Each competitor had the right to call a 'lay-day', a day off from racing. The *Eagle* camp exercised their prerogative, clearly intending to use the following day for assessment of damage.

To Illich, it was an opportunity for a brief respite for the crew. The following day would be leisurely. They would congregate in the afternoon for a brief sail practice, and to assess several newly cut sails in preparation for the following day.

After supper, on the evening of the second race, Illich walked across the strip of grass from the dining area to his small bedroom in the residential block.

A flash of light in the surrounding hills caught his attention. A car was approaching the camp, its headlights on full. It descended the winding road, making brief stabs into the dark with its beams as it rocked on its suspension. On that clear evening, even several hundred yards away, he could hear its tires kicking up gravel, and it occurred to him that the Army had come for him, now that he was on Russian territory, and would take him away. He had no urge to run as it approached the gate, drew up, and waited, engine purring.

He stepped into the beam of its headlight and, putting his hand in front of his face to shield his eyes, moved forward. A figure was emerging from the car, a figure in a raincoat.

'*Tovarich*,' Aegu said, from the folding beams of darkness.

The headlights were dipped. He could make out Aegu more clearly. Aegu had by now reached the perimeter, and his short, squat fingers gripped the mesh of the fence.

'I was on my way to St Petersburg for a meeting tomorrow.' Aegu gestured towards the pale night sky, as if this explained matters. He had clearly been drinking and was unsteady, leaning against the fence for support.

Keeping the fingers of one hand on the mesh for support, with the other Aegu reached into his pocket and withdrew a cigarette packet. Steadying himself, he managed the difficult task of lighting the cigarette.

'I wanted to talk to you, and to walk,' Aegu said, throwing aside the match.

'Now?' Illich asked.

'If you can spare an hour, Comrade. We can walk over the hills.' Aegu's face was turned up to the evening sky.

One of the two Estonian militiamen who patrolled the

perimeter of the camp at night approached. Illich recognised Anton Paalvelt, the taller of the two.

'Anton,' Illich said. 'If anyone in the camp enquires, tell them I am on a night route march with Comrade Aegu over the St Petersburg hills. I expect to be back by dawn.'

Paalvelt opened the gate.

Aegu's state Zil was a relic of the old association with the Soviet superpower. He used it as monarchs used horse and carriage, out of a respect for tradition. It was a melancholy thought that the relics of the former Communist superstate now held the nostalgic familiarity of old landmarks, as history left them behind.

Aegu's two security men sat in the front. They turned briefly to acknowledge his presence. Then the shorter, older man started the engine and turned the car round.

Built for Russian roads, the Zil's suspension had a motion like a ship at sea. They returned up the gravel road to the highway. Aegu ordered them to turn right, away from St Petersburg. He was silent while they motored west for several miles, until he ordered the driver to take a left turning down an unmarked road.

They travelled for several further miles, past farmworkers' houses, old grain silos, ghostly outbuildings. A dog came out to bark from the direction of some whitewashed farm storage barns, and ran alongside the car for several yards. Then they were in open country, the trees passing by in the moonlight. For several miles they drove.

'Here,' Aegu said without warning.

The car slowed and turned through an open gateway. Swaying, they crossed the ruts of an open field, then drew to a halt. The headlights were doused. The two bodyguards got out, closed their doors, and leaned casually against the car. Aegu also stepped out into the velvet darkness, walked several yards, and urinated.

He returned and lit another cigarette.

'Let us walk,' he said.

*

They set out, the four of them, the bodyguards several yards behind. As their eyes became accustomed to the dark, the terrain became clearer. A pale half-moon helped to illuminate their path. They were crossing a huge field, Aegu forcing the pace with short, driving steps, as if he were trying to dispel his inebriation by physical effort. The night was moist. Illich could smell leaves, mosses, the earth beneath their feet.

'History teaches us what to expect,' Aegu said, 'when the Communist Party has lost its grip.'

Illich knew no response was required. Aegu was already in the full song of his night thoughts, on the darker side of the Russian soul.

'The political power of the Army became apparent in 1980, in Poland, when Solidarity showed signs of displacing the Polish section of the Party. Under First Secretary Kania, the Party was showing signs of failure. Who was it who took over? The Polish Army, under Marshal Jaruzelski. A fascinating development. And who oversaw the takeover? Brezhnev? A politburo member? Who travelled to Poland to stage-manage the historical transfer of power, this crucial stage in the development of communism? Marshal Kulikov, Commander of the Warsaw Pact.'

They had reached the periphery of the field, bounded by a rusty barbed-wire fence. They began to skirt its perimeter, keeping parallel with the fence.

'And in China, in 1989, when the Communist Party lost its grip, who was it who restored the status quo? The Army. And did a politician order the Army to do so? Perhaps, but the man who ordered the 27th Army into Tiananmen Square was a Field Marshal, a professional soldier whose son-in-law commanded that same army.'

They were walking fast now, Aegu maintaining the pace, talking as if to clear his mind. 'So the process is this. The reformist wing of the Party is responsible for moving the state towards a position where the Party is in danger of losing control over the organs of state. Liberalism flourishes. After which the Army restores the *status quo*. That is the pattern of history. The Communist state does not lead to a reformed democracy, but to a military interregnum.'

Aegu paused only to draw on his cigarette, and continued walking.

'In the case of the former Soviet Union, there were intermediate stages, but the pattern is beginning to emerge. The Army stood by while the Supreme Soviet voted to eliminate Article 6, abandoning the automatic right of the Party to the leading role in society. They waited for the civil authorities to attempt to liberalize the economy. They waited patiently while the shortages worsened and the outlying republics became independent. They waited with exemplary patience while their own resources were cut and their men, the officers in particular, became demoralized.'

There were ruts in the field, and Illich was forced to concentrate merely to keep his footing. Once he heard the amiable curse of one of the security men as he stumbled briefly and recovered.

'As a former member of the diplomatic corps, as an ambassador, I was trained to be aware of political developments. I sense in the new Russia the same process. In democratizing the state, the political authorities have, in the opinion of the Army, lost control. To give the Army its credit, it is not a snap judgement. They have waited for more than a decade while events unfolded.'

Aegu's cigarette end glowed in the dark. Illich glanced behind at the two bodyguards, walking a few feet apart, talking occasionally in low voices. He could not hear what they were saying above the sound of their shoes on the soft earth, and the relentless flood of Aegu's own spoken thoughts.

'As you yourself will no doubt understand, the military mind is in sympathy with a command economy. It is the structure with which he is most familiar. It does not matter to him that such an economy is inefficient, that it cannot compete with the economies of individual incentive. He has

397

his tanks and his rockets. He has his support structures. From his point of view, the command economy produces the materials he requires. He sees the world in terms of the motto. 'Order, and it shall be done.' The complex and messy processes of democratic decision are anathema to him. The idea that citizens select their leaders is absurd. Private soldiers do not, after all, discuss and then present their decisions to him.' Aegu paused. 'Excuse me, comrade, I am not often in a position to talk so freely. One can seldom step outside the very processes that require analysis.'

'Please continue,' Illich said. To lend an ear occasionally to Aegu's discourses was a small, a minute price to pay for his patronage and help over the last two years. And besides, though Aegu was carried forward by his own loquacity, to Illich's mind at least there seemed to be some substance in what he said.

'I can smell the adversary stirring, looking around him, testing the ground. How far can he go? If Pridilenko's death is what we believe, he is able to remove senior members of the civil authority effectively at will. It must not be too obvious, of course, and it requires patience. The tactical procedures are complex, the importance of stealth is critical, but the overall strategy is clear.

'For most of my early life I myself have been under an illusion. In my youth I was a member of the Party and I believed in the Party ideology. Only later did I understand. The geography of the Soviet Union was not the construction of the Party, but of the Army. The Soviet Union was not the amalgamation of workers' republics who had turned voluntarily to Communism; it was the occupied area of the Soviet Army in the Second World War. The nature and structure of the Soviet Union was not the product of the Party, but of the Army. When the Soviet Union faded away, what was left, a liberal democracy? No, the Army remains, its true character revealed.'

There was something obsessive about Aegu's discourse that Illich had not seen before. It occurred to Illich suddenly that perhaps, with Pridilenko gone, Aegu now felt himself to be in the front line of resistance. Like individuals whose parents die, there is a sudden awareness that nothing separates them from death except time. And time is always short.

They crossed a small rickety wooden bridge over a dry ditch. On the other side was a sloping hillside. At the top were moonlit larches.

Aegu settled again into the rhythm of his walk. The red stub of his cigarette glowed in the dark. They began to climb the slope.

'As a student,' Aegu continued, 'I learnt as much about philosophy as I could. We were encouraged to acquaint ourselves with the petty-Marxist philosophers like Marcuse, Adorno, who supposedly had exercised an influence on the international student movement. But the library also contained the giants: Russell, Wittgenstein, Popper; Popper above all. I read them with all the burning interest of the amateur.'

Illich knew that Aegu had studied at the Moscow Institute of International Relations, the most prestigious school in the former Soviet Union. It was something known by most Estonians. They were as familiar with the *curriculum vitae* of their favourite son as any proud father.

'In the mornings we studied the means of spreading Soviet influence and power. In the afternoons a GRU major would teach us how to take apart and reassemble light weapons, sometimes with our eyes closed. In the evenings, in the library, I would study, like an antidote to all my day's activities, Popper's *The Open Society and Its Enemies*, an analysis of the dangers presented by totalitarians like ourselves.' Aegu added, 'A heady mixture, I think you will agree.'

Aegu the young genius, the outstanding student of his generation, later the distinguished diplomat, a full ambassador at the astonishingly young age of thirty-one, continued to stride forward. His footing was surprisingly sure. In the concentration of his discourse, however, once or twice he stumbled. Illich felt the temptation to help him, but he knew Aegu would have brushed aside any offered assistance.

'When one is brought up to promulgate Marxist centralist orthodoxy, to organize subtle conspiracy, to dismember the opposition slowly and methodically, by means of careful, paralysing blows, when one is taught all this, imbued with it, when one not only learns it but thinks and dreams it, one has the right to ask oneself: who is one fighting? What is the true nature of the enemy? This itself was not a seditious question; in the Institute we functioned like Jesuits; we were given latitude to consider all the arguments of the heretics in order to strengthen our own case. Define the enemy, identify his weak points, and strike. I took my mission seriously, perhaps too seriously. The nature of this enemy intrigued me, obsessed me. If it is some top-hatted capitalist, some international arms dealer, then I wished to know his more intimate aspects. In Popper, I expected to see the features of a petit bourgeois scoundrel. Instead I felt – and this is of course a subjective impression – instead I felt I was staring into the face of an angel.'

Angels were everywhere, Illich thought, in the reports of journalists, in the minds of politicians.

Aegu had a headcold. Perhaps high up, in the *St Petersburg*, he had been in a breeze on one of the opening balconies of the great airship's gondola. Now he stopped and turned his head aside to sneeze. He blew into a handkerchief. Then he was in motion again, walking fast.

'Do you know what I mean by an angel? I'll tell you. An angel is above all, light. I don't mean light, *lumen*, lumeniferous: I mean that he is not heavy with material things, he is immaterial. We say that someone is immaterial as a form of criticism. We say he has no substance. That is our condemnation. But that is exactly what an angel is; an immaterial being, a being with no substance.'

Illich was lost. Aegu, it seemed to him, was now raving. But as with the case of favourite sons, it was not one's place to say so.

'That is what I found in Popper; a detached objectivity, a mind without clutter, a former socialist who had moved on, who had jettisoned preconceptions. Marx was a nineteenth-century philosopher, and he dominated the twentieth. Popper was a twentieth-century philosopher, and perhaps he will dominate the twenty-first.'

They were almost at the brow of the hill, and for the first tune Aegu was forced to rest, breathing heavily. They were facing East. Ahead of them, like a pre-dawn, was the glow of Leningrad's streetlights. Illich glanced at the two body-guards, who were also grateful for the rest.

Aegu exhaled smoke slowly. They waited for a few moments, each in his own silence.

After a while Aegu said: 'It is the misfortune of Marxists, and I was one then, that we are taught to worship one saviour. We are as extreme in our beliefs as any religious fanatic. So that when we turn, we turn completely. I did not need bribes or women, or subtle appeals to different responsibilities, to turn me. I did not convert to capitalism out of any material influence. I merely lost my Marxist soul. In the library of the Moscow Institute of International Relations, it fluttered away from me. Or rather,' Aegu added with a slight flourish, 'since it is a materialist soul, it would be truer to say that it fell away, like a bar of lead.'

For several further moments he was silent. The dew was already heavy. In the nearby larches Illich could hear moisture falling from the dew-laden branches. Aegu gazed towards the lights of St Petersburg.

'Communism springs from the conscious mind, capitalism from the subconscious. The terrible thing that we learn, as we grow older, is that the subconscious is superior.'

Then they were walking again, fast down the slope, towards the sea.

'I do not assume that either is correct. All knowledge is

tentative. The best we can hope for are closer and closer approximations to the truth. There is no absolute truth, and no one – communist, capitalist, fascist, religious zealot – no one man or dogma has any fundamental claim to truth. It does not appear, at first, a very inspiring philosophy. But it is the inspiring philosophers who have left behind a somewhat unfortunate legacy of genocide.'

Now they were on the downward slope of the hill, and even Aegu had to hold back from a headlong flight downwards. From here they could see over the landscape into the still glowing streets of St Petersburg. To the north was the dark line of the sea. Clouds were moving across the sky, brushing the weak moon. Aegu halted once more to light yet another cigarette. Behind them the guards were silent, as if they too were absorbed by the view. Then the party set off on the final walk down the slope.

'Forgive me, *tovarich*, I am reaching my conclusion. These ramblings, I hope, are not in vain. I am describing to you how I was converted finally from a Marxist to an Estonian nationalist.'

The slope was more gentle now, and the going was easier. Here and there small, white stones jutted from the rich soil. Occasionally Aegu drew on his cigarette, and Illich could see, in a red glow, the concentration in Aegu's face.

'There is no single answer to any question of importance. Therefore, we must have many different sources. No single system can hold sway. Knowledge cannot be dominated by a single theory. There would be no progress.

'The same, I would argue, is true of nations. No single nation should hold sway. There is only progress if there are numerous small nations. I foresaw a world rich in diversity. So,' Aegu said, 'I found a logical reason, not for Estonia in particular, but for all such small, independent states.'

They had walked in a semicircle, and were approaching the area where the car had been left. Clearly Aegu knew the area well, and had used this knowledge to exercise his insomnia and to express his vision of a new world.

'Speaking of angels, and lightness,' Aegu continued, 'Lydia Teemant made a special request of me. She wanted me to promise her that you would be afforded physical protection. She believes, you see, that you are a kind of holy fool, who cannot protect himself. I am obliged to take notice.'

Though it was a long introduction to the subject, Illich understood from this a number of things. Lydia Teemant would only ask a favour of Aegu if she could give something in return. It was the time he became certain that Lydia Teemant was Aegu's mistress.

When the Zil returned Illich to the gates, it was well past three in the morning. Paalvelt the militiaman opened the gate for him. Behind Illich, the Zil reversed, turned, and began its climb of the hill towards the main road. Tired from the race that day, and exhausted from the walk with Aegu, Illich had hardly reached his room when, fully clothed, he fell into a disturbed, sweating sleep.

Seventy-Eight

The day of the third race against *Eagle* was full of slanting rain and strong winds. The anchorage for the great sailing ships had been considered unsafe. Most, warned in advance of the impending low pressure system, had left for easier anchorages. Others laid out extra cables, ready to weather the expected blast. The bad weather had not visibly shrunk the spectator fleet, which now faced into wind, riding the short seas. The engines on one or two failed, but the coast-guard patrol vessels which were on hand were able to throw a line and haul them back to safety in one of the three great St Petersburg marinas.

Despite the weather, the sky was filled with aircraft. The huge airship *St Petersburg* hovered like a gigantic fish, though lack of sunshine turned its bulk from silver to grey. In the overcast day the lights of its gondolas could be seen lit up, like a steamer in the night, 'anchored' into wind by the slow revving of its engines. Its guests partied and surveyed the scene below them.

In the small Estonian anchorage, the incoming swell was such that extra fenders were placed on *Novy Mir* to prevent her being damaged against the sides of the basin. Swinging with the wind, it was necessary for the towboat to put on full power to avoid drifting against the harbour entrance.

Outside, the motion of the yacht, without the steadying influence of sails, was fierce.

'Twenty-eight knots,' Brod read from the instruments. 'Gusting to thirty-five.'

The surface of the water was combed white. Under bare poles they heeled noticeably. The pitching of the yacht imposed fierce tugs on the tow-rope. Illich ordered that no one should go onto the foredeck in case the towrope split and backlashed.

At sea, water finds its way through the best oilskins. Thankfully, it was still humid and warm. The drenching explosions of spray were, from this point of view, merely refreshing. Like the American crew, in this weather they made use of watertight goggles. The surface of the glass was treated with a film which reduced viscous tension, causing water droplets to fall off. Several also wore white lip-salve against the heat and wind. A combination of dark glasses and white lips gave them the appearance of extra-terrestrials.

The wind changed the nature of the waiting. To keep pace against the wind and waves, the towboat had to use moderate engine power. In some ways, however, the howling wind, the punch of advancing waves against the hull and the rising and falling roar of the towboat engines were preferable to the eerie silence of waiting under calm conditions.

'What will Ericson do today?' Illich had asked Jim Shaw earlier that morning, when they were studying weather forecasts.

'He'll come for us again. He's been stung enough.'

'That makes sense,' Illich said. 'But today we won't run.'

'That's fine by me,' Shaw shrugged. 'I just hope he doesn't try something desperate.'

Illich hadn't liked the way Shaw said that. There was an edge of serious concern in it.

'What could he do?'

'I don't know. Nothing, I guess. You have to remember, though, that he'll realize now that the chances are running against him. He hasn't got the boatspeed to stand off and blast us. And that guy wants to win above everything else in the world. If I didn't know that half the big corporate guys around him feel exactly the same way, I'd say he was crazy.'

But Illich was a military man, and saying your opponent was crazy was not a clear analysis. It was what the opponent might do as a consequence of his theoretical state of mind which should be analysed. Neither of them could easily think of a desperate measure outside the normal rough and tumble of match-racing, in which both were well versed.

The exchange put Illich in mind of an aspect of his past life. During his training as a young major at military college, the privileged position allowed them unusual access to foreign ideas. In explaining the importance of assumptions, his tutor, a Colonel V. Rublov, liked to illustrate the point by means of a story about the British mathematician Hardy. At high table at Trinity College, Cambridge, a fellow diner was reported to have asked him. 'Hardy, if two and two make five, can you prove I am the Pope?' 'Certainly,' replied the distinguished mathematician. 'If two

405

and two equal five, and by the accepted rules two and two also equal four, then five equals four. Subtract three from both sides of the equation, and you have two equals one. Now, you and the Pope are two, therefore you are one.' With incorrect assumptions, you could prove anything.

Illich had another habit from the military, one which was perhaps a little more mundane than the refined examination of assumptions. If there is no clear threat, then one should put the thought from one's mind and get on with the work in hand.

The big motoryachts around *Eagle* seemed less comfortable today. Their high superstructure made them roll, pitch and, occasionally, produce strange combinations of both. Without forward speed, they lost steadiness. Illich, watching them briefly, knew that the motion on one or two of the higher bridges must have been unusual, to say the least,

'Course laid,' confirmed Brod, listening to the radio. 'Twenty minutes to the ten-minute gun.'

Today even *Novy Mir* would require a smaller genoa. It was important to set it up well.

'Mainsail,' Illich shouted. 'Prepare to cast off!'

Initially, as the yacht slipped backwards, he applied reverse helm. Then the mainsail began to develop power, the yacht generated forward speed, he turned the helm to normal, and they were away.

The genoa was being hauled up. Raised, but not yet sheeted, it shook its metal clew like an angry dog. One of the automatic reactions of a sailor in a heavy wind was to steer a little wide of the whipping clew; it could break a wrist or knock teeth out; on a larger boat, it could kill.

Sheeted, they began to move forward fast, heeling strongly at first to gather speed. Their goggles were needed against the almost incessant spray. Every second wave exploded against the bow, dousing them with spray. In the aft part of the yacht it was not so bad. The bulk of the spray blew across the boat's midsections. It was the winchgrinders who took the full brunt, in addition to their other, not inconsiderable, strains.

'Eight six,' Brod intoned, 'eight six, eight six, eight seven . . .'

They opened the leech of the foresail, as they had done the previous race on the larger genoa, but this time the indication was that the boat was faster with the leech set as in the textbooks, all tell-tales flying and no sector stall. Just as Illich had insisted on adoption of the open leech the previous day, so he was moved by entirely practical considerations to adopt its opposite today. Brecht said: 'Grub before ethics'; in sailing the motto was: 'Practice before theory'.

Once again, *Eagle* was a little late in setting sail. The white rhomboid palace of Ericson's father's yacht edged backwards to give *Eagle* sea-room for tuning.

'Tack!' shouted Illich.

Now it was necessary for Soren Gir and Edvigs Tarku, the trimmers, to become familiar with the new setting of the sail, and to throw yesterday's assumptions out of the window.

It took several minutes to reach a satisfactory setting. At length Brod said: 'Six minutes to starting gun.'

The winchgrinders were looking miserable against the spray. Inactivity was bad for nerves, even in the most professional crew. To keep them occupied, Illich took the boat through four tacks. Then they tuned the boat briefly for close reaching.

'Two minutes,' Brod warned.

In this wind, they could spare another minute of tuning. On the other end of the starting box, *Eagle* wheeled.

Shaw said: 'They're carrying a full-size genoa.'

Illich followed his gaze. They were, it was true. But what were the implications? Overcanvassing a yacht in these winds was as detrimental to performance as too little sail. If

407

the yacht heeled too much, it became unbalanced, and lost efficiency.

In manoeuvre too, the bigger genoa would be a handful in such winds, taking longer to haul in. A small error in the opponent's logic is a blessing; a large error is unsettling. Did Ericson know something Illich did not?

'One minute,' Brod called.

They started to move in towards the starting box, picking up speed fast on a reach.

'Twelve knots, twelve five, twelve nine . . .'

It was gusting now, howling in the rigging.

'Fourteen knots, fourteen two, fourteen five . . .'

Prem adjusted the mainsheet further.

'Fifteen zero, fifteen zero, fifteen one. . .'

Eagle was reaching in fast at the other end, her boom out to counteract the weather helm she would be experiencing.

'Five, four, three, two . . .'

Five seconds later they crossed into the starting box.

Now both yachts were on a collision course, *Novy Mir* on starboard, combined closing speed thirty knots.

Illich felt his mouth go dry.

Would Ericson duck low or go high? When he made his move, there would be only a second or two for him to make his own. Ericson would wait until the last moment before disclosing his game.

Only a hundred yards separated them. Ericson did not budge.

Illich swung *Novy Mir*'s bow five degrees up, to indicate his own intention of going high. Ericson, instead of swinging low or maintaining course, also swung five degrees high.

Seventy yards between them, closing speed thirty knots.

Illich pointed down ten degrees. Ericson pointed down ten.

'Oh, Jesus,' Jim Shaw said behind him.

Forty yards, collision course.

Illich pointed a further ten degrees down. *Eagle* followed suit.

408

'Get back,' Jim screamed at the bowman.

The two yachts collided at a closing speed of 28 knots, bow to bow. The impact flung the crew off their feet, the momentum destroying both backstays instantaneously. Unstayed, the two masts broke at deck level, continued to fly forward, struck one another, and then, like two drunks amiably reeling, they fell locked together with a scream of tearing metal. Flung against the wheel, winded, Illich saw a seven foot hole in the bow. The sails floated down like an afterthought, covering the wreckage of the two yachts.

Within five seconds of the impact *Novy Mir* was down at the bow, and sinking fast. Shaw was already on his feet, furiously hurling back the mainsail to uncover the middeck. Soren Gir emerged, clutching a gashed shoulder. Tarku rose from the sails, his face covered in blood, confused. Brod pulled him towards the rear. With a roar like the minotaur, Berol Baltir fought out from beneath the mainsail. Graf Ulder, the other winchgrinder, was dazed but showed no signs of damage.

'Kingissep!' shouted Illich. As the two masts had collided and fallen, beneath them he had seen Victor Kingissep dive like a jackrabbit towards the open forehatch.

The boom had fallen across the main hatch. Sinclair was beside him as he tried to raise it. It was too heavy. Brod and Jim came up to help. The four of them could not move it. Graf Ulder it was who saved the day. Lying underneath it on the floor of the cockpit, he placed his great legs against it and forced it upwards. The four of them were able to push it to the side. The greatest relief of all was to see Kingissep's face appear in the main hatch as he helped Herman Maask out of the dark interior. The boat was already half flooded, the inside dark with water. They helped out the stunned Maask.

Eagle too was going down. Her crew, gathered at the stern, were signalling to the great white motor yacht blasting towards them. Illich had seen them move towards the aft of a boat in a body a full twenty seconds before the collision . . .

The sinking of both yachts occurred with horrifying swiftness. Fifteen seconds later *Novy Mir*'s sidedecks were at the water, her bow fully submerged. At Illich's order the crew jumped and slid into the water, the healthy and the wounded. Waves were washing across the decks. They had only swum a few feet when she started to go down, a gust of locked air hiccuping from the forehatch, pulling *Eagle* down with her. Only *Eagle*'s stern showed above the water now, as the last of the Americans dived into the sea.

From collision to disappearance of both yachts was less than seventy seconds.

Seventy-Nine

The cold bit into his bones.

Gasping for air, Illich looked around at the other swimmers. They all seemed to be treading water reasonably. Only Maask was still looking groggy, and Shaw and Sinclair were supporting him at each shoulder. Prem faced him with bloodshot eyes.

'I'll kill them,' Prem said in a voice which was more threatening because it was matter of fact. Brod, silent, did not take his eyes off the Americans. It was difficult, though, to work up aggression against a group of heads bobbing in the water.

Even as they gathered, the American launch had reached the American crew, a ladder had been lowered, and Ericson and his men were being hauled aboard over the midship topsides.

Illich could see a patrol vessel about three hundred yards

away. Not far behind was their own slower tender. Now that *Eagle*'s men had been hauled aboard their own support craft a tanned, grey-haired man, who Illich knew was Ericson's father, called: 'Can we help you guys?'

Illich felt the coldness of rage in his heart. A thousand ripostes and accusations came to mind, each one more bitter than the last. He shook his head.

Their two minute immersion was freezing and uncomfortable – the Baltic is never a warm sea. But they refused the MVD launch too, pointing instead to the grey tender with the Estonian tricolour that pitched towards them over the swells as slowly as an old bloodhound.

On board the tender Illich could begin to take account of the physical damage to his crew. Soren Gir's gash on the shoulder was a light flesh wound. Herman Maask, the sewerman, had been thrown against a bulkhead while he packed sails and was suffering from concussion. The rest were in reasonable shape. Carefully they laid Maask out on the single stretcher carried by the tender.

They sat down facing one another while the MVD patrol vessels kept the press at bay and the tender moved at the centre of the convoy towards the shore. There was a pause, half-way through the journey, when a hospital vessel came alongside to take off Herman Maask.

It was only after Maask had been removed that Brod said to Illich what was in all their minds: 'That was deliberate.'

Illich glanced at Shaw, who nodded once, carefully, in agreement. No one was in any doubt. They looked to Illich to provide a remedy. But for the time being at least, Illich was so appalled by the notion of premeditation that inside he felt numb, unwilling to contemplate the minds that could perpetrate such a thing.

The hearing was held that same evening at a baronial hall set aside for the duration of the races to form an administrative office, and to handle protests.

The chairman of the five-man enquiry was Alexei Vikunov, a former Olympic bronze medallist who was current Secretary of the Russian Sailing Union. The others comprised an Italian, Stephano Bruscati, representative of the International Yacht Racing Union; a German, Heidrich Arendt, selector of the German Admiral's Cup team; the Australian former helmsman Jim Richmond, and the experienced Finnish administrator Reijo Serensen; distinguished judges all. The five-man panel sat at the head of a long table of Siberian pine. At the far end was a draped Russian flag.

Each syndicate was allowed three representatives. Illich, Shaw and Sinclair faced across the table John Ericson, his father, and the international lawyer Frank Mulvinney. Mulvinney was famous for his New York practice and, as an ardent yachtsman himself, for his work on protest committees.

Vikunov began ponderously with the quaint expression: 'Comrade gentlemen.'

He glanced around the table.

'We are here to decide the outcome of the accident today between the defending yacht *Novy Mir* and the challenger *Eagle*. In the course of the first manoeuvres after the ten-minute gun, the yachts were subject to a head-on collision. This resulted in the sinking of both yachts before assistance could be brought to bear. A most unfortunate incident, I am sure we all agree. I will ask the representatives of both sides to put their respective cases. Before I do so, it is obvious that the majority of participants here speak English. My four colleagues here are also fluent in English. Therefore I propose that we conduct the investigation in the common language.'

It was a courteous introduction, as Illich would have expected of Vikunov. Illich looked across the table into the eyes of John Ericson. Ericson returned a fixed, unwavering stare. Illich turned to look at his father, and saw, this time,

412

a trace of amusement there, a laconic element. This was a man to fear.

Vikunov was saying: 'I ask the captain of the defending yacht, Ivan Illich, to speak.'

'Thank you, Mr Chairman. What I will say is brief. After the ten-minute gun we were closing with one another in the normal manner. We were on starboard, with right of way. These confrontations are naturally tense. At such fast closing speeds mistakes can be costly. In the final moments, each yacht will usually exhibit its intentions. Although I had right of way on starboard tack, seeing no shift away on the part of *Eagle*, I exercised caution and turned upwind by five degrees. *Eagle*, instead of turning downwind or continuing on course, turned upwind. Aware of the danger, I then turned ten degrees down to avoid collision. *Eagle* followed suit, bringing her back on a collision course. In the last seconds, I turned downwind a further ten degrees. There was a chance at this stage that, if *Eagle* maintained course, we could have missed one another. Instead she turned downwind by ten degrees, making collision inevitable. On three consecutive occasions, she copied what I did, in each case bringing herself onto a collision course. I cannot help but assume this was deliberate, and if this is so, then the collision was intended. That is my case.'

There was a pause. The three men opposite Illich showed no visible sign of emotion. Mulvinney removed his glasses and thoughtfully swung them from his hand.

'Thank you,' Vikunov said in his courtly English. 'I shall now ask the captain of *Eagle*, Mister John Ericson, to put his case.'

'I shall ask Mr Mulvinney to speak for us,' Ericson said. Mulvinney replaced his glasses and carefully, without hurry, opened a file in front of him. He looked towards the five judges.

'Frankly, gentlemen, I am astonished by both the evidence and the imputations made by Mr Illich. I have to say I am sufficiently amazed that I hardly know what to say.

However, let me begin by examining the evidence. We have run through various videos of the incident in question, which we would be happy to show. Mr Illich says that he made a move, and that *Eagle* followed. He says he made another move, and *Eagle* followed. This happened a third time. Each of these reactions placed *Eagle* on a collision course. This is the essence of his evidence. I say that there is no evidence of this at all. The moves that were made by *Eagle* were simultaneous with his own, or so close to simultaneous that they can be assumed to be simultaneous. If they were simultaneous then we cannot infer a deliberate intention to collide, and Mr Illich's case collapses. The fact is, as I shall now demonstrate, both yachts were taking avoiding action. It happens that they took the same kinds of avoiding action at the same time. This was unfortunate indeed, I agree. But a lot of what happens in the world is unfortunate.'

Mulvinney paused.

'Now you may say that's too much of a coincidence. And that would be a reasonable suggestion. But I should like to ask you gentlemen a question in good faith. Have you not, at least once in your life, been walking down a street, when someone appeared walking in the other direction on what could be called a collision course? Out of courtesy, you move to the right. So does he. You move to the left. So does he. To the right again. So does he, and you collide. You apologize profusely. So does he. Or am I the only one in the room who has had that experience, not once, but several times?'

It was breathtaking. Russian justice was heavy-handed and ponderous. It rolled over the accused with all the subtlety of a tank. The defending attorneys are sullen, intimidated by the power of the court. But Illich had never seen a display like this, turning night into day.

Mulvinney was continuing: 'Gentlemen, all justice is based on the assumption that the accused is innocent until proven guilty. If you had assumed, in all the street collisions to which I have been a party, that I or the person facing me must have been guilty, say, of molestation, and if all the other parties to such collisions were similarly treated, then I submit to you most respectfully, we would have placed virtually the entire population of our two countries behind bars.'

Mulvinney paused again for rhetorical effect. His eyes were shining with candour, with righteous astonishment, even with a hint of amusement at such a ridiculous thought.

'In this particular matter I joke, of course. But,' his voice dropped to a controlled monotone, 'to assume that because a collision occurred here, which is in substance exactly like those innocent street collisions that occur between hurrying parties every day, to assume in this case, unlike all those others, that one party deliberately engineered it, would be to flout all the known rules of justice.'

There followed several seconds of complete silence. Illich looked at the five judges. They seemed transfixed. After a prolonged pause, Vikunov said: 'Mr Illich?'

'A most impressive speech, Mr Chairman,' Illich replied. 'But I believe it is based on an important error. Mr Mulvinney says that there was no time between the avoiding actions made by *Novy Mir* and the reactions of *Eagle*. As I remember, there was time between each of the three actions and reactions for *Eagle* to change course. This is the key point. I suggest that we see the video evidence.'

Vikunov said to Mulvinney: 'Would you be so kind?'

'Certainly, Mr Chairman, certainly. I'd be happy to do that.'

There was a large screen television at the other end. Mulvinney clipped in the video disc.

The sequence was shot from above, from one of the helicopters. The first few frames showed only *Eagle*, then the field expanded to include *Novy Mir*. The two were moving in towards one another. *Novy Mir* swung upwind by five degrees. About two seconds later, *Eagle* too turned five degrees upwind. *Novy Mir* swung downwind ten degrees.

Eagle followed after a two second interval. *Novy Mir* swung another ten degrees downwind. The two were close now, hardly more than a few boatlengths apart. About two seconds later *Eagle* swung downwind. The collision occurred a few seconds later. Within eight seconds of impact the two boats had become a tangled heap of wreckage, sails, rigging. There was no sound. Mulvinney clicked it off.

'Mr Chairman, I suggest to you and your distinguished colleagues that what we have shown proves conclusively that the reaction times between the two boats were so close that one cannot possibly infer that a collision was intended. These were two boats advancing towards each other like pedestrians in the street, both manoeuvring to avoid.'

'Mr Illich?'

'Mr Chairman, the video we have seen showed exactly what I described. There was a significant lapse of time between each of my manoeuvres and the counter-man-ouevres of *Eagle*, which placed her on a collision course on each of the consecutive three occasions.'

'Mr Chairman, I object most strongly. You should take into account that the boat does not respond immediately to the wheel. There is a time lapse. This time lapse is quite enough to explain any small difference between the actions taken by *Novy Mir* and *Eagle*'s own attempts to avoid collision. I put it to you, sir, that on the basis of this most flimsy evidence, to accuse the helmsman and crew of *Eagle* of deliberately engineering this terrible accident would be a travesty.'

'Mr Illich, have you anything further to say?

'No, Mr Chairman.'

'Mr Mulvinney?'

'I rest my case, Mr Chairman.'

'Mr Chairman?' There was a silence. Sinclair was speaking. The panel of five judges turned towards him.

Sinclair waited several seconds: 'I was asked by Mr Illich to act as physically non-participating witness on his yacht

416

Novy Mir, in accordance with the rules. I would like your permission to ask one question of Mr Ericson.'

Vikunov was taken aback. He leaned sideways to speak to Arendt and Bruscati. But their deliberation was interrupted by Mulvinney.

'Mr Chairman, I object, the case has now been put by the two sides. This is an unwarranted intrusion.'

Vikunov said amiably enough: 'We will decide when the hearing is over.'

Vikunov turned: 'Mr Sinclair.'

'Thank you. In the film that you showed, one aspect of the collision was not commented upon. On a sailing yacht, the crew are distributed in a predictable manner. I noticed that, even in the first frames, some considerable time before the collision was unavoidable, the crew of *Eagle* is unusually well aft. The bowman is not in his normal position forward of the mast; the mastman is not in the forward part of the cockpit. There is a remarkable aggregation of crew in the aft sections, almost as if the crew were expecting a collision and had moved to the aft, the safer, part of the yacht well before the collision. Could I have your permission to ask Mr Ericson directly how he explains this unusual behaviour?'

There was a moment's silence.

'Mr Chairman,' Mulvinney's voice was loud, authoritative: 'I object most strongly to this irregularity. I am representing my clients in this case and I have already spoken for them.'

Vikunov smiled with understanding: 'Nevertheless, Mr Mulvinney, my colleagues and I should be interested in Mr Ericson's response.'

'I place it on record that I am advising my client this is irregular and I advise him not to answer it.'

'Mr Ericson?' asked Vikunov. 'You are perfectly at liberty not to answer if you do not wish.'

They watched Ericson's face, the fair lashes of his almost albino eyes. At first they thought Ericson would obey the advice of his formidable advocate. But Ericson was preparing to answer.

'Frankly, Mr Chairman, my crew and I thought the manoeuvres of the other yacht were somewhat erratic, even though they had right of way, and naturally that made us all a little nervous.'

There was an expulsion of breath from Jim Shaw, the only comment he made in the entire hearing. Even Sinclair was silent with amazement.

'Mr Sinclair?'

'Very droll, I am sure, Mr Chairman. In my view Mr Ericson is a liar.'

But now Mulvinney had sprung up with such swiftness that the glasses of water on the table clinked with the violence of his upheaval; he was pounding the table with his fist. 'You just say that on American soil, you whippersnapper, and I'll slap a defamation writ on you so goddamn fast you won't even know whether you're coming or going!'

But now Vikunov too was rising to his full height. It was a moment when the whole space of the room seemed charged with anger. A giant of a man, Vikunov towered above the table and roared: 'Comrade gentlemen, be seated!'

There was a pause of several seconds. Slowly, with some reluctance, the participants sank back into their chairs.

'Gentlemen,' Vikunov continued, 'we have arranged two separate waiting rooms for the parties at the other end of the hall. Please wait there while my colleagues and I discuss the matter and reach a decision.'

Illich glanced at the three opposite him. Mulvinney was shuffling papers together. Ericson's father's jaw was an angry white line.

'To save further embarrassment,' Vikunov added, 'I suggest that the *Novy Mir* representatives leave first, and then those of *Eagle*. Thank you.'

Vikunov remained standing while they moved from the hall.

Seated in the sideroom, Illich heard a loud whoop of mirth from Ericson across the corridor.

'I don't mean to be a pessimist,' Sinclair said, 'but I think that Mulvinney introduced enough doubt and obfuscation to prevent them judging against *Eagle*.'

They waited for twenty-five minutes while Vikunov and his colleagues debated the matter. Then the two groups were called into the room.

'Gentlemen, our finding is that there is not sufficient evidence to apportion blame in this unfortunate incident. *Novy Mir* had right of way, and therefore *Eagle* is disqualified. But the rules state that in order to win, *Novy Mir* should have completed the course. Therefore she too is disqualified.' Vikunov paused. 'That having being decided, we have two choices. We can await the raising, salvaging, and repair of the two yachts, if indeed this is possible. This will take at least two months, perhaps longer, and it will severely disrupt the many thousands of spectators and guest boats who have come here to watch this great event. We have therefore decided in favour of a second option. The two syndicates must enter their second boats after a recovery period of three days, and the series will be continued.

'Gentlemen, I know that tempers are high. I have been in protests where emotions have also run high. I remind you, nevertheless, that you are our guests here, and we trust that there will be no more hostilities until you meet again on the water. I trust further that when you do so, both parties will strictly maintain the rules. Thank you.'

Illich, glancing at the faces of the other party, could not help but notice the hardly suppressed smile which played around the mouth of John Ericson. In his heart, Illich felt sure that he had planned this manoeuvre exactly, that it was planned to destroy the opposing superior yacht, and that now Ericson had achieved precisely the result that he wanted. In three days time the Americans would enter the course with a perfect replica of *Eagle*, whereas they would be forced onto the course with the older, outdated *Leningrad*.

419

The American party departed first. As Illich left the room, Vikunov's huge hand squeezed his arm, as if in sympathy over the decision. It was a well-meant gesture, but it did not help their situation.

Eighty

They started that very night to prepare *Leningrad*, working all through the following day and night. It took Vagir's men a full thirty-six hours, operating in shifts, to bring her hull surfaces up to *Novy Mir*'s standard. They resurfaced her underwater sections, refairing until the shed was white with the dust of their labours. They stripped out her gear, checked and cleaned and re-oiled her winches and working parts. The rigging was replaced. On the second morning, with the grey dusk hovering, they were ready to launch her, and as they loaded the sails and put out to sea for an early practice sail, they saw Vagir's men, their eyesockets hollow with dust and exhaustion, fade like ghosts, disappearing into the buildings behind them for a few hours of rest.

Without a rival boat it was more difficult to tune effectively. Here Sinclair again came to their rescue. The British challenger yacht was not yet packed for the voyage home, and would be loaned to the Estonian second crew. Sinclair took the helm. They practised for three hours, coaxing *Leningrad* as best as they were able to squeeze out the last residues of speed. It was difficult with the crowds of spectator boats to sail for any distance without interruption, despite the best efforts of the course patrol vessels. After lunch, they went out and practised again, before turning *Leningrad* over once more to Vagir and his men for a night's work of further preparation in fairing her underwater sections to a mirror finish.

Illich was so engrossed in preparation he almost overlooked the envelope left on his desk. Ilena, who filtered his mail and replied on his behalf to the majority of the letters of congratulation and condolences which came in each day now, had written 'URGENT' on it. Sitting down at his desk, slumping after the second practice of the day, he slipped the paper out of its open envelope. It was a telegram, no more than a few words. The name at the bottom froze his mind.

CAN YOU MEET ME? I AM IN TALLINN. WILL CALL BY FLAT TOMORROW, FIVE THIRTY P.M.
    ANNA

After the first shock, the first hope. His mind soared. They had broken off relations for good. Now here she was asking to talk. He did not allow himself to think what had made her change her mind. Perhaps it was merely to tie up matters, to finalize everything. But everything had already been finalized. Perhaps it was just an emotional whim, without further consequence. A woman who has spent her life with a man cannot easily forget him. It did not mean anything. It meant everything. He thought the girls might be with her. He would plead with her to see them one more time. It was grossly inconvenient. It was understandable. He knew that he had no time to spare, that he would have to forgo tomorrow's second practice. It was also a test of his commitment. Perhaps she had planned it, as a means of assessing his response. But these were thoughts that were washed aside in the expanding torrent of his hope. Despite everything, he would go.

Jim Shaw agreed to conduct the next practice against Sinclair. Illich himself took the early practice, in a suppressed fever of impatience. He was able to hold off Sinclair in a long tacking duel on the first leg before they were forced to adjourn by the press of spectator craft which had taken to gathering around them, even at that hour. He held the usual debriefing with Brod and Shaw at ten-thirty, and worked in his small office to answer the mound of correspondence that had built up in the last few days. It helped to keep his nerves in check.

His own car had been left in Tallinn, and he would have gone by train, but Shaw insisted that he take the small Lada which he and Maria had bought two months before. At two-thirty in the afternoon, Illich set out south, joining up with the main motorway, and drove through Narva, past Kohtia-Jarve, towards Tallinn. The Lada stood up reasonably well. It was several months since he had driven himself, and it took him a short while to feel comfortable once again. Traffic was surprisingly heavy. There was reputed to be a car for every two people in Estonia, a higher average than anywhere else in the former Soviet sphere. At Rakvere the engine showed signs of overheating, so he stopped on the hard shoulder and opened the bonnet. It was a false alarm. He drove more slowly, though, to Tallinn. An image of Anna and the children waiting in the staircase sustained him, an image of their departing reluctantly down the stairs drew him forward.

The traffic seemed heavier still in the outskirts of Tallinn. A new one-way system confused him, causing him to detour a mile on the bypass to Parnu and Riga. He started to feel sweat form. His watch said five-fifteen. When he reached Laidoner Street it was five-twenty-eight, and despite himself, in his hope he bought carnations from the flower stall at its Eastern end. He ran the final fifty yards to the door, paused outside to comb his fingers through his hair, and then he entered the main hallway. Irkut's door was locked. The place felt curiously empty. A builder's sign, leaning against the wall of the entrance hall, said 'Kirip and Partners, Reconstruction'. He walked up the stairs. It was five-thirty-four, and no sign of them.

They would come, she was always late. He unlocked and

opened the door. Perhaps out of instinct, he waited several seconds on the threshold before going inside. The porchway was as he had left it, except that a pile of letters had accumulated on the doormat, most of them swept sideways by the opening door. He went in. In the small living room there was dust on the floor. A movement, less than a movement, a shadow, caused him to stop. As he did so a man's voice ordered 'Don't move.'

Eighty-One

'Drop the package,' the man said and he knew then, with certainty, the identity of its owner.

He let the bouquet of flowers fall to the floor. They lay there, unmoving as his own frozen mind.

'Keep your hands away from your body. Turn slowly.'

Standing braced against the furthest wall, his feet slightly apart for better aim, his two hands held forward in the classic stance of the small-arms instructor, was Major-General Vorolov. The fine eyes were level with the top of the gun; the side of Vorolov's face furthest from the window was in shadow.

'Raise your hands, palms towards me,' Vorolov said quietly. Illich did so, waiting for the furious beating in his temples to subside.

Did she know what they intended to do? The thought was too terrible. At the same time, why had she cried so bitterly at their last meeting? Was it the grief of betrayal? Was she already collaborating with them? No, he decided, no one, not even a woman in the full bitterness and anguish of an abandoned love, could be so wicked. They had trapped and used her, as they now had trapped him.

He did not take his eyes off Vorolov. Vorolov's face was devoid of expression. He stood, short and square and unmoving, his broad hands held from him as if he were holding out an offering.

Illich looked at the squat shape of the gun in Vorolov's hands. It was a Makarov, out of date now, no longer in use in any modern armed force. But its slow, heavy bullet could smash the skull. It was an executioner's gun. How many people had been executed in prisons, in police cellars, using this blunt instrument?

Its user surveyed him carefully, without apparent hostility.

'Sit down,' Vorolov said, pointing with the gun to a chair close by.

A flare of anger went through Illich. He would have liked to have walked towards Vorolov, watching his face as he approached, assessing what fear there was behind his efficient exterior. He would have liked to watch Vorolov's eyes as he took each step closer.

Lowering his hands slowly, he leaned against one of the curtainless windows.

'Very well.' Vorolov made a movement of his shoulders which was like a shrug.

'Perhaps you would be kind enough to explain,' Illich said.

Vorolov smiled: 'Your impudence, Citizen Illich, never ceases to astonish me.'

'You are in my flat, having gained illegal entry, and you appear to be threatening me with a weapon.'

'We do not recognize bourgeois property,' Vorolov reminded him.

'Or the rights of the individual within it.'

Vorolov's face grew more serious: 'I am not here to fence with pretty phrases. I carry a message from General Chernavin.' Vorolov paused only for the briefest of moments. 'He asks you, as a soldier, and as a citizen of the Russian Republic, to renounce your past course of action, and to return voluntarily for trial as a deserter. If you do so, the Army will take into account your previous record, and perhaps it will show lenience.'

'I have been legally discharged.'

'Legally, yes,' Vorolov said, as if legality was a concept for lawyers, a bourgeois deception.

How long had they stood like this? Illich could hear the traffic in the street, the occasional passing of a bus, once or twice the noise of one those small, neat cars from the West with its tight, low-fuel engine.

'Are you suggesting some moral precedent?' Illich asked.

'The precedent of loyalty.'

'To whom?' asked Illich.

'To the Army.'

'The Army tried to assassinate me when I removed *Leningrad*. Is that how it rewards loyalty?'

'You committed a serious crime,' Vorolov said.

'I took possession of property that belongs to Estonia.'

'A bourgeois legalism,' Vorolov assured him. 'You took it from the Army.'

Illich paused. Something about this relentless recantation of old grievances was unsettling. Something was missing. It was as if Vorolov was using the argument to further some other aim, something of which Illich was unaware. For a moment he had a vision of himself as a hare being hunted by hounds, a hare which has narrowly avoided his pursuers until now. But hounds hunted in pairs, and he felt, suspected, that Vorolov had an accomplice.

'Why are you here?' Illich asked.

Vorolov did not move. A half-smile crossed his features, the smile of someone who addresses a hopeless case.

'What lies have you been telling my wife?'

Vorolov merely smiled again, a fleeting expression, almost of irritation, like the tail of an ox brushing aside a fly. The barrel of the gun did not waver.

The gun itself, the ugly, blunt instrument in Vorolov's hand, was predominant. Its presence defined their relationship. While they talked, Illich tried to work out the ulterior motive of Vorolov's visit. Look behind the tactics for the strategy, his instructor at military college had informed him.

If he wishes to kill me, Illich thought, why has he not already done so? And if he has not done so, what is the function of these questions, whose purpose appears merely to waste time? Is he waiting for someone?

Is he waiting for my wife?

The thought that Vorolov would use his wife to persuade him now was absurd. His wife was now married to another man, apparently happily, and had discontinued all contact. No, his wife's name had been useful in recalling him here, that was all.

Chernavin?

But that too, was absurd. Chernavin would surely deal with him on home ground, not in some small, troublesome republic. Vorolov was based nearby, at Pirita, and this was, physically at least, within a small distance of his base of operations.

Yet it was difficult to suppress the suspicion that Vorolov was setting the stage for some further aspect at which he could only guess. If he engaged in further debate, he was merely walking along a path already prepared for him by Vorolov. His mind turned again to the question of the gun. He worked again over the ground he had passed before. If Vorolov had intended to murder him, he would already have done so. Therefore he did not intend to use the gun. Illich began to consider whether he should challenge Vorolov directly, physically, in terms that the Army could understand.

It was tempting, nevertheless, to buy time. Time to think. Within the Army self-assertiveness was always balanced by subjugation, obedience to the larger force, to the ideal. Individuals exercised power by virtue of their obedience to this wider law. It was deeply engraved on the soul of any soldier. Obedience became an end in itself, a *sine qua non*, a driving, autonomous moral imperative. To question this, to remove oneself from the sphere of obedience, struck deeper than the mere breaking of a rule. It was an offence against the order of the universe. He saw this, and still it did not explain the situation in which he and Vorolov were the two poles.

His mouth was dry. Was Vorolov challenging him to act? Was that what he sought? It was then that he heard the thuds, and their regular echoes, as if someone was working in the basement with hammers. The thumping increased slowly in volume. It was coming closer. It was the sound of boots, army boots walking up the stairs. The sound changed slightly in pitch as the outside landing was crossed. The handle of the door was turned, the door confidently opened.

It was Chernavin. For a moment Illich's mind ran backward, nervous, amazed.

For several seconds Chernavin stood on the threshold, studying the two figures in front of him, as if assessing the stage that had been reached.

Vorolov, without taking his eyes off Illich, inclined his head once, a gesture of respect. For several further moments Chernavin waited. Then, with a nod to Vorolov, he turned and closed the door behind him. Illich heard his footsteps down the stairs.

Eighty-Two

For several moments Illich felt numb, then nauseous. Chernavin had not merely been a witness. He had passed sentence, and now it was merely time before it would be carried out. Perhaps not now, perhaps not even in this room, but sometime. He was afflicted with, in absurdly quick succession, a sense of grief, sudden terror at the prospect of leaving life, the desire to make any concession, no matter how ignoble, for a few further precious minutes, hours, days. He felt his head grow light, and his knees weaken, and he wondered whether Vorolov noticed.

Would Vorolov shoot him now, or would he wait for Illich to offer some provocation, some excuse, before the final act? At the thought of Vorolov's dilemma, he again gathered himself. Though his mouth was dry, he could speak.

'Tell me,' Illich asked. 'Was it you who ordered the military police to assassinate me when we transferred *Leningrad*?'

Vorolov paused. For a moment, Illich thought this would be provocation enough. Vorolov's hands seemed to tighten; then he shrugged, nodding almost to himself, as if acknowledging a mildly interesting but unimportant fact.

Illich felt another of those cold, intense intuitions enter his mind, not because of what Vorolov had just admitted, but because he knew now, for certain, what to expect.

Vorolov's willingness to talk about such things was the surest sign, the final proof if he needed it, of Illich's imminent death. Merely for conversation, to prolong matters,

Illich said, as if stating a banal fact: 'You're going to kill me.'

He knew it to be a superfluous comment. Vorolov watched him carefully. The barrel of the gun appeared to survey him like a single eye.

Why?

Too many questions crowded his head. If, as he was now certain, Vorolov intended to kill him, why did he not organize it at a distance, arrange an accident like Pridilenko? Why must he do it himself, take the risk of being discovered? At first his perceptions grew cloudy, but after a little while certain things became clearer. This was a personal matter. In this respect, Vorolov would risk his own neck to see Illich die. It was curiously touching. He wondered how much hate that would take, whether he himself felt similar hate towards anyone else.

There are those who, like Don Juan, raise this hate in others without being touched by it themselves. He had raised this emotion in Vorolov. And in Chernavin too. Illich remembered this same sublime hatred projected at him across the discussion table in Moscow. What was it that they hated? Time was flowing forward too fast to think it all through. Perhaps it was that Illich, with all his faults, his irresponsibilities, was free, could leave them and walk away. Chernavin was Vorolov's commanding officer, a short step away in the chain of command. He too was risking everything in the manner of this execution.

He wanted to say to Vorolov, 'Comrade, this is a personal matter, one of individual dislike, individual hatred. This is not the execution of an enemy, or even a matter of punishing a deserter, but a squalid personal murder. Your very presence here proves it.' But in a curious way this was also understood. To have said so would have been superfluous. Nevertheless, Vorolov seemed to be waiting for him to say something. So at length he observed:

'Your motive for killing me will be obvious.'

An expression passed over Vorolov's face, one which he

could not easily interpret, though it might have been one of relief.

'On the contrary. If we had chosen to execute you when the defender trials were in progress, that would have pointed to us. No, Comrade, at this time, with you engaged against the Americans, it is the enemy who apparently have the motive.'

'The shots will be heard,' Illich said. 'You will be traced.'

Again there was that faint trace of relief, almost of satisfaction.

'The janitor, Irkut, is one of ours. He arranged that the flats should be empty today for rewiring work. There is no one above and no one below. I will leave by the fire-escape. It has been carefully planned.'

In the course of this brief conversation, Vorolov again used the code words of a closed mind. When he referred to the Americans he used the phrase *glavnyi vrag*, the main enemy, the traditional reference of the Army. Speaking of Irkut, he used the word *nash*, ours, a word which extends beyond possession, which means 'our creature', a word filled with the shadows of authoritarian neurosis.

Yet Vorolov, this creature of the system, was waiting nevertheless, waiting for something. Illich tried to think carefully. For what?

His mind threshed ineffectually. Some detail escaped him. It was like a splinter which cannot be prised out, which irritates by its presence more than its pain. Below the window, the traffic moved by in the street, vibrating a loose frame. He fancied he could hear Vorolov breathing, deeply and regularly, like someone sleeping.

The answer was absurdly simple.

At 6 p.m. the bells would strike. Their sound was so much a part of him, of this flat, that he had forgotten them. They would drown the sound of Vorolov's gun. No passerby would hear the muted thump of the silencer in the closed room above or below. He should have known. Vorolov's formal training would seek out such details. There was a certain irony in using the sound of church bells to drown out the sounds of a murder. Vorolov would work to just such a carefully prepared plan.

He could smell Vorolov's fear, the fear of death. He had detected the same smell on Chernavin, not this evening, but on other occasions, when Chernavin's hatred reached out towards him. On those who killed others it hung, like a sexual scent. Something else became clearer to him. These two, Chernavin and Vorolov, were creatures from a different realm. They were driven, but their obsessions were different, inexplicable in his own terms.

He would never understand them, and perhaps they would never understand him. And what was about to happen, short and intense and brutal, would be a black poem of misunderstanding.

They were heavy, and he was light, and growing lighter. He did not fear his own death.

From his position he could almost see the nearby clock tower. By shifting to the left a short distance, no more than a few inches, he could see one side of the tower through the open window.

He shifted position slightly. Vorolov did not move. Now he could see the entire clock, the second hand moving across the face.

Vorolov was starting to sweat. He, Illich, did not need to see the shining film on his face, or watch him grip the handle of the gun tighter to prevent it slipping, to know. Vorolov was a man approaching the time of death, a religious ritual of great significance, dread, and fascination. Illich watched him coldly. Vorolov studied him almost passively. In a short while the bells would begin to chime and Vorolov, sweating, fearful, ecstatic with his own terror, would plunge the trigger and the gun would punch him down. But before that Illich would begin his own count, would make his own time.

Fifty seconds.

Illich was used to countdowns. He seemed to have spent

his entire life at starts of races with the seconds falling as slowly as drops of water. He stared at Vorolov's eyes. They showed no visible expression. Both men were waiting.

Thirty seconds.

Vorolov's grip on the gun tightened. A bead of sweat ran into his eye, and he blinked once, in irritation. It seemed to Illich that his own soul was emptying. In his death, though he was light, he would not be passive. He had already decided to make Vorolov pay, forcing him to fire before the peal of the bells. He moved slightly, balancing himself on the balls of his feet.

Ten seconds.

His body, prepared, spoke for him. In hardly more than a moment, he had covered almost half the distance between them when Vorolov's eye tightened and he felt the first blow of a bullet into his chest. A second bullet punched into him almost simultaneously. Time slowed, wavered. Only his momentum was carrying him forward. Now heavy, regular blows were striking him, blows like a sledgehammer. He seemed to be running down the mouth of the gun, a tunnel of fire. Yet from somewhere he gathered strength, reaching forward with his hands over Vorolov's gun to his unprotected face. Vorolov seemed to pause, hesitate. With his helmsman's hands Illich did the terrible work, turning the thumbs to gouge out Vorolov's eyes. The next explosion flung Illich backwards. Then he was floating downwards, was lying on the floor; a pool of peace was spreading. He could hear Vorolov gulping with pain, making small mewing sounds to stop himself screaming. Vorolov's fingers, the almost gentle fingers of a blind man, were feeling the back of his head, his neck. A muzzle was placed against the base of his skull. Someone's heavy breathing. Vorolov's? His own? As the bells started to peal he felt the final blow, a discharge of pain, and he was a piece of dust, floating.